I0640725

Cornelius Walford

A Statistical Chronology of Plagues and Pestilences

as affecting human life, with an inquiry into their causes

Cornelius Walford

A Statistical Chronology of Plagues and Pestilences
as affecting human life, with an inquiry into their causes

ISBN/EAN: 9783337370732

Printed in Europe, USA, Canada, Australia, Japan

Cover: Foto ©Andreas Hilbeck / pixelio.de

More available books at **www.hansebooks.com**

A

STATISTICAL CHRONOLOGY

OF

PLAGUES AND PESTILENCES

AS AFFECTING

HUMAN LIFE,

WITH

AN INQUIRY INTO THEIR CAUSES.

BY

CORNELIUS WALFORD, F.I.A., F.S.S., F.R. HIST. SOC.,

BARRISTER-AT-LAW.

HARRISON AND SONS, ST. MARTIN'S LANE,
Printers in Ordinary to Her Majesty.

1884.

[*For Private Circulation.*]

PREFACE.

———◆———

THIS paper was prepared for and read at a Meeting of the Statistical Society (19th December, 1882); but being deemed too lengthy for, and in some other respects not entirely suited to, the pages of the *Journal* of that Society, is now printed separately, in an Edition of 100 copies.

It constitutes only one section of an inquiry into Plagues and Pestilences, as affecting Human, Animal, and Vegetable Life. The other sections are far advanced towards completion, but the author has not yet determined in what form they shall appear.

London, May, 1884.

TABLE OF CONTENTS.

CHRONOLOGY OF PLAGUES AND PESTILENCES.

Introductory.

INQUIRIES which I have had occasion to make during a series of years into the duration of life, and the causes affecting that duration in various parts of the globe, have drawn my attention in a forcible manner to what I may designate in broad terms the " Enemies of Human Life." These may be divided into five great classes :—(1) Physical convulsions, such as EARTHQUAKES, INUN-DATIONS, &c.; (2) FAMINES; (3) PLAGUES and PESTILENCES; (4) LEGISLATIVE and SOCIAL REGULATIONS, out of which have proceeded war and all its attendant evils; (5) ACCIDENTS, CASUALTIES, and SELF DESTRUCTION. The first three causes act and react upon each other to a very large degree.

In my paper on FAMINES, read before the Statistical Society several years since (1878-79, see *Journal*, vol. xli, pp. 433—535; vol. xlii, pp. 33—275), I dealt with the physical convulsions and legislative restrictions as affecting these. I now propose to deal with Plagues and Pestilences, so far as they affect human life, and to survey their causes and consequences so far as available records permit.

Magnitude of the Inquiry.

The initial difficulty which stares me in the face is the magni-tude of the inquiry. If I were to wait until I had made myself familiar with the question in all its ramifications, an indefinite period must elapse. But the time has come for me to do the best that is possible out of the materials at command; and here it will be convenient for me to say, once for all, that the mode of inquiry I shall pursue is chronological and statistical, and not scientific. It may be, and I trust will be, that the cause of science will be aided by the records here adduced. I am more than surprised sometimes, that science should even attempt to evolve solutions, and construct theories, without any groundwork of chronological sequence, or of statistical consequence, upon which to lay a sub-stantial foundation. The truly logical method is surely to take the facts in the most complete form available, and follow whither-soever they may lead.

It was upon this principle that I prepared the extended tables regarding Famines. I am glad to know that they have been of great service to scientific inquirers; and it is no fault of mine if they have proved destructive to the sun-spot theory of periodical influence upon the seasons.* It is upon this principle of comprehensive inquiry that I have prepared the Appendix to the present paper. It follows, as of course, that if the facts are to be so used, there must be the element of completeness in them. Just so far as they are incomplete, so they may be misleading. The facts omitted, indeed, lessen the force of those presented. What is required is complete chronological sequence. The bare examination of a completed table of any observed phenomena, recording time and place, affords, in my view, greater facilities for instruction than the most elaborate theories constructed upon spasmodic observation. From such a table there is to be elicited cause and effect; it sweeps away, as if by magic, preternatural surmises; it breaks down ill-founded theories of special interposition.

Of course the difficulties of preparing on a uniform plan a table extending over and through all the recorded ages of the peopled globe, are very considerable and varied. There is the primary difficulty of divergent chronologies; these have to be reconciled; there is the almost greater difficulty of the fabulous records, wherein even the most ordinary events are warped out of their true significance by the mode of relation; there is the age of Pagan superstition, when all occurrences are set down as judgments consequent upon the displeasure of the gods! There is the age of Christian superstition, wherein all occurrences which seem out of the ordinary course are either surrounded with a halo of suppositious light, or attributed to the direct wrath of an offended deity. There are the dark ages, when records are almost entirely absent, or when merely local occurrences are surrounded with all the importance of national calamities. There is the age following the advent of the printing press, when a plethora of recording power brings before us events out of all numerical proportion to those of pre-existing periods when such facilities of record did not exist. There is the yet later period of extended locomotion and communication, when events in far distant countries are for the first time brought under record—not indeed because it was the first time they or the like had occurred there, but because the means of communication are

---

* My lamented friend, the late Professor Jevons, so regarded their results. See also "The Doomed Comet," by Mr. J. A. Westwood Oliver, 1882, p. 30. I may take this opportunity of acknowledging the aid received from Mr. Oliver in the preparation of the present paper.

for the first time in existence. Finally, there is the age of scientific scepticism, when, in reviling the infatuated credulity of former periods, all causes but those apparent on the surface are ignored and even despised. The judicious historian and inquirer has to make allowances for the consequences resulting from these several stages of diversity; and in the process has to undergo much labour and meet with many discouragements and perplexities, which only those who have travelled over the same or like roads can comprehend or appreciate. The results are largely negative to the merely casual observer.

The preceding is no imaginary picture; the record of difficulties encountered might indeed be much extended if any purpose were served by it. The real object of referring to them is to bespeak considerate indulgence if conflicting, or apparently conflicting, records shall be presented in the Table of Plagues and Pestilences given in the Appendix. No pains have been spared to secure accuracy, no labour to ensure completeness. On this point of completeness I may here say, that at an earlier period I took no small trouble to see if it were possible to select any typical period wherein the laws affecting the production or removal of plagues and pestilences might be sufficiently illustrated without repetition of constantly recurring details. I tried the method of dealing with the so-called plagues only, leaving out of account the merely pestilential periods; but any such partial mode of treatment only became confusion worse confounded. I consulted my lamented friend and neighbour, Professor Jevons, thereon; but the opinion at which we separately arrived was that there was no useful course open but complete enumeration, whatever the labour involved might be.

While on this portion of the subject I must not omit to make proper acknowledgment to those who have preceded me. Here I have to speak with thankfulness of Bascome ("History of Epidemic "Pestilence," 1851),* of Haviland ("Climate, Weather, and

---

* "A History of Epidemic Pestilences from the Earliest Ages: with "Researches into their Nature, Causes, and Prophylaxis." By Edward Bascome, M.D., London. This book, to which reference is often made by subsequent writers on the subject of pestilences, as also in this paper, is composed of two parts, which are of very unequal merit. The larger portion of the work is a chronological history of pestilences, murrains, famines, insect plagues, earthquakes, storms, floods, droughts, and so on, the value of which is much lessened by the inaccuracy of the dates and non-citation of the authorities. The remainder, dealing with the nature, causes, and prevention of epidemic diseases, is more instructive. The views put forward are summed up in the following proposition: That atmospheric disturbance, consisting of variations of temperature, hygrometric influence, atmospheric pressure, electrical tension, &c., are the *exciting* causes, while want of light, impure air (especially from defective ventilation), malarial and other noxious vapours, scanty diet, and habits induced by an irregular and artificial manner of living, are the *predisposing* causes of epidemic pestilence or disease. The latter enervate and spoil the system, and render it more susceptible to the operation of the former. The theory is ingenious, but defective at many points. The work is

" Disease," 1855), of Howe (" Epidemic Diseases," 1865), of Parkin (" Epidemiology," 1880), and lastly, but by no means least, of the Commissioners of the Irish Census of 1851, by whom vast stores of information have been brought together; but in each case associated with so much that could not be made available, that the process of selection and elimination, to say nothing of harmonising the dates and occurrences, has been most considerable. Numerous other authorities have been consulted, and hundreds of cases added which had escaped previous record. I have, too, paid very especial attention to the literature of the subject. This literature is very vast, far more so than could at first sight be supposed. The object of incorporating it in its proper place in the table, is that future investigators may have the sources of more extended information as to particular outbreaks than it is possible in the present paper to supply ready to hand. It is, however, far from complete even yet.

Divisions of the Subject.

By way of completing this explanatory statement, it is necessary to say that while the several branches of the inquiry into plagues and pestilences as affecting human, animal, and vegetable life have to a large extent been pursued simultaneously, yet it now becomes necessary to treat of them separately. The chief reason is that of space; but there are in this also some advantages. There will be time for those so disposed to examine and reflect upon the facts now presented. I too shall have time for reinvestigating some of the considerations involved. On this occasion, then, I shall deal only with those outbreaks of plague and pestilence which have affected human life, or more correctly speaking, with these so far only as they have affected human life. In a subsequent paper or papers, plagues as affecting the lower animals, and as affecting the vegetable kingdom—and these are far more numerous than I at one time supposed—will receive detailed elucidation.

Causes of Plagues and Pestilences.

One purpose of the present inquiry is to furnish the data for arriving at some solution, or approximate solution, of the causes of the recurring phenomena which induce or produce plagues and other pestilential outbreaks. Are these physical?—*i.e.*, resultant from the physical condition of the globe. Are they climatic?—as the term is generally understood. Are they planetary?—*i.e.*, regulated by position or conjunction of the planets; or are they the result of any combination of these influences? Do they recur at stated or uniform intervals, so as to presuppose a law of periodicity? If the latter, does the sun-spot theory throw any light upon their

chiefly of interest as one of the earlier attempts to place the whole subject of pestilential diseases upon a scientific basis. I may add that the quotations I have made from it here have been verified by the aid of Mr. Raymond H. Vose.

recurrence? Are plagues directly produced at all, or do they always result from some infraction of nature's laws, and thus rank as only secondary, and possibly avoidable effects? Again, are they designed for the subjugation and punishment of man? Are they manifestations of divine wrath—judgments, in fact? Or are they designed as a counterpoise to over-population? Further, do they commence with man, and pass from him, and through him, to the lower branch of animal creation, and thence down to the vegetable kingdom? Or is their order entirely the reverse of this, beginning with the vegetation, and so affecting the food of man and the lower animals alike? Or have those who avoid animal food any special exemption? Are there any parts of the world, or any known conditions of life, which are exempt or can secure exemption from these dread destroyers? Do the dark races suffer equally with the white?. (see Table, 1837). These are some of the enigmas which meet us at the threshold of the inquiry. Others follow in rapid succession, as its successive phases dawn upon us. For instance, have plagues and pestilences been all the same in character, although varying in designation, from the beginning? Or do they change their character with the changing social condition of the inhabitants of the globe? Is there such a thing as a *new* disease of an epidemic character?* Why are pestilences sometimes light and gentle in their effects, at other times virulent? Can there be more than one pestilential disease operating amongst the same people at the same time?† Is there any progressive development?‡ Many of

---

* Bascome answers this question from a medical point of view in the following passage:—
"If we refer to the histories of ancient nations, as well as to the modern annals of medicine, we shall find therein recorded the same character of diseases, arising from like causes, occurring during similar seasons, happening in similar localities, and marked pretty generally by the same circumstances." "The supposition of the existence of any new disease in our day is . . . . untenable, but to be accounted for because of our inability to trace diseases under the same names and precise characteristic symptoms described by our predecessors in the study of nature; in fact, the comparatively modern origin of some diseases may be said to rest on the absence or deficiency of distinct and express notice of them in the writings of the ancients, arising in some measure from false or imperfect translations from the original, and from the practice of the ancients in referring different malignant maladies to the same pestilential constitution."—" Hist. Epid. Pest.," pp. 186 and 187.

† It has frequently been observed that epidemic anginas, catarrhs, measles, &c., precede great and destructive plagues and pestilences. It is so in our day. The terrible pestilential cholera of 1817 and subsequent years was preceded by influenza, &c. For the constitution of the seasons by which these diseases are caused, becomes increased in its malignancy and powers by the repeated accumulation of the peculiar poison, and it consequently induces the highest gradation of disease, pestilence, or plague—all these distempers being essentially similar, differing in appearance only, as modified by climate, season, &c., and also by the duration and energy of various efficient causes.—BASCOME, pp. 92 and 93.

‡ Thucydides noticed that during the plague of *Athens* other diseases declined:

these points will present themselves for consideration and solution as we proceed.

Different Theories.

I need hardly say that the theories of different writers, at different periods, and in different countries, regarding pestilences, present an infinite variety—ranging from the sweeping assertion that they are but the natural outcome of the operation of the physical causes which affect the destiny of terrestrial existence, down to the more precise and narrower issue of their being special manifestations of divine wrath directed against the commission of particular transgressions. If they be part of the general law of the universe, and therefore not to be avoided, they must be regarded as designed to check redundant population, or for some other wise if inscrutable purpose. I have not hitherto seen any argument, nor observed any indications which go entirely to support this view. If they be only the manifestations of divine displeasure (which I should be sorry to feel compelled to believe) consequent upon special causes of transgressions, physical or moral, there is hope of the future; but there is also despair. Then there is the cosmical theory, that the globe has been passing through stages which will no more recur, and hence the cause being removed, the consequences can no more ensue. But, as I have said, all the theories extant have been deduced from a very partial and incomplete survey of the premises, and as a consequence are, in my judgment, entitled to very little weight. I will ask my readers to do what I have myself endeavoured to do—to discard all former teachings, or even surmises, and be content to follow the weight of evidence as it may be revealed by the following survey, deduced mainly from the facts contained in the chronological table which forms the Appendix to this portion of the inquiry; although for reasons of brevity and clearness I have usually omitted reference to the supposed causes in the table.

Classification of Causes.

After this preliminary survey, I may now attempt a classification of the causes of plagues and pestilences, as recorded by historians, as gathered from scientific and other writers, or as resulting from the present inquiry generally. These may be stated as follows :—

" And, besides this, none of those diseases to which they were accustomed afflicted them at that time, or whatever there was, ended in this."—" Hist.," lib. ii, 51. This phenomenon has neither been unrepeated nor passed unnoticed in later days. In treating of the nervous fever of 1771, in *Ireland*, Sims (" Observations ") says that the disorder claimed " the prerogative of the plague, almost all others vanishing before its sovereign presence."

1. DIRECT OR IMMEDIATE CAUSES, viz. :—

   i. Judgments.

   ii. Abnormal state of the atmosphere, arising from :—

     (*a*). The introduction of extraneous matter or gases from space—meteorites, cosmic dust, &c.

     (*b*). Dust, sulphurous gases, &c., ejected from active volcanos; or the liberation of gases, and atmospheric commotions, consequent upon earthquakes.

     (*c*). Noxious gases, from decaying vegetable matter left after the subsidence of floods; and consequent upon blight, &c.

     (*d*). Effluvia from putrefying bodies uninterred during sieges, after battles, wars, floods, &c.

     (*e*). Putrefying animal or other matter, affecting the surface water, or vitiating the atmosphere.

     (*f*). Exhalations from the soil.

     (*g*). Contamination of the general water supply, which may be affected in ways too numerous for detailed specification.

2. PREDISPOSING CAUSES, as :—

   iii. Abnormal condition of the system induced by :—

     (*h*). Want of food; famine; change of food.

     (*i*). Sudden change of climate; hence the frequency of pestilence in *marching armies*.

     (*j*). Fatigue.

     (*k*). Fear.

     (*l*). Excessive luxury or debauchery.

     (*m*). Crowded and unhealthy dwellings.

     (*n*). Excessive crowding in cities during wars, &c.

3. INDIRECT CAUSES :—

     (*o*). *Drought*, by permitting the accumulation of foreign matter in the air.

     (*p*). *Floods*, by inducing an excess of moisture in the air.

     (*q*). Plagues of insects, and all the direct causes of *famine*.

It is clear that this classification is too involved for detailed consideration here, and I have been seeking for a broader one, as, for instance—I. Celestial, and II. Terrestrial influences. But here I am brought face to face with another difficulty, that of definition. The word "celestial," in its strict sense, means matters relating to heaven—spiritual influences. In its broadest sense it includes the entire planetary system—the sun, the moon, and stars—seen and unseen; as also "the twelve celestial signs," with all their occult associations; and, since the earth is a planet, it therefore forms part of the celestial system. In this sense all the considerations would fall under the first division. It becomes necessary, therefore, to seek some modification, and I think this may be found in the assumption that to us who dwell on this planet, the incidents which affect it physically are to us terrestrial influences; the celestial being (from this point of view) such as are not dependent upon the physical condition, and, so to speak, local operations of our globe. This distinction admitted, we have secured on the terrestrial side earthquakes and volcanic eruptions with their accompaniments. But other difficulties yet arise. The seasons, which so greatly affect our health and our lives, are believed to be mainly dependent upon the influence of the sun and on the relative positions of many other planets. Their operations hence fall to be classed on the celestial side. Then as to effluvia from putrefying animal bodies and noxious gases from decaying vegetable matter, these seem at first sight peculiarly terrestrial. But are they so? Do they not rather come within the range of those

> "Pestilential vapours
> Which the *sun* sucks up from bogs, fens, flats."

And hence demand to form a branch of the influences classed as celestial?

In this perplexing conflict I turn to the scientific writers for some light; but the result is confusion, mystification, and manifest uncertainty! Science has hitherto dealt piecemeal only with the phenomena of plagues and pestilences. The subject, as a whole, has entirely eluded its grasp. This I regard as in some degree fortunate: it leaves me at all events free to follow such an arrangement as may seem best suited to my present purpose. I shall in the main, therefore, adopt the celestial and terrestrial classification, keeping in view immediate or direct causes, as distinguished from the predisposing and more remote influences. That certain overlapping and apparent contradictions will arise, appears to me a foregone and unavoidable conclusion.

Direct or Immediate Causes—Celestial and Terrestrial.

Upon these the weight of the investigation falls. They may be ranged under two main divisions: I. Judgments. II. Disturbance of the earth's surface, and the consequences thereof. These will be separately examined:—

JUDGMENTS.—I take a few of the recorded cases, treating them entirely historically, and naming them chronologically, as far as the authorities quoted admit. Here are first a few taken from the

Pagan mythology, which is particularly indifferent about chronology, although the location is indicated :—

Phanidæ (Attica). Plague, a punishment for the slaughter of a sacred bear.

Luceria (Thessaly). Plague of Coronis. "Coronis being pregnant with Æsculapius, and having shown disrespect to a young Arcadian named Ischys, Apollo was so irritated by it that he sent the goddess Diana, his sister, to Luceria, where Coronis lived, for the purpose of exciting a plague, of which Coronis herself died."—PINDAR.

Sicyon. Apollo and Artemis, after the destruction of the Python, had wished to be purified at Sicyon-Ægyallia ; but being driven away by a phantom, they proceeded to Carmanor, in Crete ; upon this the inhabitants of Sicyon were attacked by a pestilence, and rites seem to have been ordered to appease the gods. —SMITH'S " Greek and Roman Antiquities."

Samaria. This is what we find written of Shalmaneser in the Chronicles of the Syrians :—" Now the new comers in Samaria are called Chuthites, from a country of Persia of that name, and from the river Chutah, from which they had their origin. There were five nations of them, and they brought as many of their own country gods along with them, highly provoking the true and the Great God to indignation against them for the worship they paid to these idols, so that they were visited with so dreadful a plague that the place was well nigh unpeopled with it ; and, finding no relief from any human means, they were advised by the Oracle to have recourse to the worship of the Great God . . . . They had the law of Moses read, with an explication upon the practice, and the reason of their religion and discipline, which had so powerful an effect upon them that they gave themselves wholly up to the study and exercise of it ; and soon after the pestilence ceased."—JOSEPHUS'S " Antiquities," lib. ix, c. 14.

Then follows another series, wherein time as well as place is indicated :—

Troy. 1184 B.C. " Homer [" Iliad," book i] speaks of the plague which prostrated the Greek camp at the siege of Troy, and ascribes it to the wrath of . . . . [Apollo], who was offended by an insult offered to Chryses, his high priest. But though deep-rooted superstition was fain to impose on the gentle god the blame of the hurtful visitation, the great poet does not forget to indicate a powerful auxiliary to the god's malevolence in the filth lying about the camp, and introduces Agamemnon, who orders it to be thrown into the sea. This, if the first recorded step in sanitary reform, is certainly a notable one, and shows the inclination, even in those distant days, to break through the barriers of ignorance and credulity by seeking out and removing the real causes of pestilential diseases."—FLEMING, " Animal Plagues," Introd., p. xx.

B.C. 1105.—"Corvina was instituted to Apollo upon Hyppolitus killing a prophet of Apollo, which was followed by a plague."—" Univ. Hist.," vol. xix, p. 195.

Delphi, B.C. 581.—Plague and famine, as a punishment for the ill-treatment of Æsop.—PLUTARCH.

Rome, B.C. 260.—" A dreadful plague raged, when, the Sibylline books being consulted, a vestal was convicted of incontinence, and condemned to be buried alive ; to prevent which she strangled herself."—BOYLE, i, 114.

Now if we turn to the Scripture records, we find the following :—

The Plagues of *Egypt*, B.C. 1491.—It seems that these were rather torments than plagues, as we are here regarding them. The mortality to human life is believed to have been small.

Taberah (in the wilderness), B.C. 1480 (about).—" The fire of the Lord burnt among " the Israelites in the wilderness, because they were discontented. Numbers xi, 1.

This is supposed to refer to an outbreak of venereal disease.*

Kibroth-hattaavah (in the wilderness).—About the same period. Angered at the Israelites lusting after flesh-meat, the Lord sent multitudes of quails, "and while the flesh was between their teeth . . . . the Lord smote the people with a very great plague." Numbers xi, 33.

Kadesh, B.C. 1471.—Plague among the Israelites, because they murmured at the punishment of Korah, Dathan, and Abiram for rebellion; 14,700 died. Numbers xvi, 49.

Canaan, B.C. 1017.—David having sinned in taking a census of Israel without divine permission, the Lord gave him the option of (1) seven years' famine, (2) three months' flight before the enemies' swords, or (3) three days' pestilence. David chose, and "the Lord sent a pestilence upon Israel, and there fell 70,000 men." 2 Samuel xxiv.

The same account is repeated in 1 Chronicles xxi, except that the alternative famine is for three instead of seven years.

Here is a remarkable instance of supplicating for a judgment: it seems almost necessary to say that this is attributed to the sister isle. The authority is perhaps as reliable as in some of the other instances quoted :—

Ireland, A.D. 665.—Over-population caused a dearth of food, and famine prepared the way for the pestilence, which had broken out in England the year

---

* The following is a more modern instance of a pestilence of the same character :—

In the latter part of March, 1493, the venereal disease broke out in Rome, and continued until 1499. It produced such mortality in Spain that the royal physicians were instructed to attend to the sufferers, and numbers of the first physicians of the land investigated the symptoms, but without being able to find a remedy. It was accordingly regarded as a *chastisement from Heaven*. In Rome the cure employed was a mercurial ointment mixed with lead—a specific said to be due to a Portuguese—but with what success we are not told. In 1495 the disease appeared in the army of Charles VIII at Naples. Respecting the cause of this singular outbreak in Europe there have been various opinions. It began, according to Dr. Bascome ("Hist. Epid. Pest ," p. 72), in the form of a pestilential fever, communicable through the genitals and otherwise. Its source was traced by some to the troops of Admiral Christobal Colon, which were said to have brought it over from America. Astruc has shown, however, that the disease was unknown before its appearance in Europe. The first notice of it is to be found in the work of Arden, surgeon to Richard II, which was published sometime about the middle of the twelfth century. From Bishop Winton's records of the public stews, it appears that the disease was known in England more than three hundred years before it became so prevalent in Italy and Spain, its name being "brenning" or "burning." When it broke out in the French army, in 1495, the French people called it "the disease of Naples," and attributed it to the eating of human flesh, which some merchants had packed in barrels and sold to the soldiers for tunny. As Bascome remarks, it is certain that cannibals are much infected with the venereal disease; but we need hardly adopt such a fanciful explanation, when we know that the complaint was very prevalent in Rome at the time of the siege of Naples (?), and could easily have been communicated to the invaders. The medical writers of the time mostly ascribe it to the baleful influence of certain conjunctions of the planets.

An outbreak of venereal disease in Cork, in 1735, which caused much scandal, was traced to a monthly nurse employed in confinements. In "drawing the breasts" of her patients she imparted the disease. The discovery was made by Dr. Barry, an eminent physician in that city.

before. It carried off great numbers. It is recorded that two of the kings called a council at Temora, and that a general fast was decreed in order that God might be solicited "to remove by some species of pestilence the burthensome multitudes of the inferior people." A faction headed by St. Gerald moved "to supplicate the Almighty not to reduce the number of the men till it answered the quantity of corn usually produced, but to increase the produce of the land, so that it might satisfy the wants of the people." The nobles carried the day; a pestilence was prayed for, and they themselves were among the victims to the disease.—*Vide* "Report of Irish Census, 1851," part v, vol. i, p. 51.

Nor is this view confined to Ireland. Mr. JACKSON, Consul at Mogador, in his "Travels in Africa," describing the plague which depopulated Western Barbary in 1799 and 1800, says that the Mühamedans regard the plague as a good or blessing sent from God to clear the world of a superfluous population.

In JOHN BALE'S "Tragedy or Interlude" of the "Promises of "God," (1537), *Pater Cœlestis, loq.*:—

> "Whych wyll compell me agaynst man for to make
> In my dyspleasure, and sende plages of coreccyon
> Most grevouse and sharpe, hys wanton lustes to slake
> By water and fyre, by sycknesse and infeccyon,
> Of pestylent sores molestynge hys compleccyon."

Rapin (Book X), after speaking of the exultation consequent on the success of the English army on the field of Cressy in 1347, and the subsequent surrender of Calais in 1348, says :—

"During the prosperity enjoyed by the English, it is no wonder that ease and plenty threw them into the excesses that are the usual attendants thereof. All the historians unanimously affirm that an unbridled debauchery at this time prevailed through the kingdom; and the women, laying aside their modesty, the great ornament of their sex, seemed to glory in the loss of their virtue. Nothing was more common than to see them riding in troops to the tournaments, dressed like cavaliers, with swords by their sides, and mounting their steeds, adorned with rich trappings, without any regard to their honour or reputation. The men's excesses were no less scandalous. *God permitted not these disorders to go long unpunished.* A terrible plague, after raging in Asia and part of Europe, spread itself into France, and from thence into England, where it made such desolation that one-half of the nation was swept away. London especially felt the effects of its fury; and it is observed in one year [1348-49] above 50,000 persons were buried in a churchyard belonging to the Cistercians [Charter House]."

The belief in these direct judgments has remained down to very modern times. Here is an instance :—

In Burton's "Judgments upon Sabbath Breakers" (1641), he narrates certain incidents regarding the erection of a maypole at Dartmouth, and some disregard of authority associated therewith; and he concludes as follows :—"Now although this revelling was not on the Lord's Day, yet being upon any other day and especially May day, the maypole set up thereon giving occasion to the profanation of the Lord's Day the whole year after, *it was sufficient to provoke God to send plagues and judgments* among them."

Dr. TIMONE, who practised at Constantinople for many years, says, in a paper on the plague at Constantinople ("Phil. Trans."

for 1720), that "the common people, and especially the poorer
" sort, not only of the Turks, but also of the Christians and Jews,
" believing the plague to be sent as a punishment from Heaven,
" take no measures whatever to avoid the contagion."

In this connection, the belief in plague *omens* is noteworthy :—

In the Archiepiscopal Library at Lambeth, there is a MS. "Caxton's Chronicle,"
differing from the printed chronicle, which records that in 1461 "ther bred a
raven at Charyng Crosse at London. And never was seen noon brede there before.
And after that came a gret dethe of pestilence that lasted iij yer. And peple dyed
myghtely in every place, man, woman, and chyle. On whose soulys God have
mercy. Amen."

Witchcraft.—The dread inspired by pestilence has resulted in superstitions far
less elevated than these. Among the fragmentary remainder of a great aboriginal
people one illustration survives. In a village of the North American Indians the
chief men died of a plague. The "medicine men knew well that the bird of
death which flapped its wings and uttered its cries every night over the cabins of
those doomed to destruction, could be none other than a transformed wizard ; but
all their arts availed nothing. At last a deputation from the doomed village
visited the lodge of The-Man-With-Very-Long-Hair, a hermit of the wilderness,
to implore assistance. He made them some charmed arrows. With one of these
they wounded the fatal bird. The next day a young man living in a poor wigwam
with his mother was reported to be very ill. Some of the elders visited him, and
found, as they expected, the magical arrow sticking in his flesh ; under pretence of
withdrawing it, they gave it such a thrust as to kill him."

EARTHQUAKES.—These are the more potent of the terrestrial
causes of plagues and pestilences. There are certain Scriptural
associations. Thus in the 14th chapter of the book of Zechariah
there is a prophecy that an *earthquake* shall precede the plague
which he foretold should destroy the enemies of Jerusalem. In
St. Luke (xvii, 2), "and great *earthquakes* shall be in divers
places, and famines and *pestilences.*"

Athens, 435-30 B.C.—Thucydides mentions that this plague was
associated with the occurrence of serious earthquakes, which prevented the annual invasion of Attica. I judge that the plague had
commenced before these occurred ; but the chronology is not clear.

Black Death, 1348.—During the prevalence of this disease, and
preceding its appearance in Italy and other parts of Europe, fearful
earthquakes, fiery meteors, and terrestrial commotions of all descriptions are recorded.

1517.—There was a violent earthquake shock in central Germany. In this year the third visitation of sweating sickness
occurred ; but still more striking, encephalitis became epidemic in
central Europe. At the same time there broke out in Holland an
unusual but malignant disease—now known to have been diphtheria.

There are yet other considerations arising out of the influence
of earthquakes upon the human system in pestilential periods,
chiefly in the production of *fear.* This part of the subject will fall
to be considered in more detail in another division of the inquiry ;

but I may take the following passage from Haviland (*climate, &c.*) :
—" We know not the effect of an earthquake upon the minds of
" those who witness this convulsion of nature ; we cannot estimate
" its remote effect upon children that are still in the womb ; we
" know, however, full well the extraordinary consequences, both
" physical and mental, that succeed to the impressions made on the
" mind of the mother. May we not infer, therefore, that the effect
" of the shock of an earthquake has not merely an immediate but a
" remote effect upon the people ?" The point of which is that an
earthquake occurring either before or during the existence of a
pestilence may very largely increase the mortality, even without
reference to consequences of the earthquake in the direction of
noxious vapours or ashes.

VOLCANIC ERUPTIONS.—The exact relations between earthquakes
and volcanos I believe is not yet by any means understood.
Mr. Haviland said (1855) :—" A history of volcanic eruptions,
" earthquakes, and their sequels, so far as regards the *health of*
" *nations*, would be a valuable and interesting addition to the lite-
" rature of our [the medical] profession. The incandescent bowels
" of the earth appear to me to be a powerful instrument in the
" hands of the Almighty, with which He punishes and terrifies His
" children in order to make them sensible of His wrath and their
" sinfulness." (p. 143.)

1783.—During this year there was a great eruption of Mount
Hecla, the most tremendous one on record. It was accompanied by
violent wind and rain and a darkness of the heavens. The inhabitants (of Iceland) thought their end had come, and not without
reason : the end of their little world seemed at hand. The fire
spouts from the volcano, after rising to a considerable height in
the air, formed a torrent of red-hot lava, that flowed for six weeks,
and ran a distance of 60 miles in the sea, in a broken breadth of
nearly 12 miles. Twelve rivers were dried up, twenty-one villages
totally overwhelmed by fire or water, and thirty-four others were
materially injured by fire and water. In the same year there were
most destructive earthquakes in Italy and Messina. Dreadful
pestilences prevailed all through Europe ; but we are most concerned to consider the consequences which befell the people of
Iceland :

" Diseases of the most inveterate kinds, in the form of scurvy, broke out in
sundry places, and those even far distant from the fire ; as for instance in the
districts of Guldbringue, Borgefiorde, and Myhre, especially in the first. The
district of West Skaptefield was, however, the chief seat of this distemper ; and
in only six parishes there, no less than 150 persons were carried off between the
commencement of the new year and the month of June following ; but some of
these perished by famine. The same symptoms showed themselves in this disorder
in the human race as among the cattle. The feet, thighs, hips, arms, throat, and
head were most dreadfully swelled, especially about the ankles, the knees, and the

various joints, which last, as well as the ribs, were contracted. The sinews too were drawn up with painful cramps, so that the wretched sufferers became crooked, and had an appearance the most pitiable.

In addition to this they were oppressed with pains across the breast and loins; their teeth became loose, and were covered by the swollen gums, which at length mortified, and fell off in large pieces of a black or sometimes dark blue colour. Disgusting sores were formed in the palate and throat, and not uncommonly, at the termination of the disease, the tongue rotted entirely out of the mouth. This dreadful, though apparently not very infectious distemper, prevailed in almost every farm in the vicinity of the fire during the winter and spring . . . It is necessary here to remark that the disorder principally attacked those who had previously suffered from want and hunger, and who had protracted a miserable existence by eating the flesh of such animals (not even excepting horses) as had died of the same distemper, and by having recourse to boiled skins and other most unwholesome and indigestible food."—HOOKER, "Tour in Iceland," vol. ii; BRUGMAN's "Verhandeling over een Zwavelagtige nevel," p. 11; "Kuobloch Sammlung," v, ii, p. 522; Lord DUFFERIN, "Letters from High Latitudes," p. 113.

MEPHITIC VAPOURS.—These are more particularly, though not exclusively, associated with earthquake and volcanic phenomena. The term "mephetical" is defined by Webster as being "offensive " to the smell; foul; poisonous; noxious; pestilential; destructive " to life." De Quincy speaks of the "mephitic regions of carbonic " acid gas." Carbonic acid gas is sometimes called mephitic acid, or mephitic air. Thus the meaning is made plain.

These mephitic vapours appear to have played a more important part in the history of pestilences than they have heretofore had credit for.

The first reference I find is that in the year 140 B.C. The Roman armies operating in Algeria had charged the atmosphere with mephitic vapours, with the view of producing pestilence amongst the inhabitants; but the army itself fell a victim to these! This at least shows that their noxious character was well understood at that early period. The next instance belongs to the class fabulous:—

A.D. 168.—A disease appeared in *Rome* during the reign of Marcus Aurelius Antoninus and Lucius Verus, preceded by a more destructive plague in Asia, which the great Ammianus Marcellinus, the philosophic hero, asserted *arose from the foul air of a small box* which a Roman soldier had opened at the capture of Seleucia. This statement, which has been regarded by some writers as founded upon superstition, finds support, or at all events solution, from some facts which follow.

A.D. 561, *Ireland.*—" A poisoned pool made its appearance in " that region [Meath] through a chasm of the earth, and a vapour " proceeded from it, which produced a fatal disease in men and " beasts of burden."—ST. ÆDUS, vol. i, p. 422.

Coming nearer to modern times: it is recorded in Cooper's "Annals of Cambridge" (i, 39), that in 1223, at *Barnwell* (near

Cambridge), March or April, as the Bishop of Ely was giving orders, in the first week of Lent, there arose such a tempest of rain and thunder, "that all in the church were readie to fall to the "ground, and such flashes of lightning entered the church that each "man thought it had been set on fire; and *such a filthie stench* "*arose withal, that manie of the companie fell sick thereof and hardly* "*escaped death.*"

In A.D. 1345-49 a plague spread over the world, which, it is —— said, left scarcely a fourth part of the human race alive. Guido de Gaullaco tells us that it broke out in Spain in the month of March, and from other medical writers (Andres Laguna, Martinez de Leyva, and Duarte Nunhez) we learn that it lasted five years. An Arabian physician asserts that the pestilence first broke out in Africa, thence spread to Egypt and Asia, and finally attacked Italy, France and Spain. Villanius, the historian of Florence, gives yet another account. He says that the disease first appeared in Cathay or China, *where it arose from the vapour proceeding from a certain fiery body which fell from the atmosphere or was eructated from the earth.* The pestilence spread throughout Asia, entered Egypt, Greece, Italy, France, Spain, England, and lastly, Germany. The mortality was awful. In the city of Florence, St. Anthony computed the number of victims to have been 100,000. (Villanius says about 60,000.) In London, 50,000 deaths are said to have occurred in one week. 100,000 perished at Venice; 90,000 in Lubeck; and the deaths in the kingdom of Spain were computed at 200,000. For further particulars, see Bascome, pp. 48 and 49.

At *Foggia* (Naples), in A.D. 1731, pestilential vapours issued from rents in the ground made by an earthquake on 20th March. Many persons perished by inhaling the fumes.—BOYLE, ii, 65.

The *Grotto del Cani*, or *Bocca venenosa*, by the Lake of Agrano, near Naples, still exhales noxious vapours, powerful enough to kill any animal entering the *mafetta*, unless its stature is such as to prevent its inhaling the gas, for the vapour does not rise far from the ground.

Professor Rogers ("Agriculture and Prices," i, 293) adopts the theory—after a careful review of the progress of the *Black Death* in the fourteenth century—that it was very likely consequent upon the great physical convulsions which had preceded the outbreak, that foreign substances of a deleterious character had been projected into the atmosphere, and permanently infected its lower regions, and could not, by the ordinary powers of dispersion possessed by the air, be easily eliminated or neutralised. He supports this view as follows:—"We are informed, as part of a "physical theory which may account for the prevalence of "bronchitis accompanied by severe depression of the vital powers,

" that such a state may be induced accidentally by inhaling very
" small quantities of the vapour of selenium; and if this sub-
" stance—a product of volcanic action—were dispersed in the air,
" that there might be, probably is, a general affection of all who
" are subject to its influences."

But the great champion and exponent of the mephitic vapours
theory is Dr. John Parkin, whose work on "Epidemiology" will
receive attention in my investigations into the other branches of
pestilence. Those who are familiar with Humboldt's "Cosmos,"
will remember the many instances he gives which are confirmatory
of the theory.

METEORIC OR COSMIC DUST.—One of the most modern theories
regarding pestilences is that they may be the result of an hitherto
unexpected and therefore unexplained cause, viz., the prevalence in
the atmosphere of metallic particles, designated most suggestively
cosmic dust. Experiment has shown that this prevails in considerable quantities, much more in dry than in wet seasons; for the
rain washes it out of the air into the earth. This dust is found to
be composed of iron, nickel, cobalt, and other substances known in
chemistry. Mr. Ranyard is of opinion that its presence and its
purposes will throw much light upon hitherto unexplained phenomena regarding the earth and the conditions of our existence upon
it. His paper, which contains references to all previous writings
upon the subject down to 1878, is printed in the Monthly Notices of
the Royal Astronomical Society (vol. xxxix, p. 161). The consideration of this question was referred to a committee of the British Association, and a brief report will be found in Proceedings of that body
for 1881 (p. 88).

It is there suggested that some systematic observations be made.
Pending these, I will merely append a few notes which I have
made in the present investigation, having, as I think, a bearing
upon this question :—

A.D. 92.—The Jewish writer Philo describes a pestilence which occurred after
the great eruption of Vesuvius in A.D. 88. "The clouds of dust suddenly falling
on men and cattle, produced over the whole skin a severe and intractable ulceration : the body immediately became tumid with efflorescences or purulent phlyctenæ,
which appeared like blisters excited by a secret fire beneath. Men necessarily
undergoing much pain and universal soreness from ulceration and inflammation,
suffered not less in body than in mind by the severe affliction, for a continuous
ulcer was observable from head to foot."

In A.D. 590, while a pestilence prevailed at Rome, the air was observed to be
filled with a sort of mist, which induced violent sneezing. At that time it became
the custom to salute a person sneezing with the expression, "Dominus tecum."
Bascome says (p. 27), "the practice has descended to our own time." May this
"mist" have been not vapour but cosmic dust ?

Here, as at every branch of the inquiry, we meet with the
confusions of mythology.

Mephitis was one of the titles of Juno, and she was supposed to wield the destructive powers of noxious vapours.

HAZE.—A haze or "dry fog" has been the frequent accompaniment of modern cholera visitations. There was such a haze seen in 1782. When viewed in the mass it was of a pale blue shade, possessed peculiar drying properties, and had a strong and peculiar odour. This was the year of the eruption of Mount Hecla (Iceland). There were also great and most destructive earthquakes in Italy. Hence the haze has been supposed to be connected with the earthquakes, and the epidemics with the haze. This haze, which has usually been regarded as associated with moisture—and so associated with the vapours arising from the earth—seems more likely hereafter to be properly classed with fire, with the eruptions of volcanos, with the escaping gases from the upheaval of the surface of the earth by earthquakes. The dispersion of the haze in 1783 was attended with a severe thunderstorm. Have we not in this metallic haze a gas which may account for lightning, and the formation of meteoric stones ?

Dr. Prout regards it as highly probable that some such mineral as selenium—nearly allied to sulphur, and a volcanic product—when combined with hydrogen gas in the form of seleniuretted hydrogen, is *capable of producing all the effects which characterise influenza.* A bubble of this gas, about the size of a split pea, deprived Berzelius completely of his sense of smell, and induced a severe catarrh, lasting fifteen days. At another time he suffered most severely from accidentally inhaling this gas.

All this seems to point to the fact that the haze may be associated with the powerful agents which do seem to pervade the air after volcanic and earthquake eruptions. See table, A.D. 568. And it is clear on scientific grounds that some diseases may be so occasioned.

POISONING THE WATERS, &c.—Amongst the direct causes, I ought to mention this as associated more particularly with the "Black "Death" of the fourteenth century. It arose out of the superstitions of the people, who were not only unduly terrified, but the different sects and parties were led to accuse each other of poisoning the waters, and other similar mal-practices. Both Christians and Jews in their turn appear to have been persecuted unto death in great numbers. At Mentz, 12,000 Jews are stated to have fallen victims to the fury of an ignorant and brutal populace, under the pretext that they had poisoned the waters of the wells of that city.—MARSHALL, 1832, p. 10.

In the pestilence which prevailed in *Italy*, A.D. 190-95, when the diurnal mortality was stated to be 2,000, it was believed that this outbreak was propagated by thrusting poisoned needles into people's bodies.

Of the same class is the following:—The city of *Milan* suffered from a severe visitation of the plague in 1630. There was a popular belief in the propagation of the disease by persons who were supposed to have anointed the walls of the houses with a poison fatal to those who touched it. Many persons accused of being *untôri* (anointers) were subjected to torture in order to procure confessions and accusations; and, being tried, were found guilty, and executed with circumstances of appalling cruelty. The house of a barber named Mora, who was supposed to have compounded the poison, was pulled down and a column erected on the site, which remained standing near the Via Ticinense till 1778, and was called the Colonna Infame, or Column of Infamy.

It was upon these incidents that the late Italian poet and historian Manzoni founded his famous "Storia della Colonna "Infame." Published 1842.

Indirect Causes—Celestial and Terrestrial.

The indirect influences which lead to the production of plagues and pestilences cover a very wide range; and being indirect, it may chance that they cannot all be enumerated with exactitude. The line too between the direct and the indirect causes is at some points a very narrow one. I do not profess to have drawn it very accurately in all cases, but I do claim to have drawn it impartially. I give the planetary influences priority, but not without some misgivings.

PLANETARY INFLUENCES.—There seems always to have been an opinion that epidemical diseases are largely associated with planetary influences. It is sometimes said that this belief originated in the "dark ages." Uneducated people are always superstitious. It is in the ordinary course of things that they should be so. They see the grand operations of nature, but understand them not. Comets, eclipses, lightning, storms, meteors, and other signs of the heavens—the aurora borealis more especially—are regarded by them as supernatural portents; and the next succeeding disaster, be it pestilence or otherwise, is forthwith associated with the latest of these. Cause and effect are not determined by exact processes of reasoning in such cases. But we may go back far beyond what we regard as the dark ages for the origin of such beliefs. Those who have had occasion to consult ancient medical literature—such for instance as the Iatro-meteorology of Hippocrates—will know that the enlightened Greek philosophers left little in this line of speculation to the benighted ecclesiastics of the middle ages.

Hecker remarks hereon:—" That Omnipotence which has called " the world with all its living creatures into one animated being, " especially reveals Himself in the desolation of great pestilences.

" The powers of creation come into violent collision, the sultry
" dryness of the atmosphere, the subterraneous thunders, the mist
" of overflowing waters, are all the harbingers of destruction.
" Nature is not satisfied with the ordinary alternations of life and
" death, and the destroying angel waves over man and beast his
" flaming sword." That view profoundly impressed itself upon
nearly all the chroniclers of plagues and pestilences, and in following and quoting from their records I have not attempted its entire
obliteration.

In recent years there seems something of a revival of the
pedantry—it may be the wisdom—of astrology. The Royal
Astronomical Society had before it a paper by one of its own members a few years since (1878, I believe), dealing with the several
coincidences of great epidemics with the perihelia of the superior
planets. Dr. Knapp, writing to the " New York Medical Journal,"
in 1878, remarked that " at former periods it has been observed
" that the approach of one or more of the great planets of the solar
" system occasioned disturbance in the atmosphere, causing great
" heat and cold, rains, drought, blighting of crops and fruits, epi-
" demic diseases among the human race, and epizoötics among
" animals, consequent on the interference with or abstraction of the
" usual amount of light and heat."

Mr. Alfred J. Pearce (" Times," May, 1879) said, " Having
" prosecuted an inquiry into planetary action on our atmosphere
" for nearly twenty years, I may be allowed, perhaps, to suggest to
" Mr. Lowe that he should pay particular attention to the conjunc-
" tions and oppositions of the sun and planets, and their angular
" positions at the solar ingresses into Aries, Cancer, Libra, and
" Capricorn. For instance, at the vernal ingress this year the sun
" was very nearly conjoined with Saturn in the northern angle
" (the meridian under the earth). Hence the weather of the
" spring quarter has been cold and stormy, vegetation has been
" backward, and farmers and gardeners have experienced great
" losses. On the 30th of June next there will happen a conjunction
" of Mars and Saturn in the 16th degree of the sign Aries."

Another correspondent to the same journal (H. A. R.) said,
" Coincident with the theory of the sun's cycle, another reason why
" extraordinary atmospheric phenomena may be expected till 1885
" is not unworthy of notice—viz., the perihelion periods, or nearest
" to the sun of the four largest planets, Jupiter, Saturn, Uranus,
" and Neptune. The perihelion of all these planets coincidently
" has not occurred for more than 1,800 years."

I did not know all these things when I commenced this branch
of the inquiry: if I had, the work would probably have been left
to others. I knew that Dr. Parkin said in the introduction of his

" Epidemiology " (1880), that " we are now living in an epidemic,
" or pestilential epoch." That fact has induced me to persevere in
an inquiry which at times has seemed hopeless and overwhelming.
I have not yet learned precisely all the ramifications of planetary
influences in association therewith. I am glad, therefore, that the
more formal consideration of this branch of the subject has to stand
over until another occasion.

ELECTRIC TENSION.—It has long been recognised that the electric
condition of the atmosphere has played a more or less important
part in the promulgation of epidemic and perhaps other diseases.

In 1864 Mr. William Craig (of Ayr) published a work " On the
" Influence of Variations of Electric Tension as the remote cause of
" Epidemic and other Diseases." He contends that all the usually
regarded influences of filth, impure air, contagion, miasmata, are
as nought in the production of epidemics compared with variations
in electric tension.

This same point has since been under the investigation of Dr.
Hirsch, a learned physician in Dantzic, but I have not yet heard
the result.

COMETS.—These have been largely associated in the popular
mind with pestilential visitations.

Hecker, in his " Epidemics of the Middle Ages," states that
comets were seen in 1505 and 1506, and that an eruption of Mount
Vesuvius took place in 1506, the year of the second visitation of
the *sweating sickness* in England.

Dr. Theophilus Thompson, editor of the " Annals of Influenza,"
points out that comets have repeatedly attracted attention about
the time of catarrhal epidemics, and he instances the years 1510,
1557, 1580, 1732, 1737, 1743, and 1763.

In 1529, on the authority of Hecker, three comets appeared.
This was the year of the great visitation of the trousse-galant in
France, and of the fifth outbreak of the sweating sickness in
England.

In the pestilential year 1554 a comet appeared. Various other
instances occur in the table.

I do not intend to pursue this branch of the inquiry on the
present occasion. The instances cited in the superficial survey
here taken may be but coincidences. There are pestilential outbreaks of some kind in some parts of the world nearly every year;
comets and meteors are of very constant occurrence. There *must*,
therefore, be coincidences in point of time. These may mean something or nothing. Certainly anything less than a thorough and
exhaustive inquiry will not justify any conclusions, positive or
negative. I have for some years been making notes in view of such
an inquiry. On some convenient season I shall place the collected

results before the public; but a wide range of investigation has yet to be entered upon before they can be so presented. In the meantime I commend to the attention of all interested therein, the words of one who I had hoped would have taken an active personal part in the elucidation of the question.

Haviland, in his "Climate, Weather, and Disease," 1855, says (p. 140) :—

"How comets should influence epidemics is by no means a question likely to be solved yet. The *modus operandi*, however, of volcanic eruptions and earth-quakes may be easily conceived when we consider what really takes place during their occurrence. Vast volumes of mephitic fumes, impalpable but heavy dust, ashes, cinders, stones, and gases of all descriptions are vomited from the craters of volcanos in activity. These deleterious matters get hurled with prodigious force into the higher regions of the atmosphere, where the current rapidly wafts them over distant lands, and thus impregnates the air with an invisible poison, which, *as the unseen hand of Providence, fulfils its fatal mission* by sapping the health and destroying the life of thousands and tens of thousands. Probably *meteors* or *aerolites* were often mistaken for comets; their origin, however, is highly proble-matical, although they come under the denomination of foreign bodies suspended in the atmosphere, and perhaps owe their origin to the same cause that produces what are called 'dry fogs,' which were noticed in the remarkable year 1782, when the influenza was more widely epidemic than ever it had been before."

SEASONAL OR TERRESTRIAL INFLUENCES.—These have always been intimately associated with plagues and pestilences. Whether they are to be classed with the natural or direct causes may be left an open question.

Quoting a few authorities, by way of introduction, Bascome remarks (p. 161) :—"All authors who have given descriptions of "catarrhal epidemics . . . agree in saying that they have almost "invariably followed cold and moist seasons, and that they seemed "most immediately to be produced by·sudden atmospheric vicisi- "tudes."

Professor Rogers, in his "History of Agriculture and Prices" (1846, i, 292), writing of the "Black Death" in 1333, says :—"It "is said that it was accompanied at its outbreak by various terres-"trial and atmospheric phenomena of a most destructive character " —phenomena similar to those which characterised the first appear-"ance of the Asiatic cholera, of the influenza, and even in more "remote times of the Athenian plague."

It is recorded that during the period this Black Death was still desolating Europe (1348), the island of Cyprus was visited by a remarkable *pestiferous wind*, which in its progress killed numbers of the inhabitants.

An able American writer has said :—"The gentle air that brings "refreshment to all organised life amid the heats of a sultry sun, "may become a whirlwind of fury and desolation to a wide circle. "Even in its gentleness it may be laden with health-giving odours, "or bear the germs of corruption and disease. At certain times

" and under favouring circumstances the seeds of pestilence acquire
" unusual vitality, and the angel of death sweeps with his scimitar
" over a circuit of many lands."—" Insurance Times," N. Y., May,
1879.

In the period 1528-34 Europe was invaded with a serious pestilence, of which some details are contained in the Appendix under
that date; but it is further recorded that a damp heat prevailed in
the autumn and winter, causing the trees, which had just shed
their leaves, to bud again and burst into blossom. Violets were
gathered at Erfurt in the middle of February. Floods and storms
succeeded, inundating whole districts. "The sun was rarely seen
" through the dark clouds during the latter part of summer and the
" whole of the autumn." Earthquakes in Italy, blood coloured
rain at Cremona, and a comet completed the measure of natural
horrors.—BASCOME, pp. 80—82.

Graunt, in his famous "Index of the Positions, Observations,
" and Questions contained in this Discourse" (*vide* "Natural and
" Political Observations," edition 1665), says :—" 33. That altera-
" tions in the air do incomparably more operate as to the plague
" than the contagion of converse [*i.e.*, association]." Again : "35.
"A disposition in the air towards the plague doth also dispose
" women to abortions."—See table, B.C. 296-91, p. 60.

At a more recent period (date not given) a peculiar fog or
vapour was observed in New York during the most fatal period
of pestilential fever, especially in the month of September.—See
Haze.

A correspondent (E.T.T.) in the "British Medical Journal"
(1882, p. 366) says :—

" In the several outbreaks of scarlet fever we have had in the villages around,
and of a fatal type too, strange to say, they have always been early in the year,
when the seasons have been mild, and when the gardens of the cottages (where the
excrements of fever patients have been buried) and the fields around are being
prepared for the sowing of the different vegetables and crops. I am inclined to
think that we living in the country have more illnesses in early spring than our
town friends, and I cannot help regarding the emanations from the soil as being
in a great measure accountable for it."

The table in the Appendix abounds in instances falling within
this category.—See *Decomposing Matter.*

DROUGHT.—The effects of drought are manifested in several
forms, as :—(i). In permitting the accumulation of foreign matter
in the atmosphere—as cosmic dust, for instance—rain being the
great purifier. (ii). In retarding the growth of vegetation, and
so producing a scarcity of food. (iii). As being the visible result,
or accompaniment, of undue heat, arising from solar or other
causes, detrimental to human life, and which rain would have
removed or modified. See table, B.C. 1100; A.D. 1230.

It is a noticeable fact that many epidemics have occurred after very dry seasons. I will name a few of them :—

Spain, B.C. 1100.—Before the outbreak of pestilence this year there had been a continuous drought of twenty-five years. Rivers and springs were dried up, the water in the deeper reservoirs had become stagnant. There was neither pasturage for the beasts of the field, nor proper food for man. The country was "full of " dreadful mortalities, plagues, and misery of every description, " which, with emigration to other lands, nearly depopulated the " country."

China, A.D. 1334.—Hecker says, " Here a parching drought, " succeeded by famine, commenced in the tract of country watered " by the rivers Kiang and Hoai." This was followed by such violent torrents of rain in and about Kingsai, that more than 400,000 people perished in the flood. *Op. cit.,* p. 12. Another drought occurred at Tche in China, followed by pestilence, which carried off, it is said, 5 millions of people. These two incidents are a good deal confused by various writers.

Constantinople, A.D. 1541.—This plague succeeded a remarkable drought in the preceding year.

Ramesey, who wrote a treatise on foretelling weather in 1665, says that such a conjunction happening in a fiery sign (Aries) shows that "the earth shall be barren through extremity of heat and " drought."

The cholera year, 1854, was remarkable for its drought, the rainfall at Greenwich being but 18·7 inches, or 7·3 less than the average of thirty-nine years. Mr. Lowe, of Highfield House, Nottingham, wrote to the "Times" (16th January, 1855), " The long " drought of 1854 was another remarkable feature; the deficiency " in the amount of rain falling being nearly 12 inches. The amount " of rain which fell in February, March, April, June, September " and October, being for the *six months* less than *three inches,* and " in this period, out of 180 days, 129 were fine. In March, April, " and September, there were 42 cloudless nights—September being " particularly free from clouds."

Other instances will be found in the table given in the Appendix.

DECOMPOSING MATTER.—This ranges under three heads :—

      i. Putrid animal or insect bodies;
      ii. Decaying vegetable substances;
      iii. Stagnant pools, marshes, &c., breeding Malaria.

Animal Substances.—The abnormal state of the atmosphere arising from the presence of putrid animal substances has from the earliest times afforded instances of directly creating or attracting pestilences. I quote a few notable instances from ancient and modern history :—

Africa, B.C. 125.—" In the reign of Micipsa, and the consulate of Marcus Plautius Hypsæus and Marcus Fulvius Flaccus, according to Orosius, a great part of Africa was covered with locusts, but at last they were thrown in vast heaps upon the shore. A plague ensued, which swept away an infinite number of animals of all sorts. In Numidia only perished 800,000 men, and in Africa proper 200,000; amongst the rest 30,000 Roman soldiers quartered in and about Utica. At Utica in particular the mortality raged to such a degree that 1,500 dead bodies were carried out by one gate in one day."—" Univ. Hist.," vol. xviii, p. 152.

B.C. (Place and date not stated.)—A pestilential epidemic was attributed to the unwholesome exhalations from the dead bodies of a great number of animals which had perished during an epizoötic.—" Dict. de l'Acad. Franç. Médecine," art. Peste.

Roman Empire, A.D. 314.—Plague. Eusebius ("Chronicon.," Paris, 1628) thus describes the atmospheric conditions which prevailed :—" The air was so noxious and everywhere so deranged with corrupt vapours, fumes from the earth so putrid, winds from the sea, exhalations from marshes and rivers, so injurious, that a certain poisonous liquor, as it were from putrid carcases, was brought by the elements, and covered the subjacent seats or benches, walls, and sides of houses, and the dew appeared like the sanies of dead bodies."

Note.—This greatly resembles some of the atmospheric conditions consequent upon PLANETARY INFLUENCES. See that head in this section of the paper.

France, A.D. 874.—A pestilence, caused by the stench arising from dead locusts, destroyed about a third of the inhabitants of the French coast.—" The Magdeburg History."

Shakespeare makes the king say before the battle of Agincourt:—

> " A many of our bodies shall no doubt
> Find native graves ; upon the which I trust
> Shall witness live in brass of this day's work ;
> And those that leave their valiant bones in France,
> Dying like men, though buried in your dung-hills,
> They shall be fam'd ; for there the sun shall greet them,
> And draw their humours reeking up to heaven ;
> Leaving their earthly parts to choke your clime—
> The smell whereof shall breed a plague in France."—HENRY V.

Vegetable Substances.—Decaying vegetable substances have always been regarded as peculiarly detrimental to human life. Innumerable plagues and pestilences are attributed, and no doubt justly, to their influence. I shall here quote one or two instances remarkable in history :—

Syracuse, B.C. 210-12—A pestilence supervened to afflict the besieging armies of Rome and Carthage. " At first the contagion commenced in the country. The heat of the climate and of the season had corrupted the air, and the refuse of the sea-board and other vegetable substances which the sea ordinarily leaves upon the shore when the waters retire, had still further determined it. The two camps of Himilco and Crispinus were first attacked. Then the malady communicated itself to the army of Marcellus, from the intercourse of that of Crispinus with it. Soon after Acradina was attacked by it; and the famine which was prevailing there would of itself have caused it. Thus around the place and in the interior of it nothing was seen but the dead and the dying. From the fear of catching infection by approaching the dead bodies, they were left without burial, to poison the places where they lay decomposing........ The evil committed incomparably less ravages in the two Roman camps than in that of Himilco and Hippocrates. The army of Marcellus had been long before Syracuse. It was seasoned to the air and water of the country. With regard to the Carthaginians, they died without distinction of officer and soldier. Hippocrates and Himilco themselves died of it. The proconsul comforted the sick of the camp of Crispinus; he caused the part of his army that was encamped without the walls to change their ground; he put the soldiers of it under shelter and under roofs. In fact they used every precaution, and the mortality was only moderate."—CATROU et ROUILLÉ, "Histoire Romaine," tome viii, p. 152.

An important modern instance is given in the Appendix; see *South America*, 1838.

Against these views as to the effects of vegetable or animal substances in decomposition, stands forth Dr. John Parkin, M.D. (" The Causation and Prevention of Disease," 1859), who has paid great attention to the subject of pestilences, and whose opinions on other points of vital importance are reviewed herein, who not only refutes the influence of contagion, but denies (and brings a striking array of figures in support of his denial) that either "the products " of decomposing matter on the surface, or the alteration of the air " by overcrowding, or the use of impure water, have any influence " in the production of the two classes of disease termed epidemic " and endemic." He traces these in many remarkable instances to telluric exhalations, or the escape of malaria from the ground, the particular miasm depending on the nature of the soil and its geological peculiarities. Dr. McWilliam, C.B., lends confirmation to this view by showing that the water-side officers employed in the customs, who are peculiarly exposed to exhalations from decaying organic matter in the foul water and festering mud banks of the Thames, are, if anything, less liable than others to fever and cholera.—*Vide* " Rumsey's Fallacies of Statistics," 1875, p. 60.

MALARIA.—Dr. Aitkin (" Science and Practice of Medicine," 1864, ii, 909) asks what is the nature of the noxious agent of malarious districts, and what circumstances are necessary to its formation or extrication? and answers the joint inquiry as follows: —" It seems certain that the deleterious agent is neither heat alone " nor moisture alone, nor any known gas extricated from the marsh. " It cannot be heat, for many of the hottest parts of the West " Indies are free from fever; it cannot be moisture, for no persons " enjoy better health than the troops of clean ships at sea, even " when cruising in tropical climates, as long as they have no com- " munication with the land. While carbonic acid, azote, oxygen, or " carburetted hydrogen—the gases collected by stirring the bottom " of marshes—have all been inspired without finding any disease " similar to paludal fever, it seems to follow almost as a necessary " consequence that the remote cause must be a miasma, poison, or " malaria, whose presence is solely detected by its action on the " human body; and two hypotheses have been imagined to account

" for its origin : the one, that it is a product of vegetable decompo-
" sition ; the other, that it is an exhalation from the earth, favoured
" by the conditions of marshiness."*

He further says that the general evidence in favour of vegetable
decomposition being the remote cause is, that all countries are for
the most part free from the diseases associated with malaria while
the crops are growing, and only become unhealthy after the
harvest, when large quantities of vegetable matters are left on the
ground at the time the rain begins to fall. Marshes are generally
healthy till the summer sun or other cause has diminished their
waters, and bared the greater or less portion of their bed. The part
thus exposed almost always contains a large portion of vegetable
matters, which running into rapid decomposition, generates a
poison that gives origin to malarial fevers, and it is during the
periods of the year when the drying process is in greatest activity,
that unhealthiness prevails with the greatest severity in the East
Indies, namely, before the commencement and after the termination
of the rainy season.

From the same source we obtain some solution of the numerous
pestilential attacks which fell upon the ancient city of Rome, as
shown in the early pages of this table in the Appendix. Their
frequency led to the erection of a temple to the goddess Febris—
but still they did not stop. Their origin was found to be in the
great masses of water which poured down from the Palatine,
Aventine, and Tarpeian hills, becoming stagnant in the plains below,
converting them into swamps and marshes. The elder Tarquin
ordered them to be drained, and led the waters by means of sewers
to the Tiber. This system of drainage, which was continued as late
as the Cæsars, rendered Rome proportionately healthy, and the seat
of a larger population than has since probably been collected within
the walls of any European city. On the invasion of the Goths,
however, the public buildings were destroyed, the embankments of
the Tiber broken down, the aqueducts laid in ruins ; the sewers
thus became filled up, or obstructed, and the country being again
overflowed, Rome once more became the seat of an almost annual
paludal fever, as in the times of her earliest foundation.

It may perhaps be here stated with advantage that as, in the
vegetable world, *sulphur* has been found an antidote to mildew and
other diseases associated with moisture, so the same agent *sulphur*
appears to be efficacious in the case of malaria outbreaks. It is

---

* There was published in 1871—" What is Malaria ? and why is it most
intense in Hot Climates ? An Inquiry into the Nature and Causes of the
so-called Marsh Poison, with Remarks on the Principles to be observed for the
Preservation of Health in Tropical Climates and Malarious Districts." By
C. F. Oldham, Assistant Surgeon of Her Majesty's Indian Forces. London and
Calcutta. 8vo., 184 pp.

stated to be a fact that in malarious places where marsh fever has raged so virulently as to attack 90 per cent. of the inhabitants, workmen in the sulphur mines of the vicinity are comparatively exempt from its ravages. And further, with negative force, that the town of Zephyria, in the Grecian Archipelago, once containing 40,000 inhabitants, and exceedingly prosperous, is now deserted, because no one has been able to spend a night there since its sulphur mines were exhausted, without being stricken down with fever.—*Vide* "Insurance Times," New York, 1882, p. 627.*

FLOODS.—These are the result of an undue degree of moisture in the atmosphere. Their influence operates variously, as: (i) on the constitution of persons, by predisposing them to disease; (ii) by destroying vegetation, and hence producing shortness of food; or (iii) by superinducing deadly vapours—malaria.

PLAGUES OF INSECTS.—These again destroy vegetation, and hence (i) produce scarcity of food for man and beast; (ii) corrupt the atmosphere; and (iii) pollute the water. They constituted a peculiar feature in the plagues of Egypt (B.C. 1491), as they have in many later ones to which reference has been made under *Decomposing Matter—Animal.*

Mildew or *Rubigo.*—This substance, "impregnated with highly " corrosive powers " (HIRD on *Pest.*), was anciently deemed one of the causes of pestilence.

The Romans deified its noxious principle as *Robigus*, and held sacrificial "*festæ rubigalia*," offering sucking whelps, whence Columella :—

"*Hinc malo rubigo, virides ne torreat herbas, sanguine lactentis*
" *catuli placatur et extis.*"

RAMAZZINI (*Constitut. Epidem.*) ascribes an epidemic to this " *lues rubigalis.*"

So HOFFMANN, on the "*ros valde corrosivus*," in his treatise *de Temp. Ann. Insalub.* (tom. i).

Predisposing but Remote Causes—Terrestrial.

The circumstances which may predispose individuals or communities to the ravages of plague, or to attacks from pestilence, are very varied. I will review a few of the most prominent :—

---

* *Influence of Railways on Malaria.* Dr. W. S. King, U. S. Army, broaches in the " New York Medical Record " the theory that the passage of railway trains through low lands may lessen the effects of malaria in those localities. He thinks the heated locomotives, by continually passing through the infected districts, rarefy the air, and create a constant atmospheric disturbance by inducing warm upward currents, such currents acting, with the pure air which rushes in from all directions, as agents in the dispersion or annihilation of the miasmatic influence.—" Lancet," 11th March, 1882, p. 421.

The introduction of railways is said to have caused abundant rainfall in districts where it was previously unknown.

Overcrowding.—Densely crowded towns and cities have always been found to be the favoured haunts of plague, particularly where the dwellings are of an inferior class.   See table, B.C. 463.

Rome, A.D. 291.—The pestilence broke out "when the city was thronged with the peasants who had taken refuge in it, with their property, from the enemy.   The dejection generally prevalent may have acted as a predisposing cause, as in Cadiz in 1800.   The want of fodder and even of water for the cattle driven within the walls could not fail to breed diseases among them, which rendered the men likewise more susceptible of contagion, and even prompted its development; and the fugitives, who, for want of a hospitable roof, passed their nights under porticos or in open places in the dog days and September, were liable to the malignant fevers of the country and season, even within the enclosures."— NIEBUHR'S " Lectures on Roman History," vol. ii.

Warfare—(i) deprivations ; (ii) mental anxieties.   See table, B.C. 473.

Absence of Efficient Sanitary Regulations—(i) debilitating the health ; (ii) attracting disease germs.*

Want of Food.—Famines are nearly always succeeded by pestilential outbreaks.   Thus B.C. 366, " after their famine followed a " pestilence, for the vncustomed nouryshement of the vnholsome " meates they did eat, wyth the trauayle of their journey and the " care of the mynd, spread diseases amonges them."—BRENDE, " Quint. Curt.," fol. 283.

Change of Diet.—Mere change, as such, seems to produce epidemics in many instances, even where the new food is not of a character to affect the enteric habits.   Early in this century (I have not the date at hand), one of the finest regiments of Sweden, consisting of Dalecarlions, lost nearly half its men by such a disorder. The corps had been transferred from its own district to Stockholm, and the more nutritious food of the capital so undermined the health of the men, that to save the few who had escaped the disease, their wonted diet of black bread and peas was restored to them.   See GRAVES.   It is needless to remark upon the frequency of epidemic diseases among troops led into fruit districts.

Bodily Fatigue.—Armies marching or undergoing great hardships.

Sudden Change of Climate, as excessive heat after cold or damp seasons.

* " Until this time (1760), extraordinary as it may appear, there was not any such thing as a privy in Madrid ; it was customary to throw the ordure out of the windows at night, and it was removed by scavengers the next day.   An ordinance having been issued by the king that every householder should build a privy, the people violently *opposed* it as an arbitrary proceeding, and the *physicians* remonstrated against it, alleging that the filth absorbed the unwholesome particles of the air, which otherwise would be taken into the human body !   His majesty, however, persisted ; but many of the citizens, in order to keep *their food wholesome*, erected their privies close to their kitchen fire-places."—BASCOME, pp. 129 and 130.

Excessive Luxury or Debauchery.

B.C. 101.—" The mild softness of the Venetian climate, early and excessive heats, debauchery, excess in wine, and, if we may believe some writers, the use of bread and of cooked meat, produced great ravages among the *Cimbri;* so that from these causes, at the end of a short time, they found themselves considerably weakened in numbers and in vigour."—THIERRY, " Hist. des Gaulois," tome ii, p. 232.

Boccaccio implies that the state of debauchery prevailing in Florence during the fourteenth century, accounted largely for the dreadful mortality in that city.

The table in the Appendix contains many examples applicable to the conditions here enumerated. Some I have noted under the different heads.

Dr. William Farr (" Statistics of British Empire," 1846) offers the following observations bearing upon several of the preceding heads :—

" In a thinly peopled and uncultivated country the indigenous plagues may be generally traced to marshes, to famines, or to congregation of great multitudes in the same spot for superstitious or warlike purposes. As civilisation dawns, cities are constructed; but they are all first rude inventions, where the supplies of air, water, and food are irregular; the narrow streets shut out the sun; the dirt, the animal secretions, and decayed organic matter are suffered to infect the air. In a high temperature the effluvial atmosphere becomes a deadly poison; and it is only as science advances, and the construction of cities is improved, that epidemics decline."

In another portion of the same article he says, "If any proof " were wanted of the inadequate supply of food, and the unhealthy " dwellings of the English people down to the seventeenth century, " it would be found in the famines and plagues which still pre- " vail[ed] with little mitigation."

Geographical Distribution of Diseases.

A mere cursory review of the records of plagues and pestilences indicates what a wide field remains open for the study of the geographical distribution of diseases. In those countries which sustain the most frequent outbreaks, or where these appear in the greatest intensity, there is most assuredly a cause which may be fathomed. It may be the soil (*i.e.*, the geological formation); it may be the location, as exposed to pestilential currents, or as to being too much sheltered from "the free winds of heaven," by moun- tain ranges or otherwise; it may be the climate. And while speaking of climate, is it not worthy of special remark that we rarely hear of any pestilential outbreaks in the more arctic regions? It is not habits of cleanliness which protect them. May it not be that the pestilential virus is killed by the cold? Or is it the sparse popula- tion that acts as a protection? Again, in many of the more *tro- pical* regions the outbreak of pestilence is by no means frequent. I think this may be said of India, taken as a whole. Considering the climate, and the density of the population, that vast continent appears particularly free from pestilential casualties. These points seem worthy of further elucidation.

The American continent, alike north and south—except in certain malarial districts, where yellow fever finds a congenial home—has been peculiarly free from pestilential devastation. Yet its peoples are largely composed of all nationalities. It cannot be that there is any protective influence in its climate, for it has in its vast range all climates; nor in its geology, for it embraces all known formations. It is reasonably free from volcanos; but many portions of its surface suffers severely and periodically from earthquakes. Light upon these points will come from its own foremost men in the ranks of science in due course. They are receiving growing attention there as here. In 1876, Mr. James T. Gardner, director of the New York State Survey, said, " From " the united results of topographical, geographical, and sanitary " surveys of a larger area, I believe it possible to deduce, with " absolute certainty, the principal causes of prevailing diseases, " and to point out practical remedies that will reduce the death " rate one-half its present amount, and banish from the world an " untold weight of suffering and sorrow."

Is it to be regarded as a fact (implied in the foregoing brief review) that pestilential epidemics are chiefly confined to the *temperate* zones ? and is it true that ancient cities are more subject to such incursions than modern ones. Rome and London are two remarkable instances. I think it may be said without contradiction that but for the great fire of 1666, which burnt out the elements of pestilence so thoroughly that they have never reappeared in any virulent form—that but for that fire and this result, London would have been unfit to be the emporium of the world's commerce! With respect to Rome, I have already shown the cause of its frequent pestilential outbreaks, and the remedy.

PLAGUE SPOTS OF THE WORLD.—In this connection I have to say something concerning certain periodical assemblies held at locations which may be aptly designated " Plague spots of the world." These are more especially *Hurdwar* (Hindustan), where is held one of the greatest religious fairs in the world; *Mecca* (in Arabia), the birth-place of Mahomet ; and *Nijni Novgorod*, where is held the great mercantile fair of Russia. From these three great centres (and many lesser ones) are annually disseminated the germs of such diseases as may at the moment prevail. It seems desirable to take a further survey of the facts :—

Hurdwar is situated on the west bank of the Ganges. It is one of the celebrated places of Hindu purification. Pilgrims from every part of India resort annually to its temples, and to obtain purification in the waters of the holy river at this spot. The gathering takes place in the month of April, and the occasion is employed for the holding of a mercantile fair, at which merchants from all parts of India, from China, Arabia, Persia, Tartary, and Bokhara attend. It is said on credible authority that, one year with another, some 2 millions of persons attend. Every sixth year the fair is larger, and greater numbers attend; every twelfth year still more extended. The country round about is then formed into one vast camp, composed of the different nationalities. What may be expected to occur under such conditions of camp life too often does occur. I have at hand a paragraph from the " Times' " telegraphic correspondence with India, published 19th May, 1878, as follows :—

" Cholera has been making fearful havoc among the pilgrims returning from the Hurdwar fair, and is being spread by them through Northern India. It is asserted that between 20,000 and 30,000 hill-men from the Himalayan districts near Nynee Tal died on their homeward journey. Several cases, most of them fatal, appeared among the 15th Hussars almost immediately after their arrival at Meerut from Candahar, and it is supposed that the outbreak is due to some men having travelled from Mooltan in railway carriages which had been used by infected pilgrims. The disease has appeared in most cities of the Punjab, and the fear of the spread of the epidemic to Peshawur has induced the authorities to remove the greater portion of the garrison there." It is added " the Government might well consider whether it is not time to put an entire stop to those great religious fairs, seeing that they almost invariably form centres whence pestilence spreads throughout the country, and that the effective sanitary control of the masses of pilgrims assembled is almost impossible."

There are other religious fairs in India : *Kansat* (Bengal), 1868, and *Karagola* (Bengal), 1872. See table.

Mecca.—A famous city in Arabia ; the reputed birth-place of Mahomet, and the first seat of his power. It is situated in a rocky country about 50 miles inland from the port of Jedda on the Red Sea. It is the only place where the faithful may worship with his face to every point of the compass. The place has no trade beyond the manufacture of pilgrims' chaplets ; and is entirely supported by the concourse of pilgrims from every part of the Mahommedan world. During the residence of the caravans, which bring an annual addition of about 100,000 to its inhabitants, it is converted into an immense fair, with sheds and booths in which the productions of the most distant regions of the earth are exposed for sale. They drink water from the holy well and kiss the miraculous stone. This kissing and drinking are each suspected of aiding in the dissemination of disease.* Nearly every year some such paragraph as the following appears :—

" Cholera among the Mecca pilgrims. Alexandria, 12th December.—An official report from Elwedj, dated 7th November, states that out of 3,500 pilgrims

---

* In support of this view we quote from a Hungarian scientific journal some observations of Otto Herrman, which are very much in point. His observations

detained there to perform quarantine, only twenty-seven died of cholera during the ten days preceding the above date. At the same time the report says that the mortality from sickness produced by the fatigues of the journey to and from Mecca was very great."—*Vide* " Times," 13th December, 1881.

In the same journal of the previous October there had appeared in the Constantinople correspondence the following :—

" The question of taking measures to prevent the extension of cholera, which is raging at present in Mecca, is causing a good deal of trouble to the Turkish Government. The medical authorities are of opinion that pilgrims should be prevented from going to the holy places, for the epidemic would certainly be intensified by the aggregation of many thousand people in a small town which has no proper accommodation for them, and it would be rapidly disseminated over the whole Mussulman world by the pilgrims returning to their homes. The Sultan, however, is afraid lest fanatical believers should condemn him as an infidel, and political intriguers should make capital out of the religious discontent. It was supposed on Tuesday that a compromise had been found; for the International Commission was allowed to pass a resolution that no ships having pilgrims on board should be cleared for the Red Sea ports, and a Russian steamer, as I reported, was obliged to land the pilgrims whom she was taking to Jeddah. The compromise, however, has since been withdrawn, for the next day a director of a company which is under the control of the Admiralty, went to the place and declared that he had 350 pilgrims waiting impatiently to be transported to their destination. The matter was submitted to the Sultan, and his majesty replied laconically, ' Let them go.' They have accordingly been despatched, but it is expected that they will be stopped at Port Said, and that the affair may cause some difficulties between the Porte and the Egyptian Government."

In 1847, more than 30,000 pilgrims in the return caravan bound from Mecca to Damascus died of Asiatic cholera.

Nijni Novgorod (Russia).—Here is held annually in August, at were made of the kissing of the image of the Holy Virgin at the Szenkut place of pilgrimage. His description of the proceedings is as follows :—" Pilgrims were coming to this place from all quarters, Magyars, Swabians, men of various races were all herded together. As a matter of course, men worn out with sickness dragged themselves along side by side with the faithful wearing the cross. Blenorrhœa, leprosy, and every species of contagious disease were represented. The long procession of pilgrims was terminated by those of extreme old age and of extreme youth, pregnant women, blooming girls, and mothers with children at the breast. When the procession arrived at the shrine, the *ne plus ultra* of horrors began. A prayer having been offered, infected lips imprinted a kiss in turn, first upon the pedestal of the image, then on the face, the feet, and so on; the lips of the well touched the same places. The next day I found a brown crust 0·5 millimetre in thickness, which had been formed by the kisses. The basin of the holy fountain, which contained 10 or 15 litres of water, presented a still mere disgusting spectacle. All the pilgrims washed themselves in this same water, people with ulcers, caries, and limbs which had already begun to mortify, all used the same 15 litres of water. Mothers, with children on their arms, stripped them naked and bathed them in the water from the crown of their heads to the soles of their feet, so that no harm might touch them. Language fails me to describe the horror I felt at the sight. It, however, explained satisfactorily enough how it happens that children, and young men and young women, mysteriously contract the vilest diseases, without having committed any acts that ought to entail such a curse upon them. These diseases, when developed, bring these same persons back to the holy shrine again, and the holy place propagates anew fresh contagion far and wide. The evil has become so great that whole villages and races have become infected with the poison."—" Deutsche Versicherungs Zeitung," 1877.

the confluence of the Oka and Volga rivers, the great modern commercial fair of Europe. Merchants from all trading countries throughout the East attend it. Merchandise from other great fairs is here exhibited. Upwards of 200,000 people are congregated together during the pestilential season. Great precautions have been taken of late years to prevent the outbreak of pestilence, and on several occasions the holding of the fair has been prohibited. There can be no doubt that pestilence has been disseminated in Europe by its agency.

Students of the geographical distribution of disease will find much to learn in the light of these and other Holy Shrines and similar gatherings. They were formerly much more general if not so largely attended, as now. Here is an early instance :—

B.C. 1614.—*Ireland.*—Pestilence killed *Tighearnmeas* and three-fourths of the men of Ireland with him, at the meeting to worship the idol Crom Cruach, held at Magh-Slecht (now Tullyhaw, in Cavan).—Irish Annalists.

Plague Preventives and Remedies.

My task will be considered incomplete unless I offer some observations upon, or at least publish a review of, the various remedies which have been propounded for the cure on the one hand, and the prevention on the other, of plagues and pestilences. An obvious advantage in studying the proposed remedies is that we ought thereby to gain an insight into the views which prevailed in former periods regarding the nature of the disease, and the causes of its recurrence. Hence a survey of the remedies forms but a necessary counterpart to the enumeration of causes already reviewed. The items almost spontaneously range themselves under two heads —saintly and secular:—

SAINTLY REMEDIES (*Incense*).—" And Aaron took as Moses com-" manded, and ran into the midst of the congregation; and behold " the plague was begun among the people: and he put on incense, " and made an atonement for the people."—Numbers xvi, 47.

Saints' Blessings.—In Michael Wodd's " Dialogue " (1554) we read : " If we were sick of the pestylence we ran to St. Rooke ; if " of the ague to St. Pernel, or Master John Shore." . . St. Sebastian is also said to have an influence against pestilence.

In Googe's version of " Naogeorgus," there is the following couplet :—

> " There is a saint whose name in verse cannot declared be,
> He saves against the plague and each infective maladie."

Rich, in the " Irish Hubbub " (1619), has the following passage :—" There be many miracles assigned to saints, that (they " say) are good for all diseases . . . They have saints that be good

" amongst poultry, for chickens when they have the pip, for geese
" when they do sit, to have a happy successe in goslings; and to
" be short, there is no disease, nor sicknesse, no greefe, either
" amongst men or beasts, that hath not his physician among the
" saints."

Prayer and Fasting.—The King of Scotland (Malduin) A.D. 668
went to Scolmakill to visit the sepulchres of his ancestors. At
this time rang ane horrible pest, to the great mortality of the
people in sundry parts of the world, and ceased not until the
people, by continual prayer, fasting, and good works, pacified the
wrath of God. The Scots in these days knew no manner of hot
fever, and were preserved from the same by temperance of the
mouth; for this cruel pestilence rang never among the Scots until
they left the wholesome temperance of their elders, and made them ·
selves ready to receive all infirmities. Colmaine, bishop of Lindis-
farne, states, that ane huge multitude of Saxons perished in this
pestilence.—Boece, " History of Scotland," book ix, p. 3.

But the " Divine Wrath " theory of pestilence-generation was
always in view. In the " Newe Booke," 1561, there was the.
following mock prescription : " Take a pond of good hard penaunce,
" and washe it wel with the water of youre eyes and let it ly a
" good whyle at your hert. Take also of the best fyne faythe,
" hope, and charvte y^t you can get, a like quantite of al mixed
" together, youre soule even full and use this confection every day
" in youre lyfe, whilst the plages of God reigneth. Then, take
" both your hands ful of good workes commaunded of God, and
" kepe them close in a clene conscience from the duste of vayne
" glory, and ever as you are able and se necessite so to use them.
" This medicine was found wryten in an olde Byble boke, and it
" hath bene practised and proved true of mani, both men and
" women."

In Lower Bengal the natives have for a long time past
worshipped the Goddess of Cholera, as the *Oola Beebee*. According to the traditions associated with the temple to this goddess,
which was erected in Calcutta, at a date which cannot now be
ascertained, a female, while wandering about in the woods, met
with a large stone, the symbol of the Goddess of Cholera. The
worship of the deity through this stone was, according to the
prevailing ideas of Hindoos, the only means of preservation from
the influence of this terrible disease. The fame of this goddess
spread, and people flocked from all parts of the country to come
and pray at her shrine in Calcutta.—Macnamara's "Hist. of Asiatic
" Cholera," 1876, p. 34.

In 1565, at *Ayr* (Scotland).—" The plague was at that time
" very terrible, and John Welch being necessarily separate from his

" people, it was to him the more grievous. But when the people of
" Ayr came to him to bemoan themselves, his answer was, that
" Hugh Kennedy, a godly gentleman in their own neighbourhood,
" should pray for them. This counsel was accepted, and accord-
" ingly the plague was stayed."—" Spiritual Watchman."

Religious Feast.—At *Huesca* (Aragon), in 1439, pestilence.
Alonzo de Burgos says, "the disease in Huesca only yielded to a
" solemn and general vow which the city made, to celebrate a feast
" on the day of the Conception of the Virgin, and to observe its
" vigil with an absolute fast."—See also Appendix, 1092.

Repentance.—Therefore He [the LORD] lifted up His hand
against them, to overthrow them in the wilderness : To overthrow
their seed also among the nations, and to scatter them in the lands.
They joined themselves also unto Baal-peor, and ate the sacrifices
of the dead. Thus they provoked *Him* to anger with their
inventions, and the plague brake in upon them. Then stood up
Phinehas, and executed judgment : and *so* the plague was
stayed.—Psalm cvi, 26—30.

But this penitence was sometimes by way of what Jeremiah
calls backsliding. Thus we read, in the chronicle of "the
" venerable BEDE," that during the plague of A.D. 665 (see table),
the East Saxons, *Sighere* with the people under him, "*forsook the
" mysteries of the Christian Faith, and began to adore idols and
" restore the abandoned temples.*"

In " Preservatives against the Plague Pest, at the Request of
" the City of London " (in 1665), by Francis Herring, Doctor in
Physic, a work dedicated to the king, and in which dedication
the plague is spoken of as " not a disease, but a monster, over-
" watching, and quelling ofttimes both art and nature," is the
following :—" The plague (if you will have his true characterism
" and essential form) is *Ictus Iræ Divinæ pro Peccatis Hominum ;*
" the stroke of God's wrath for the sins of mankind. This is not
" only the opinions of divines but of all learned physicians, and
" acknowledged by the blind heathen in all ages by the light of
" nature. Therefore his appropriate and special antidote is, *seria
" pœnitentia* and *conversio ad Deum :* unfained and hearty repent-
" ance and conversion to God. Till this be practised, I tell you
" plainly, I put small confidence in other by-causes. The cause
" remaining, who can look for the taking away of the effect ? Let
" me therefore be an humble suitor, that your highness would be
" pleased to command a general humiliation of the people by
" prayer and fasting." He however follows this up by some
excellent advice regarding burial of the dead, cleansing the streets,
and keeping the body in a condition of cleanliness and exercise.

1832.—The cholera prevailed in Canada, and a man named

Ayres, from the United States (said to be a graduate of the University of New Jersey), was given out to be St. Roche, the principal patron saint of the Canadians, and renowned for his power in averting pestilential diseases. He (Ayres) was reported to have descended from Heaven to cure his suffering people of the cholera; and many were the cases in which he appeared to afford relief. Many were thus dispossessed of their fright in anticipation of the disease, who might, probably, but for his inspiriting influence, have fallen victims to their apprehensions. The remedy he employed was an admixture of maple sugar [compare *table*, A.D. 1565, *Europe*, where *treacle* is mentioned], charcoal, and lard. —PETTIGREW'S "Medical Superstitions," p. 53.

The "Tiflis Messenger," May, 1879, reported that a disease with terrible mortality, was raging in ten villages in the Caucasus. Holy pictures had been carried in solemn procession through the village of Metkha, in the district of Gori, with prayers for the preservation of the inhabitants.

Holy Wells.—Many wells and fountains have had various virtues and superstitions attached to them. Those which were considered medicinal were usually named after some patron saint, and hence they were called "holy wells" or "holy springs," and sometimes "wishing wells," &c.; and various rites were performed at them at Easter, upon Holy Thursday, and other particular days. Offerings were made to propitiate, or to obtain the favour of their patron saints, and among the rest a custom was very prevalent to deposit rags. Grose (from a MS. in the Cotton Library) relates that between the towns of Alton and Newton, near the foot of Rosberrye Toppinge, there is a well dedicated to St. Oswald. Those resident in the district had an opinion that a shirt taken off a sick person and thrown into that well would show whether the persons would recover or die: for if it floated it denoted recovery; if it sunk there remained no hope of their life. And to reward the saint for his intelligence, they tore off a rag of the shirt and left it hanging on the briars thereabouts, "where," says the writer, "I have seen such numbers as might have made a fayre rheme in a "paper-myll." Pennant, Heron (Pinkerton), Sinclair, Macaulay, Brand, and many others relate similar practices in different parts of the world. In view of the discoveries of 1852 concerning water being the chief medium for conveying cholera infection, it might be curious to know the fate of those who used such wells for their legitimate purposes.

Sacrifice.—At *Carthage*, B.C. 534. A terrible plague. The people sacrificed their children to appease the gods.—BARONIUS.

At *Corinth.* A terrible plague, when Melicerta was thrown into the sea.

During the pestilence which prevailed in Spain about 470 B.C., the Carthagenians, to appease the ire of the gods, to whom they attributed these fatal visitations, offered up human sacrifices, and made incisions on their arms and legs and on other parts of their bodies; they also immolated cattle of all kinds, according to the severity of the pestilence.

The Roman pestilence of B.C. 366 was said to have been ended by the sacrifice of Marc. Curtius, who threw himself into a chasm which opened in the ground. Was this the chasm from which mephitic vapours were supposed to proceed?

SECULAR REMEDIES.—These are various, and as to some of the items enumerated (*Bells* and *Music* for instance) it may be said that both natural and supernatural results are invoked.

Bells.—" Great ringing of Bells in populous cities disperseth " pestilent air, which may be from the concussion of the air and " not from the sound."—BACON, " Natural History."

Music.—This has at all times been supposed to have a healing power; and in the middle ages it was believed to cure epilepsy, madness, convulsions, hysteria, and all forms of nervous affections. —VIGNOLI, " Myth and Science," p. 304.

At *Sparta*, B.C. 665. A plague, which Thalates *cured by the influence of music.*

Perfumes—Athens, B.C. 500. Actius and Galen both make mention of Hippocrates entering Athens during a pestilence, and advising the inhabitants to kindle large fires in the streets, and throw into the flames flowers of herbs and drugs of sweet odour to purify the air.

In Rome, A.D. 195, where 5,000 persons died daily for some time, the physicians advised the filling of the nose and ears with sweet-smelling ointments to prevent contagion. The distemper continued unchecked, however, for three years.

De Foe, in his " Journal of the Plague Year, 1665," referring to the practice which had come into use—consequent upon the belief that the plague was often spread by the contagion of the human breath—of employing perfumes, aromatics, and essences, says that if you went into a church where any number of people were present, " there would be such a mixture of smells at the entrance " that it was much more strong, though perhaps not so whole- " some, than if you were going into an apothecary's or druggist's " shop. In a word, the whole church was like a smelling bottle: " in one corner it was all perfumes; in another aromatics, balsamics, " and a variety of drugs and herbs; in another, salts and spirits; " as every one was furnished for their own preservation." He adds (p. 199):—" The poorer people, who only set open their windows " night and day, burnt brimstone, pitch, and gunpowder, and such

" things in their rooms, did as well as the best."—" Collected
" Works," v, 169.

Frugality, Cleanliness, &c.—Herodotus and Justin have recorded
the destruction of the *Grecian* (? Carthaginian) army when retreating into Asia after defeat at the battle of Salamis (B.C. 480),
by a grievous pestilence, which attacked both the land and sea
forces.   This army was largely composed of Spaniards, who were
a frugal race, and practised habits of personal cleanliness.   They
contributed very slightly to the 150,000 victims who are recorded
to have perished by this outbreak.   But it had already been
observed in Athens that those who lived frugally, drank water alone,
and wore clean garments, suffered much less than those who pursued an opposite course.   Some Roman historians asserted that the
secret of the Spanish soldiers was that they washed their bodies
with urine; whilst Galen, the Greek physician, had said of the
Syrians that they avoided the plague by drinking their liquid ex-
crement.   The learned Dean Swift admitted no other remedy into
the *materia medica* of his " Utopia of the Houyhnhnms."   It is
admitted that the Spaniards did use ablutions of urine with good
effect under certain conditions.   And even at the present day, the
oil-impregnated garments of whaling crews are washed in this
fluid—a barrel being placed under the topgallant-forecastle for the
preservation of their micturations.   This custom has perhaps not
been without influence in the depopulation of the South Sea
" freshwater stations," by *lues venerea.*   May not the curse in
2 Kings xviii, 27, have referred to plague in this way ?

Physical Changes.—The Greek philosopher Empedocles, who
flourished B.C. 444, is said to have shut out the pestilential sirocco
by stopping a mountain gap, and to have remedied intermittent
fever by changing the course of the Hypsa.

The Sacred Nail.—*Rome*, B.C. 360 and again 260.   The plague
raging, a nail was driven in the temple of Jupiter Capitolinus.

A Serpent.—*Rome*, A.D. 167.   Plague, supposed to be of the same
nature as that which occurred twenty years later.   Æsculapius, in
the form of a serpent, being invoked on both occasions.

Incantation.—The *Anglo-Saxon* remedy for flying venom, *i.e.*
plagues, as also for every venomous swelling, was this:—On a
Friday, churn butter, which has been milked from a neat or hind
all of one colour; and let it not be mingled with water; sing over
it nine times a litany, and nine times a pater noster, and nine
times this incantation—words which seem to belong to no known
language, and which, therefore, I do not attempt to give.   The
charm is said to have been originally Gaelic; but other authorities
say Irish.—" Leechdoms," &c., ii, 113.

Russian Preventive Remedy.—Mr. Wallace, in his " Russia,"

1879 (vol. i, p. 118), speaks of an incident which occurred in a village near which he had been living in 1871 :—

"Cholera had been raging in the district for some time. In the village in question no case had yet occurred, but the inhabitants feared that the dreaded visitor would soon arrive, and the following ingenious contrivance was adopted for warding off the danger :—At midnight, when the male population was supposed to be asleep, all the maidens met in nocturnal costume, according to a preconcerted plan, in the outskirts of the village, and formed a procession. In front marched a girl holding an icon ; behind her came her companions, dragging a sokhá—the primitive plough commonly used by the peasantry—by means of a long rope. In this order the procession made the circuit of the entire village ; *and it was confidently believed that the cholera would not be able to overstep the magical circle thus described.* Many of the males probably knew, or at least suspected, what was going on, but they prudently remained within doors, knowing well that if they should be caught peeping indiscreetly at the mystic ceremony, they would be unmercifully beaten by those who were taking part in it."

This custom is believed to be a remnant of old pagan superstition ; but the introduction of the ban is a modern innovation, and illustrates that curious blending of paganism and Christianity which is often met with in Russia.

Flagellation.—In 1349 a dreadful pestilence, after ravaging Africa and Asia, extended to Europe, and proved especially fatal in France and England. To appease the wrath of Omnipotence, persons wandered through the country lacerating their shoulders with whips ; whence arose the sect called Flagellants.—BOYLE, i, 466.

In " Froissart's Chronicle " we find the following :—

" In this year of our Lord, 1349, there came from Germany persons who performed public penitences by whipping themselves with scourges having iron hooks, so that their backs and shoulders were torn ; they chanted also in a piteous manner canticles of the nativity and sufferings of our Saviour, and could not, by their rules, remain in any town more than one night. They travelled in companies of more or less in number, and thus journeyed through the country, performing their penitence for thirty-three days, being the number of years Jesus Christ remained on earth, and then returned to their own houses. These penitences were thus performed to entreat our Lord to restrain His anger, and withhold His vengeance : *for at this period an epidemic malady ravaged the earth, and destroyed a third part of its inhabitants.*"

Herbs, Flowers, and Fruits.— On the Assumption of the Virgin Mary (15th August), it was the custom of the Romish Church to implore blessings upon herbs, plants, roots, and fruits. "Naogeorgus" (Googe's version) contains the following hereon :—

" Great bundles, then, of hearbes to church, the people fast do beare,
The which against all hurtfull things the priest doth hallow theare.

    ＊   ＊   ＊   ＊   ＊

For sundrie witchcrafts by these hearbs are wrought, and divers charmes,
And each in the fire are thought to drive away all harmes,
And every painefull griefe from *man* or *beast*, for to repell,
Far otherwise than nature or the word of God doth tell."

In 1588 Dr. Cogan published in his " Haven of Health " " A " Short Treatise on the Plague," wherein he advises, in order to escape the pestilence, "take in your hand an orange, or a posie of " rew, or mint, or balme." See *Perfumes.*

Medicine.—In 1616 Dr. Francis Anthonie published his "Apologie, " or Defence of a verity heretofore published concerning a Medicine " called Aurum Potabile, that is, the pure substance of Gold, pre- " pared and made potable and medicinable without Corrosives, as " an Universal Medicine." 4to.

Herein is given the names and addresses of many eminent persons who had been cured through the agency of this nostrum, also the different diseases, and amongst them the *plague.*

Fires in Streets.—The practice of lighting fires in the streets, so largely resorted to in London in 1665, had a significance in Pagan rites associated with the "summer solstice" and midsummer eve observances. In the homily *De Festo Sancti Johannis Baptiste,* there occurs the following :—

"In worshyp of Saint Johnn the people waked at home, and made there manner of fyres : one was clene bones and noo woode, and that is called a Bone Fyre; another is clene woode, and no bones, and that is called a Wode Fyre, for people to sit and wake thereby ; the thirde is made of wode and bones, and it is callyd Saynt Johannes fyre. The first fyre, as a great clerke Johan Delleth telleth, he was in a certayne countrey, so in the countrey there was soo greate hete, the which caused that dragons to go togyther in tokenynge that John dyed in brennynge love and charyte to God and man, and they that dye in charyte shall haue parte of all good prayers, and they that do not, shal never be saved. Then as these dragons flewe in the ayre, they shed down to that water froth of ther kynde, and so enveynomid the waters and causeth moche people for to take theyr deth thereby, and many dyverse sykennesse. *Wyss clerks knoweth well that dragons hate nothyng more than the stenche of brennynge bones,* and therefore they gaderyd as many as they might fynde, and brent them ; and so with the stenche thereof they drove away the dragons, and so they were brought out of greete dyseuse."—BRAND's "Popish Antiquities," p. 166.

—— It is recorded that during the raging of the plague at Avignon, in 1347, Pope Clement VI ordered great fires to be kept up by night as well as by day in every room within his palace; and by this means the disease was unknown within its walls. It was no doubt the record of this fact which led to fires being lighted in the streets (and probably very generally in the houses) during the plague visitation of which we are now speaking.

This practice will be referred to under legislation, 1563, as by order of Queen Elizabeth.

Fire Ordeal.—In the "Mirror," for 24th June, 1826, there is the following account of an attempt to purify by fire. on the occasion of a cattle epidemic in Perthshire :—

"A wealthy old farmer having lost several of his cattle by some disease very prevalent at present, and being able to account for it in no way so rationally as by witchcraft, had recourse to the following remedy, recommended to him by a weird sister in his neighbourhood, as an effectual protection against the attacks of the foul fiend. A few stones were piled together in the barnyard, and wodd coals having been laid thereon, the fuel was ignited by *will-fire*—that is fire obtained by friction; the neighbours having been called in to witness the solemnity, the cattle were made to pass through the flames, in the order of their dignity and age, commencing with the horses and ending with the swine. The ceremony having been duly and decorously gone through, a neighbouring farmer observed to the enlightened owner of the herd, that he, along with his family, ought to have followed the example of the cattle, and the sacrifice to Baal would have been complete."

It is stated on the authority of Kemble ("Saxons in England," i, p. 361 *note*), that *will-fire* has been used in Devonshire for a like purpose within the memory of man. It is believed to be an Anglo-Saxon custom.

Cold-water Cure. — CLIMSELL, "London's Vacation," 1637, describes the virtues of hydropathic treatment:—

> " The sheet being wet, and he stark naked in it,
> About his body he did strait way pinne it;
> Which being done, away to bed he went.
> The morning being come, and the night spent,
> He found himself well, and his body cleare
> From all those spots which before did appear."

He adds, that the gentleman having prudently procured the sheet to be buried, it was "covetously dug up," and those concerned in the operation died of the plague caught from the infected linen.

Charms.—For *cholera* the "lapis porcinus," according to Bontius, is declared to be good. During its prevalence in Continental Europe, it was common in many parts of Austria, Germany, and Italy, to wear an amulet at the pit of the stomach, in contact with the skin. " I have (says Dr. Pettigrew) seen one of " these, sent from Hungary; it consists merely of a circular piece " of copper $2\frac{1}{2}$ inches in diameter, and is without characters. In " Naples, I learn, they were very generally worn."—PETTIGREW, p. 103.

Regarding the use of charms, amulets, talismans, and all this class of trifles, there is this indirect, or it may almost be said direct advantage, they remove the feeling of fear, which on many sensitive constitutions operates so fatally. "The hope entertained by " the possession of a charm, to avert pestilence, may have operated " in many instances so as to counteract the taking of the plague, " for which disease such numerous amulets have been found."— PETTIGREW, p. 149.

In Hill's "Natural and Artificial Conclusions" (1650), is set forth " the virtue of a rare cole that is to be found but one hour in " the day, and one day in the yeare." "Divers authors (he adds) " affirm concerning the verity and virtue of this cole, viz., that it " is only to be found upon Midsummer Eve, just at noon, under " every root of plantine and of mugwort, the effects whereof are " wonderful: for whosoever weareth or beareth the same about " with them, shall be freed from the *plague*, fever, ague, and " sundry other diseases. And one author specially writeth, and

" constantly averreth, that he never knew any that used to carry of
" this marvellous cole about them, who ever were, to his know-
" ledge, sick of the plague, or (indeed) complain of any other
" maladie."

Coffee.—In 1720 there was published in England a tract " On
" the Virtue and Use of Coffee with regard to the Plague."

Tobacco.—The popular belief in the efficacy of tobacco as a
specific against the infection of the plague was in former times
approved by DIEMERBRORCK and other great authorities. But
modern practice, following CHENOT and RIVINUS, classes this
among obsolete prophylactics. The exceptional prevalence of
plague at *Aleppo*, where both sexes smoke constantly, seems con-
clusive; and the better opinion is that tobacco has only the
antiloimic virtue of opium and wine, in soothing the mind and
rendering it less prone to the anxious fear which unquestionably
excites infection. And in this case, as in others, the sedative
effect of smoking is more than counterbalanced by the subsequent
agitation induced by nervous reaction.

In the "Reliquae Hearnianai," touching the plague of 1665, it
is stated that " none that kept tobacconist's shops had the plague.
" It is certain that smoaking is looked upon as a most excellent
" preservative. In so much that even children were obliged to
" smoak . . . Tom Rogers, . . . yeoman beadle . . . that year a
" school boy at Eaton . . . was never whipped so much in his lyfe
" as he was one morning for not smoking." Yet such is the
progress of science that in 1881 a boy was expelled the Charter-
house for smoking.

Influence of Royalty.—I must not omit all notice of the supposed
influence of royalty in the matter of plagues and pestilences.

In 1661 Captain John Graunt first published his " Natural and
" Political Observations on the Bills of Mortality," and therein he
offered some very curious and original remarks on the plague,
several of which I have quoted in this paper. Then there is the
following :—

" As to this year 1660, although we would not be thought superstitious, yet it
is not to be neglected, that in the said year was the king's restoration to his
empire over these three nations, as if God Almighty had caused the healthfulness
and fruitfulness thereof to repair the bloodshed and calamities suffered in his
absence. I say this conceit doth abundantly counterpoise the opinion of those,
who think great plagues come in kings' reigns, because it happened so twice, viz.,
anno 1603 and 1625; whereas as well the year 1648, wherein the present king
commenced his right to reign, as also the year 1660, wherein he commenced the
exercise of the same, were both eminently healthful, which clears both monarchy,
and our present king's family, from what seditious men have surmised against
them."—P. 21.

The process of touching for the "king's evil" I have already
noticed. Did queens ever exercise the supposed curative touch,

and did the idea originally arise from the " laying on of
" hands ?"

Many of our sovereigns propounded remedies for the cure of the
plague : among these may be specially noted Elizabeth and Mary,
James and Charles. Their nostrums were mostly amusing and
palatable. Lord Bacon followed in the same line with this recipe :—

" Take a pint of Malmsey wine, burnt, with a spoonful of bruised grains, *i.e.*,
cardamon seeds; of the best treacle a spoonful; and give the patient to drink of
it two or three spoonfuls pretty often, with a draft of Malmsey wine after it, and
so let him sweat. If it agree with him, and it stay with him, he is out of danger ;
if he vomit it up, repeat it again."—MARSHALL, 1832, xvi.

Legislative Measures Concerning the Plague.

I have here to speak of the various precautions taken by kings,
queens, and council, and orders made concerning the plague by the
lord mayor and common council of London, a few of which I here
set forth :—

1563.—Command came from the queen (Elizabeth) that the
inhabitants of a house which the plague had visited should not go
to church for a month ; and a blue cross was to be placed on the
door of every house visited, with an intimation in writing. A man
was hired to kill all dogs in the streets ; and all vagabonds and
sturdy beggars were to be taken up and placed in Bridewell.

Four days after, a commandment was issued out that every
man in every street and lane should make bonefire three times in
the week, in order to the ceasing of the plague, if it so pleased
God, and so to continue these fires everywhere Mondays, Wednes-
and Fridays.—STOW.

1570.—Orders were issued to the various officers of the city
regarding what was to be done :—

Howses having some sicke, though none die, or from whence
some sicke have bene removed, are infected houses, and such are to
be shutt upp for a moneth. The whole familie to tarrie in xxviii
daies.

Common Hunt.—To kyll doggs, &c., or to loose his place. None
shall kepe dogge or bitche abrode unled, none within howling or
disturbing theire neighbours. To have no assemblie at funeral
dynners, or usual meeting in houses infected.

If the increase of the sicknes be feared, that interludes and
plaies be restreyned within the libertyes of the cyttye.

That all maisterlesse men, who live idelie in the cyttye, without
any lawfull calling, frequenting places of common assemblies, as

D

interludes, gaming howses, cockpitts, bowling allies, and such other places, may be banished the cyttye, according to the lawes in that case provyded.

The increasing of the citie by buildings and inmates was look'd as very dangerous to the city and of very ill consequence. Wherefore the queen, at the cities desire, set forth a proclamation against new buildings.—Stow, B.V., p. 436.

1593.—In consequence of the plague prevailing in the city this year, the queen (Elizabeth) issued a proclamation prohibiting the holding of St. Bartholomew Fair.

1603.—The plague outbreak of this year caused the issue of several proclamations. 1. Dated Windsor, 11th July, postponing the holding of St. James's Mayfair for eight or ten days after the usual time of holding the same. 2. Another, dated 29th July, to the effect that "the solemnities of our coronation being now per-" formed," the nobility of Scotland, and all English noblemen and gentry, not the king's servants in ordinary, are commanded to repair homewards into the country, to prevent the spreading of the contagion of the plague. The knight-marshal was to prevent persons "from infesting the court," and petitions of suitors were to be received at Kingston. 3. The other, dated at Hampton Court, 8th August, forbidding the holding of Bartholomew and Stourbridge fairs at the usual times (in September), or until they should be authorised by the king.

The lord mayor of London addressed a letter, bearing date 18th April, 1603, to the lord high treasurer of the realm, informing him of the steps taken to prevent the spread of the plague in the counties of Middlesex and Surrey.

1604.—The Act 2 James I, cap. 31, for affording charitable relief during plagues, will be cited in a later division.

1606.—The lord mayor addressed a letter in October to the lords of the council, acknowledging a letter from their lordships, and informing them of the steps taken to preserve the city from the spread of the infection, and reciting that the following Order had been passed:—"That every infected house should be warded and " kept with two sufficient watchmen, suffering no persons to go " more out of the said house, nor no searcher to go abroad without " a *redd roade* in their hand;" and that a marshal and two assistants had been appointed to keep the beggars out of the city, &c.

1607.—The lord mayor addressed a letter, 12th April, to the lord chamberlain, informing him of the increase of the plague in the *skirts* and *confines* of the city, "which is likely to spread thro' " the great heat of the season, and requesting that all stage plays " may be interdicted, and that the justices of Middlesex may put

" into execution such ordinances in Whitechapel, Shoreditch, and " Clerkenwell, and such other remote parts as they are advised, " for the stay thereof."

1625.—The plague again appearing in various parts of the country, Charles I, by royal proclamation, issued from his palace at Woodstock, probably in August, prohibited the holding of St. Bartholomew or Stourbridge fairs, specifying generally any fairs within 50 miles of the metropolis.

The lords of the council address a letter, 4th December, to the lord mayor and court of aldermen, requesting them to have infected houses cleansed and secured from further contagion, and specially the household stuffs and bedding therein; the using diligence wherein may encourage His Majesty to approach sooner to the city, and give confidence to all to repair thither.

1636.—The lords of the council address a letter (7th April) to the lord mayor and court of aldermen, upon the apprehended increase of the plague, requiring them to meet the justices of Middlesex, Surrey, and Westminster, once or twice a week, and advise with them as to the courses taken upon former like occasions, and as to the best means to be now taken for the prevention of the increase of the plague.

An Order in Council, dated 27th April, for levying of rates in Middlesex and Surrey for the erection of Pest Houses and other places of abode for infected persons; also directing the justices of the peace for Middlesex to join with the lord mayor and court of aldermen in making additional Orders, to be printed, for preventing the increase of the infection, and authorising them from time to time to make such further Orders thereon as they shall think fit; also directing the churchwardens, overseers, and constables of every parish to provide themselves with books for their directions; and requiring the physicians of the city to renew the former book touching medicines against infection, and to add to, and alter the same, and to cause it to be forthwith printed.

The lords of the council address the lord mayor (11th May), complaining that the *Red Cross* and the inscription, " Lord have " mercy upon us," are placed so high, and in such obscure places, upon infected houses, as to be hardly discernible; and that they are so negligently looked to, that few or none have watchmen at the doors, and that persons have been sitting at the doors of such houses; and requiring that the crosses and inscriptions be put in the most conspicuous places, and that the houses be strictly watched, and none permitted to go out or in, or sit at the doors, and that such as wilfully do, be shut up with the rest of the infected persons; and that such officers that have failed in their duties therein be committed to Newgate as an example to others.

The lords of the council address the lord mayor (13th November) with respect to the money collected for the relief of the poor in the cities of London and Westminster and the suburbs, which had been entrusted to him for distribution in all those places, though out of his jurisdiction—requiring him, having regard to the long continuance of the plague, which must have very much impoverished the poor, whether infected or not, to extend his care to both sorts.

The lords of the council address the lord mayor and aldermen, under date 9th December, upon the decrease and abatement of the plague, and requiring them to take effectual order that all houses that have been infected this summer, and the goods therein, be aired, cleansed, and purified in the best manner that can be thought of, &c.

The king addressed the lord mayor (29th December), expressing His Majesty's anxiety at the sudden increase of the plague during the last week, which he believed had arisen from want of care, especially by the streets being pestered with beggars, rogues, wanderers, and dissolute persons, many of whom probably came from infected places, and with plague sores about them; and forwarding further instructions for the guidance of the lord mayor and the justices of the peace of Middlesex, Surrey, and Westminster.

1639.—The lords of the council address the lord mayor and aldermen (31st July) with respect to the recent spreading of the plague, and requesting them to revive the execution of such of the former Orders sent in the time of the late infection as they shall find requisite, and especially those for the removal of infected persons to the pest houses, and to see that the houses from which they are removed, and any houses in which infected persons remain, be shut up and guarded, so that none come out or go in, or have speech with them at doors and windows.

1641.—Was published, "Orders thought meet to be put into "execution against the Plague." And amongst them the following: " That the bill, '*Lord have mercy upon us,*' with a large crosse, be " set upon the door of every house visited by the plague."

[*Note.*]—ROGER SHARPE, in "More Fooles Yet," published 1610, tells of "A doore belonging to a house infected whereon was plac't (as 'tis the custome still) *Lord, have mercie upon us!*"

Pepys, in his immortal diary, under date 7th June, 1665, records:—" This day, much against my will, I did in Drury Lane see two or three houses marked with a red cross upon the doors, and 'Lord have mercy upon us!' writ there; which was a sad sight. . . . It put me into an ill conception of myself and my smell, so that I was forced to buy some roll tobacco to smell and to chaw, which took away the apprehension." " By water home, where weary with walking and with the *mighty heat of the weather.*" . . . . " Twelve at night, when it begun to lighten exceedingly, through the greatness of the heat."—(COLBURN's 1848 edit., iii, 23.)

Departing the City.—The practice of residents absenting them-selves from the city during plague outbreaks became very general, but was much and unfavourably commented upon by the pamphleteers of the period.

1665.—Among the very few advertisements in the early news-papers, was the following in the "Intelligencer," June 22—30, 1665:—

"This is to certify, that the master of the Cock and Bottle, commonly called the Cock Alehouse, Temple Bar, hath dismissed his servants, and shut up his house for this long vacation, intending (God willing) to return at Michaelmas next; so that all persons who have any accounts or farthings (tokens) belonging to the said house, are desired to repair thither before the 8th of this instant July, and they shall receive satisfaction."

This old hostelry is still standing, although its demolition is threatened by the Temple Bar improvements.

In the present generation we seek general remedies only in the improved condition of the public health, and in the improved education of the medical profession.

Influence of Pestilence upon Nations, Communities, and Associations.

It is hardly to be supposed that calamities of such magnitude as plagues, or of such frequent occurrence, did not leave their im-press upon the nations who were most subject to them. The mode in which this influence was exerted it is not always easy to discover; and the inquiry, if made in any detail, would be too wide for my present purposes. But on the other hand it is certain that no survey of the history of pestilences could be considered at all complete which left this portion of the subject unnoticed. I shall, however, only attempt to deal with those effects which lie nearest the surface—remarking that here is an abundant field for study by those who are looking for a new subject of investigation.

Early Sanitary Laws.—It is believed that the sanitary regula-tions recorded in the Book of Leviticus resulted from the plague visitation which fell upon the Egyptians in the desert, B.C. 1471. See Table, 1832. Other instances are given in this paper.*

Decline of Roman Empire.—It is admitted by Gibbon that the great plague of A.D. 250-65, which had such a depletory effect upon

---

* Dr. Guy, a long and earnest labourer in the cause of Public Health, says : " There are three diseases which no longer, under any name, figure on our registers of death : I mean the Black Death of the fourteenth century, the Sweating Sickness of the sixteenth, and the Plague of the seventeenth. For the disappear-ance of these diseases " (he adds) " neither science nor the labours of individuals, nor such local occurrences as the great fire of London, can claim any credit. We must attribute the happy result to the natural progress of society from barbarism to civilisation, to the onward march of the peaceful arts, and to the growth of the habits of decency and cleanliness."—" Public Health," 1870, p. 19.

the nations then under the sway of Rome, was one of the earliest steps which led first to its decline, and then to its final fall.

Saxon Invasion of England.—It has been assumed that the invasion of England by the Angles, Jutes, and Saxons in the middle of the fifth century, was in consequence of the island being decimated by pestilence. I confess to not finding any historical authority for the statement. What population remained after the Roman abandonment had been sadly harassed by the Picts and Scots, and but little fighting power was left.

Depopulation of the Eastern Nations.—One of the plagues which appear to have exerted the greatest influence upon the destinies of race, is apparently that of A.D. 544 (sometimes spoken of as A.D. 568), and usually designated the "Plague of Constantinople." We know upon authority that it depeopled many of the cities of the East. May it not account for the general depopulation of the ancient cities of Persia?

But it probably had an influence to preserve as well as to destroy. May it not be fairly supposed that from *its* teachings Mahomet was induced to enjoin strict temperance upon his followers, as also habits of personal cleanliness? But, further, the Mahometan Empire could hardly otherwise have maintained its existence in the midst of plague surroundings. The "Levantine plague" has been always regarded as of the most deadly character.

QUARANTINE REGULATIONS.—These arose directly out of the known dangers of infection, and they have had, and still continue to have, an influence upon the commerce of the world. Lines of freight and passenger ships are still arranged with reference to the requirements of certain ports in the way of quarantine.

The first regulations of this character which I meet with in history were enforced in *Venice* in 1127. All merchants and others coming from the Levant were obliged to remain in the house of St. Lazarus (hence lazar house?) or the Lazaretto forty days before they were admitted into the city. The Lazaretto of Venice was built in the water, and is still standing.

Quarantine regulations appear to have been first instituted in England during the plague outbreak of 1499-1503. The first act of parliament on the subject appears to have been the 9th Anne, cap. 2 (1710). Since which their number has been almost indefinite.

LABOUR LAWS.—Out of the "black death" of the fourteenth century arose important events. The mortality was so great amongst the craftsmen (artisans), as also amongst the lower class designated as labourers, that some branches of industry were brought practically to a standstill. The survivors, finding their labour so much in demand, began to demand wages altogether beyond anything previously known or contemplated. Prices of commodities came to be seriously enhanced. Petitions were poured into parliament, and finally there was enacted in 1349 the *Statute of Labourers*, 23rd Edward III; which was amended and re-enacted two years later, by 25th Edward III, stat. 2.

This was the commencement of a long line of legislative infatuation in the way of interference with the laws of supply and demand, which have only been finally exploded (if I may say finally) in our own time. I shall hope on some future occasion to address this Society more particulary on some of the consequences which resulted.*

Laws of Inheritance, &c.—In the parliament 25th Edward III (1350-51), there came a communication from the king touching the laws of inheritance, which was in substance as follows :—

" The king, considering how much mischief and damage have come to the people, as well from the neglect of guarding and observing the statutes heretofore made, as *by reason of the mortal pestilence* which lately obtained, has, for the quiet and the well being of his people, ordained, with the assent of lords and commons, that the law of England be reaffirmed to be that children (or subjects) of the king, born abroad, may inherit their ancestors' lands in England as if born there, so long as their parents are liege subjects when the children are born."

In A.D. 1399 the loss in Spain was such that the king suspended the law requiring a year's widowhood before remarriage.

Religion and Literature.—Out of this same "black death," the ravages of which extended entirely through Europe, came other, if remote, consequences than those relating to labour and to property. A belief had gained ground (amongst uneducated people any belief may take root) that the plague was in some way associated with usurpation by the Papal power. The Romish Church has always been astute in grasping at temporal advantages—and such a period of extended depopulation must have afforded many opportunities. Wycliffe, then a youth, was pondering upon a much needed reformation in this Church. He saw the aid this view would lend to his cause. Thus enthusiasm was imparted, and in the end the result obtained.

With regard to the influence upon literature. This is seen in the writings of Petrarch and Boccaccio. The "Decameron" of the latter is founded upon the incidents of the plague. May it not have suggested the idea of Defoe's "Journal of the Plague," after

---

* " The plague of 1348, and the consequent depopulation, brought the opposition between the interests of the working classes and the employers for the first time on a large scale to a crisis. As the clergy took advantage of the small number of those who could say masses and prayers in conformity with the intentions of the faithful, in order to increase their fees, and as merchants and tradesmen took advantage of the small supply of wares to raise their prices ; in like manner the workmen continued to use, for a general rise in wages, the distress into which the propertied class had been plunged through the universal dearth of labour."—BRENTANO'S " Preliminary Essay on English Guilds," p. 142.

the visitation in 1665?   Petrarch is hailed as the first restorer of letters in a popular sense.

A curious instance of literature arising from a plague is that of a poetical tract by John Singer, a comic actor of Shakespeare's day, entitled " Quips upon Questions . . . Clapt up by a Clowne of " the Towne in this last restraint, having little else to doe to make " a little use of his fickle Muse."   The "last restraint" was the forbidding of plays during the pestilence of 1600.

The Passion Play at Oberammergau, which to-day occupies so unique a place in dramatic art, owes its origin to a pestilence which visited the little Bavarian town in 1635, when the devout Oberammergauers vowed to God the performance of a play of the Divine Passion of Christ.

Sanitary Regulations, 1388.—In 1361-62 England was again visited by a pestilence; and it was in view of its approach from the continent of Europe that Edward III wrote to the mayor and sheriffs of London a letter enjoining certain sanitary precautions. These precautions, if taken, were not continued, as we may learn by the following passage from Stow, 1580 :—

> "Another matter that required remedy and regulation, in these suburbs especially, was this: It was customary for the people to carry their filth, as entrails of dead beasts and other noisome things, and to throw them into the ditches, waters, fields, and highways, whereby the air was in danger of being corrupted : and so to create infectious diseases in the city."—Book iv, p. 36.

The ancient oath of office was this year taken by Thomas Mereward, provost of Dublin, anno 12th Richard II.   The following clause is extracted from it :—

> " Ninthly,—You are not to suffer any cattle to be slaughtered within your walls, neither to suffer any swine to run about the streets, and to banish all beggars in the time of any sickness or plague."

Plague Refuges.—In a lease of some lands of St. Peter's Abbey, at Gloucester, granted in 1515, was contained the following reservation :—

> " And upon reasonable summons by the abbat made to the lessee, when the plague shall be at Gloucester or Over, the abbat reserves a convenient part of the mansion house at Hyneham for the residence of himself and his men during the continuance thereof, 12th March, 7° H. 8."—RUDDER'S " Gloucestershire," 1779, p. 141.

Highnam was a manor house situate 2 miles from the city.

Charitable Relief.—On the occasion of any serious outbreak of plague the town or district suffering had to make a public appeal, and gather up means of supporting its sufferers as best it could. Here is an instance :—

> " 1597-98.—The Plague.   Carlisle, Cumberland.
> " In the 40th and 41st Elizabeth, the plague raged exceedingly at Carlisle and other parts of the country, insomuch that there died of it at Carlisle alone 1,196

persons, which was about one-third part of the whole number; during which time collections were made as set forth in the following report:—

" 'A brief note to posterity of all such sums as did accrue for the relief of the diseased of the plague, which began in this city at Michaelmas, in the year of God 1597, and continued until Michaelmas, 1598; with a remembrance of the bene-volence of the county there, and the particular gifts of certain well affected gentle-men, with the assessments of the citizens themselves, and the charge taken forth of the common chest.

	£	s.	d.
Imprimis, From the justices of the peace of this county, received and brought in by Mr. Richard Bell, then mayor....	20	0	0
Item, More sent by Mr. Lawson, then high sheriff of the county, about the 10th of June	10	0	0
Item, From the dean and chapter at several times, which came to the sum of	5	7	0
Item, From the bishop of Carlisle, then being (Dr. Meye)	6	13	4
Item, From the bishop of Carlisle that now is, upon his entry (Dr. Robinson)	2	0	0
Item, From John Dalston, esquire, of Dalston	1	10	0
Item, From Mr. Dethick, chancellor	1	0	0
Item, From Mr. Francis Highmore, of Harby-brow	0	18	0
Item, From Mr. Warwick, of Warwick hall	0	10	0
Item, From Mr. Pearson Warwick, of Marpitt	0	10	0
Item, Taken out of our common chest at several times, for relief of the said sick persons	85	2	0
Item, The whole remainder of the revenue upon Chamberlain Pattinson's account the year before, being the sum of	61	14	8
Item, The several collections of the citizens themselves	14	4	10
The total sum	209	9	10' "

—From NICOLSON and BURNS's "History of Westmoreland and Cumberland," vol. ii, p. 234.

With a view to remedy this state of things, the aid of parliament was evoked, and in 1604 the first Act of the legislature in favour of sufferers from the plague was passed, viz., the 2nd James I, cap. 31: *An Act for the Charitable Relief and Ordering of Persons infected with the Plague,* which recited :—

" Forasmuch as the inhabitants of divers cities, boroughs, towns corporate and of other parishes and places being visited with the plague, are found to be unable to relieve the poorer sort of such people so infected, who of Necessity must be by some charitable course provided for lest they should wander abroad and infect others; (2) and forasmuch as divers persons infected with that disease, and others inhabiting in houses and places infected, as well poor people and unable to relieve themselves that are carefully provided for, as others which of themselves are of ability, being commanded by the magistrate or officer of or within the place where the infection shall be, to keep their houses, or otherwise to separate them-selves from company for the avoiding of further infection, do notwithstanding very dangerously and disorderly misdemean themselves."

Wherefore it was enacted that the mayor and others in authority have power to tax every inhabitant and all property for the relief of the sick of the plague. All contributions so levied to be reported to and certified by next quarter sessions. The Universities, cathedral churches, and Eton and Winchester colleges were excepted from the operation of the Act.

I believe it was under the authority of this Act that *pest houses* were provided in the vicinity of many, if not of most, of the towns in the kingdom. Many of these are still existing, bearing their original description.

Cases still arose which were too serious even for its machinery to grapple with. Here is one in 1645 :—

MANCHESTER.—" The town was again visited with the scourge of pestilence, and the number of burials in Manchester increased from about 200, which was at that time the general average, to upwards of 1,200. This visitation was so ruinous that parliament, on the 9th of July, directed that 1,000*l.* should be appropriated to the relief of Manchester ; and on the 9th of December the House of Commons issued an ordinance, directing a collection to be made in all the churches and chapels of the metropolis for the town of Manchester, which is described to have been for a long time ' so sore visited by the pestilence, that none were for many months permitted either to come in or go out of the said town.' The Rev. Adam Martindale, in his autobiography, speaking on this subject, says— ' Manchester was sadly visited by the pestilence in the year 1645. So sore was the visitation, that persons sickened and died in one night ; public fast were held at Blackley and other places in the neighbourhood, and the markets of Manchester were for a time wholly discontinued.' [MS. Life of Adam Martindale in British Museum.] Before the end of the year the malady was stayed, and in the following year the burials were reduced from 1,200 to 144. The disease was, however, far from being subdued in the country, for between the 22nd of June, 1647, and the 14th of October in the same year, the burials in Chester amounted to the almost incredible number of 1,875. [*Harl.* MSS., Codex 1921, fo. 27.]"—BAINES'S " Lancashire," 1836, vol. ii, p. 280.

The Act however must have been of great service in many instances. Here is a case in point :—

" BRIDPORT (Dorset), anno 2 Carolo I, was visited by the plague ; and an order of sessions was made to raise money in Dorchester division for their relief. In 1672 an order of sessions was renewed, allowing 12*l.* out of the county stock, for the poor of Bridport, in the lazary of Altington."—*Vide* HUTCHINS'S " Hist. of Dorset," i, 234.

But out of these special collections of charity some abuses arose. Thus in 1760-71 there was enacted the 22nd and 23rd Charles II, cap. 16, "An Act for the discovery of such as have " defrauded the Poore of the Citty of London of the Moneys given " for their Releife at the Times of the late Plague and Fire, and for " the recovery of the Arrears thereof." These collections had been made under proclamation bearing date 6th July, 17th Carlo II ; 13th September, 18th Carlo II, and 26th September, 1668, and recited that a great part of the money so contributed had been mis-applied. The Act was to enforce restitution.

The ill-paid and shiftless actors of the seventeenth century must have suffered bitterly from the closing of the play-houses in time of pestilence. In " Jocabella," a jest book of 1640, occurs this *conceit*, numbered 122 : " A gentleman meeting a stage player

" in a great sicknes time, who had formerly plaid women's parts,
" told him he was growne grave, and that he began to have a
" beard. The other answered, while the grasse growes the horse
" did starve, meaning, because there was then no playing, and
" therefore he did let his beard grow." [See *supra* : " Legislative
" Measures," 1570.]

Popular Traditions.—That many traditions arose or were invented concerning the plague, which did not bear serious reflection
or investigation, is but too probable. Graunt, in his " Natural and
" Political Observations, 1665," thought it necessary to declare
" that the opinion of plagues accompanying the entrance of kings
" is false and seditious." I have an impression that this idea
became diffused from the former prevalent practice of " touching
" for the evil." When a new sovereign ascended the throne, there
was always a great rush to be touched, and to receive the golden
" touch piece," which was one of its accompaniments. It has
been suggested that crowds assembling for the coronation and its
accompanying festivals have been factors herein. But I have
found no reason for thinking so.—*Note*, Table, 1603.

It appears upon reference to the Civil Statutes of *Genoa*,
promulgated 1610, that it had been customary at an earlier period
to make the approach of the plague—and probably also its continuance—the subject of insurance wagers; and henceforth, as such
were prohibited, " They shall not be made upon the *plagues* or wars
" being impending or not."

The author of " Every Man his own Broker," of which several
editions appeared during the last century, thought it necessary to
caution his readers that the great variety of rumours conveyed in
letters from the continent, as deaths of certain great personages,
" breaking out of the plague," &c., were too often made subservient
to the great purpose of stock jobbing !

Special Prayers.—I have not been able to discover when the
words " From plague, pestilence, and famine .... Good Lord deliver
" us," were first introduced into the Litany.* They are found as
far back as 1633, in the Book of Common Prayer published at
Cambridge in that year. There was a special form of prayer
against plague issued in 1721, when pestilence was raging with
great violence in France and other parts of Europe.

Board of Health and Registration.—It was to the cholera outbreak in 1832 that we may trace the establishment of a General
Board of Health (now superseded by the Local Government Board),
whose reports I have herein repeatedly referred to; but, still more

---

* Litanies primarily were (in the Gallic Church) the outcome of the practice of
invoking the Divine mercy in times of excessive drought, by means of rogations
and processional supplications.

important, to this same cause we owe the improved system of registration of deaths, &c., and indeed the foundation of the office of
the registrar-general, from which most of the reliable statistics we
now have regarding the births, marriages, and deaths of our population have emanated.

On a recent occasion Mr. J. Foster Palmer read before the
Royal Historical Society an excellent paper, "Pestilences; their
" Influence on the Destiny of Nations." He therein refers to many
of the points here spoken of. He supposes the breeding ground of
plagues and pestilences to lie in that region where the three conti-
nents of Europe, Asia, and Africa meet, and near to which so many
great nations have risen and passed away :—

> " We thus find that pestilence has been, from more than one point of view, a
> most important factor in the composition of history ; and though we may hope for
> the future to prevent its reappearance among ourselves, at any rate on so large a
> scale as formerly, we cannot eradicate the past, nor can we over estimate its
> influence upon the past and present condition of the world. I beg to submit,
> therefore, that in judging of the probable fate of nations from the analogy of the
> past, we must not lose sight of the fact that all the great empires of antiquity—
> the Egyptian, the Assyrian, the Babylonian, the Persian, the Grecian, and to a
> certain extent also the Roman, had their seats in this plague-stricken region of the
> globe, and were thus subject to an adversary from which the powers of the present
> day have less to fear, and which civilisation promises finally to overcome."

Has the periodical overflowing of the Nile any influence upon
the locality indicated; and is the diffusion mainly in the caravan
routes ? These are amongst the points that here arise for reflection.

Influence upon Associations.—We at the present day can hardly
realise the influence of plague visitations upon the minds of men
at the period when they most prevailed. All the affairs of life
were rendered more especially uncertain by their influence. Take
one instance—that of life insurance associations, whose purpose is
to equalise as it were the individual uncertainties of human life.
Their operations are necessarily based on averages; but under the
influence of spasmodic visitations of pestilence, and in the absence
of all sound statistical knowledge regarding their fatality, the
notion of average was out of the question. Life insurance then
was simply a *lottery;* and the founders of such associations—wise
in their generation—treated them as such, by adopting the principle of *mutual contribution.* No fixed sum was guaranteed at
death, but all the then members were to be called on to contribute
in a certain ratio, and the aggregate of these contributions was to
constitute the measure of the fund available to meet the death
claims. To this fund all the members usually contributed equally,
irrespective of age.

When, in 1762, it was proposed to set on foot an association
having a more certain basis of financial operation—where indeed a
specific sum should be paid in respect of a given annual premium,

determined by the age of the contributor and the amount to be paid at his death, the consequences of plague (although there had been no such visitation in England for nearly a century) were still in the minds of the founders of the association, viz., *The Society for Equitable Assurances on Lives and Survivorships*—and in its deed of settlement it was provided that in case of plague or contagion three directors might constitute a court, and there was introduced the following clause :—

"And the said court of directors shall and may, during the continuance of such sickness or contagion (if it shall appear to them that the fund or affairs of the said society shall require it), *reduce the payments of the several and respective sums of money which shall become due by reason of the deaths which shall happen in such a time of public calamity, to any sum not less than one quarter part of what shall so have become due;* and for the remainder of the said sums which shall have so become due, and which shall not then be paid, credit shall be given to the respective claimants, their executors, administrators, and assigns in the books of the said society: and the said remainder of the said sums due, together with interest for the same at the rate of 3 per cent. by the year, shall be paid to the said claimants, their executors, administrators, or assigns, as soon as the affairs of the said society will admit thereof."

What seems more surprising is that the deeds of some of the life offices founded in the present century contain like provisions. Thus the *London Life Association*, founded 1806, has such a clause (87 of its deed); the *Atlas*, 1808, the like ; *Mutual Life*, 1834, and the *Gresham*, 1848, the same. Thus do customs descend from generation to generation.

Such precautions are not alone confined to England. When in 1828 the *German Life Assurance Company* of Lubeck was formed, its business operations were restricted to healthy lives in Europe, or to countries not theretofore subject to plague or yellow fever.

Again, the outbreak of cholera in Europe in 1831 is said to have greatly helped forward the operations of the Gotha Life Assurance Bank, then newly founded, but now and for many years the most powerful life office in Germany.

Conclusion.

I now have to bring this paper to a close. I am painfully aware how much has been left unsaid ; but considerations of time and space have intervened. There is hardly a branch of the subject here treated concerning which I have not additional facts. Those given must be regarded therefore as illustrative only. The table I have endeavoured to make complete as to the occasions of pestilence affecting human life. There remain to be treated the "Periodicity " of Plague Visitations," the "Spontaneous Origin of Disease," as also "Pestilential Cyclones." These will each receive considera- tion hereafter, when I shall endeavour to notice some of the local customs which have arisen out of plague visitations.

APPENDIX.

Plagues and Pestilences affecting the Human Race, from the Earliest Records, Chronologically Arranged.

B.C.

2500 .... *Egypt.* A great plague in the reign of Semempses, about this date.
—MANETHO.

2450 .... *Ireland.* Severe epidemy and epizoöty.—*Irish Annalists.*

2311 .... *Ireland.* Pestilence [*Tamh*] in the island of Ard-Neimhidh (now
Barrymore, near Cork). of which died 2,000 or 3,000 persons.
After this period Ireland was a wilderness for two hundred
years.—*Irish Annalists.*

1997 .... *Ireland.* Pestilence in Westmeath, or, as some annals say, in county
Cork, of which died " twenty hundred.''—*Irish Annalists.*

1921 .... *Canaan.* Plague.

1867 .... *Ireland.* Pestilence.—*Irish Annalists.*

1651 .... ,,   Pestilence in Roscommon.—*Irish Annalists.*

'14 .... ,,   Pestilence at the gathering of people to worship the idol
Crom Cruach. Three-fourths of the men of Ireland perished.—
Irish Annalists.

1503,1541, *Greece.* The islands of *Rhodes, Tenedos, Cos, Chios, Samos, Mity-*
or 1548   *lene,* and *Lesbos,* immediately after the Deucalion deluge, suffered
from famine and pestilences.—HOWE, p. 30.

1401 or   *Egypt* (Pharaoh IV king). The ten plagues of Egypt, not generally
1625   destructive of human life. See Exodus xii. Another plague about
this period is said to have swept away millions of human lives.
—Numbers xi.
There was published in 1810 *Bryant's Observations upon the
Plagues of the Egyptians, the Peculiarity of these Judgments and
their Correspondence with the Rites and Idolatry of the People.*
In 1873, *Signs and Wonders of the Land of Ham, a Description of
the Ten Plagues of Egypt, with Ancient and Modern Parallels,* by
the Rev. Thomas S. Millington.

1490 .... *In the Wilderness.* A very great plague among the children of
Israel.—Numbers xi, 1 ; xvi, 33. " Fire of the Lord."

'71 .... *Kadesh* (Desert of Paran). 14,700 persons died in the camp of the
Israelites while travelling from Egypt to Palestine.—Numbers xvi,
49.

'52 .... *Egypt.* Of the riotous and drunken worshippers of Baal-poor,
24,000 men and women perished.

1398 .... *Ireland.* Pestilence. "Muinemon, the monarch," died of this
epidemy.—*Irish Annalists.*

'32 .... *Thebes.* Amphion, his family, and multitudes of the inhabitants
destroyed by plague.

'10 .... *Ægina* (Greece). Epidemic pestilence fatal to great numbers.

1280 .... *Greece.* A pestilential fever after the return of Idomeneus and
Merion from the siege of Troy.

'60 .... *Troy.* Epidemy and epizoöty.

'50 .... *Ægina.* Plague.—OVID's *Metamorph.,* lib. viii, p. 253.

'07 .... *Peloponnesus.* Plague of the Heraclidæ. See ROLLIN's *Ancient
History,* vol. ii, p. 163.

1200 .... *Ægina.* A plague common to man and beast, described by OVID
(*Metamorphoses,* book vii) ; PAULET (*Maladies Epizoötiques*)
supposes the disease to have been a form of gangrenous sore-throat,
with acute fever and perhaps erysipelas ; probably also contagious.
The long-continued heat and damp weather mentioned by the poet
may have been the predisposing causes. The pestilence appeared
amongst animals and birds before mankind.

Plagues and Pestilences affecting the Human Race—Contd.

B.C.

1190	*Troy.* Plague in the Grecian army.—*Iliad*, lib. i.
'84	*Greece.* During the Trojan war, the Greeks invited Podalirius to their camp to stop a pestilence which had baffled the skill of the physicians.—LEMPRIÈRE'S *Classical Dict.*, p. 543.
'41	*Syria.* The people of Ashdod (Philistines) visited by an affection of the bowels—a malignant dysentery which proved very fatal.—1 Samuel, v.
'01	*Ireland.* As Sirna, with the men of Ireland, was fighting the Fomorians, in Meath, a pestilence was sent upon them. The Fomorian leaders and " countless numbers " of the men of Ireland perished.—*Irish Annalists.*
1100 or 1017	*Spain.* The first recorded pestilence in Spain, which destroyed 70,000 persons in three days. During a twenty-five years' drought, the land was full of " dreadful mortalities, plagues and miseries of every description."
1060	*Greece and Asia Minor.* Pestilence.
1022	*Ireland.* "There was great faintness generally over all the whole kingdom once every month during that year."—*Annals of Clonmacnoise.*
'17	*Canaan.* A grievous pestilence, destroying 70,000 in three days.—2 Samuel xxiv; 1 Chronicles xxi.
951	*Ireland.* Pestilence, destroying "great numbers."—*Irish Annalists.*
884	*Greece.* Before the revival, by Iphitus, of the Olympic Games, the country was almost ruined by war and pestilence.—*Univ. Hist.*, vol. vi, p. 269.
807	*Britain.* After a plague of flies, "ensued great sickness and mortality, to the great desolation of this land."—GRAFTON, *Chronicle, &c., of England.* Lond., 1569.
790	*Rome.* Great pestilence; killing almost instantaneously.
774	*Paria.* Epidemic, attributed to the blockade of the town by Charlemagne.
767	*Universal.* The first recorded plague in all parts of the known world.—PETAVIUS.
753	*Rome.* Pestilence, fatal alike to animals and men.—PLUTARCH, *Life of Romulus.*
740–38....	*Rome.* Dreadful plague and famine.
717	„ (?). Plague during the war of the Camerians.
717	„ (?). An epidemy carried off 50,000 inhabitants, according to some historians.
710	*Judah.* The Assyrian armies perished at the siege of Jerusalem, to the number of 185,000.—PLUTARCH.
710	*Italy.* Pestilence greatly ravaged the country, especially the capital.
694	*Rome.* Pestilence, described by LIVY.
675	The army of Hippotes, on the march to invade Peloponnesus, attacked by pestilence in consequence of the murder of Carnus.
671	*Rome.* Pestilence, mentioned by Zosimus.
665	*Sparta.* Approximate date of the plague of *Thaletes.*
631	According to HERODOTUS, plague attacked the Scythians who plundered the temple of Venus.
608	*Athens.* Pestilence, cured by Epimenides.
594	*Jerusalem.* About one-third of the inhabitants perished from pestilence, during the siege of the Chaldeans.
581	A serious epidemy prevailed in the Grecian army which besieged Syracuse during the sacred war.
544	*Rome* and Campania again suffered. This pestilence spared neither age nor constitution, and yielded to no remedies. It destroyed its victims rapidly, but disappeared on the approach of continuous cold weather.
540	*Ægylla* (Tuscia). Pestilence whilst the Phocaeans were waging war with the Tyrians and Carthaginians.

Plagues and Pestilences affecting the Human Race—Contd.

B.C.

538............ *Rome.* Plague and famine; the city besieged by Vitages.

534............ *Carthage.* Dreadful plague. The people sacrificed children to appease the gods.

515............ *Rome.* Disastrous plague; particularly fatal to children.

506............ „ Plague, during which Tarquin sent his two sons to consult the oracle at Delphi.

493............ *Latium* (Volscian). A dreadful pestilence overspread the Volscian country, causing such mortality at Velitra that hardly a tenth part of the inhabitants survived.

489............ *Rome.* Distempers consequent upon a famine.

488............ „ Animals and men affected by a plague. " The mortality among mankind, however, was not great, for they escaped the dangers arising from this disease."—DIONYS. HALICAR., *Antiq. Rom.,* vii, 68.

480............ *Greece.* The army of Xerxes, while retreating to Asia after defeat at the battle of Salamis, afflicted by a grievous pestilence, which attacked both land and sea forces. The army under Mardonius lost victims to the extent of 150,000.

476............ *Spain.* A series of pestilences and minor diseases, " by which a multitude of persons perished."—FLORIAN DE CAMPO, i, lib. ii.

473............ *Rome.* A dreadful plague suspended for a few months the furious contest between the patricians and the plebeians concerning the Publilian law.

472............ *Universal.* " According to Mariana (Historia General de España), a plague reigned throughout nearly the whole world. It began in Egypt, and at length reached Spain, the disease generally commencing among the cattle. A peculiar feature in its progress was that it nearly always appeared in the country districts before it reached the towns."—FLEMING, *Anl. Plagues,* p. 12.

464............ *Italy.* Pestilence broke out among the animals, extended to the herdsmen, infected the country generally, and finally raged in Rome, where it carried off the flower of the Roman youth.—LIVY, lib. iii.

464............ *Rome.* Plague.—LIVY, iii; DIONYS. HALICAR., x.

463............ „ Pestilence caused by overcrowding in the city, owing to the incursions of the Latins and Hernici.

461-59 .... *Rome.* 100,000 persons in and around the city carried off by plague. It swept away a fourth part of the senators, the tribunes, the two consuls, the two augurs, and many distinguished Romans.

454............ *Italy.* This year the above sequence was reversed. Plague broke out in Rome, and destroyed nearly half the people. It spread to the country, the herdsmen, and ultimately the flocks. A famine ensued.

452-53 .... *Rome.* A pestilence, known as *loimikié,* which was also communicated to the Æqui, the Volsci, and the Sabines, and caused a great mortality among them.—LIVY, iii, 32 ; DIONYS., x, 53.

450............ *Rome.* A pestilence, which carried off two consuls, the high priest of Jupiter, the augur Horatius, four tribunes, and a great number of the wisest senators, almost all the slaves, and half the citizens.— LECLERC, *Hist. de Médecine,* p. 2, v. iii, chap. 1. Temple raised to the goddess Salus in consequence of plague.

448............ *Italy.* A great plague.

448 to 443 *Rome.* Grievous pestilence, lasting five years. So frequently had the imperial city been scourged by epidemic pestilences, that Livy styled it " urbs assiduus exhausta funeribus."

437............ The *Roman Republic* reduced to the brink of ruin by a famine, plague, and seditions of the people.—CATROU et ROUILLÉ, *Hist. Rom.,* vol. i, p. 317.

435-30 .... *Athens.* In the second year of the Peloponnesian war, consequent upon the crowding of the Athenians from their territory into the

Plagues and Pestilences affecting the Human Race—Contd.

B.C.	*Athens—Contd.*
435–30	city to avoid the ravages of the Lacedæmonians. It destroyed 5,000 of the prime of the armies, and a vast number of poor people. Pericles died from it.

This was the great plague so eloquently described by Thucydides (*Bello Pelop.*, ii, 39). He attributes the plague to the practice of the inhabitants of living in booths during the summer season. In them there was hardly room to breathe, so that when the epidemy broke out there was much to favour its development.

Egypt, Libya, Ethiopia. All visited by similar pestilences. Said by some writers to have originated in Ethiopia.

433–32 .... *Rome.* Pestilence showed itself among the troops, and afterwards affected the city and the country. In the second year it caused great ravages.—CATROU et ROUILLÉ, *Hist. Rom.*, vol. iii, p. 373. Revolt of the Veientes and Fidenates.

431............ *Rome.* Pestilence, followed by a murrain. It began in the country.—LIVY, iv, 25, 30.

430............ *Athens.* Visited by the first of the œcumenical plagues.

427............ *Europe.* A cruel pestilence is said to have spread almost through the world. It commenced in Egypt, and travelled through the intervening countries until it reached Spain. It usually commenced with the cattle, then attacked the country people, and finally entered the towns. At Athens it broke out afresh.

428............ *Italy.* Pestilential epidemics.

426............ *Rome.* Plague.—COPLAND'S *Dict. of Med.*, vol. i, p. 771.

425............ *Greece.* Dreadful plague.

424............ *Rome.* Drought, famine, and pestilence.

419............ „ Epidemic disease.—NIEBUHR.

413............ „ Plague breaking out, "every one shut himself up in his house, minding nothing but to preserve himself from the contagion." The disease passed away after causing a few deaths.—CATROU et ROUILLÉ, *Hist. Rom.*, iii, 452.

413............ *Sicily.* A plague broke out in the Athenian army before Syracuse, occasioned by the unwholesome air of the fens and marshes near which it was encamped. This determined Nicias to abandon Sicily.

412............ *Italy.* Pestilential epidemics.

412............ *Rome.* Plague and famine made the city desolate.—LIVY, lib. iv.

406............ *Agrigentum.* Plague during the siege, of which Hannibal died.

404............ *Carthage* suffered greatly through its armies, sent to subjugate Sicily, being decimated by pestilence. Many fell dead as soon as they took the disease, the chief features of which were violent dysentery, severe fever, acute pains in all parts of the body, anguish, and great depression of both mind and body.—JUSTIN, xix, 2 ; DIOD. SIC., xiii and xiv.

401............ *Italy.* Pestilential epidemics.

400............ *Rome.* A cold winter and hot summer were followed by great mortality among men and beasts.

400............ The *Sabines* afflicted with plague.

396............ *Italy.* Pestilence, from which Rome especially suffered, "occasioned by strange change of weather."

395............ *Carthage.* The people reduced to a miserable state by plague.

394............ *Sicily.* Plague destroyed 150,000 of the Carthaginians.—BOYLE, *Chron.*, i, 84.

393–83 .... The armies of Gaul and Rome afflicted with sore pestilence; at the latter period occasioned by famine consequent upon drought.

389............ *Roman territory* afflicted by contagious distempers.

387............ *Italy.* Pestilence, after the invasion of the Gauls.

"The Roman consuls of this year commenced their office with magnificent games in honour of Jupiter, but a contagious distemper ensuing, they were deposed, and a short interregnum followed."—BOYLE, *Chron.*, i, 85.

E

Plagues and Pestilences affecting the Human Race—Contd.

B.C.

378............ | *Carthage.* Plague raged with unprecedented violence immediately after the arrival of the troops from Italy.

374 or 375 | *Rome.* A plague followed the death of Manlius.

373............ | „ The plague had disappeared the previous year, but now broke out again, preventing the troops being led into the field to subdue the Volsci.

366............ | *Rome.* Pestilence, lasting for three years; when at its height it was reported that 10,000 citizens died daily. It was very heavy during the months of September, October and November. The Sibylline books and the ceremony of the Lectisternium were resorted to in vain.—LIVY, vii, v; SHORT, *On the Air.*

362............ | *Spain.* The city of Saguntum (now Murviedro) was visited by an epidemic pestilence consequent upon famine.

361............ | *Rome.* Plague. It continued the following year.

360............ | *Italy.* Plague, during which the sacred nail was used.

345............ | *Rome.* At this period of tranquillity pestilence carried off as many citizens as war would have done.

333............ | *Syria* ravaged by famine and pestilence.

332............ | *Italy.* Pestilence.

330............ | *Rome* ravaged by pestilence.

329............ | „ Cor. Rufinus was chosen dictator, but the augurs compelled him to abdicate on account of a raging plague.—BOYLE, i, 101.

296............ | *Italy.* Pestilence.—LIVY, x, 31; GROTIUS, iii, 21.

296–91 ... | *Rome.* A pestilence, peculiarly fatal to pregnant women and breeding cattle.

291............ | *Italy.* Pestilence.

289............ | *Ireland.* Pestilence.

288–80 ... | *Rome.* Plague. In accordance with the directions of the Sibylline books, the god Æsculapius was fetched from Epidaurus, and at once put an end to the plague.

287............ | *Rome.* Severe plague.

278............ | *Rome.* "A grievous pestilence invaded the city and its environs, which attacked all, but especially the women. The fœtus was killed in the womb, and discharged from it. Miscarriages exposed mothers to great danger; so much so, that it was feared that a future population and breed of animals would be wanting."—(P. OSORII, *Hist.*, lib. iv, p. 2). This disease was known as the *Abortus Epidemicus.*

262............ | *Rome.* Destructive pestilence. A vestal virgin was doomed to be sacrificed, but she committed suicide.

260............ | *Rome.* Pestilence again. "A nail fastened in the temple of Jupiter Capitolinus."

256............ | *Rome.* "A contagion broke out that made a dreadful havoc."

234............ | *Sardinia.* The Prætor P. Cornelius went to make war in Sardinia, but pestilence broke out in his army, the air in that country being bad, and the water partly salt and partly stagnant.—OROSIUS, lib. iv, c. 12; LIT. LIV., lib. xx; CATROU et ROUILLÉ, *Hist. Rom.*

224............ | *Cisalpine Gaul.* Plague in the Roman army.

223............ | *Sardinia.* Cornelius Asina, the prætor, died of the plague.

218............ | The Carthaginian armies, on their route to besiege Saguntum, suffered greatly from pestilence.

216............ | *Carthage.* Great pestilence began in the neighbourhood of this city in the summer. Supposed to have resulted from crowding and scarcity of food, as also from the stagnant air. Rich and poor alike fell victims. Hamilca, the wife of Hannibal, and their offspring, were among those carried off.

212–207... | *Syracuse.* Plague, of which Hamilcar, Hippocrates, and almost all the Carthaginian army died.

206............ | *Naples.* A great pestilence, preceded by immense swarms of *locusts*, which invaded the country near Capua.

Plagues and Pestilences affecting the Human Race—Contd.

B.C.	*Naples—Contd.*
206............	The Roman and Rhodian fleets, anchored at Pharselis, in the Gulf of Pamphylia, in an unwholesome situation, and in the middle of summer, suffered severely from pestilential disease, especially the rowers, who were subjected to hard labour and the burning rays of the sun.
201............	*Italy.* Plague occasioned by decomposition of swarms of locusts.
193............	*Bruttium* (Calabria). Plague made great havoc in the Roman and Carthaginian armies. " Hannibal wasted by pestilence."
188............	*Syria, Egypt, Greek Islands.* Plague destroyed 2,000 persons daily. —PLINY.
187............	*Rome.* Three years' pestilence.
182............	*Italy.* Plague.—LIVY, xli, 21.
182–81	„ Violent pestilence ravaged the whole country during three years. There was a severe *drought*, followed by terrible storms, pernicious seasons, and awful commotions of the elements ; coldness, dampness, moisture and dryness, noxious vapours, and putrid exhalations. The cattle also suffered.
177............	*Rome.* Pestilence among the inhabitants and the cattle. It continued for four years. Dogs and vultures did not attack the bodies of the dead. *Locusts* appeared in prodigious swarms.
176–75	*Rome.* A dreadful pestilence raged, chiefly among the lower classes. —LIVY, lib. xli, 18—21. " An epidemic malady, which in the preceding year had attacked animals, broke out this year amongst men. The mortality was so great that the dead could not be interred."—*Dict. de l'Acad. Franç. Méd.:* art. Peste.
144............	*Rome.* Another pestilence, of which an account is given by Orosius.
140............	*Algeria.* The Roman armies in this country fell victims to the measures taken by their generals to produce pestilence amongst the inhabitants. One of the methods adopted had been to charge the atmosphere with *mephitic vapours.*
128............	*Egypt.* 800,000 persons perished from a plague caused by the putrefaction of vast swarms of locusts.
126............	*Rome.* Plague.—WEBSTER.
126............	*Africa.* Great pestilence, which destroyed in Numidia alone 800,000 of the inhabitants ; and on the coast of Carthage 200,000 were reported to have perished. This outbreak was attributed to the stench arising from the putrid *locusts* washed up on the seashore. —LIVY, *Epist.*, 60 ; OROS., lib. v.
89............	Whilst Cneus Pompeius was marching his army against Marius, a plague broke out in it, and carried off 11,000 men in a few days. —LEMPRIÈRE'S *Classical Dictionary*, p. 550.
87–86	*Rome.* Great mortality caused by plague and famine.
78............	„ A dreadful pestilence raged, during which 10,000 persons were known to die in one day.—BOYLE, i, p. 233.
70 or 73	*Jerusalem.* The first wall entered by Titus, " under pestilence and famine."
69............	*Albania.* Epidemy.
65............	*Rome.* A grievous plague.
49............	*Spain.* Epidemic pestilence affected the army of Julius Cæsar, which was waging war against the Pompeians. The year was marked by *heavy rains* and *tempestuous seasons,* and the pestilence was ascribed to excessive moisture in the air, together with the poisonous exhalations from the ground, which had been submerged by the overflowing rivers.
48............	? A pestilential epidemic was attributed to the unwholesome exhalations from the dead bodies of a great number of animals which had perished during an epizoötic.—*Dict de l'Acad. Franç. Méd.* art. Peste.
44............	*Italy.* Plague.—WEBSTER.

Plagues and Pestilences affecting the Human Race—Contd.

B.C.	
30............	*Asia Minor.* A pestilence which lasted five years, and seems to have afflicted the whole world more or less; destroyed vast numbers of people at Jerusalem, in Palestine generally, and at Rome.
28............	*Judæa.* A great plague in the time of Herod Archilaus.
22............	*Italy.* Plague in Rome and other cities. The land being untilled, famine ensued.
21............	*Rome.* Another plague in the time of Tullus Hostilius.
21............	*Arabia.* Ælius Gallus had penetrated far into the country, when a fatal disease obliged him to return.—(*Ency. Brit.*, 3rd ed., vol, xv, p. 600.) After two years spent on the expedition, he returned with but a small remnant of his army of 10,000 men.—STRABO, lib. xvi, p. 1126; DION. CASSIUS, lib. liii, p. 516.

A.D.	
7............	*Palestine.* Horrid butcheries were committed, which brought on a famine and pestilence.
14............	*Asia Minor.* A pestilence, described by Tacitus. Suetonius mentions one at *Babylon* about the same time. Also in *Greece* and *Italy* during the reign of Claudius Cæsar. The period was marked by a famine, an earthquake, and the appearance of a comet.
40-54	*Italy.* Pliny and Tacitus both give an account of the remarkable mortality of this period, when most of the officers of Rome died of pestilential disease: "Ex omnium magistratum genere plerique mortem obierunt." *Babylon* was almost depopulated.
50-100....	*Ephesus* cleared of a dreadful plague by Apollonius of Tyana, to whom the citizens erected a statue.—PHILOSTRATUS, *De Vitâ Apollonii Tyaneus*, lib. iv, c. 1, p. 159; CAVE'S *Lives of the Apostles*, v. i, p. 249.
65............	*Rome.* Pestilence carried of 30,000 of all ranks and conditions.
68............	„ Plague.—TACITUS, *Annal.*, xv, 47; xvi, 13; OROSIUS, lib. vii; *Univ. Hist.*, vol. xiv, p. 159.
78............	*Rome.* A pestilence, which in one day carried off 10,000 persons.—TYTLER'S *Univ. Hist.*
88............	*England.* A pestilence appeared in the northern counties, and continued for some time.
88............	*Rome.* Pestilence, carried off 30,000 of the Roman people.
92............	*Scotland.* Pestilence, said to have carried off 150,000 persons (?).
92............	*Palestine.* The Jewish writer Philo describes a plague caused by a fall of hot dust.
114 (about)	*Wales.* A pestilence, followed a hot summer and inclement autumn; 45,000 victims. Possibly due to frequent inundations of the Severn.
133............	*England.* Pestilence, preceded by drought.
141............	*Arabia.* A pestilence and a comet are mentioned by Capitolinus as having marked this year.—LYNAM'S *Rom. Emperors*, ii, p. 477.
146............	*Scotland.* Severe epidemy.
158............	*Arabia.* The country ravaged by a pestilence.
162............	*Rome.* "A general infection in the air," caused by a great inundation of the Tiber. Lucius Verus brought the plague in his army from Syria.
— 167............	*Europe.* The real oriental plague was carried into Europe by the army returning from the Parthian war, and spread all over the western world—Asia Minor, Greece, Italy, Gaul, Africa alone excepted.—NIEBUHR'S *Lect. on Rom. Hist.*, vol. iii, p. 251; *Ammianus Marcellinus*, lib. xxiii; ECHARD'S *Roman History*, vol. ii, p. 315, &c.
— 168............	*Egypt, Italy, &c.* According to Ammianus Marcellinus, plague broke out in Seleucia, was carried thence into Egypt, extended to the country of the Parthians, and there infected the army of Lucius Verus, by which it was introduced into Italy and Rome. It affected the most distant countries that had any communication with Rome or the Romans.

Plagues and Pestilences affecting the Human Race—Contd.

A.D.	
169............	*Wales.* Plague.—SHORT.
169............	*Aquileia.* The emperors repaired to Aquileia in the depth of winter, but were forced to retire on account of the plague raging there.
173............	*England.* A severe winter, a famine, and a pestilence in the summer following.
173–78	*Rome.* A pestilence.
180............	*England.* Plague.—*Univ. Hist.*, vol. xix, p. 560.
180............	*Italy.* Plague.
180............	*Sirmium* (now Sirmich, in Sclavonia). Marcus Aurelius died of the plague.
183............	*Rome.* Pestilence.
188............	*Italy.* A dreadful plague lasted three years. In Rome alone it frequently carried off 2,000 persons in a day.—HERODIAN,*Hist.*,lib. i.
190-95	*Italy.* "About this time a great pestilence raged over all Italy, and became most violent in Rome by reason of the great concourse of people assembled from all quarters of the world."—HERODIAN, *Hist.*, lib i.
	In the year 192, when the diurnal mortality was stated to be 2,000, it was believed that this outbreak was propagated by thrusting poisoned needles into people's bodies.
	"The assertion is quite true that the old world never recovered from the great plague in the time of M. Antoninus, brought by the army from the Parthian war."—DRAPER : *Intellectual Devel. Europe,* vol i, p. 250.
207............	*Britain.* 50,000 of the troops of Severus died of the plague.
211............	*London.* Plague.
216............	*Italy.* Widespread pestilence.—HELVETIUS CAVRIOL, *Hist. Brix.*
218............	*Scotland.* Pestilence killed 100,000 (?).
218............	*Ceylon.* A great plague, which Forbes thinks was small pox.—FORBES, *Eleven Years in Ceylon.* App., p. 286.
250............	*Europe, Asia.* A pestilence ravaged *Italy, Ethiopia, Egypt, Asia, France, Spain,* and almost the entire globe.
	It began in Ethiopia, and was the second general great plague after Christ (recorded by Eusebius). It was attended with extraordinary evacuations, to the great weakening of the sick, and continual vomiting.
250-65	*Roman Empire.* Plague. 5,000 deaths occurred daily for some time in Rome. Many towns were entirely depopulated. This destructive plague, which lasted fifteen years, is recognised by Gibbon as having had an influence in promoting the decline of the Roman Empire.
252............	*Egypt.* Alexandria and other districts suffered from pestilence for twelve or fifteen years. Several different disorders appeared at the same time. Cedrenus ascribed them to singular *exhalations* and *dews,* like "the ichors of dead bodies," which were noticed at the time.—IONAIAS, lib. xii ; GIBBON.
261............	*Egypt* (?). A general famine and terrible plague, so that the numerous inhabitants were soon reduced to a small number.
261............	*Greece.* The plague extended here.
261............	*Rome.* 5,000 citizens perished daily from a pestilence, which Aurelius Victor ascribes to *depressed spirits* and a *pestiferous state of the atmosphere.* Bascome (p. 21) remarks that in this disorder we may recognise all the symptoms of *cholera,* which first appeared in 1817. Earthquakes prevailed.
268............	*Sirmium* (Lower Pannonia). The Emperor Claudius died of the plague, with great numbers of his troops.
268-69	The Goths, preparing to invade the Roman Empire, sailed to Crete, Rhodes, and Cyprus, but lost great numbers of their men by the plague. They returned to Macedon to winter, where the contagious distemper completed their ruin.

Plagues and Pestilences affecting the Human Race—Contd.

A.D.

270........... *Europe* and *Asia.* Plague at Rome and throughout the world.

282........... *Italy.* This pestilence, which was so fatal at Rome, visited the rest of Italy.—DIONYSIUS, ix, 42.

287........... *Gaul.* Famine and plague in the Burgundian army. In the *East* a plague broke out, "which particularly fell upon the eyes, and rendered abundance blind."

291........... *Rome.* Pestilence to man and animals from overcrowding.

292........... *England* and *Wales.* Pestilence and famine.

30)........... *Rome.* Plague. Among the victims are mentioned one of the consuls, another one elected to fill his place, four out of the ten tribunes, an augur, one of the three great flamens, many senators, half the free inhabitants, and all the slaves.—(LIVY, iii, 32; DIONYSIUS, x, 53.) This pestilence attacked the neighbouring States, the Volscians, Æquians, and Sabines with equal fury.

302........... *Syria. Famine* and *drought* caused a pestilence which made great ravages. The disease was carried to the army of Gallienus in Armenia, and thence spread to every city in the Eastern provinces. The pestilence is described by Cedrenus, Eusebius, and Nicephorus. Bascome hints that it was confluent small pox. It produced a horrible stench, and affected the eyelids, causing total blindness.

307........... *Wales.* Great Pestilence.—IOLO. *MSS.*

310........... *England* and *Wales.* Pestilence carried off 40,000 persons in Wales alone.

312........... *Asia.* Ravaged by pestilence.

314........... *Rome.* Pestilence from vitiated atmosphere.

325........ ... *Great Britain.* Pestilence, preceded by famine.

333........... *Syria, Cilicia,* and *Thrace.* Plague and famine.

336, 355, } and 358 } *Great Britain.* Famine, earthquakes, and pestilence.

359........... *Persia.* A plague broke out in Amida, during its investment by Sapor. It was attributed to the corruption of unburied bodies lying about the streets.

362........... *Europe.* A dreadful plague about the shores of the Mediterranean.

362, ... } 367-68.... } *Great Britain.* Famine, earthquakes, and pestilence.

375. .... „   Famine, earthquakes and pestilence. 43,000 deaths in Wales alone.

376........... *Europe.* A deadly epidemy.—FLEMING, i, 28.

377........... *Roman Empire.* A terrible plague swept away vast numbers of people in all the western provinces.

381........... *Constantinople.* A contagious disease destroyed many thousands of people.—FLEMING, i, 29.

384........... *Africa.* Plague in most of the cities. Also at *Antioch.*

394........ *Magdeburg.* Plague.—COPELAND'S *Dict. of Med.*, i, 772.

394 or 395 *Palestine.* Pestilence, occasioned by the effluvia of decaying locusts. ·—*The Magdeburg Hist.*

400-407... *Europe, Asia,* and *Africa.* Pestilence desolated these countries; details wanting.

406........... *Egypt.* Plague caused by the stench arising from dead grasshoppers.

407........... *Europe, Asia,* and *Africa.* Plague.—NICEPHORUS, lib. xiii, 6, 36; *Magdeburg Ant.*, b. v, 13.

409........... *Rome.* Plague and famine during investment by the Goths.—BOYLE, i, 288.

409........... *Spain.* The country ravaged by a dreadful plague.—IDATIUS.

425........... *Thrace.* Plague in the army of the Huns, which was laying waste the country.

430........... *Great Britain.* A plague followed an invasion of the southern parts by the Picts and Scots.

442........... *England.* Severe pestilence.

Plagues and Pestilences affecting the Human Race—Contd.

A.D.

443............ | *Spain.* Disease consequent upon famine.
444............ | *Turkey.* Fever, followed by the plague.
446............ | *Constantinople.* "Stench of the atmosphere killed a great number of men."—BEDE, *Eccles. Hist.*, ii, 66.
446–47 .... | *Roman Empire.* Terrible plague in most of the provinces.
446............ | *Turkey.* An earthquake occurred, followed by pestilence and famine.
448............ | *Great Britain.* The plague of Vortigern. The precise date is uncertain.—GILDAS, c. xix, p. 119; BEDE'S *History*, c. xvi, p. 157; *Univ. Hist.*, v. xix., p. 575.
450............ | *Rome.* Pestilence.
458............ | *England.* Pestilence again broke out.
458............ | *Europe.* According to Nicephorus, it prevailed in Cappadocia, Galatia, and Phrygia, about the same time.
466............ | *Britain.* A pestiferous smell in the air killed both man and beast.
466............ | *Wales.* Great pestilence from the effluvia of the corpses of the Gwyddolians.—*Welsh Annals.*
472............ | *Rome.* Famine and plague whilst besieged by Ricimer.
484............ | *Africa.* Drought and famine caused a grievous plague.
502............ | *Scotland.* Severe epidemy.
517............ | *Palestine.* Pestilence.
527............ | *Wales.* Pestilence.
532............ | *Constantinople* visited by an œcumenical plague.
532............ | *Ethiopia.* Great pestilence.
538............ | *Italy.* Plague and famine.—BOYLE, i, 310.
538............ | *Rome.* During the siege by Vitiges, famine and plague made dreadful havoc among both the besieged and the besiegers. The city was invested for a year and ten days.
530 to 569 | *Ireland* and *Wales.* The great epidemic constitution of the sixth century, and the first special pestilence recorded in the Irish Christian annals, commenced about this period, and lasted nearly thirty years. It was preceded by famine, and followed by leprosy. The disease was called *Blefed, Crom, Chonnaill,* or *Buidhe Chonnaill* (literally, the corn or stubble-coloured yellowness), or *Buidhechair,* jaundice, and was probably a form of yellow fever, or the bilious remittent, still observed in the West Indies and America. This epidemic is, in the Cambrian Annals, styled *Vall Velen, Lalwellen,* or *Vad Velen*—Flava Pestis—expressive of the same disease, known in Ireland as *Buidhe Chonnaill.* It probably spread from Wales to Ireland. The leprosy, which began about 550, is in one instance described by the annalist as small pox, but as this is not corroborated by the other chronicles, it is probably an error. Colgan, in the *Acta Sanctorum* (St. Ædus, vol. i, p. 422), says of the origin of this outbreak, "a poisoned pool made its appearance in that region (Meath) thro' a chasm of the earth, and a vapour proceeded from it which produced a fatal disease in men and beasts." The *Liber Landavensis* says, "It appeared to men as a column of watery blood, having one end trailing along the ground and the other above, proceeding in the air, and passing thro' the whole country like a shower" [waterspout?]. *Tables, Irish Census,* 1851.
540–42 .... | *Europe; Asia.* A plague, with intermissions, in most parts of the world.—NICEPHORUS, xviii, 11; *Eccles. Hist.*, lib. iv, p. 29. *Persia* especially devastated.
543............ | *Egypt.* The plague of Justinian.
544............ | *France.* Dysentery, so severe as to be like the true plague, made great havoc for four years.
547............ | *Great Britain* and *Ireland.* Pestilence in Wales. The yellow plague of Rhos, called by physicians the Iliac Passion.—(See GIRALDUS DE BARRY and Welsh Tryads in Myvyrian Archæology.) Men afflicted with this pest are said to have looked like "charcoal wood."

Plagues and Pestilences affecting the Human Race—Contd.

A.D.	
547............	*Constantinople.* " A depopulating plague at Constantinople and the countries about, that daily there died 5,000, and some days 10,000."—ALSTED in *Thesaur. Chron.*
548............	*France.* Epidemic dysentery, with high fever and "vomiting of yellow or green bile." Vesicles appeared on the body.—SHORT.
554-55	Pestilential disease in the German army, from wet, bad air, and bad food.—BARONIUS.
558............	*Europe, Asia,* and *Africa.* A plague commenced in Europe, and extended into Asia and Africa. It lasted many years ; some writers have stated fifty or more. *Constantinople* was nearly depopulated. The disease, when at its height, carried off 10,000 persons daily. It is described by Paulus Diaconus and Procopius. Nicephorus relates that a white crust-like coating was deposited from the air upon things. This is one of the great plagues of history.
561............	*Ireland.* A dreadful pestilence.—ST. ÆDUS, vol. i, p. 422; ST. BRIGIDA, vol. ii, p. 536.
565 to 610	*Europe, &c.* "France, Germany, Italy, and various other countries of Europe—in fact, the whole inhabited globe—suffered awfully from pestilence."—BASCOME, p. 25. In 589, St. Gregory of Tours describes this pestilential period, and says the disease was in Spain characterised by pustules, with buboes in the groin ; such great havoc did it make, that the houses were so many tombs, and the town was one vast cemetery. It had previously raged in France in 580. It carried off great numbers of children and young persons.—GREGORY's *History of the Franks.* Evagrius describes this as the longest. plague ever known, and says it was called " Pestis Inguinaria."—BARONIUS.
569............	*Germany, France,* and *Italy.* " A great disease, accompanied by dysentery and variola."—MARIUS, *Episcop. Chron.;* DUCHESNE, *Scrip. Rev. Fran.,* vol. i, p. 215.
580............	*France.* A plague appeared after "great floods, tempests, earth-quakes, hail, and several prodigies." It is stated that the corpse of the Count d'Angoulême, who died of the pestilence, appeared black and charred, as if it had been burned.
589............	*Italy.* After an inundation of the Tiber, the fields were left covered with mud and slime. The hot and steamy state of the atmosphere gave rise to a plague.—BARONIUS, *Imper. Hist.*
589............	*Spain.* St. Gregory, Bishop of Tours, describes a pestilence which broke out in Spain, having been introduced, it was supposed, by a ship from Marseilles, where the disease was raging the year before.
590............	*Italy* and *France.* Pestilence.
590............	*Rome.* A destructive pestilence. A peculiar mist in the air induced violent sneezing. The pestilence prevailed in *Spain* at the same time. " The plague of 590 was mortal almost beyond example."—WEBSTER.
591............	*Great Britain.* A pestilence called *inguinaria* broke out.
591............	*Italy.* Great mortality caused by the putrefaction of locusts. In *Britain* and *France* an epidemic called *inguinaria* prevailed. St. Gregory relates (*Francor. Histor.,* vol. x, p. 30) that " in the second month of this year a great pestilence destroyed the people " of *France* and *Belgium.*
595............	*Constantinople.* "Chogan, king of the Avari, in conjunction with remnants of the Gepidæ, Sclavi, &c., broke into the empire, and vowed its total destruction........ He advanced as far as Constantinople, when a sudden plague breaking out among his troops, vast multitudes were swept away........upon which the invaders retired." —BOYLE, i, p. 317.
599............	*Africa.* A dreadful pestilence.

Plagues and Pestilences affecting the Human Race—Contd.

A.D.

601........... *Rome.* The Romans being distressed by a pestilence, Chogan, king of the Avari, invades them.

605–6........ *Italy.* Plague.—BARONIUS, *Imper. Hist.*

610........... *Arabia.* Pestilential small pox committed great ravages at Mecca.

614........... *Italy.* Epidemic elephantiasis.

617........... „ An epidemic resembling the true plague.

628........... *Persia.* King Khobas Schironjeh died of the plague.

639–40 .... *Syria, Arabia, &c.* A great pestilence.

644........... *London* ravaged by a great plague.

654........... *Turkey.* Severe pestilence in Constantinople.

656........... *Ireland.* The second appearance of the *Buidhe Chonnaill* or yellow plague. Some of the annalists chronicle this pestilence as following the eclipse of 664. See *L'Art de Ver. les Dates.* "In the plain of Itha the pestilence was first kindled in Ireland."—*A Morte Patricii,* anno cciii, *Prima mortalitas,* cxii.

664........... *Great Britain.* Pestilence began on the southern coasts and spread in all directions. It was similar to the kind of pestilence arising from famine.

664........... *England.* "There was a great pestilence in the Island of Britain." —*Anglo-Saxon Chron.* *Vide* NENNIUS and BEDE.

664........... *Egypt* also suffered.—PAUL DIAC., 980.

664........... *London.* The city ravaged by the plague.

665........... *Ireland.* The plague carried off great numbers. It is reported that this pestilence came in answer to a prayer "to remove the multitudes of the inferior people." The incident is referred to in the preceding paper under *Causes of Pestilence.*

665........... *Italy.* Pestilence reached Italy.—BARONIUS.

669........... *Europe.* General mortality.

672........... *England.* A great plague.—WEBSTER.

672......... ... *Syria* and *Mesopotamia.* Pestilence at the same time.

675........... *Ireland.* The first small pox. "There reigned a kind of great leprosy in Ireland this year, called the pox, in Irish, *Bolgagh.*"— *Annals of Clonmacnoise.*

679........... *England* and *Ireland.* Pestilence from July till September.

680........... *Europe.* "At this time, that is, in the reign of Maldwine, a plague
(about) desolated Europe, from which the Picts and Scots are said to have escaped."—BUCHANAN's *History of Scotland,* vol. i, p. 189. [Fergahard, Maldwine's predecessor, reigned from 652 for eighteen years, namely, to 670 A.D., and Maldwine reigned twenty years. This plague seems to have been towards the termination of Maldwine's reign. Is it Bascome's plague of 683-86?]

680........... *Rome.* Pestilence.

681........... *Saxony.* Pestilence.

682........... *Syria.* Pestilence : (WEBSTER says, 683) accompanied by famine.

683........... *England.* Pestilence, lasted three years.

685........... *Ireland* suffered at the same time.

685........... *Syria* and *Lybia.* Pestilence.

695........... *Ireland.* Pestilence for three years, so that men ate each other.— *Chron. Scot.*

696........... *Turkey.* Pestilence at Constantinople.

708........... *Scotland.* Pestilence.

708........... *Ireland.* The *Baccach,* or epidemic lameness, with *ventris profluvio* (dysentery).—*Irish Annalists.*

713........... *Scotland.* Another pestilence.

714........... *Spain.* Epidemic small pox caused great mortality.

717........... *Turkey.* 30,000 deaths in Constantinople.

724........... „ Pestilence at Constantinople again.

729........... „ Another pestilence at Constantinople.

731........... *Scotland.* "Two most glorious jewels, Brigitto and Maura, daughters of the king of the Scots, were born on the same day, at

Plagues and Pestilences affecting the Human Race—Contd.

A.D.	Scotland—*Contd.*
731..........	whose birth famine and pestilence, which had so long devastated that whole land of Scotia, are said to have ceased."—COLGAN's *Acta Sanctorum.*
732..........	*England.* Pestilence at Norwich.
732..........	*Syria.* Pestilence.
734..........	*Ireland.* Plague almost depopulated *Leinster.*—*Annals of Innisfallen.*
740..........	*Europe, Asia,* and *Africa.* General pestilence over the whole world. "This was the beginning of a pestilential period, which lasted for two hundred and sixty years."—BASCOME, p. 29.
742..........	*Ireland.* Small pox.
744..........	*Calabria.* A terrible plague broke out, and spread into *Sicily, Greece,* and the islands of the Ægean Sea, and then to *Constantinople,* where it lasted for three years, causing such mortality that the living could scarcely bury the dead.
746..........	*Europe* and *Asia.* A dreadful pestilence prevailed for three years.— BOYLE, i, 341.
746–49	*Constantinople.* A plague, of which 200,000 inhabitants perished. It extended into *Calabria, Sicily,* and *Greece.*
750..........	*Rome.* Plague. Sternutation was a fatal symptom. [See text, *Meteoric Dust.*]
759..........	*Britain.* "There happened a tribulation of mortality, and continued almost two years, several grievous distempers raging, but more especially the dysentery."—*Continuation of Bede.*
759..........	*Ireland.* The great pestilential period of the eighth century, characterised by extreme cold, fearful thunder, scarcity and dysentery, with small pox and murrain, began about the year 760, and continued for upwards of twenty years.—*Tables, Irish Census,* 1551. *The Annals of Ulster* record an irruption of water and fish from the mountain peak, Bennmuilt, in 759.
762..........	*England* and *Wales.* Pestilence, which afterwards extended all over England, continuing until 771.
772..........	*Chichester (England).* An epidemic disease carried off 34,000 persons.—WILLIAM OF MALMESBURY. [Other authorities state that this plague occurred in 762.]
772..........	*Ireland.* Small pox all over the kingdom.—*Annals of Clonmacnoise.* *England.* A desolating mortality.—SHORT.
776–77	*Ireland.* Dysentery and other diseases prevalent.—*Annals of Ulster.*
778..........	„ "Small pox all over Erin."—*Annals of Ulster.*
779..........	*France.* Pestilence.
784..........	*Germany.* Plague among men and animals.—HAGEK and LIBOCZAN, *Annal Bohemor,* vol. i, p. 348.
784..........	*Scotland.* Pestilence.
785..........	*Ireland.* The plague called *Scamach,* a peeling of the skin. Probably a kind of leprosy.—*Annals of Ulster.*
798..........	*Ireland.* An extraordinary storm of thunder and lightning was followed by a pestilence.—*Irish Annalists.*
800–801....	Plagues in various places mentioned by various authors; no definite details.
802..........	*Europe.* By reason of the "warmth and unseasonableness of the weather, the plague broke out."—SHORT.
803..........	*France.* Plague followed an earthquake near Aix-la-Chapelle.— SHORT.
804..........	*Bohemia.* Plague.—HAGEK and LIBOCZAN, *Annal. Bohemor.,* vol. i, p. 413.
805..........	*Ireland.* Great plague.—*Annals of Ulster.*
806.........	„ A great epidemy.—*Chron. Scot.*
813 & 814	„ Pestilence.
817 & 820	*Europe.* LAUCISIUS and BARTIANUS give an account of a pestilence which arose from excessive rains and cold damp weather.

Plagues and Pestilences affecting the Human Race—Contd.

A.D.	
823............	*France.* Unusual weather, followed by a plague, which extended through the country "in a fearful manner, destroying multitudes of different sexes and ages." *Germany* suffered from the same unknown disorder.—EINHARDI'S *Annales.*
825............	*France* and *Germany.* Both countries almost depopulated by a pestilence consequent upon *drought.*
829............	*Greece, Thrace,* and *Bulgaria.* Plague.—FRARI, *Della Peste,* ii, 211.
853............	*Scotland.* Pestilence.
863............	,, Another epidemic.
868............	*England.* In the twentieth year of King Alfred's life there was a severe famine, and in the next year famine and "mortality of men." —ASSER.
863............	*Europe.* Great mortality all over Europe, but chiefly in France.— DUCHESNE, iii, p. 473; ASSER., *De Rebus Gestis Alfredi,* p. 20.
869............	*England.* "Mortality of men."—*Chronicle of* FABIUS ETHELWERD; *Chron. of* ST. EVROULT.
874............	*Europe.* Pestilence destroyed a third part of the maritime inhabitants of Gaul. Its origin was referred to the putrefaction of swarms of enormous grasshoppers or locusts, which were driven into the English Channel by a strong wind and then cast up on the shore.
878............	*Germany.* A plague amongst oxen, followed by a pestilence in man. —*Annal. Fuldens.*
878	*Rome.* Pestilence.
883............	*Italy.* Famine and pestilence.
884............	*England.* Pestilence at Oxford.
896............	*Europe.* Pestilence prevalent. Possibly transmitted from the domestic animals, which were suffering from anthrax.
897............	*England.* "The nation....was weakened in these three years by the disease in cattle, and, most of all, in men, so that many of the mightiest of the king's thanes that were in the land died within three years."—*Chronicles of the Saxons.*
917............	*Ireland.* "There reigned a great plague this year."—*Annals of Clonmacnoise.*
922............	*Scotland.* Pestilential fever very prevalent.
929............	*England.* Severe winter, followed by famine and pestilence.
937............	,, Pestilence, arising from great heat and drought.
940............	*Great Britain.* A murrain amongst the cattle was followed by a pestilence, of which 40,000 persons died in Scotland alone.
941............	*Winchester (England).* Plague.—DUGDALE's *England,* x, p. 1549.
941............	*Europe (North).* An epidemy followed a great mortality among cattle.
945............	*France.* A furious mortality caused by the "faim canine."— MEZERAY, *Hist. de France,* vol. i, p. 677.
954............	*Scotland.* Pestilence; 40,000 perished.
959............	*Britain.* A great plague happened in the month of March.—*Chron. and Mem. of Great Britain,* p. 24.
959......... ...	*Ireland.* A "bolt of fire" or "arrow of fire" killed thousands of men and cattle.—(*Annals of the Four Masters; Annals of Ulster*). FLEMING thinks that a plague is thus referred to.—*Animal Plagues,* i, 53.
962............	*London.* Plague.
964............	*Italy* or *Germany.* Pestilence almost entirely destroyed the Emperor Otho's army.
965............	*London.* A malignant fever or plague.
975............	*England.* Sickness (ascribed to a comet) prevalent.—GRAFTON, *Chron. Hist. England,* 1569.
981............	*Greece.* Great mortality amongst the Lacedæmonians.
986............	*Britain* and *France.* "A great sudden destruction, which caused a loss of people."—*Annals of Ulster.*

Plagues and Pestilences affecting the Human Race—Contd.

A.D.

987 .... *Great Britain and Ireland.* "In this year two plagues of an unknown character appeared in England, to wit, fever among men,
and pestilence (dysentery) among animals and men........ These
ravaged the whole of England, and the destruction to men and
animals was quite incredible."—SIMEON DUNELMEN, p. 161;
BROMPTON, *Hist. Angl.*, p. 878; HENRY DE KNYGHTON, *De Event.
Angl.*, p. 2314; *Annals of* TIGHERNACH; FLORENCE *of Worcester.*
In *Ireland* a great and unusual wind [bearing mephitic vapours ?]
was followed by "demonical colic."—*Annals of the Four Masters.*

988 .... *Wales.* A great mortality took place among the people through
famine.—*Brut y Tywysogion.*

988 .... *Germany.* Plague.

992 .... *Ireland.* A "great mortality" upon man.—*Annals of Ulster.*

992-94.... *France.* Widespread mortality, caused by ergotism (*feu sacré*);
destroyed more than 40,000 persons.—DULAURE'S *Hist. Phy.
Civ. et Morale.*

994 .... *Saxony.* A terrible plague. Ergotism in *France.*—*Annales Quedlinburgens.* PERTZ, *M. V.*, p. 72.

995 .... *England.* A deadly form of dysentery prevalent. "A worse year
in *Saxony* than the former, for so great a pestilence, which .was
named 'osterludi,' raged amongst them, that not only their houses,
but many of their towns remained empty, their inhabitants being
dead."—SHORT, p. 93; *Annales Quedlinburgens.*

997 .... *England.* Burning fevers and agues.

1003-1008 *France.* Pestilence and famines.

1005 .... "Pestilence in the shape of the true plague, began and continued
for three years in various parts of the globe, more than half the
human race perishing therefrom."—BASCOME, *H. Ep. Pest.*, p. 31.

1005 .... *England.* Plague.

1006 .... *Europe.* Pestilence for three years.

'09 .... *England.* A plague among the Saxons.—WEBSTER.

'10 .... *France.* Great pestilence amongst cattle and reptiles, causing
famine and pestilence in the human race.

'11 .... *Ireland.* Epidemic colic.

'12 ....   „   Epidemy; boils, cramp, and colic.

'12 .... *Germany.* Endless multitudes died of famine and plague.—SHORT.

'12-24.... *England.* BASCOME speaks of these as "dreadful pestilential
seasons."

'13 or '15 *Ireland.* A "disease of the legs" (scurvy ?) among the Danes.—
Chron. Scot.

'20 .... *Saxony.* A dreadful pestilence.

'25 .... *Europe.* A cold and wet summer, with pestilence in England and
other parts of Europe. In *Flanders,* constant rain for six months
was followed by a plague which swept away the greatest part of
men.—SHORT.

'27 .... *Europe.* Choro-mania, chorea, or St. Vitus's dancing madness,
appeared in Germany, and subsequently spread over the continent
of Europe and to the British Isles.—HECKER.

'28 .... *Europe.* Pestilence, caused by dense foul vapours and a plague of
caterpillars.—HAGEK and LIBOCZAN, *Annal. Bohemor,* vol. v,
p. 152.

1031 .... *India, Persia.* Prof. Hirsch contends that Asiatic cholera spread
over these countries and as far as Constantinople.

'33 .... *England.* Pestilence.

'33 .... *Cappadocia, Paphlagonia* and *Armenia,* were so afflicted by plague
that the inhabitants forsook those provinces.

'35 .... *France.* Famine and "Une maladie contagieuse appellée 'La
Peste' dans les chroniques. Cette de Fontenelle nous décrit les
désastres de ce double fleau. Les villes, les bourgs, devinrent
déserts et n'offraient que des ruines. La maladie contagieuse

Plagues and Pestilences affecting the Human Race—Contd.

A.D.	*France—Contd.*

1035 .... atteignat les hommes et les animaux. Les chemins, les carrefours, les cimetières, les églises, étaient remplis des malheureux qui répandaient des exhalations insupportables, et qui de toutes partes venaient chercher des remèdes à leurs maux."—DULAURE'S *Hist. Phys. Civ. et Morale.*

'41 .... *England, France,* and *Germany.* Diseases prevalent, amongst others ergotism or erysipelas.—*Chron. St. Bavonis, Corp. Chron. Flandr.,* i, 385.

'42 .... *Europe.* Famine, and a pestilence affecting both men and cattle, in England, Gaul, Germany, &c. It rained throughout the summer, and snowed in harvest time.

'44 .... *Ireland.* "Clonmacnoise was plundered by the people of Conmhaicne (co. Longford), whereupon God and Ciaran sent upon them the unknown distemper (*Pamh Anaithinidh*), which killed almost all their people and cattle."—*Chron. Scot.; An. Four Masters; An. of Clonmacnoise.*

'47 .... *England.* Great mortality. "A destruction of men" in *Ireland.*— *Annals of Ulster.*

'51 .... *Europe.* 300,000 of the Patzinacæ, a Scythian nation, descended upon the eastern Roman empire, but a contagious distemper breaking out among them, the Roman general gained a victory.—BOYLE, i, 394.

'51 .... *England.* Plague.

'53 .... *France.* Famine and pestilence for five years.

'54 .... *Germany.* "A pestilential disease smote the country, so that the living had not strength to bear away the dead, and this great affliction was endured throughout the whole summer."—CEDRENUS, *Hist. Comp.,* ii, 609.

'59 .... *Bavaria.* "A direful plague smote man and beast."—STANDELII, *Chron. Æfele Scrip. Boic,* i, 477.
 France. Famine bred pestilence.—DULAURE, *Hist. Phys., Civ., &c.*

'60 .... *England.* Plague.—SIGEBERT.

'60–62.... *France.* A contagious malady destroyed a great number of persons.

'61 .... *Ireland.* Epidemic colic and small pox.

'64 .... *Italy.* Fluxes, pleurisies, and fevers carried off many hundreds of Saracens marching to invade Rome. The pestilence continued until 1066.

'67 .... *Egypt* and *Arabia.* An awful plague swept away a great part of the inhabitants.

'68 .... *England.* A pestilence raged in York and Durham.

'68 .... *Constantinople.* A terrible plague.

'77 (about) *Europe.* Locusts, famine, and pestilence made great havoc in Italy, Russia, Flanders and England.

78 .... *Ireland.* "Great mortality among the people."—*Annals of Innisfallen.*

'84 .... *Ireland.* Pestilence (possibly typhus fever) began at this time, and continued for thirteen years.

'85 .... *France.* Erysipelas.

'87 .... *England.* "The people in all places were pitifully plagued with burning fevers, which brought many to their end."—HOLINSHED, *Chron.; Annal. Waverleiens.*

'87–89.... *Europe.* Cold, wet summers, and hard winters, caused famine and pestilence in England, Gaul, Germany and Italy.

'89 .... *France.* Erysipelas prevailed epidemically, causing great mortality.

'89–91.... *Europe.* "Ignis sacer," or ergotism, very prevalent.

'92–94.... „ Fatal distempers prevalent in England, France, Germany, Italy, and at Constantinople. The mortality continued for three, and in some places four years. At Constantinople the plague was caused by putrefying locusts.—POLYDORUS; ZONARIUS; CRANTZIUS; SPANGENBERG, p. 228; HOPMANNI, *Annal. Bamberg.;* LUDWIG, *Scrip. ver. Bamberg,* p. 90; AGRICOLA, DE PESTE, *Briet. Annal*

Plagues and Pestilences affecting the Human Race—Contd.

A.D.	Europe—Contd.
1092-94...	*Mund.;* FABRICIUS, *Origin Saxon,* p. 218; ÆLNOTHIN, *Hist. S. Canuti Reg.;* LANGABEK, *Scrip. rer. Dan.,* iii, 375; *Saxo Grammaticus,* p. 222. The plague at *Tournai* was so severe that a sacred procession was formed of the heads of the Church to perambulate the city. This event is still perpetuated by an annual procession leaving the old five-towered Cathedral every 9th September.—See Gallait's great picture, " The Plague of Tournai " (see 1426).
'94	*England.* Plague ; *London,* great mortality.
'95	*Ireland.* Pestilence. The celebrated judge, Brehan O'Manchan, died of it.
'95	*Europe.* Plague in many parts of the continent.
'96 to 1105	*England, North of Europe, Palestine.* Inclement seasons, famine, pestilence.
'99	*France.* Severe epidemy (gangrenous erysipelas).—*Chronic.* URSPERG., *edit. Mylius,* pp. 177, 180. *England.* An epidemy.
1108-11...	*Europe.* Pestilence in various parts.
'09	*England.* Erysipelatous diseases were epidemic, affecting and destroying many people, whose limbs were covered with black spots like carbuncles.—WEBSTER.
'11	*London.* A dreadful plague caused terrible mortality amongst the citizens.—HOLINSHED, *Chron.*
'12	*England.* " A great mortalitie of men."—STOW, *Chron.*
'13	„ " People were afflicted with grievous and long diseases, especially a dysentery and most destructive plague."—SHORT.
'13	*Palestine.* Pestilence ravaged Judea.
'14	*Ireland.* A great epidemic disease seized upon Murtagh O'Brien, whereupon he abdicated his kingdom.—*Annals of Kilronan.*
'15	*Ireland.* Mortality of men.—*Chron. Scot.; Annals of the Four Masters; Annals of Boyle.*
'20–25...	*England.* Erysipelas cut off about a third of the population.—BASCOME, p. 35. A pestilential period of two hundred and seventy-two years said to have commenced.
'25	*Europe.* Pestilence in men and cattle.
'26–28...	*England.* A destructive pestilence.
'27	*France.* The " divine plague " (perhaps ergotism).—ST. BAVONIS, *Chron.*
'29	*Europe.* " Ignis divinis."—ANSELM GEMBLAC, *Chron. Pistor.*
'33–46...	*England.* Famine and pestilence.
'37	*Ireland.* A great storm of wind was followed by epidemic colic, which killed many.
'41	*Ireland.* " There was a great disease of biles [*sic*], patches, and scabs in Connaught and Munster in this year."—*Annals of Clonmacnoise.*
'42–43...	*England.* " Small flying worms which darkened the air, ate all up." A plague from " bad air."—SHORT, i, 119.
'50–69...	*Europe, Asia,* and *Africa.* Famine and pestilence swept the world, especially Scotland, Ireland, Italy, Gaul, Sicily, Judea, Asia, and Africa. The period was marked by severe winters, dry summers, inundations, and earthquakes. " A most grievous pestilence."—LEIBNITZ, *Access. Hist.,* vol. i, p. 344.
'53	*Scotland.* A dearth, followed by a violent pestilence.—HECTOR BOECE, *Chronicles of Scotland,* vol. ii, p. 308.
'62	*Aquitania.* Plague.—*Chron. Magdeburg.*
'66	*Saxony.* Plague and mortality in children. — *Chron. Saxo.;* LEIBNITZ, *Access. Hist.,* vol. i, p. 308.
'67	*Italy.* " The emperor, who had entered Italy at the head of an army to place the anti-pope, Pascal, in possession of the holy see, became master of Rome ; but a malady which spread through his army compelled him to retire to Campania."—BOYLE, i, 419.

Plagues and Pestilences affecting the Human Race—Contd.

A.D.

1171 .... *Germany.* Great mortality of men and cattle.—*Chron. Magdeburg;* HOFFMAN, *Annal. Bamberg.*

'72 .... *England.* Dysentery very prevalent. The distemper was introduced by the army, in which it broke out through too much fresh food.—SHORT, p. 124.

'72 .... *Ireland.* Pestilence and famine.—WARBURTON'S *Hist. of Dublin,* i, 153.

'73–74.... *Europe, Asia,* and *Africa.* "This year the whole world was afflicted with a cloudy corrupt air, which occasioned a most universal cough and catarrh fatal to many." This is the first instance of influenza on record.—SHORT, i, 125; *Chronogr. Saxo.,* p. 310; YMAGINES, *Hist. Twysden,* p. 579.

'73 .... *Ireland.* Plague and famine.
Germany. An epidemy among children.—CELLEUSUS.

'74 .... *England.* Small pox, measles, epidemic catarrh, scarlet fever, quinsies, and pleurisies, very prevalent.

'75–93.... Similar maladies were rife in other parts of the world.—BASCOME.

'83 ...... *England.* Pestilence.

'83 .... *Rome.* A plague raged at the same time.

'85 .... *Spain.* Castile, and principally the city of Leon, suffered from plague.

'87 .... *England.* Great mortality.—BENEDICT ABBAS. Grievous and pestilent.—SHORT.

'90 .... *Asia Minor* (the *Crusades*). A famine and pestilence appeared in the army of the crusaders at the siege of Acre, and carried off 1,000 men a day. The famine was caused by the stoppage of the supplies by the Governor of Tyre; the pestilence was doubtless due to the famine and continuous heavy rains together. The events are described by the old chronicler GEOFFREY DE VINSAUF.

'93–94.... *England.* "The common people perished in every quarter for lack of food, and the fiercest pestilence followed, in the form of acute fever, which destroyed such numbers that scarcely any were left to minister unto the sick; the customary funeral service ceased, and in many places large ditches were made, into which the dead were thrown."—(*Chron.* W. HUMFORD, v. ii, p. 546—47). This pestilence continued until 1196.

'96 .... *Spain.* A great famine and plague in the principality of Catalonia.

'96–1201 *Europe.* "Ignis sacer" widely prevalent in England and on the continent.

'99 .... *Cordova* (Spain). Pestilential fever. The celebrated physician Averhoes observed that every patient who was bled before purging invariably died.—BASCOME, p. 37.

1200 (1185 to 1211) *Portugal.* "A disease never before seen sprang up. The viscera of mankind were disturbed as if by some raging heat, which caused raving as if of madness."—DE VERA, *Reg. Portugal; Hispania Illustrata,* vol. ii, p. 1257.

1200–1201 *England.* Epidemic pestilence.

'04 .... *Ireland.* Plague destroyed a prodigious number.

'06 .... *Spain.* Heavy rains, inundations, and a severe epidemic. (Total eclipse of the sun in February; darkness as great as midnight.)

'06 .... *Poland.* A famine, produced by the ravages of the Tartars, was followed by a plague that depopulated one of the most populous countries of the north.—*Encyc. Brit.,* 3rd edit., vol. xv, p. 281.

'07 .... *Ireland.* "A great destruction of men and cattle."—*Annals of Ulster.*

'13 .... *France* and *Spain.* Gangrenous erysipelas (*feu sacré*).—VILLALBA, *Epidemiologia Española,* vol. i, p. 54.

'17 .... *Egypt* and *Italy.* Plague, it is said, left scarcely a tenth part of the inhabitants of Italy alive. In the city of Damietta [besieged] only three persons out of 70,000 survived.—BASCOME, p. 37.

Plagues and Pestilences affecting the Human Race— Contd.

A.D.	
1217	*Spain.* Pestilential disease fatal to men and cattle.
'18	*Egypt.* The camp of the Christian Crusaders was overflowed in consequence of the waters of the Nile (then in flood) being held back from their proper outflow by a north wind ; the provisions, arms, and baggage of the Knights Templars were destroyed. An epidemic fever ensued, which carried off many of the brethren.— *The Knights Templars*, 2nd edit., p. 292.
'21	*Europe.* "Excessive rains, floods, frosts, and inclement heats induced a famine and pestilence, which almost desolated the whole of Europe....In some cities scarcely a person survived the terrible destruction."—BASCOME, p. 38.
'21-23....	*Poland.* "Three years' famine and plague, whereof died myriads of people and cattle."—*Chron. Magdeburg.*
'22	Plague raged with uncontrollable fury in Germany, Hungary, Gaul, Egypt, and other countries.
'24	*Ireland.* During the prevalence of an epizooty, the persons who ate flesh or milk were attacked by "various belly sicknesses." A great mortality was caused by this, as well as by "teasca" (probably typhus), which broke out in Connaught.—*Annals of Connaught ; Annals of Kilronan.*
'28	*England.* Heavy rains, a hot summer, and a severe winter, induced fatal disease.—BASCOME, p. 38.
'30	*Europe.* A severe epidemic broke out in Denmark, Italy, Gaul, and other countries, lasting till 1236.
'30	*England.* Pestilence here also, which decimated the population.
'30	*Rome.* Pestilence raged until 1235. It was preceded by an inundation of the Tiber, a hot summer, and famine.
'30	*Denmark* desolated by plague.
'30	*Majorca.* When King Don Jayme seized on the island, a terrible pestilence broke out. He was obliged to send galleys to Catalonia in search of colonists. The hospital of St. Anthony was established for the treatment of those suffering from "the sacred Persian, or St. Anthony's, fire." For details, see BASCOME, p. 39.
'30	*Russia.* A plague, believed to be the same epidemic that visited the Scandinavian countries, and especially Denmark.—BROBERG, *on the Plague in Stockholm.*
'33	*England.* Famine and disease.
'35	„ Plague and leprosy ; 20,000 died in London.
'37	„ "A most epidemic ague. A rainy, stormy, sickly year ; agues were epidemic beyond compare."—SHORT.
'37	*Germany.* The dancing mania broke out at *Erfurt.*—HECKER.
'38-39....	*Europe.* Pestilence.
'40	*England.* A pestilence appeared in various parts of the country. The seasons were inclement, and the fish on the coasts died. "Sore and heavy diseases on man and beast."—SHORT.
'42	*France, Italy,* and *Greece.* Plague.
'43	*England.* Pestilence in various parts. The year was remarkable for meteors and drought.
'47	*England.* Pestilence broke out in September. "A great plague was in England."—STOW.
'48	*Britain* and *Ireland.* Plague.—*Annales Cambria.*
'49	*Palestine.* JOINVILLE describes a pestilence which ravaged the armies of St. Louis the Crusader. The bodies of the slain were thrown by the Saracens into a river, where they accumulated so as to cover it from bank to bank. Being Lent, the French soldiers were obliged to live on fish, and the only kind obtainable was the eel-pout—a gluttonous fish which fed on the dead bodies. For details, see BASCOME, pp. 40 and 41.
'49-50....	*Friesland.* Pestilence followed a famine.—UBBON, *Emmii Ber. Fries. Hist.*, 1516.

Plagues and Pestilences affecting the Human R ice—Contd.

A.D.	
1251	*England.* Epidemic pestilence throughout the country. The summer was intolerably hot. "In many parishes 100 died a month."— SHORT.
'52	*England.* "Great mortality among men and cattle."—WILKES'S *Chronicle of English Affairs.*
'52–53....	*England.* "At Michaelmas the plague began to rage in London, and pervaded all England, continuing until August in the following year; thus affording an instance of this disease beginning in autumn, running through the winter, and terminating in the summer."—(BASCOME, p. 41.) There was a drought in the previous year, a late frost in spring which destroyed all vegetation, and heavy rains in July.
'55–56 and 1258	*England.* Wet seasons, storms, and floods destroyed the crops; famine ensued, and fatal fevers carried off great numbers of the populace.
'62	*Ireland.* "A great destruction of people this year from plague and hunger."—*Annals of Ulster.*
'70	"The Crusaders, under Louis IX, disembarked near Tunis, and were seized by a pestilence, which destroyed the king, his eldest son, and the greater part of the army in a few weeks."—BOYLE, i, 446.
'71	*Ireland.* War produced famine and pestilence.—*Irish Annalists.*
'75–76....	*France.* "A dreadful famine, followed by a still more dreadful pestilence."—HOFMANNI, *Annal Bamberg.;* LUDEWIG, *Scrip. ver, Bamberg.*, p. 176.
'78	*Germany.* The dancing mania at *Utrecht.*—HECKER.
'80	*France.* Pestilence.—DULAURE, *Hist.*
'81	*Scotland.* Great mortality caused by the pest.—BOECE, *Hist. and Chron. of Scot.*, vol. ii, p. 359.
'82	*Scotland.* Hector Boetius gives an account of the plague as having first visited Scotland.—HAILE'S *Annals.*
'82	*Denmark.* A great plague.
'83	*Spain.* Pestilence killed about 4,000 men of the army of Philip of France when at Gerona.
'85	*England.* Severe dysentery prevailed in various parts of the kingdom; also an epidemic resembling the influenza of the present day. It was about this period that water was conveyed to London by means of leaden pipes.
'86	*England.* Great mortality followed a boisterous spring and an exceedingly hot summer.—STOW, *Chron.*
'94	*Ireland.* Famine and pestilence.—*Irish Annalists.*
'96	*Scotland.* Famine and pestilence.
'97	,, Famine and plague.—SHORT.
'99–1302	*England.* Inclement seasons. Severe catarrhs with fluxes pervaded the country.
1308	*Ireland.* March. "A destruction of men and cattle."—*Annals of Connaught.*
'14	*Europe.* Plague raged.
'15	*England.* After dearth, "a grievous mortality of people."—STOW.
'15	*Ireland.* The pestilential period of the fourteenth century, which began this year, and continued almost without interruption for eighty-five years, is the most disastrous in the annals of Ireland. It commenced with the Scots invasion under Edward Bruce. Epizoötics succeeded, followed by small pox; then dearth, severe seasons, influenza, and an outbreak of the barking mania. Subsequently appeared the black death, the "king's game," and the third pestilence—portions of the five general and fatal epidemics which commenced in the reign of Edward III, and the fourth and fifth pestilences in the beginning of the reign of Richard II. Starvation and distempers this year. See *table in Irish Census Report*, 1851.
'15	*Germany.* Famine and pestilence.

F

Plagues and Pestilences affecting the Human Race—Contd.

A.D.

1316 .... *England.* A deadly form of dysentery caused great mortality equal to that of plague. — (DUCHESNE, *Histoire Gen. d'Angleterre,* p. 728.) Disease in other countries also.

'17 .... *England.* Upon a scarcity ensued " a great death and mortality of people."—HOLINSHED.

'17 .... *Ireland.* A "horrible plague" carried off numbers.—GRACE'S *Annals.*

'23–45.... *Northern Europe.* Plague raged.—BROBERG.

'25 .... *Ireland.* Influenza "affected, during three or four days, every person, so that it was second only to death." This is the first instance of influenza in Ireland.—*An. of Ulster.*

'27 .... *Ireland.* Small pox was epidemic.—*Irish Annalists.*

'30 .... *Glasgow.* Plague.—*Stat. Acct. Scot.*

'32 .... *Ireland.* A disease called *Mauses* spread throughout the country; apparently a sort of influenza.—GRACE'S *Annals.*

'33 .... *Barcelona* (Spain). According to the diary of Ramon Vila, famine and pestilence carried off 10,000 persons about this time.

'34 .... *Tche* (China). Plague said to have carried off 5 million people.— DEQUIGNES, *Hist. of China,* p. 226.

'35 .... *England.* "So great a death........ that scarce could the living, bury the dead."—HOWE.

'37 .... *China.* Pestilential epidemic caused by famine.

'38 .... *Germany.* Great mortality. "Worms were bred in human bodies, so that many people died."—HAMSFORTII, *Chronologia; Langebek,* v. i, p. 303.

'39 .... *Denmark.* Desolated by war, famine, and pestilence.

'41 .... *Ireland.* An epidemic of the barking disease, similar to that described by Calmeil and Hecker, appeared in Ireland in 1341. This was a species of Lycanthropy, one of the many nervous disorders common in the middle ages, and which especially heralded in the great mortality or black plague of the fourteenth century. It was a form of disease similar to the dancing mania, the affection of the *convulsionnaires* of France, the Jumpers of Wales and Cornwall, the Tigretier of Abyssinia, and several affections of a kindred nature in North America in modern times. Grace and Camden, in their respective annals, say that this epidemy originated in Leinster, where a certain man, travelling along the road, found a pair of gloves, the which donning, he lost his speech, and began to bark like a dog : " nay, from that moment the men and women, old and young, throughout the whole country, barked like dogs, and the children like whelps "—this strange seizure remaining upon the persons affected sometimes eighteen days, again a month, and in some cases for two years ; finally infecting the neighbouring counties. (Note *Table, Irish Census,* 1851, *passim.*) This extraordinary madness is treated of by Ætius, Paulus, Schenkius, Hildesheim, Forrestus, Olaus Magnus, Vinc, Bellaircensis, Pierius, Bodine, Zuinger, Zeilger, Peucer, Wierus, Spranger, and others ; and it is difficult to adopt the belief that the accounts are all fabricated, although that view has been advanced.

'42 .... *Scotland.* A plague swept away a third part of the inhabitants.— BUCHANAN'S *Hist. of Scot.*

'46–55.... *Europe, Asia,* and *Africa.* **BLACK DEATH.** This pestilence ravaged the greater part of the Eastern hemisphere, and is said to have carried off a fourth part of the human species. According to several writers, it originated in China in 1346. MEZERAY says that a globe of fire issued from the earth, burst, and spread the infection around. From *China* it proceeded westward to Constantinople and *Egypt.* From Constantinople it passed into *Greece, Italy, France,* and *Africa ;* from the Mediterranean coasts to *England, Scotland,* and *Ireland,* and from Britain into *Germany, Hungary, Poland,*

Plagues and Pestilences affecting the Human Race—Contd.

A.D.	*Europe, Asia,* and *Africa—Contd.*
1346-55....	*Denmark,* and other northern kingdoms. *Greenland* is said to have been depopulated; all the mercantile classes were killed off. It reached England* in 1348 (DUGDALE). In the first six months of the year 57,000 persons are said to have died in London and Norwich. The churchyards in London not being sufficient to receive the dead, Sir Walter de Mauny purchased 13 acres of ground belonging to St. Bartholomew's Hospital in Smithfield, and there alone about 200 interments per day took place from Candlemas to Easter (LYTTLETON'S *Hist. of England,* vol. i, p. 565). 100,000 persons are said to have perished in the city (CRUTWELL'S *Gazetteer,* vol. ii). The contagion spread into Wales and Ireland, proving chiefly fatal to the common people. "The Scots, invited by the prospect of an easy prey in this season of dearth and desolation, made an irruption into the northern counties, and, together with a large booty, carried back the contagion to their native country, where it raged with uncommon violence" (LYTTLETON'S *Hist. of England*). According to Antonius, Archbishop of Florence, the distemper carried off 60,000 people in that city, among whom was the historian John Villanini (*Ency. Brit.,* vol. xiv, p. 795, art. Plague). The only notable English victim was Jane, the king's second daughter, who succumbed at Bordeaux, on her way to Castile. It is recorded that this Black Death had many symptoms similar to those of yellow fever. Dr. HECKER estimates that Europe lost 25 million inhabitants.

Cyprus. This island suffered most severely.

Bristol. For effect of pestilence on this city, see CORRY and EVANS'S *Hist.* (1816), i, 188.

Coventry. See SHORT, *Hist. of Air, &c.* (1749), i, 177.

Dublin. For long and curious contemporary account, see WARBURTON, WHITELAW, and WALSH'S *Hist.,* i, pp. 172 and 173.

---

* "The pestilence began, as Fabian and the generality of our historians say, in this county [Dorset], on the sea coast, passed thence into Devon, Somerset, and through the whole nation. It was the greatest plague known since that in the time of Vortigern, mentioned by Bede. Few survived the seizure above two or three days, some not half a day. Sir William Manny purchased 13 acres near Smithfield for a burial place, in which were interred 50,000. At Leicester, in St. Leonard's parish, died 380; in St. Cross's, 400; in St. Martin's, above 700, and great multitudes in other places. Walsingham says, scarce a tenth part of the people remained alive. The Scots took this opportunity to invade England, but the disease speedily invaded their army. They retired to the forest of Selkirk, and died in great numbers. They invented an oath to celebrate the occasion—'by the foul death of the English.' At Oxford the schools, colleges, and halls were all shut up, and the parliament was obliged to be prorogued. H. Knyghton says, things were sold almost for nothing............He further says that the great pestilence had swept away so many priests, that a chaplain could hardly be got to serve a church under x marks or x pounds *per ann.,* whereas before they might be had at v or vi marks, nay, at ii with their diet; and men would hardly accept of a vicarage of xx marks or xx*l. per ann.* This, I suppose, was because vicars were thought to be obliged to stricter residence, which in pestilential seasons was, doubtless, hazardous. The Sarum registers from 8th August, 1348, to Lady Day, 1349, contain the admissions of seventy incumbents. In many villages all inhabitants died, the houses fell down, and were never inhabited again. This plague continued till Michaelmas, 1349. Yet, as it began in this county [Dorset], we may suppose its rage abated sooner here than in other parts of the nation, which received the infection later. Our historians, especially the more ancient ones, give a very melancholy account of its ravages. See FABIAN, KNYGHTON, RYMER'S *Fœd.,* FREIND'S *History of Physick,* FLEETWOOD'S *Chron. Pret.*"—HUTCHINS' *Hist., &c., of Dorset,* 1774, vol. i, Introduction, pp. xxiv and xxv.

Plagues and Pestilences affecting the Human Race—Contd.

A.D.	*Europe, Asia,* and *Africa—Contd.*
1346-55....	*Glasgow. Stat. Account of Scot.,* vi, 107.

Lancaster. "At this time a pestilence of the most fatal character raged in the county of Lancaster, and indeed in all the other counties of the kingdom; and so malignant were its effects, that one-third of the inhabitants became its victims."—BAINES's *Lancashire* (1836), i, 332.

London. STOW, in his *Chronicle,* gives a description of the whole pestilential period, from 1348 to 1357, as it affected this city.

Manchester. "In consequence of the pestilence which raged in the parish of Manchester in 1352, a commission was granted by the bishop of Lichfield for the consecration of a burial ground at Didsbury, to be appropriated to the interment of such persons as died in that hamlet of this grievous epidemic."—BAINES's *Lancashire,* ii, 193.

Yarmouth. The mortality in 1349 was over 7,000 persons.—GILLINGWATER's *Lowestoft,* pp. 58 and 59.

Some writers have asserted that the pestilence took its rise in a monastery crowded with idle voluptuous monks. I have seen no authoritative statement on the subject; but in addition to what HUTCHINS has said (see note on preceding page) regarding its fatality amongst the clergy, there is evidence that it caused serious mortality among the monks in France. One society in Montpelier lost 133 members out of 140; in Marseilles the whole 140 died; and 66 Carmelites perished in Avignon.

The actual number of victims in specified places during the foregoing pestilential period has been thus summed up:—

Venice	100,000
Basle	14,000
Erfurt	16,000
Strasburg .... about	16,000
Paris	50,000
Norwich	50,000
Marseilles (in one month)	56,000
Florence [Petrarch says 100,000]	60,000
Avignon	62,000
London	100,000
Lubeck	90,000

Germany lost 1,244,434.—SHORT.

Spain, two-thirds of the population.

Ireland, nearly depopulated.—BASCOME, *Hist. Epid. Pest.* p. 53.,

One of the most accurate accounts of the pestilence is supplied by Guy de Chauliac, physician to Pope Clement VI, who was at Avignon in 1348. According to the most credible data and the most moderate figures, the black plague made more than 40 million victims. Guy de Muisit, prior of the Abbey of St. Martin at Tournay, states that there were towns where of 20,000 inhabitants scarcely 2,000 survived, and villages where of 1,500 persons scarcely 100 escaped. People fell in the street as though struck by a thunderbolt. From one country to another the scourge spread all over Europe, till after depopulating Iceland, it reached its last stage in Greenland. In its fatal progress it caused a sullen despair and extinguished all natural feelings. "The father," says Chauliac, "refused to visit his son, and the son his father. Charity was dead, and hope downcast." It was this pestilence which so impressed Boccaccio, Petrarch, and Wycliffe, as seen in their works.

It has been broadly asserted that one-fourth of the population of the globe was destroyed on the occasion; and that fully one-half of the productive population of Europe was carried off. Certain it is that it had a considerable influence upon the destinies of certain

Plagues and Pestilences affecting the Human Race—Contd.

A.D.	*Europe, Asia,* and *Africa—Contd.*
1346-55...	European countries. In England it gave rise to that branch of legislation known as the Labour Laws, to which fact reference has been made in the text.
'52	*China.* Pestilence and famine are supposed to have killed about 900,000 Chinese about this time. [This may be only another account of the mortality from the Black Death.]
'55	*England.* A peculiar kind of madness became epidemic, causing those affected to flee into the woods and wander about the fields.
56	*Germany.* "Pestilence.......first attacked the flocks of sheep, then passed on to the cattle, and finally destroyed a great multitude of men."—MUTIUS, *Chron. Pistor. Scrip. rer. German,* ed. *Sruve,* ii, 896.
'59 and 1361	*Sweden.* Plague.—BROBERG.
'60	*England.* Heavy rains and storms destroyed the crops, and pestilential fevers followed.
'60	*England.* "A mortality of people, called the 'second plague,' because it was the second in the reign of Edward III."—SHORT, i, 178.
'61	*England.* "A plague raged in England, which, in allusion to the great plague in 1349, Barnes calls the 'second plague.' 'Nothing near,' says he, ' so dismal and universal as the former, but much more destructive to the nobility and prelacy.'"—(BAINES'S *Lancashire* (1836), i, 142.) "Second pestilence" is also mentioned in EARNSHAW, *East Cheshire* (1880), ii, 235.
'61	*Ireland. The King's Game,* or the second pestilence. It seems that the Black Death spent its force earlier in Ireland than elsewhere, as the Irish annals contain no notice of it after the middle of the century. This *King's Game* was perhaps a return of the Black Death, but more probably a return of the dancing mania. It ended with this decade.
	Milan, which escaped in 1348, suffered severely from the Black Death this year.—WEBSTER.
'62	*London* and *Paris.* Great mortality.
'62	*Scotland.* A plague, which cut off great numbers of every rank and age.
'63	*Spain.* A pestilence, known as the "second mortality"—that of 1350 being the first—carried off vast numbers of the Spaniards.
'65	*Cologne* (Prussia). 20,000 of the inhabitants perished from pestilence.
'66	*England.* A disease prevalent, "so as many who went well to bed at night were found dead next morning."—SHORT, i, 180; WALTER'S *Hist. of Eng.*
'68	*England.* "The third pestilence began in England, and continued for two years."—OTTERBOURNE.
'68	*Scotland.* Famine and pestilence.
'68-70....	*Europe.* An epidemic pestilence ravaged England, Ireland, Italy, and Gaul.
'70	*England.* The "third mortality." The west country suffered most. —SHORT, i, 180; GRAFTON.
'70	*Scotland.* A grievous pest, imported with English booty. "The third part of the people deceasit."
'70	*Ireland.* The third pestilence; probably a true bubonic plague. It lasted three or four years, and "made awaie a great number of people."—HOOKER, *Chron.*
'71	*Barcelona.* Pestilence lasted for a year. On 13th June imprecatory processions were instituted.
'72	*Europe* and the *East.* Pestilence raged in Germany, Egypt, Greece, and all the East. Lubeck lost 90,000 of its inhabitants.
'73	*England.* Epidemic madness among the lower classes.—(WEBSTER.) Thought to have been the dancing mania by SHORT.
'74	*Europe.* St. Vitus's dance raged at Aix-la-Chapelle, and extended to nearly all the towns in the Low Countries.

Plagues and Pestilences affecting the Human Race—Contd.

A.D.	
1374	*England.* The fourth pestilence plagued England for a year.— OTTERBOURNE.
'74	*Shetland Islands.* Dancing mania, or a similar disorder, prevailed in the *Shetland Islands,* where it had previously appeared from time to time.
'74	*Milan.* Plague.—HECKER.
'75	*Scio.* Pestilence broke out and continued for a year. An imprecatory procession was formed on 20th June.
'79	*England.* Pestilence, especially in the northern counties.
'80	*Scotland.* A contagious disease prevalent, which was imported into the country by the borderers.—SIR W. SCOTT'S *Hist. of Scotland,* vol. i, p. 221.
'80	*Spain.* A great inundation, followed by pestilence resulting from an atmosphere surcharged with moisture.
'80–81...	*Glasgow.* Plague.—*Stat. Account of Scot.,* vi, 107.
'81–82...	*Europe.* A severe pestilence appeared at *Avignon* in *France,* which raged for four or five years. It prevailed in Italy, France, Germany, England, Ireland, Greece, and the East.—WEBSTER.
'82	*Ireland.* Another epidemic constitution commenced at this date, and was marked by the advent of the *fourth pestilence,* the characters of which have, however, not been determined. Like the two first, it extended over a period of about ten years.
'82	*Italy.* Final visitation of the Black Death.—HECKER.
'83	*Milan.* Plague.—HECKER.
'83	*Seville.* A pestilence, called the "third mortality," broke out. It was preceded by inundations and rains. An earthquake occurred in the previous year.
'84	*Spain.* Great pestilence and mortality from this period until the end of the century.—BASCOME, p. 60.
'84	*Lisbon.* Numbers of the soldiers of the army of Don Juan, first king of Castile, fell ill in consequence of the severity of the atmospheric changes, to which they were unaccustomed. The king was obliged to remove the garrison to Seville.
'84	*Majorca.* The "third plague" broke out this year, causing considerable mortality. It is described by VINCENT MUT, the historian of the island.
'85–87...	*Mallorca, Lisbon,* and *Gallicia.* Influenza and other diseases prevalent. "At the commencement [of 1386] there was in Gallicia much sickness among the soldiers of Tornas Moraix. The character of the epidemic is but imperfectly given, but history states the mortality to have been very great."—BASCOME, p. 60.
'87	*Benavente* (Spain or Portugal ?). "The armies of the king of Portugal and of the Duke of Lancaster suffered from severe pestilence in Benavente, and in the towns of Matillas, Arzon, Villalobos, Rales, and Valderas, owing to the scarcity of provisions."—BASCOME, p. 60.
('88–91...	*England.* Drought, followed by violent tempests, produced a famine, which in turn gave rise to anginas and dysenteries throughout England and in other parts of the world. The disease affected children principally, and was especially mortal in Norfolk and at York.
'91	*England.* The fifth pestilence began, and continued in the northern parts of England from the nativity of St. John the Baptist to the festival of St. Luke.—OTTERBOURNE. This disorder is described by SHORT as a "bloody flux," and ascribed by him to the eating of much green fruit in harvest.
'91	*Ireland.* The last of the five great pestilences began, and lasted until 1400. Perhaps typhus, as that fever is specially recorded in the annals a few years later. See *Irish Annals.*
'94	*Spain.* Pestilence in the kingdom of Valencia and in the principality of Catalonia, arising from *great heat.* Nearly 10,000 persons, mostly young, died in the city of Valencia alone.

Plagues and Pestilences affecting the Human Race—Contd.

A.D.

1394 .... | *Greenland.* It is supposed that the plague called the "black death," must have prevailed in Greenland at this time.—Howe's *Epidemic Diseases*, p. 107.

'96 .... | *Barcelona.* A pestilence here again. On 9th December, King Don Martin retired to the city of Perpignan for safety.

'99 .... | *North of England.* The English borderers, wasted by a raging pestilence, could scarce offer any resistance to the depredations of the Scottish borderers.—Sir W. Scott's *Hist. of Scotland*, vol. i, p. 234.

'99 .... | *Italy.* Plague.—Hecker.

1400 .... | *Seville.* Famine and pestilence, caused by heavy rains. The author of the *Annals of Seville* asserts that this plague occurred at centenary periods.

'01 .... | *England.* 30,000 persons died in London.

'01 .... | *Bordeaux.* Dysentery killed 14,000 persons.

'01 .... | *Italy.* Pestilence broke out in Florence.

'04 .... | *Ireland.* Epidemic fever.

'05 .... | *England.* The country visited by severe pestilence.—Sir W. Scott's *Hist. of Scotland*, vol. i, p. 241 ; Walter's *Hist. of England.*

'05 .... | *Denmark.* Famine and plague.

'06 .... | *England.* Pestilence again in London.

'06 .... | *France* (Bordeaux). A malignant dysentery destroyed 14,000 persons. A like disease was equally fatal in Aquitaine and Gascony.

'06 .... | *London.* Great plague ; 30,000 deaths.

'07 .... | *England.* "A dreadful pestilence destroyed multitudes of people throughout the kingdom, especially in London, where, within a short space of time, no less than 30,000 were swept away."— Lyttleton's *Hist. of Eng.*, vol. ii, p. 10.

'07 .... | *Wales.* Pestilence, from putrid fish cast ashore.—*Iola MS.*

'08 .... | *Ireland.* Leprosy.—*Monast. Hib.*

'10 .... | *Spain.* Epidemic pestilence at Niebla, Gibraleon, Frigueros, Seville, and Barcelona. At the latter place its appearance was preceded by an earthquake.

'11 .... | *France.* Two diseases, called respectively "tac" and "ladendo," became very general. Both were attended by a cough, and, notwithstanding alarming symptoms, were seldom fatal.
Note.—"Tac" is the French equivalent for "sheep-rot." I follow the statement made by the historian.

'13 .... | *Ireland.* Small pox.—*Annals of Ulster.*

'13 .... | *Ostergötland* devastated by a great pestilence, "probably a continuation of the *Copenhagen* plague."—Broberg.

'14 .... | *France.* Another epidemy of a similar nature, called "coqueluche," appeared. It was attended with severe hoarseness, and was so general that all public business in Paris was interrupted by it.

'14 .... | *Germany.* Dysentery prevalent.

'15 .... | The *English army* under Henry V was wasted down to a fifth of its numbers by a contagious distemper, before the famous engagement of Agincourt took place.—(Tytler's *Univ. Hist.*, p. 306.) Henry V descended upon Normandy with an army 50,000 strong ; but after the taking of Harfleur, a contagious dysentery carried off three-fourths of his men.—Voltaire, *Univ. Hist.*, vol. ii, p. 35.

'16 .... | *England.* Plague.—Dugdale, vol. v, p. 691.

'16 .... | *Durham.* Plague.—Dugdale's *England*, vol. v, p. 691.

'18 .... | *Paris.* Plague ; 50,000 persons said to have died in five weeks.

'19 .... | *Wales.* Pestilence caused by intense heat.—*Iola MS.*

'19 .... | *Ireland.* Plague, after a hot summer.—*Annals of Connaught.*

'19-24.... | *Scotland.* "A contagious distemper, resembling a fever and dysentery, wasted the land universally, and cut off many victims. Amongst other distinguished persons who died of this disease [were], the Earl of Orkney ; Douglas, Lord of Dalkeith ; and George, Earl of March."—Sir W. Scott's *Hist. of Scotland*, vol. i, p. 263.

Plagues and Pestilences affecting the Human Race—Contd.

A.D.

1421 .... *France.* The English army, before *Meaux,* suffered an epidemy.

'21 .... *Sweden* invaded by the plague, after constant rains and famine. — BROBERG.

'23 .... *Dublin.* A mortality among men. — *Registry, All Saints' Priory.*

'25 .... *Ireland.* Inclement weather, and "loss of people."—*Annals of Clonmacnoise.*

'26 .... *Dantzic.* Famine and pestilence.

'26 .... *Tournay (Flanders).* "*A propos* of the last great picture of M. Gallait, the 'Plague at Tournay,' now at the Vienna Exhibition, the *Revue Générale* says that the period referred to is probably A.D. 1426, when the plague broke out with great violence at Tournay.'—SPECIAL CORRESPONDENT, 1873. [See 1092.]

'27 .... *England.* Pestilence. An earthquake occurred 14th July.

'29 .... *Scotland.* Pestilence. beginning at *Dumfries,* succeeded a dearth.— *Scotch Acts of Parliament.*

'29 .... *Barcelona.* Pestilence. It is recorded that 8*l.* and 16 sueldos were paid to a chaplain for his labours in removing for burial the dead bodies found in the churches and elsewhere—"which would seem to indicate a great mortality."

'30 .... *Scotland.* "Flying pestilence" (*pestilentia volatilis*) appeared at *Edinburgh,* and prevailed until 1432, visiting *Perth* and *Hadding-ton.*—FORDUN and TYTLER.

'30 .... *Italy.* An epidemy.

'31 .... *Ireland.* Plague.—*Irish Annalists.*

'31 .... *Augsburg (Germany).* A great mortality of people.

'33 .... *Spain.* A vast number of people perished. Whether this mortality was caused by intense cold, or by an epidemy, is not known.— VILLALBA, *Epidemiologia Española,* i, 95.

'36 .... *Europe.* "Epidemic coughs, small pox, and fevers swept away many thousands from the face of the earth." There was much rain, and a dearth of corn in various parts of Europe.

'37 .... *Ireland.* Plague.—*Annals of Kilronan.*

'37 .... *France.* Plague raged.

'39 .... *England.* Plague. The Commons petitioned Henry VI that "a sekenoss called the pestilence universelly thorough this your Roialme more comunly reyneth than hath bien usuell bifore this tyme, the whiche is an infirmite most infectif," by reason wherof they asked that the kissing of the king in doing homage should be dispensed with for the time being. His majesty granted their prayer.

'39 .... *Scotland.* Pestilence very severe.—*Chron. Reign James II.*

'39 .... *Sweden.* Plague during this and the year following.

'40 .... *Europe.* An epidemic constitution set in, which affected most of the countries of Europe with several diseases, especially small pox, influenza, epidemic pneumonia, and dysentery. SHORT calls this a "tragical time of great destruction."

'42 .... *Sweden.* Plague and famine.—BROBERG.

'43-50... *Europe and Asia.* Famine and pestilence destroyed millions of the human race, especially in Asia, and in Italy, Gaul, Germany, and Spain. "In Italy, Gaul, Germany, Spain, and other countries, and also in Asia, famine and plagues reigned for nearly seven years."— FLEMING's *An. Plagues,* i, 119.

'47 .... *Ireland.* Plague; mortality unusually great. 700 ecclesiastics said to have died in Meath.

'48 .... *Spain.* A severe pestilence, attributed to excessive moisture and unprecedented heat. Public prayers were offered up at Barcelona on account of the infliction. A great mortality occurred in the army of King Alonso V, encamped in the neighbourhood of Pomblein (? Pombelinho, in Portugal).

Plagues and Pestilences affecting the Human Race—Contd.

A.D.

1448 .... *Ferrara* (Italy). The plague raging at Ferrara, the council moved to Florence, where the union was effected between the two churches.

'49 .... *Italy.* Plague raged for some years. *Milan* is said to have lost 60,000.—WEBSTER.

'50 .... *Spain.* In June, pestilence broke out in the city of Saragosa. It extended to Barcelona, and lasted for two years. On 13th June 1452, the queen, with her court, retired from the city for fear of the pestilence. [Further, see BASCOME, p. 67.]

'51 .... "*Sweden* was visited by a great and fatal epidemic, so fatal as to be compared with the *Digerdöd.* In *Stockholm* alone 9,000 people died."—BROBERG.

'56 .... *Scotland.* Plague.—TYTLER, and *Scotch Acts of Parliament.*

'61 .... *England.* Plague.

'63 .... *Saxony* and *Thuringia.* Plague.

'64 .... *England.* The Thames frozen; a great pestilence.—(STOW, *Chron.*) 200 deaths per diem.—*Sforza Archives, Milan.*

'64 .... *Ireland.* Epidemic colic or cholera.—*Annals of the Four Masters; Annals of Connaught.* FLEMING thinks that this must have been anthrax.—*An. Pl.,* i, 120.

— '64 .... *Stockholm* visited by destructive pestilence, which spread throughout Sweden; bubonic.—BROBERG.

'65 .... *Italy.* Pestilence.

'65–66.... *Spain.* Pestilence appeared at Barcelona. Cadiz was nearly depopulated. Processions were organised to propitiate the powers.

'66 .... *England.* "An infection prevailed in the pestilent air over the dwellers in the land to such a degree, that a sudden death consigned to a wretched doom many thousands of people of all ages, just like so many sheep destined for the slaughter."—INGULPH'S *Chronicle of the Abbey of Croyland,* p. 443.

'66 .... *Ireland.* Plague, superinduced by famine.

'67 .... ,, Plague.

'68 .... ,, Epidemic colic.—*Irish Annalists.*

'68 .... *Parma* (*Italy*). Pestilence.

'70 .... *Dublin* wasted by a plague.

'71 .... *England.* A plague destroyed more people than the continental wars for the fifteen preceding years.

'72 .... *France.* Plague; 40,000 perished in Paris.—WEBSTER.

'74 .... *Valencia* (Spain). A severe epidemy consequent upon excessive heat and drought.

'75–76.... *Majorca.* Pestilence devastated the island. A "morbeira," or board of health, composed of a magistrate, a knight, a physician, a surgeon, a tradesman, and a merchant, was formed by the governor, Don Berengario Blanels, in order to consider and prescribe remedial measures. Quarantine for forty days was established.

'76 .... *Barcelona.* Pestilence seems to have been rife here again, for we read that the Council of One Hundred ordered an imprecatory chapel to be consecrated at St. Roque, and on 13th July a solemn procession took place, in which were exhibited the bodies of St. Severus and St. Innocent. The plague lasted from 27th March until 13th November. — BASCOME, *Hist. Epid. Pest.,* p. 68.

'77 .... *England.* Pestilence.—(WALTER'S *Hist. of Eng.*) Caused by heat. —SHORT.

'77 .... *Dublin* wasted by plague.—HARRIS'S *Dublin.*

'77 .... *Spain.* Leprosy prevailed epidemically.

'77–85.... *Italy.* Epidemic pestilence, attended with buboes.

'79 .... *England.* A great mortality lasted from September (1478) to November (1479), "in the which space died innumerable of people in London and elsewhere."—HOLINSHED.

Plagues and Pestilences affecting the Human Race—Contd.

A.D.	
1480–81....	*Europe.* Heavy rains and floods, followed by disease. Malignant epidemics in Switzerland and southern Germany, and putrid fevers prevalent in Westphalia, Hesse, and Friesland.—(MEZERAY, *Hist. France*, ii, 720; *Annals of Langebek*, i, 195.) Encephalitis in *Germany.*—HECKER.

"The number of *ignes fatui* during this period was remarkable."
'80 .... There was published about this date (1). *A passing gode lityll boke necessarye and behovefull agenst the Pestilence. Sine ullâ notâ.* 4to., black letter, 12 leaves.

(2). *Here begynneth a litil boke, the whiche traytied and rehcrced many gode thinges necessarie for the infirmitie and grete sekenesse called Pestilence, the whiche often times enfecteth vs, made by the moost expert Doctors in phisike, Bisshop of Arusiens, in the realme of Denmark.* 4to., 9 leaves.

(3). *Here begynneth a treatise againste Pestylence, and of the Infirmities, &c.* London, by Wynkyn de Worde. 6 leaves. Woodcut on title.

'82 .... *France.* Two years of scarcity induced a plague. "It raged in the form of an inflammatory fever, with delirium, accompanied by such intense cephalalgia, that many are reported to have dashed out their brains against the walls of their houses, or to have rushed into the water."—(BASCOME, p. 69.)   Febrile cerebritis.—HECKER.

'82 .... *Italy.* Epidemic pleuritis.—HECKER.

'83 .... *England.* The river Severn overflowed: pestilence was the consequence.—BASCOME, p. 69.

'83 .... *Wales.* Sudor Anglicus or sweating sickness broke out in the army of Earl of Richmond, afterwards Henry VII.

'83 .... *Barcelona.* Pestilence again appeared, lasting upwards of a year.

'84 .... *Denmark.* Famine and plague.

'84–85.... *Europe.* Malignant fever in Germany and Switzerland. Plague in Spain.

'85 .... *England.* Pestilence.—WALTER's *Hist. of Eng.*

'85 ....   „   "SWEATING SICKNESS." Epidemic visitations of the "sweating sickness."—HECKER.

"A disease hitherto unknown, which, from its symptoms, was called the 'sweating sickness,' prevailed at this time in Lancashire, and in other parts of the kingdom. Happily the malady, which was most fatal, was of short duration, having made its appearance about the middle of September, and run its course before the end of October in the same year."

"The complaint was a pestilent fever (says LORD VERULAM), attended by a malign vapour, which flew to the heart, and seized the vital spirits; which stirred nature to strive to send it forth by an extreme sweat. If the patient were kept in an equal temperature, both for clothes, fire and drink, moderately warm, with temperate cordials, whereby nature's work were neither irritated by heat, nor turned back by cold, he commonly recovered; and the danger was considered as past in twenty-four hours from the first attack. But infinite persons died suddenly of it, before the manner of the cure and attendants were known. It was conceived not to be an epidemical disease, but to proceed from a malignity in the constitution of the airs, gathered by the predisposition of seasons; and the speedy cessation declared as much."—BAINES's *Lancashire*, i, pp. 442 and 443.

'85 .... *Italy.* Glandular plague.—HECKER.

'85 .... *Milan.* "Black Death."—HECKER.

'85 .... *Spain.* Pestilence broke out in Seville. Heavy rains and inundations in the subsequent winter aggravated it. In the following year it appeared at Saragossa and in other parts of the kingdom of Aragon.

Plagues and Pestilences affecting the Human Race—Contd.

A.D.	
1486	*Germany.* Epidemic scurvy.—HECKER.
'88	*Andalusia (Spain).* " Pestilence prevailed, which must have been very fatal, especially in the army which King Don Ferdinand commanded, although no correct accounts of its mortality are on record."—BASCOME, p. 71.
'88	*Ireland.* Epidemic small pox.
'89	*Low Countries.* Plague raged.
'89	*Barcelona.* A pestilence broke out on 3rd November, and lasted until 16th September of the following year.
'90	*Europe.* Fevers were prevalent in various parts of Europe. A putrid fever appeared, which some supposed to have arisen from the unburied bodies in Granada; and others stated to have been imported by some soldiers who came from the island of Cyprus, in which place this kind of fever was endemic.
'91	*Ireland.* The sweating sickness.
'92	„ " The air grew so pestilential that a multitude of people died of the plague."—*Hibernica Anglicana.*
'92	AMERICAN CONTINENT. " Epidemic variola was unknown to the Indians until it was conveyed to the East by the commercial intercourse of the Dutch; it was also supposed to have been introduced into America by a negro slave of Pamfilo Narvaes, when that Spanish general proceeded to Mexico against his enemy Hernando Cortés. The inhabitants of Zempoala lost great numbers, and 16,000 Indians fell its victims."—BASCOME, p. 71.
'93	*Italy, Spain.* Remarkable outbreak of venereal disease, said to have been introduced from the Indians of South America; but afterwards traced to have been known in England previously.
'93	*Barcelona.* Pestilence again broke out, and lasted from 13th June until 4th October.
'93	*Majorca.* A loimic disorder; called the plague of Boja, from the name of the man who was supposed to have introduced it into the island.
'95	*Naples.* Syphilitic pestilence among the mercenary army of Charles VIII; also in Rome.—HECKER.
'95	*Spain.* Bubonic plague.—*Chron. Monast. Mellic. Pez. Scrip. rer. Austriac.*, vol. i, p. 273.
'95-96....	*Spain.* Pestilence at Saragossa, in consequence of which the king convoked the Cortes in the city of Tarragona. In 1496 a petechial pestilence appeared among the soldiers employed in Granada.
'96	*Europe.* Epidemic scurvy appeared in Germany, Portugal, Ireland, and other countries.
'97	*Barcelona.* Epidemic pestilence raged from about 18th July until November.
'98	*Ireland.* Small pox.—*Annals Four Masters.*
'98	SCURVY. " Juan de Banos, in the first ten numbers of his 'Voyages of the Portuguese to the East Indies,' gives a circumstantial account of a pestilence which seized on the crews of their fleet after they had passed the Cape of Good Hope. This disease was evidently scurvy."—BASCOME, p. 74.
'99	*Europe.* Pestilence in Germany, and disease in many other parts.
'99-1503	„ Pestilence broke out in various parts of Europe, and continued until 1503. It prevailed throughout Britain, carrying off 30,000 lives in London alone. The king and his court retired to Calais. Brussels lost 500 citizens daily. France and Germany also suffered severely. In October, 1501, pestilence appeared at Barcelona, and soon spread to other parts of Spain. The viceroy of Sicily prohibited the entry of ships hailing from Barcelona. This period of pestilence was preceded by very remarkable seasons. The winter was so cold that the brute creation died on all sides; the summer was so hot that the trees were dried up and set on fire

Plagues and Pestilences affecting the Human Race—Contd.

A D. | *Europe—Contd.*

1499-1503 | by the sun. BASCOME remarks that these extreme seasons marked the commencement of a century of malignant disease. Mould, or "plague spots."—HECKER.
This is the earliest recorded instance of QUARANTINE REGULATIONS being instituted in Great Britain.

1500 .... | *England.* The king (Henry VII) and court removed to Calais in consequence of the plague which prevailed throughout the country. In London alone there were 30,000 victims. Bishop Langton died of the plague.

1500-03.... | *Germany.* Signacula and glandular plague.—HECKER.

'02 .... | *Brussels.* Plague.—SHORT.

'03 .... | *France.* A severe glandular pestilence, to avoid which the inhabitants fled to the woods.—HECKER.

'03 .... | *Germany.* Glandular plague.—HECKER.
Cologne. Violent plague.—MOCENIGO, *Despatches to Venice.*

'03 .... | *Sweden.* Plague. People "perceived with terror the spot-like precipitations from the air, known as *Signacula.*"—BROBERG.

'03 .... | *India.* During the spring 20,000 men died in the army of Zamoryn, sovereign of Calicut, the enemy of the king of Cochin, mostly from "a disease which struck with pain in the belly, so that a man did not last out eight hours' time." MACNAMARA is of opinion that this was cholera.—See GASPAR CORREA, *Lendas da India.*

'04 .... | *Ireland.* The second *king's game.* Mortality very great.

'04-23.... | *Lombardy.* Epidemic demonolatria. 1,000 victims burned in one year for sorcery in the district of Como alone. The maniacs accused themselves of horrid crimes.—CALMEIL.

'04 .... | *Germany.* "Encephalitis, putrid fever, and malignant pneumonia." —HECKER.

'04 .... | *Spain.* Plague.—(HECKER.) Earthquake.

'04 .... | *China.* Said to be nearly depopulated by plague!

'05 .... | *Europe.* Spotted fever very prevalent in many places. "Pestilence for several years."—SPANGUENBERG, *Mansfield Chron.*, book i, p. 402.

'05 .... | *Italy.* "First epidemic petechial fever."—HECKER.

'05 .... | *Portugal.* Plague.—HECKER.

'06 .... | *London.* Second outbreak of the sweating sickness.—HECKER.

'07 .... | *Spain* (especially Barcelona) suffered greatly from pestilence. The diary of Ramon Vila states the pestilence to have been at its height in the months of April, May, June, and July. On the 14th of August the court returned to Barcelona, in consequence of the cessation of the plague there. It continued to rage elsewhere however, especially at Cadiz. It is stated that during 1507 and 1508, the neighbourhood of Seville, and indeed the whole of Spain, was overrun with locusts.

'07 .... | *Germany.* Plague.

'07 .... | *Constantinople* ravaged by pestilence.

'08 .... | *Sweden.* Plague.—BROBERG.

'10 .... | *Europe.* A universal catarrh, called in France (where it was specially destructive) "coqueluche," from the practice of covering the patient's head with a cap, the air being considered very detrimental.—See *Annals of the Influenza, Sydenham Society's Works.*

'11 .... | *Verona* (Italy). A plague.

'11 .... | *Spain.* Theomania —CALMEIL.

'12 .... | *Poignez.* Lycanthropy.—CALMEIL.

'13 .... | *England.* Plague.—SHORT.

'13 .... | *Verona* (Italy). A malignant dysentery.

'13-14.... | *England.* Plague. In October the deaths reached 300 a-day.— SANUTO.

Plagues and Pestilences affecting the Human Race—Contd.

A.D.

1513-14 ...	*Edinburgh.* The plague raged with great violence. Regulations were instituted by the magistrates to preserve the public safety. All vagrants were forbidden to walk the streets after 9 p.m.—(*Stat. Account of Scot.*, i, 735.) Shops shut, and doors and windows closed, for fifteen days.—MAITLAND.
'13-14...	*Italy.* An epidemic prevalent. According to Schenkius, a malignant epidemic dysentery broke out in Venice and Padua, through the importation of diseased meat from Hungary.—SCHENKIUS, *Hist. Hanover*, ch. xi.
'14	*Aberdeen.* Pestilence.—*Stat. Account of Scot.*, xii, 20.
'15	*Holland.* An epidemy of suffocating catarrh.—SHORT.
'15	*Spain.* Epidemic pestilence.
'16	*Scotland.* Plague.—LESLEY.
'16	*Germany.* Plague.—DAUBIGNY'S *Hist. of the Reformation*.
'17	*England.* In most of the capital towns half the inhabitants died of the sweating sickness, and Oxford was depopulated.—STONE. "In the beginning of this year (says TYENIUS) raged a pain and inflammation of the throat, so pestiferous, malignant, and contagious, that whoever, within six or eight hours' seizure. had not proper remedies applied, died in sixteen or twenty hours."— (SHORT, i, 88.) The sweating sickness appeared at midsummer.
'17	*London.* Third visitation of the sweating sickness in July.— HECKER.
'17	*Ireland.* Pestilence, continuing until the end of 1528. Succession of wet seasons.
'17	*Europe.* Sweating sickness. An epidemic encephalitiax, or brain fever, appeared in Germany. In *Holland* an epidemic œcophagitis (diphtherita), which only lasted eleven days, caused great terror. "It was so malignant and rapid in its course, that unless assistance was procured within the first eight hours, the patient was past all hope of recovery before the close of the day. Sudden pains in the throat, with violent oppression about the region of the heart, threatened suffocation, and at length actually produced it.". This epidemic spread towards the south, and in the summer appeared at Basle, where it carried off 2,000 persons in the space of eight months. Epidemic disease also prevailed in Spain.—(BASCOME, p. 78.) The *Hauptkrankheiten*, a great epidemic brain fever, raged.—HECKER.
'17	*Hayti* (West Indies). Small pox produced great mortality.
'18	*England.* "The sweating sickness raged with such violence, that several towns lost one-third, and others one-half of their inhabitants; the patient generally dying in three hours after he was seized with the disorder."
'19	*Aix-la-Chapelle.* Plague.—ROBERTSON'S *History of Charles V;* D'AUBIGNÉ's *History of the Reformation*, vol. ii, p. 112.
'21	*Dresden.* Plague.
'21	*Barcelona.* A dreadful pestilence again ravaged the city.
'22	*Rome.* "The Pope has determined not to quit Spain till spring, because the plague is in Rome, though he wishes to be there in order to arrange the affairs of the world."—SANUTO, *Diary.*
'23	*Majorca.* Great numbers carried off by a plague. This is the last one mentioned by Don Vincente Mut.
'23-24....	*Spain.* The city of Valencia suffered from a pestilence, which was attributed to atmospheric poison. In the following year (1324) a bubonic pestilence destroyed 50,000 of the inhabitants of Milan. Xativa was visited by plague, and at Seville occurred the most destructive pestilence that had ever been known there. It persisted for some years. *Rome.* Plague. Pope ceased to give audiences.
'24	*Milan.* Great plague. 50,000 deaths.—HECKER.
'25	*London.* 50 deaths a-day.

Plagues and Pestilences affecting the Human Race—Contd.

A.D.	
1525–30....	*Italy.* Plague.—HECKER.
'25	*Europe.* Sweating sickness prevailed in France, Germany, Holland, Norway, and Denmark.
'27	*Italy.* " Great numbers of the imperial army of Italy were destroyed by pestilence after the sacking of Rome."—BASCOME, p. 79.
'27	*Spain.* Demonopathy. In *Xativa* a pestilence.
'27	*Holland,* particularly in convents and schools, was demonopathically affected towards the middle of the century.—CALMEIL.
'28	*England.* Outbreak of the sweating sickness, designated " *la trousse galante.*" See 1545.
28	*London.* Deadly fevers were prevalent, which, in the autumn degenerated into sweating sickness. " Fourth outbreak of the sweating sickness," in the end of May.—HECKER.
'28	*Ireland.* Sweating sickness.
'28	*Aragon* (Spain). The kingdom was visited by a severe plague, which was attributed, Cardinal Gustaldi relates, to the ringing of the great bell of Velilla.
'28–34....	*Europe.* This period was one of great mortality, consequent upon the exceptional seasons. Petechial (spotted) fevers were very destructive in Italy, great numbers of the French army before Naples succumbing to them. In France the " trousse galante " is said to have carried off a fourth part of the population. Violent remittent pestilence appeared in Amsterdam on 20th September, 1529, during a foggy state of the atmosphere, and after raging with fury for five days, disappeared as suddenly as it arose. The sweating sickness broke out in Hamburg, and spread all over Germany. "In Pomerania a peculiar kind of debility or lassitude affected the inhabitants in the midst of their work, and without any conceivable cause, persons became palsied in their hands and feet, rendering them incapable of any exertion." At Brussels, a disease called " the English disease," carried off many of the inhabitants. To add to the general misery, famine arose in nearly all the countries of Europe. The animals were also affected. In some of the German States the birds fell dead in numbers, with boils under their wings. The river fish in various places became unfit for food, and a disease prevailed among the porpoises in the Baltic.—BASCOME.
'30	*London.* The plague of pest being hot, blue crosses were commanded to be set over the doors of infected houses.—STOW.
'30	*Milan.* Pestilence.
'32	*London.* Plague.—LYTTLETON's *Hist. of Eng.*, vol. ii, p. 181.
'32	*Europe.* Plague in the north of Europe, called in the Swedish chronicles " the great pestilence."—BROBERG.
'33	*Paris.* Plague in September.—TULLY's *Plague.*
'34	*Ireland.* Plague, preceded by earthquake.—*Irish Annalists.*
'35	*Cork* (Ireland). Epidemic disease. Also in Dresden.
'35	*London.* There was published about this date—*A moche profitable treatise agnst the pestilence, translated into Englyshe by Thomas Paynel, Chanon of Martin Abbey. Londini in œdibus Thomœ Bertheleti Regii Impressoris. Cvm Privilego.* Small 8vo., 12 leaves.
'36	*Ireland.* Small pox, fever, and dysentery.—*Irish Annalists.*
'36	*England.* There was published—*Hereafter ensueth a litle treatise very necessary and behouefull as well to preserue the people from the Pestilence as to helpe and recouer theym that be infected with the same made by a Bysshop and doctor of Phisick of Denmarke, and the experience thereof proued by the same Bisshop, and also of late practised and proued in mani places within the City of London, and by the same many folke haue been recouered and cured and therefore a boke myche profitable for all men and specially for suche as be farre from Phisicions.* 4to., 8 leaves. Imprinted at

Plagues and Pestilences affecting the Human Race—Contd.

A.D.	*England—Contd.*
1536	London by Thomas Gybson in the moneth of Septembre in the yere of oure Lord God a thousande fyue hundreth thirty and sixe, and in the xxviii yeare of the reigne of our most gracious soueraigne Lorde Henry the Eyghte by the Grace of God of Englonde and of Fraunce kinge, defender of the faithe and lorde of Irelande and in earthe (next under Christe) supreme hedd in the Chirche of Englande. God saue the Kinge.
This colophon indicates the work of the Reformation in placing the king at the head of the Church.

'36-39....   *Europe.* Pestilence raged in England, and mortal dysentery prevailed all over Europe. The plague appeared in Hungary during the war with the Turks. Excessive heat and swarms of locusts marked the period.

     Note.—Erasmus, who died in 1536, ascribed the plague that occurred in England to the dirty and slovenly habits of the people. The fires were kindled on the floors, and the smoke expected to make its way out by the roof, doors, or windows. Straw pallets did for beds, and logs of wood for pillows.

'39 ....   *England* and *Ireland.* Fever and " bloody fluxes."—STOW ; WARE's *Annals.*

'40 ....   *Liverpool.* This incipient commercial port was nearly depopulated by the plague. About this date Richard Bankes [Rycharde Banckes] printed and published *Tretyse agaenst Pestylence.* This is the earliest treatise on the subject I have met with.

'41 ....   *Constantinople.* Pestilence carried off vast numbers.

'41-42....   *Europe.* Plague in many parts.

'43 ....   *London.* Pestilence.—STOW.

'43 ....   *Hungary.* Plague during the war of the Turks.—HECKER.

'43 ....   *Germany.* Plague and petechial fever.—HECKER.

'43 ....   *India.* Cholera was epidemic at Goa. The natives called it moryxy.—GASPAR CORREA.

'44 ....   *Metz.* Epidemic pestilence caused frightful mortality.

'44 ....   *England.* Severe plague outbreak at *Bristol.—Hist. of Bristol*, CORBY and EVANS, i, 225.

'45 ....   *Scotland.* Dreadful plague in *Dundee.* The diseased were removed to booths or huts built for them outside the town.—*Stat. Account of Scot.* xii, 17.

'45 ....   *London.* The plague, increasing in the city and neighbouring villages, seemed as if it would devour all before it.—CLARKE's *Martyrology*, p. 359.

'45 ....   *France.* Trousse Galante. 10,000 English carried off at Boulogne. —HECKER.

'45 ....   *Scotland.*—Plague raging in *Dundee*, and at *Haddington.*

'46 ....   *Europe.*—The disease called "la trousse galante" caused great mortality. " It was equal in awfulness and mortality to the pestilence which in the days of Moses destroyed the first-born of Egypt. The disease first appeared in Savoy, and extended over a great part of France. It continued until the following year, 1546. Parè, and a Flemish physician, Sanders, describe the symptoms of this malady, which was attended, as in 1528, with the loss of the hair and of the nails. Its attack was rapid and very fatal. Patients at the onset suffered from an overwhelming weight in the body and a violent headache, which soon deprived them of all consciousness, and stupor ensued, with relaxation or loss of power of the sphincter muscles. In most cases an eruption was observed, of which no mention is made in former outbreaks of the malady. Sanders does not, however, distinctly state its nature. 10,000 English residents died from pestilence in the course of this year and the year following at Boulogne. The bubonic plague made its appearance in the Netherlands."—BASCOME, p. 84.

Plagues and Pestilences affecting the Human Race—Contd.

A.D.	
1546	*Scotland.* There was pestilence in *Aberdeen* and a severe visitation of plague at *Irvine.*
'46	*Netherlands* and *France.* Plague.—HECKER.
'47	*England.* Very severe plague visitations at Yarmouth. Weekly collections for sufferers.
'47	*Cork.* A great plague.—SMITH's *Cork.*
'47	*Europe.* Pestilence, especially in England. Holland, Germany, and Portugal. It continued to rage in England and Prussia during the year following.
'47-51....	*Germany.* Mould spots in the north.—HECKER.
'48	*London.* A plague. The court removed to Hatfield. There was published—*A newe Boke conteyninge An exortatatio to the Sycke. The Syckeman's prayer, a prayer with thankes at the purification of women, a consolation at buriall.* 8vo. Imprynted at Ippswiche by me Iohn Oswen. Cum priuilegio ad imprimendum solem.
'48	*Liverpool.* Plague broke out.
'48	*Ireland.* Leprosy and sweating plague.
'48	*Sweden.* Plague.—BROBERG.
'48	*Low Countries.* Plague.
'49	*Germany.* Pestilence und petechial fever. All herbage destroyed by caterpillars.
'50-53....	*Europe.* Epidemic catarrh and dysentery raged in France. A pestilence, attributed to the effects of damaged grain, caused great mortality among the inhabitants of Valencia. Seville also suffered from a pestilence. Epidemic influenza was rife throughout Spain, malignant fevers overran Germany and Switzerland, scurvy prevailed in Denmark, and disease in one form or another infested not only Europe, but the whole inhabited world. Senertus tells us that the spring of the year 1551 was dry and cold, and the summer wet, while " inundations, earthquakes, meteors, mock-suns, great tempests, and summer fogs were noticed."
'51	*England.* " Fifth outbreak of the sweating sickness." Began at *Shrewsbury* on 15th April, and reached *London* 9th July.— (HECKER.) *Bristol* suffered severely, " several hundreds dying every week." *Ulverston* (Lancashire) also. Sweating sickness prevailed to a considerable extent at Cambridge.
'51	There was published—*An Exhortation or Warninge to beware of greater Plagues and Tumults than are yet come vpon this Realme for the Sinnes and Wickednes that hath been and is yet dayly committed therein.* By Giles Couchman. 8vo.
'51	*France.* Influenza.—SHORT.
'51	*Swabia.* Malignant fever.
'51	*Spain.* Plague.—HECKER.
'52	*England.* Edward VI, then 16 years of age, having been attacked by measles and small pox, made a progress through part of his kingdom in the effort to re-establish his health. A letter written from Southampton by the king himself to one of his favourites, Barnaby Fitz-Patrick, concludes thus :—" We thinke it not good to trouble you any further with news of this countrey, but onely that, at this time, the most part of England (thanks be to God), is clear of any dangerous or infectious sicknesse."—WARNER's *Hampshire,* 1795, vol. i, p. 155. Plague. There was published this year, "*A Boke, or Counseill, against the Disease commonly called the Sweate, or Sweatyng Sicknesse, made by Iohn Caius, Doctour in Phisicke. Very necessary for euerye personne, and much requisite to be had in the hands of al sortes, for their better instruction, preparacion and defence, against the soubdein comyng and fearful assaultyng of the same disease.*"
'54	*Rome.* Contagious hystero - demonopathy among the Jews.— CALMEIL.

Plagues and Pestilences affecting the Human Race—Contd.

A.D.

1555 .... | *England.* A fatal hot burning fever.—SHORT.

'55 .... | *Western Europe.* A hot summer with heavy rains, followed by febrile diseases in England and France. Their prevalence increased in the succeeding year, aggravated apparently by a hot and dry summer. The city of Valencia suffered from epidemic variola. Cardinal Gastaldi relates that about this time, when the Emperor Charles V invaded the French territories, pestilence destroyed great numbers of the peasantry and of the Spanish soldiery.

'56–58.... | *Europe.* "Vienna about this time suffered from epidemic pestilence, as also did Holland in the year following; the disease continued until 1558. This disease commenced in the form of influenza in various parts of Europe, and in France, Italy, and Germany; Spain also suffered from its violence, which was greater in some countries than in others, viz., Florence and Tuscany. In France, malignant dysentery was the most predominant malady; agues in Holland, and petechial or spotted fever in Spain; the last-named disease was as fatal as the true plague. A Spanish writer, Andres Laguna, physician to Charles V, Philip II, and Julius III, wrote a work on this pestilence (as did many other eminent physicians), entitled *Discurso breve sobre la Cura y Preservacion de la Pestilentia.* In going minutely into the symptoms described by these authors, we recognise all the symptoms of bilious remittent or yellow fever, synocha, &c., as prevalent now-a-days, and termed ' Andalusian fever.'"—BASCOME, p. 87.

'57 .... | *England.* Fevers rife; the air fatal to many puerperal women; "malignant pox" and spotted fever raged amongst all.—SHORT.

— '57 .... | *Holland.* Bubonic plague. 5,000 died at Delft. FORESTUS (de Peste Delphensi) ascribes this outbreak to mouldy grain, long kept by merchants in time of scarcity. Diphtheria at Alkmaar. It attacked more than 1,000 persons in a single day.

'57 .... | *Spain.* A new disease broke out and continued until 1570, nearly depopulating the peninsula. It was supposed to have originated among the Saracens, after the conquest of Granada, as the disbanded soldiery were observed to communicate the disease to the inhabitants of the cities and towns to which they resorted. It is described by LUIS DE TORRO in his work, *De Febre Puncticulari, &c.*

'58 .... | *England.* Pestilence. 20,000 deaths previous to August.—WALTER'S *Hist. of Eng.*

'60 .... | *Cologne.* Epidemic convulsions.—CALMEIL.

'62 .... | *England.* "Men being sent for the safeguard of *Newhaven*, there broke out such a plague amongst them, that the streets lay full of dead corpses; from thence, this year, the soldiers brought the infection into *England*, whereof died, within the bills of mortality, 20,136."—SHORT.

'62–63.... | *Europe.* Plague in most of the cities.—THUANUS, lib. xii.

'63 .... | *England.* The Earl of Warwick returned with his forces from France, and introduced the plague.--(BOYLE, i, 544.) In one day there were 1,000 deaths.—WALTER'S *Hist. of Eng.*

'63 ...... | *London.* 20,000 (Stow says 17,414) deaths from plague in the city. —DUGDALE. See also SYDENHAM, *City Remembrancer,* and HODGE'S *Loimologia.*

'63 .... | *Europe.* Epidemic disease appeared in many European cities this year. Pestilence again broke out in *Barcelona*, and also throughout *France.* Among the cities which suffered were *Burgos, Frankfort, Magdeburg, Dantzic, Hamburgh, Wiemar, Lubeck, Bostack,* and *Dresden.*

'63 .... | *India.* Garcia d'Orta gives a vivid description of the cholera in Goa. The Arabs call it *hachaiga.*—GASHORN, "*Literature of Cholera,*" *Med. Chirug. Rev.*, 1867.

G

Plagues and Pestilences affecting the Human Race—Contd.

A.D.

1564 .... | *Bristol.* Plague carried off 2,500 persons.

'64 .... | *Europe.* Quinsies and spotted fever prevailed epidemically in various parts of Europe. Pestilence raged in *Barcelona* from June to November (heavy mortality). "The city of *Saragossa* also suffered from a cruel epidemy from May unto December, during which period there died 10,000 persons in the city alone. It was supposed that the disease was introduced from France by means of the clothes of persons who had died there from the disease."

"Dr. Porcell, who was singularly successful in treating the disease, wrote a work on it, and dedicated it to Don Philip II; it was entitled *Informacion y Curacion de la peste de Zaragoza, y preservacion contra peste en general, per Juan Porcell Sardo, Doctor en Medicina, Zaragoza.* The symptoms of this malady were intense cephalalgia, sleeplessness and delirium, vomiting of bilious matter, urgent thirst, nausea, accompanied by pain in the stomach; dissective showed nothing particular in the humors; the gall-bladder was extremely large, and distended with black viscid bile—sometimes, however, it was found empty. There was yellowness of the skin, and a similar tinge was observed internally."—*Vide* BASCOME, p. 89.

'65 .... | *England.* Hollinsworth says, "there was a sore sicknesse in Lancashire in 1565, which was probably some remains of the plague contracted by the English army at Newhaven in 1562."—BAINES'S *Lancashire,* i, 510.

'65 .... | *Ayr* (Scotland). Plague very severe.

'65 .... | *Europe.* An epidemic pestilence became prevalent in France, especially at Lyons. A similar disease appeared in Spain, but did not prove very fatal. The outbreak of the epidemy in January, was preceded by a sharp frost in December; nevertheless we find its origin traced to "gross vapours" in the atmosphere. At first bleeding was the cure adopted; but it was found to be fatal in many cases; so the physicians of Charles IX announced their disapprobation of the practice. In Spain the most effectual preservative was the use of treacle, great quantities of which were accordingly sent by Philip II to Charles IX. WIERUS tells us that this pestilence afflicted all mankind, "depopulating," amongst other cities, *Constantinople, Alexandria, Leyden, London, Dantzic, Vienna,* and *Cologne.* It was preceded by small pox and measles. The disease itself seems to have been an aggravated form of quinsy. *Sweden* suffered severely, *Stockholm* alone furnishing 18,000 victims, and the disease continuing during 1566 and 1568, according to BROBERG.

'66 .... | *Europe.* A pestilence began at *Comorra,* and increased at *Gewer* in Hungary, where the Christian Powers were assembled against the Turks, called in Latin "Morbus Hungariens" and "Lues Pannonica." The victims were generally covered with spots like fleabites, chiefly on the breast. The Emperor Maximilian, whilst carrying on war against the Turks, lost thousands of his soldiers by this disease. A similar spotted-fever prevailed at Paris in 1567. It subsequently broke out in various parts of Europe, and after continuing for three years, degenerated into the true plague, lasting in that form for four years more.—(BASCOME. *Note.*—BROWNE'S *History of the Hungarian Disease.*) Epidemic madness at *Amsterdam.*

'67 .... | "Small pox raging in many countries."—FLEMING'S *An. Pl.,* i, 134.

'68 .... | "*Edinburgh* had a severe visitation of the plague in October, when the magistrates issued orders to prevent it spreading. Those infected seem to have been sent to an isolated place called the muir, probably the burgh muir to the south of the city."—ANDERSON'S *Hist. of Edin.,* p. 22.—See MAITLAND.

Plagues and Pestilences affecting the Human Race—Contd.

A.D.

1568 .... *Holland.* Pestilence followed an inundation of the sea.

'68 .... *Seville.* Epidemic pestilence.

'69 .... *London.* The "plague of pestilence" raged.—STOW, *Chron.*

'70 .... *Poland.* The plague was very fatal.

'70 .... *Switzerland.* In *Basle* a malignant fever carried off numbers. Measles, erysipelas, malignant fever, &c., prevailed in various parts of the world.

'70 .... *Spain* suffered from epidemics called "*febris diaria*" and endorific fever. The diseases were carried to *America.*

'70 .... *Central America.* Great mortality in the city of *Mexico.* See 1572. Dr. Franesco Bravo, a celebrated physician, wrote an extensive work on this subject, entitled *Opera Midicinalia in quibus quam plurima extant scitu medico necessaria quatuor libros digesta.* Also (in Italian) Proposed measures for providing against the infection of the plague in London.

'71 .... *Memmingen (Bavaria).* An epidemy in mankind.—EBHARDT, *Topography of Memmingen,* p. 63.

'72 .... *Ireland.* "A great mortality of men."—*An. Four Masters.*

'72 .... *Dresden.* Pestilential visitation.

'72 .... *Stockholm.* Plague. Quarantine first introduced into *Sweden.*— BROBERG.

'72 .... *South America.* AGRICOLA records a pestilence at *Augusta de Alémania.*

'73 .... *Leyden.* During the siege the inhabitants were obliged to eat horses, dogs, leather, the leaves of trees, &c. A pestilence followed, which carried off half their number.—Sir J. E. SMITH'S *Tour on the Continent,* vol. i, p. 18.

'74 .... *Great Britain.* Plague at *Edinburgh.*—MAITLAND. In *Ireland,* after an extraordinary "hailstorm," which the annals say left lumps upon the skins of those it struck [blains from meteoric or volcanic scoriæ?], a loathsome pestilence ensued. *Dublin,* according to HARRIS, lost 3,000.

'74 .... *Europe.* Severe pestilence prevailed in various parts of *Spain* and *Italy.* In *Savoy* an epidemic madness. 80 monomaniacs were buried in one grave, according to CALMEIL.

'74 .... *London.* During the months of September, October, and November pestilence.

'74 .... *Bristol.* Very severe plague visitation.

'74 .... *Africa.* Pestilence also appeared in *Egypt* and the *Levant,* continuing for three years.

'74 .... *India.* Great pestilence (wabá) and famine in Gujarat, for nearly six months. The inhabitants fled the country; notwithstanding which, grain rose to 120 *tankas* per *man* (or maud), and cattle fed on the bark of trees.

'75 .... *Dublin.* Outbreak of the "Great Plague." The inhabitants retired to the island of Dalkey.— *Hist. of Dublin,* 1818, ii, 1278.

'75 .... *India.* "When Khán Khánán, with his mind at ease about Dáúd, returned to Tánda, the capital of the country, under the influence of his evil destiny, he took a dislike to Tánda, and crossing the Ganges, he founded a home for himself at the fortress of Gaur," compelling his soldiers and *raiyats* to accompany him. Gaur is so unhealthy that, although once the capital of Bengal, it had been abandoned. The people thus obliged to move at the height of the rains were afflicted by many diseases. The pestilence so increased that men could not bury the dead, but cast them into the river; and Khán Khánán, deaf to the warnings of death about him, and "so great a man that no one had the courage to remove the cotton of heedlessness from his ears," after ten days' illness, died.

Plagues and Pestilences affecting the Human Race—Contd.

A.D.

1575-76.... *Italy.* Plague raged in *Milan*, *Padua*, and *Prosperalpine*, being communicated from other places, without any fault of the air or weather, for this year was good and healthy, and all necessaries of life plentiful.—(SHORT.)   Also prevalent in most parts of Europe. —(THUANUS, lib. xii ; and see MERCURIALIS, *On the Plague of Venice.*)   In *Milan* great ravages.

'76 .... *Venice.*   Plague.

'77 .... *Oxford.*   During the summer assizes this year, a disease broke out, which carried off the lord chief baron (Robert Bell), some other judges, the high sheriff, many of the jurors, and numbers of the residents in the town.   Between the 6th and the 10th of July, 510 persons are reported to have died.   The disease was not the true plague, although it was quite as destructive : the physicians, strange to say, were unable to give it a name.   Respecting its origin there were diverse opinions.   See LINGARD, *Hist. of England*, 6th edit., vi, 164, for further details.

Some supposed it to have originated with prisoners who were brought up for trial in a filthy state, and who might have contracted the distemper while confined in their cells, which were at that time kept in a foul condition ; others ascribed it to natural causes, the weather at the time being hot and sultry, and a damp fog constantly rising from the river Isis, near which the court was held. Some maintained that it was contagious ; others contended that it was not.   The period was remembered as " the Black Assizes."

'77 .... There was published—*Orders thought meete by Her Majestie, and Her Privy Councell, to be executed throughout the Counties of this Realme in such Townes, &c., as are or may be hereafter infected with the Plague.*   4to., black letter, 12 leaves.   Imprinted at London by Christopher Barker, &c.

'78 .... *Provence.*   400 demoniacs were burned at *Languedoc.*—CALMEIL.

'79 .... *Europe.*   "The summer was moist and rainy, and was succeeded by a cold, dry north wind ; the winter was open and chilly.   An epidemic catarrh pervaded all Europe ; it began in *Sicily*, and showed itself in *Italy*, *Venice*, and *Constantinople ;* it infected *Hungary*, *Bohemia*, and *Saxony*, and it afterwards prevailed in *Norway*, and raged in *Sweden*, *Poland*, and *Russia*.   The symptoms were violent fever for some days—four or five generally—with pains in the head or chest, and severe cough, terminating in profuse perspiration.   4,000 persons died of it in *Rome*, 8,000 in *Lubeck*, and 3,000 in *Hamburgh ;* and great numbers were carried off in other places by epidemic pestilence.

'79 .... *Marseilles.*   The plague raged here with considerable violence.

'79 .... *Asia.*   One of the most destructive plagues ever known began at *Grand Cairo.*   Prosper Alpinus reports the deaths from November, 1580, to July in the following year—a period of eight months—to have amounted to 500,000.

'80 .... *England.*   "From the middle of August to the end of September raged a malignant catarrh ; it began with a pain of the head and feverish heat."—(SHORT.)   This influenza spread universally.   The outbreak was called "the gentle correction," for though sufferers "for three dais laie as dead stockes . . . yet such was the good will of God, that few died."   Plague at *Gloucester ;* county assizes held at Tewkesbury.   *Scotland.*   Plague at Leith.—CRAWFORD.

Ireland was also visited, and indeed, according to Hooker and others, the English army brought the disease thence to England. See the *Hibernia Anglic.*

'80 .... *Spain.*   Epidemic catarrh broke out in the month of August. Madrid was well nigh depopulated by it.   Variola appeared in the city of Seville, proving fatal principally to children.   Plague followed a year later.

Plagues and Pestilences affecting the Human Race—Contd.

A.D.

1580-81.... *Europe.* Influenza, malignant fever, and small pox.

'82 .... *London.* Plague broke out.

'82 .... *Spain.* Pestilence prevailed in various parts of the country. Cadiz suffered greatly. Dr. Juan de Carmona published a work on the disease, entitled, *Tractatus de Peste ac Febribus cum puncticulis, vulgo tabardillo,* advocating the practice of bleeding from the arm in cases where buboes, carbuncles, and fluxes were all absent.

'83 .... *Europe.* Pestilence continued in Spain. War, famine, and plague caused great havoc in Flanders. Epidemic pestilence ravaged Moravia, and was rife in London, Germany, and Holland. Egypt and Rome also suffered from famine and disease.

'85 .... *England.* Pestilence in *Exeter* gaol. Eleven out of twelve on one jury died.—STOW.

'85 .... *Edinburgh.* "The plague made its appearance on the 4th day of May, and raged till the succeeding month of January, during which time the city was deserted by all who had the means of leaving it." The professors returned to the University about the middle of January, and the students, by an order of Council, were ordered to be at their places upon the 3rd of February.—CHAMBERS'S *Scottish Biography,* vol. iv, p. 166.

'85-86.... *Europe.* Severe winters, hot and dry summers, famine, and universal catarrh prevailed throughout Europe. The plague raged at *Dresden,* and at *Narva* and *Revel,* in *Livonia,* on the Gulf of *Finland.* 6,000 persons died at Revel. THUANUS ascribed the outbreak to the effects of war and inclement weather.

'85-86.... *Spain.* Small pox broke out in the neighbourhood about *Toledo.* It was remarked that old persons only were attacked by the disease.

'85-87.... *Scotland.* Plague at *Perth.*—(*Stat. Account of Scot.,* x, 37.) The plague of pestilence which had begun in the end of the former year, raged in *Edinburgh* and " vehemently " at *Leith.*—CRAWFORD ; and *Leith Council Rec.*

'86 .... *Europe.* Plague in *Flanders, Turkey, Hungary, Austria.*—SHORT.

'87 .... *England.* Manchester was visited with a dreadful epidemic called, from the extent of its ravages, the plague.—*Historical Recorder,* p. 20.

'87 .... *London.* Plague reappeared.

'87 .... *Madrid.* Epidemic small pox broke out in the city and carried off upwards of 5,000 persons in a short time.

'88-89.... *Spain.* A pestilence similar to that of 1583 appeared, and lasted three years, causing frightful mortality in *Seville* and its neighbourhood. In 1589 the plague raged in *Barcelona* from June to December. It was supposed to have been introduced from France.

'89 .... *England.* Plague. *Durham* severely visited.—(DUGDALE, vol. v, p. 69.) The English fleet brought the Hungarian fever from Portugal.—SHORT.

'90 .... *Villadolid* (Spain). Petechial or spotted pestilence.

'91 .... *Sicily.* An epidemy.

'91-92.... *Dresden.* Plague.

'92 .... *England.* Epidemic pestilence prevailed in several parts of the country, especially in *Shropshire.* A drought occurred in the summer ; the Thames was fordable at London. Mortal plague in *London.*—WEBSTER.

'93 .... *Derby.* "The plague of pestilence, by the great mercy and goodness of Almighty God, stay'd past all expecta'con of man · for it rested upon assodayne at what time it was dispersed in every corner of this whole p'she : ther was not two houses together free from ytt, and yet the Lord bade His angell staye as in Davide's tyme ; His name be blessed for ytt."—GLOVER, *Hist. of Derby.*

Plagues and Pestilences affecting the Human Race—Contd.

A.D.

1593	*London.* 18,000 persons died of the plague.—(BOYLE, i, 560.) 6th August. Proclamation was issued prohibiting erection of booths for Bartholomew Fair, and all traffic except in horses, cattle, and wholesale goods. In TULLY'S *Plagues of the Mediterranean* it is stated that the disease was imported from *Alkmaar.*
'93	*Malta.* Plague ravaged the island.
'94–97....	*Spain.* Pestilence was rife in many provinces in 1596. At Seville it continued for four consecutive years.
'95	*Dorchester.* A dreadful plague. So many carried off that living insufficient to bury dead. Looked on as judgment by papists; several popish priests having been executed here in Queen Elizabeth's reign. *Vide* HUTCHINS's *Hist., &c., of Dorset* (1774), i, p. 374. Another edition of the *Orders*, &c., of 1577 was issued.
'96	*Europe.* Pestilence in Germany; and epidemic convulsions upon the continent, similar to the subsequent affection of the *convulsionnaires* in France. SHORT has described "that extraordinary epidemic convulsive contagious disease" from the works of Sennertus and Hortius, &c. See also BROWNE, *Hungarian Disease.*
'97	*England.* Plague. Durham again visited.—DUGDALE, v, p. 69; also *Carlisle.*
'98	*Cumberland* and *Westmoreland* suffered severely this year. On the wall in the chancel of the church at *Penrith* is an inscription giving an account, viz., "A.D. MDXCVIII. Ex gravi peste, quæ regionibus hisce incubuit, obierunt apud *Penrith*, 2,260; *Kendal*, 2,500; *Richmond*, 2,200; *Carlisle*, 1,196." "This plague is mentioned in the register book of Penrith, and also in that of Edenhall." — NICOLSON and BURN's *Hist. of Westmoreland and Cumb.* (1777), ii, 410.
'98	*Tewkesbury* (Gloucester). Plague visitation. 560 died of it. See 1603.
'98	*Germany.* Ergotism prevalent.
'99	*England.* Malignant fevers prevailed throughout the country. *London, Lichfield, Leicester, Kendal, Carlisle, Penrith,* and *Richmond* suffering severely.
'99	*Europe.* In *France* and *Upper Italy* plague. Plague and dysentery in *Venice* and *Padua.* Disease in various parts of the world.— PALLADIO, *Storia de Friuli*, ii, 235.
'99	*Spain.* Plague killed 70,000 of the inhabitants of this country.
'99	*Asia.* Pequ was nearly depopulated by famine and disease. Pestilence raged in *Constantinople*, carrying off seventeen princesses, sisters of the Sultan Mahommed.
1600	*London.* Plague. See MAITLAND.
1600	*Ireland.* The English army of Lough Foyle, under Sir Henry Docwra, were weary and fatigued for want of rest and sleep every night, through fear of O'Domhnaill; and they were diseased and distempered in consequence of their situation and the old victuals, the salt and bitter flesh meat they used, and from the want of fresh meat and other necessaries to which they had been accustomed. They were in consequence seized by a distemper, of which great numbers died.—*Annals of the Four Masters.*
1600	*Spain.* Fernando Bustos describes pestilential epidemics which visited *Granada* about this time.
1600	*Europe.* "A pestilential contagious mortal colic affected all *Europe.*" —SHORT.
1600	*Turkey.* *Gallicia* suffered from epidemic small pox.—MIGNOT's *Hist. of Turk. Emp.* 2:6.
1600	*Scotland.* Plague at *Glasgow* and at *Cumnock.* "It is related in the life of John Welsh, minister of Ayr, that about the year 1600 two travelling merchants, each with a pack of cloth upon his horse, who

Plagues and Pestilences affecting the Human Race—Contd.

A.D.	
1600	Scotland—Contd. had been denied entrance into Ayr, because Mr. Welsh assured the magistrates that the plague was in their packs, had, on their being dismissed from Ayr, gone to Cumnock, and there sold their goods. There followed upon this such a plague in the town of Cumnock that the living, it is said, were scarce able to bury the dead. There are still traditions of the melancholy event to be found among the people."—*Stat. Account of Scot.*, v, 480.
1600 and 1602	*Russia.* Famine and plague, it is recorded, destroyed 500,000 in *Muscovy*, and 30,000 in *Livonia*. In 1602 the summer and winter were cold and dry. "Catarrh and acute fevers epidemically scourged the human race; great famine prevailed for a series of years, the crops having failed for several years successively. In Muscovy the plague raged for three years; parents devoured their children, and cats, rats, dogs, &c., were also used for food; all the ties of nature seem to have been forgotten during this dreadful suffering; the powerful overcame the weak, and human flesh was exposed for sale in the shambles in the markets. Multitudes were found dead with their mouths filled with straw and other filthy substances."—BASCOME, p. 95.
'01	*Switzerland.* The air was loaded with vapours, at the sun rising especially, and trees were loaded with black rotten fruit; dysentery and fever were general.—SHORT. *Portugal.* A great plague. Black round worms crept, living, from people's nostrils.
'01	*Seville.* Plague.
'02	*Scotland.* Plague in *Glasgow.*—*Stat. Account Pest.*, vi, 107.
'02	*Ireland.* Plague in *Waterford.*—SMITH's *Waterford.*
'02	*Spain.* The plague broke out about the middle of March in Jacu, and soon extended to Seville, Madrid, Valladolid, Burgos, Saragossa, Toledo, Cordova, Malaga, Velez, Ecija, Antequera, Granada, Andujar, and other cities.
'03	*England.* Pestilence appeared to have been introduced from Flanders; 30,000 deaths after 17th November.—(WALTER's *Hist. of Eng.*) Other accounts say 56,000.
'03	*London.* 36,000 persons swept off by plague. Some accounts state much larger numbers. The weather was unusually wet, and on the accession of James I the plague raged in London. There died of that disease in one week of July 857 persons. "As the plague was raging in the city and suburbs, the people were not permitted to go to Westminster to see the coronation."—*Hist. Eng.* " The preparations for the coronation of King James were interrupted by a dreadful plague, which ravaged the city with greater violence than any similar visitation since the reign of Edward III." A person was whipped through the streets for having gone to court when his house was infected. During the year 38,244 deaths occurred from all diseases, of which 36,578 were caused by the plague.—BOYLE, i, p. 573. There was published:—(1.) *The wonderful yeare,* 1603. *Wherein is shewed the picture of London, lying sick of the Plague. At the end of all (like a mery Epilogue to a dull Play) certaine Tales are cut out in sundry fashions, of purpose to shorten the lines of long winter nights, that lye watching in the darke for us.* By THOMAS DECKER. (2.) *The Arke of Noah, for the Londoners that remaine in the Citie to enter in, with their families, to be preserued from the deluge of the Plague. Item, an exercise for the Londoners that are departed out of the Citie into the Country to spend their time till they returne. Whereunto is annexed an epistle sent out of the Country to the afflicted Citie of London. Made and written by Iames Godskall the yonger, Preacher of the Word, London.*

Plagues and Pestilences affecting the Human Race—Contd.

A.D.	*London—Contd.*
1603	(3.) *A short dialogue concerning the Plague's Infection, published to preserue bloud, thro' the blessing of God.* 12mo. London.
	(4.) *Treatise of the Plague, containing the Nature, Signs, and Accidents of the same.* By THOMAS LODGE [Dramatist and Poet]. 4to.
	(5.) Another edition of *Orders, &c.,* published 1577.
'03	*Cambridge.* On 9th November a grace was passed for discontinuing the sermons and public services in the university.
'03	*Tewkesbury* (Gloucester). Plague visitation. The "Black Book" of the corporation records that the bodies, "to avoid the perill, were buried in coffins of bourde;" which implies that wood coffins were not then commonly in use.* *Vide* RUDDER'S *Gloucestershire* (1779), p. 737.
	Chester. Plague raged sore from 1602 to 1610. It is notable that Chester was at this time the chief seaport, and in connection with Ireland.
	Ireland. In January, the municipal authorities of the Irish town in the city of Kilkenny enacted preventive laws, *e.g.,* "That henceforth everie day one proper tall man shall stand with his halbert in the oppen streete neere the gates, at everie gate within the Irish town, to keep out all strangers or suspected persons that might come from enny infected place within the kingdom."........"It is also concluded that all the poore people which be strangers in the towne, shall have twenty four hours victualls at the towne charge, and after driven out of the towne." The plague reached *Dublin* in October, and soon after attacked *Kilkenny.*
'03	*Europe.* "The plague raging in *Ostend* and the Low Counties, the soldiers returning from thence into England brought the infection with them to London, and several other parts of the nation.— SHORT.
'03	*Paris.* The plague raged in Paris for three or four years about this time, carrying off, when at its height, 2,000 persons weekly. The physicians believed the disease to have been imported into London from there.
'04	*England.* In *London,* considerable mortality from plague; one account states the deaths at 30,578; another at 68,596. Defoe says the great plague commenced in December of this year, when the bills of mortality began sensibly to increase.

---

* Coffins were not used for the common people at this date, and probably not at all generally so until after the middle of this century. *Vide* SIR HENRY SPELMAN'S *Treatise de Sepultura,* p. 173. In plague seasons indiscriminate interment without coffins was very usual.

> "'Cast out your dead!' the carcase-carrier cries,
>   Which he by heapes in groundlesse graves interres."

—The Triumph of Death, in the picture of the Plague as it was in 1603, by JOHN DAVIES. (1609.)

FULLER, in 1662, writing of the giantess Long Megg, of Westminster, says that the "long grave stone shown on the south side of the cloister at Westminster Abbey, said to cover her body, was placed over a number of monks who died of the plague and were all buried in one grave."

GEORGE WITHER, in his extraordinary poem on the plague, *Britain's Remembrancer,* 1628, says :—

> "One grave did often many scores enclose
>   Of men and women; and it may be those
>   That could not in two parishes agree,
>   Now, in one little roome, at quiet be."

Plagues and Pestilences affecting the Human Race—Contd.

A.D.

1604 .... *Nantwich* (Cheshire). The plague broke out in June, and did not subside till March, 1605. Nearly 500 persons perished.—DUGDALE's *England,* viii, p. 1232.

'04 .... *Scotland.* In *Edinburgh* the plague " raged very vehemently."— (ANDERSON's *Hist. of Edinburgh.*) Also in *Glasgow.*

'04 .... *Ireland.* A visitation of plague. "This year the plague began in Dublin in October, and continued till the September following. It broke out again the next succeeding year, and continued that and the following."—*Hist. of Dublin* (1818), i, 202.

'04–05.... *Spain.* Psuncticular fever became very prevalent all over Spain. In the following year epidemic pestilence broke out in various parts of the country. It was especially fatal in *Arbucias.*

'04–05.... *Bristol.* In 1 James I, "a pestilential disease began its ravages in Bristol, where it continued upwards of a year, during which there died 2,440 persons of the plague, and 516 of other distempers, according to the list of burials kept in the church books."—CORRY and EVANS's *Hist. of Bristol,* 1816, vol. i, p. 387.

'05 .... *England.* The plague spread into Lancashire, and became so extremely fatal, that in *Manchester* alone 1,000 of the inhabitants [according to HOLLINWORTH's *Mancaniensis,* MS.] died, which was probably equal to one-sixth of its population. Other accounts say 2,000. *Vide Manchester Historical Recorder.*

'06 .... *England.* " Heavy rains and inundations of the Severn submerged the country round about Bristol. Epidemic pestilence soon after followed in Somersetshire and Norfolk."—BASCOME, p. 97.

68,596 died of the plague in London.—SHORT.

There was published, *The Seven deadly Sinners of London, drawn in Seven severall Coaches through the Seven severall Gates of the Citie, bringing the Plague with them. Opus septem dierum.* By THO. DEKKER. 4to. London.

'06 .... *Europe.* Epidemic pestilence. Various provinces in Spain suffered from bubonic pestilence, which attacked children principally. Great mortality from it occurred at *Barcelona.* This plague is mentioned by Voltaire.

'06 .... *America.* The pestilence extended to America, where it attacked the company of emigrants taken out by George Popham, who were settled at a place in America called Sagadahor, a patent having been granted by King James to some London merchants to form a settlement there. HUTCHISON, PURCHAS, and GORGES, in their histories of New England and Massachusetts, describe this unfortunate adventure.

'06 .... *The British Fleet.* "It was about this time that a mortal pestilence broke out in the fleet of Sir Thomas Gates and Sir George Somers, who were on their way to Virginia, in America. It was a spotted fever, with yellowness of the skin, attended by bilious vomiting, hemorrhages, &c., symptoms which characterise yellow fever in the present day. It raged with an intensity equal to the true plague : it was preceded by bad weather and gales of wind lasting four days, which, with the crowded state of the ships, was sufficient to account for all their sufferings. The vessel in which Sir George Somers embarked was wrecked on the island of Bermuda, where Sir George died of the pestilence."—BASCOME, p. 97.

'07 .... *Weymouth* (Dorset). There was a great plague here, also at *Melcomb* (same county).—HUTCHIN's *Hist.,* i, 403.

'08 .... *Scotland.* Plague visited *Dunnotar.*—*Stat. Account of Scot.,* xi, 222.

In *Perth,* the magistrates and town council promptly adopted vigorous measures to prevent its entrance into the city. "All communication with the place where it was known to exist was prohibited. Watchmen were placed at the different parts of the town to prevent the entrance of anyone from without, and without the

Plagues and Pestilences affecting the Human Race— Contd.

A.D.	*Scotland—Contd.*
1608	sanction of the magistrates. But every means used was unavailing. Many of the inhabitants were seized with the pestilence and died. Of the number who died no correct account appears to have been kept, but it must have been considerable, as the interments were at the public expense, and places of burial were specially appointed..... Those who conducted the interments received for each 12*s*., and the gravemaker 6*s*. Men, designated cleaners, were employed in examining the suspected tenements, and received for each that they cleaned 13*s*. 4*d*." To show what stringent measures were adopted by the magistrates, we are told that Duncan McQueen was ordered to be imprisoned, with several others, for speaking with David Hunter in Dundee, the plague being there; "and an order was issued to close up the house of James Ross and others, they to remain during the council's will, for having purchased certain goods from John Peebles, of Dundee, who died of the pest."—*Stat. Account of Scot.*, vol. x, p. 37.
'08	*Cork.* An epidemy of dysentery.—WEBSTER.
'08-9	*Italy.* Epidemic colic.—SHORT.
'09	„ In the month of July pestilence broke out in the cities of Citaro, Potraso, Castelnuoso, Padua, and other places of Venice and Albania; in fact, throughout the entire jurisdiction of Ragusa.·
'09	*Spain.* In August the pestilence extended to Seville.
'09	*Bavaria.* The plague appeared in *Memmingen* from July to December. —ERHARDT, *Topog. of Mem.*, p. 63.
'10	*Europe.* Catarrh. Pestilence throughout *Spain*, where also demonopathy raged.—(CALMEIL.) "Garrotillo," a form of scarlatina. [But BASCOME calls it Quinsy. See 1613.]—FOTHERGILL.
'10	*Constantinople.* Plague killed 200,000.
'11	*England.* After a hot and dry summer, plague. *Sherborne* (Dorset) had a similar visitation.
'11	*Germany.* Plague at Hesse and in other parts. Malignant fevers prevailed.
'12	*England.* A dry summer, and a malignant fever.—WEBSTER.
'12	*Constantinople.* 200,000 persons died of the plague.—RIVERIUS, lib. xvii; SHORT, vol. i; MIGNOT, *Hist. Turk. Emp.*
'12	*France.* A plague visitation.
'12	*Germany.* An epidemic in Hesse and other parts.
'13	*Europe.* "Epidemic pestilence occurred in various parts of *France*, and in Montpelier there was a malignant fever, with livid spots and carbuncles. Riverius states that one-third of those who were attacked with it died. At *Lausanne*, where pestilence raged with great violence, there was such an abundance of flies as was never remembered to have occurred previously . . . Pestilence also raged at *Constantinople*, where the physicians, supposing that the *cats* spread the contagion, advised the Emperor, Achmet I, to transport them to the desert island of Scutari. *Spain* this year suffered from malignant sore throat, which raged with such severity that it was considered to have been more fatal than in the year of the *garratillos* (quinsy)."—(BASCOME, p. 98.) At *Amou*, in France, broke out an epidemic of the barking mania, *mal de laira*, which chiefly affected females.—CALMEIL and DELANCRE. (Compare 1341 and 1700.)
'14	*Europe, Asia.* The winter had been very severe, the summer cold and wet, and the autumn variable. "The most deadly *small pox* laid waste Crete, *Alexandria, Calabria, Turkey, Italy, Dalmatia, Venice, Germany, France, Poland, Flanders, Persia,* and *Asia;* it prevailed also with great severity in *England.* In some of these counties measles was also prevalent. The mortality for the natural small pox at that period equalled in fatality the plague in its worst form."—(BASCOME, p. 98.) The most universal small pox ever known.—SHORT.

Plagues and Pestilences affecting the Human Race—Contd.

A.D.	
1614	*Italy.* Epidemic colic.—SHORT.
'14	*Bohemia.* A very deadly epidemy.
'16	*Germany.* Epidemic agues, very prevalent.
'16	*Naples.* Malignant angina. Plague in *Egypt,* the *Levant, Norway, Denmark, Bergen,* and other places.
'16	*Hindustan.* (Reign of Jahángér.) Plague appeared in the Punjab, reached Lahore, spread through Sirhind and the Doáb to Delhi and its dependencies, and reduced them and the villages to a miserable condition. The native chronicles state that it was preceded by two years' famine and a deficiency of rain. Some of the "physicians and learned men" attributed it to atmospheric impurities consequent upon drought and scarcity. Jahángér records the death of one of his nobles in Dakhin from cholera about this time, but says of *this* plague *that it had never before appeared in the country.*
'17	*Naples.* Garrotillo, or quinsy, very prevalent.
'18–23....	*Europe* and the *Levant.* Malta, Naples, Hungary, France, and England suffered from epidemic diseases, such as small pox, plague, &c. Gangrenous sore throat prevailed at Seville. Pestilence appeared at many places in the Levant in 1619.
'18	*North of Europe.* The plague in *Norway, Denmark,* &c.
'18	*India.* Pestilence in Agra, by which "numbers of men" perished.
'18–23....	*North* and *South America.* A pestilence destroyed thousands of the aborigines. According to HUTCHISON the Massachusetts tribe in North America was reduced from 30,000 to 300! GORGES tells us that the disease occurred in the summer and autumn seasons. It was a sort of spotted putrid fever, and must have been of domestic origin, as there was then no intercourse between the Indians and the civilised world.
'21	*Moscow.* Plague.—COPLAND's *Dict. of Med.,* iii, 202.
'22	*England.* Pestilence in various parts.
'22	*London.* Pestilence broke out. It lasted for four years, carrying off in the first year 8,000, in the second 11,000, in the third 12,000, and in the fourth 35,417 persons.
'22	*Amsterdam.* Plague broke out, and is said to have continued eight years.—BASCOME, p. 100.
'22	*Spain.* Pestilence. In July the Council of One Hundred at *Barcelona* received intelligence that pestilence had broken out at *Argel,* whereupon they excluded slaves and goods coming thence.
'23	*England.* Severe plague visitation in *Lancashire;* the deaths in *Bolton* were over 500. Also in *Cheshire.*
'24	*London.* The effect of this visitation upon the city this year was serious in many respects. This may be gathered from contemporary authority: one instance is at hand. In January, 1625, the lords of the council called upon the city, through the lord mayor, to provide a certain specified number of ships for guarding the Thames. The lord mayor and court of aldermen replied, that having taken their requirements into serious consideration, "they begged the council to think of the existing state of the city, after many hindrances, the particulars of which were well known, *and after the late heavy affliction God had laid upon it;* and to free it from so heavy a burden, which its revenues were not able to bear."—*Remembrancia Index,* p. 248.
'25	*London.* "On the 11th of July Parliament was prorogued, in consequence of the ravages of the plague, which swept away 35,417 persons." .... "The Parliament which, owing to the plague, had been removed to Oxford, met in the divinity school, on the 12th of August." .... Towards the end of the year a thanksgiving was offered up in consequence of the abatement of the plague, similar to that which had been observed on the 29th of the preceding January.—(BOYLE, i, 586.) On the accession of Charles I,

Plagues and Pestilences affecting the Human Race—Contd.

A.D.	London—*Contd.*
1622	the plague broke out even more vehemently than at the time of his father's coronation. (See 1603.) On the 31st July, the Exchequer removed to Richmond, by reason of the severity of the plague at Westminster.
'25	*Dresden.* Plague. 9,597 of population died.

There were issued :—

(1) *Orders thovght Meet by his Maiestie and his Privy Councell, to be executed throughout the Counties of this Realme, in such Townes, &c., as are, or may be, infected with the Plague,* black letter, small 4to.

(2) *Solomon's Pest House, or Towre Royall, newly Re-edified and prepared to preserve Londoners from the Deluge of the Plague, for those departed out of the City into the Country, by J. D.; also Mr. Holland's Admonition against the Pestilence; Mr. Phaer's Prescription for Physicke, and London Looke Ba·ke; a Description of the Prodigious Plague in 1625, by A. H.,* 1630. Sm. 4to.

(3) *The Runawayes Answer to a Book called A Rodde for Runneawayes, in which are set down a defence of their Running, with some Reasons perswading some of them never to come back.* 4to. 12 leaves. [This was in answer to a tract by Decker this year.]

(4) *London's Lamentation for her Sinnes, and Complaint tŏ the Lord her God; out of which may bee pickt a prayer for priuate families, for the time of this fearefull infection, and may serue for a helpe to holinesse and humiliation for such as keepe the fast in priuate;* together with a souereigne receipe against the plague. By W. C., Pastor at Whitechappell. London, 12mo.

(5) *Cities Comfort, The; or, Patridophilus, his Theologicall and Physicall Preservatives against the Plague, together with a caveat to those that flie into the country.* Broadside. London. By G. P. [With a curious receipt for the cure of the plague, by Lo. Stourton, in manuscript, dated 1625, an advertisement relative to a specific as a preservative against the plague, &c.]

(6) *Certain Rules, Directions, or Advertisements for this time of Pestilentiall Contagion.* By Francis Hering, Doctor in Physike.

(7) Charles I issued from his Palace at Woodstock a proclamation against the holding of fairs within 50 miles of London, in consequence of the prevalence of this plague.

(8) On 30th December, a proclamation by the king declaring that the contagion having ceased, the citizens of London might freely repair to any *fair.*

'26	*London.* Plague first appeared in Whitechapel.—HODGES.
'26	There was published—*Lachrymæ Londinensis: or London's Teares and Lamentations for God's heavie visitation of the Plague of Pestilence; with a map of the cities miserie.*
'26	*England.* Plague in various parts of England. At *Bridport* (Dorset) the harbour works were stopped.
'26	*France.* At *Lyons* 60,000 are stated to have been carried off by plague. It continued in the city for several years. Some writers date this plague several years later, as 1632.
'26	*Holland.* Plague prevailed in *Amsterdam* about this period; it hung about the city for nearly eight years.
'28	There was published by George Wither, the poet, *Britain's Remembrancer, containing a Narration of the Plague lately past, a Declaration of the Mischiefs present, and a Prediction of Judgment to come (if Repentance prevent not); it is dedicated (for the Glory of God) to posteritie and to these times (if they please).* Imprinted for Gt. Britain, &c. 18mo.
'29	*England.* Plague at *Cambridge.*
'29	*France.* Plague at *Narbonne.*
'29	*Holland.* Plague at *Amsterdam.*

Plagues and Pestilences affecting the Human Race—Contd.

A.D.	
1629	*America.* Yellow pestilence on this continent.
'30	*London.* Serious outbreak of plague threatened.

There was issued :

(1) " Order of the lords of the council directing the lord mayor and the justices of the peace of Middlesex and Surrey, on account of the danger of spreading the sickness, to prohibit and suppress all meetings and stage-plays, bear-baitings, tumbling, rope-dancing, shows, &c., in houses, and all other meetings whatsoever for pastime, and all assemblies of the inhabitants of several counties at the common halls of London . . . . and all extraordinary assemblies of people at taverns and elsewhere."

(2) " Letter from the lords of the council to the lord mayor, complaining that their former directions for the prevention of the spreading of the infection were not observed, and requiring that all infected houses should be shut up (unless the inmates could be removed), and should have guards set at the door, and a red cross or the words ' Lord, have mercy upon us,' painted on the door, that the passers by might have notice." In a second letter, a week later in date, the lords of the council repeat these instructions, adding that if any are disobedient they are to be committed, and that if the disobedience be great the council should be advertised thereof ; and a fortnight later the lord mayor is admonished and required by the council to use all fitting means to stop and cut off all intercourse and passage of people between the city and Greenwich, on account of the great and dangerous increase of the sickness in that "court suburb." Similar instructions are also given in other letters, cutting off all intercourse between the city and Cambridge, Exeter, and other places where the plague was raging ; and subsequently (after the cessation of the visitation) commanding all houses in which " the sickness" had shown itself to be " right carefully disinfected."—*Remembrancia Index*, pp. 5£1 *et seq.*

'30 .... *England.* Plague still prevailed in many places. At *Preston* (Lancashire) there were 1,100 deaths; at *Dalton* 360.

The plague being in Cambridge, a royal proclamation was issued against holding the " three great fairs of special note," viz., those of St. Bartholomew, Sturbridge, and Southward.

There was published :—

(1.) *A Looking-Glasse for City and Countrey ; wherein is to be seene many fearfull examples in the time of this grievous Visitation, with an Admonition to our Londoners flying from the City, and a perswation to the Country to be more pitifull to such as come for succor amongst them.* A broadside, with a characteristic woodcut of the Londoners flying into the country in coaches and afoot. " Printed at London, for H. Gosson, and are to be sold by E. Wright at his shop at Christ Church Gate."

(2) *London soundes a Trumpet, that the Country may hear it :—*

When Death drives the grave thrives.
Coachman runne then away never so fast,
One stride of mine cuts off thy nimblest haste.
London : printed by Henry Gosson.

(3) *Treatise of the Pestilence.* By William Bornston. There was written about this date—(4) *The Historie of the Pestilence, or the Proceedings of Justice and Mercy manifested an the Great Assizes holden about London in the yeare* 1625. *wherein soe many were executed by that Plague, recorded faithfully with many pertynent circumstances for the future benefite of all Three Kingdomes, and dedicated unfaignedly to the Glorie of Almightie God, by George Wither; who being present at that arraignment and deserving death, was acquitted by the free pardon of mercy.* Psal. lxvi, 14 ; xci, 6 and 7 ; li, 15.—A MS. in the Pepysian Library, Cambridge.

Plagues and Pestilence affecting the Human Race—Contd.

A.D.

1630	In *Norwich* St. Bartholomew's Day was observed for special thanks-giving for the deliverance of the city from this pestilence. Collections were made for the poor of Cambridge and Wynndham, where the plague prevailed. That for Cambridge amounted to 164*l*. 8*s*. 8¼*d*.
'30	*Sweden.* Plague. Infected houses cruciated. Continued until 1638.—BROBERG.
'30	*Milan.* Plague, described by RIAPOMONTI in his work *De Peste Medislani.*
'30	*France.* Many provinces of France were afflicted with gangrenous ergotism, a disease which began with numbness of the legs, and ended with their sphacelation.
'30	*Upper Italy.* An epidemy.—BOTTANI, ii, 43 ; RAMAZZINI, *De Contagiosa Epidemia.*
'30	*Spain.* The principality of Catalonia suffered from what we now term Andalusian fever. A puncticular pestilence at the same time prevailed at Guadix.
'31	*England.* Plague prevailed in Manchester. "The Lord sent his destroying angell into an inne in Manchester, on which died Richard Merriott and his wife, the master and dame of the house, and all that were in it, or went in it for certaine weeks together. At last they burned or buried all the goods in the house, and yet, in midst of judgment, did God remember mercy, for no person else was that yeare touched with the infection." — *Historical Recorder.*
'31	*Europe.* An erysipilatous epidemic prevalent. In April a decree was issued in Spain, prohibiting intercourse with France, where pestilence was rife. In the year following intercourse with Narbonne was forbidden.
'32	*Dresden.* Plague continued for five years.
'33	*North America.* Pestilential fever among the Plymouth settlers.—WEBSTER.
'34	*Ratisbon* (Bavaria). Plague.
'35	*London.* Plague in the city.
'35	*Holland.* Epidemic pestilence carried off 20,000 at Leyden.
'35	*Germany.* Prevalent in several parts of Germany.
'35-36....	*Holland.* At Nimeguen, and several other places.—(DIEMERBROECK, *Tractatus de Peste.*) At Leyden the pestilence, carried off 20,000.
'36	*London.* The plague raged with great severity. Above 10,000 persons died of it. The law courts adjourned during Trinity term. It broke out first in Whitechapel, as in 1626.
'36	*Europe.* Rains induced epidemic fever during the summer and autumn in Barcelona and other parts of *Spain.* Epidemic pestilence raged in Holland, Denmark, Egypt, and Constantinople.
'36	*Asia Minor.* Plague prevailed.
'37	*England.* Plague. Great mortality at Northampton.
'38	*Dorsetshire.* Great outbreak of plague at Wimborne Minster, where 400 died ; also at Milton Abbas.
'38	*Spain.* A new disease, which continued for ten years, attacked the inhabitants, principally on the coasts of St. Andrés, Malaga, Puerto de Santa Maria, and Xeres de la Frontera. Burgos, Nieto, Viana, and other cities in the interior also suffered from it.
'38	*America.* Malignant fevers, with small pox, prevailed in North America and along the coasts of South America.
'39	*London* was visited by epidemic pestilence of a severe type.
'39	*England.* A severe outbreak of pestilence at the fort in Holy Island, North Durham.
'39	*Europe.* Outbreak in various places ; mild.
'40	*South America.* Yellow pestilence amongst the Spanish population.

Plagues and Pestilences affecting the Human Race— Contd.

A.D.	
1641	*England.* Plague in various places. At *Cambridge*, 28th September, the Corporation made the following order :—"Forasmuch as the Inne called the *Rose* and some other houses in this Towne are shutt upp, Upon suspicion of the sicknes of the Plague, one having dyed at the Rose of that sicknes as is probably supposed: It is Ordered that the Michaelmas feast shall, for this year, be wholly laid aside."—*Annals*, iii, p. 316.
'41	*Congleton* (Cheshire). "According to an old tradition the plague was brought from London in a box of clothes sent down to a person at North Rode Hall, whose relation had died of the plague in London. On opening the box the family caught the infection and died. From them it spread all over the country, and was presently in Congleton, where it made dreadful ravage. Most of the infected died, and lay dead in their houses, no person coming near them for a long time. When their neighbours were satisfied they were dead, some who had recovered from the disorder, or were more bold than the rest, went and dragged out the dead bodies, and buried them as so many dogs."—From a local MS.
'41	*Ireland.* "Loosenesses," dispnœa (stopping of the breath), sciatica, and stranguries epidemic. English army suffered.—(BOATE'S *Nat. Hist. Ireland.*) Fever and dysentery.
'42	*Oxford.* While the Earl of Essex was besieging Reading, a malignant fever broke out in his army. It carried off great numbers in both armies, and then extended to Oxford, where it assumed a greatly aggravated form, buboes appeared in some cases, as in the true plague. Indeed, we are told that during the dog days the disease was considered and treated as a mild form of plague. It affected all the villages within ten miles of Oxford.
'42–43....	*America.* Pestilence at New Haven and on the banks of the Delaware river in 1642, and at Boston and many other parts of the northern continent in the year following.
'43	*England.* Plague was lingering about. Malignant febrile epidemy at the siege of Reading by the Earl of Essex, which spread upon the dispersion of the armies.—SHORT.
'44	*England.* Fevers, followed by dysentery.
'44	*Denmark.* Plague.
'44	*Spain.* Great mortality from epidemic disease in *Madrid*, following hot summer.
'45	*England.* Plague at Keighley (Yorks); also in *Manchester*; Parliament voted 1,000*l.* for relief of the town. For several months no one was permitted to enter or leave the town. At *Bristol*, during the siege, there was a terrible pestilence, carrying off 3,000 persons.
'45	*Scotland.* At Govan (Lanarkshire) business was at a stand. At *Leith* the victims numbered 2,936, being more than one-half of the whole population. At *Dunfermline* there was a severe outbreak; also at *Falkirk.* The infected were confined to their houses by order of the Kirk Session; also in *Edinburgh.* The plague seems to have appeared at *Perth* also, for in 1645 a house without the Castle Gable Port was burnt, by order of the Council, to prevent the spreading of the plague.—*Stat. Account of Scot.*, vol. vi, p. 693—706; vol. x, pp. 37, 735.
'46	*England.* Plague raged at *Newark, Stafford, Totnes.*
'46	*London.* Plague.
'46	*Ireland.* Plague prevailed.
'46	*Spain.* The city of *Valencia* suffered severely; also other places.
'46	*Malta.* Valetta suffered severely.
'46 (about)	*Greece.* Sicyon (or Basilico). A distemper swept off nearly all the inhabitants, and the place has not been re-peopled since.—*Universal Hist.*, vol. vi, p. 150; Sir GEORGE WHEELER's *Voyages*, book iii.

Plagues and Pestilences affecting the Human Race—Contd.

A.D.	
1646	*West Indies.* Pestilential yellow fever was rife throughout, especially in Barbados and St. Kitts; it has been computed that in the two islands 12,000 perished.
'46	*America.* Epidemic catarrh prevailed, affecting equally English, Dutch, and Swiss colonists.
'47	*England.* Liverpool suffered greatly. Its port-mote court was postponed.

There was published in London, *A Sleeping Sickness, the distemper of the times, as it was discovered in its curse and cure ; in a sermon preached........January 27th, the day appointed for their solemne and publicke humiliation.* By WM. JENKYN. 4to. |
'47	*Scotland.* A pestilence of a highly malignant character spread over the country. It was especially fatal at Largs, a village on the west coast, in the Firth of Clyde. Also at Logie ; in Aberdeen ; and in Glasgow, where the students of the college were removed to Irvine. *Brechin* suffered terribly.—BLACK, *Hist. Brechin.*
'48	*Scotland.* The town of Montrose was visited by the plague. "There was no session or collection in this church of Montrose between the last of May, 1648, and 1st of February, 1649." It also appeared at Dunnotar, in Kincardineshire.—*Stat. Account of Scot.*, vol. xi, pp. 222, 264, 277. At *Kintyre* the plague depopulated the greatest part of the country. When it had subsided the Marquis of Argyle imported a colony of agriculturists from Ayr and Renfrewshire.—*Stat. Account of Scot.*, vol. vii, p. 427.
'48	*Ireland.* Small pox, plague, and dysentery.
'49	*England.* Plague in *London* and in *Shropshire.*
'49	*Scotland.* Plague in Glasgow.
'49	*Ireland.* Plague prevailed.
'49	*France.* Plague visitations ; Marseilles especially.
'49	*Spain* suffered severely, and lost, it is recorded, 200,000 of its inhabitants. Seville (Cabrera remarks) was one entire hospital when the pestilence ceased, about May. Marbella, a port on the Mediterranean, also suffered terribly.
'49	*America.* The town of Boston visited by small pox.
'50	*England.* Plague prevailed in Lancashire, especially at Cockerham.
'50	*Ireland.* Plague and dysentery ravaged the island. Very severe in Dublin. It also raged in the year following, for Ireton died of it at Limerick on 26th November, 1651.—*Life of Anthony A. Wood.*
'50	*Europe.* After an open winter, and cold, wet spring, severe influenza prevailed all over Europe, followed, when the hot weather came, by pestilence. It appeared in *Denmark* in the form of ague ; and in *France*, in that of an inflammatory fever, called by different writers *ignis sacer, fièvre St. Antoine*, and *ergot. Sologne* suffered particularly from it. The cause of the outbreak was found by some in the diseased state of the rye ; others ascribed it to a scarcity of food. The lower classes suffered most. *Genoa* was in a pestilential state. *Spain* in this and the following year was overrun with diseases, *Barcelona* especially afflicted, as usual. Locusts spreading desolation in *Russia* and *Poland*, pestilence followed in their track.
'50	*Leipsic.* Miliary pestilence among puerperal women. Called by German equivalent for frieze, on account of symptomatic cutaneous asperities.—GOTOFR. WELSCH, *Hist. Med. Nov. Morb. Puerp. qui der Friessel dicitur ;* in HALLER, *Disput. Med.*, tom. 5, § 174.
'51	*England.* Plague in *Liverpool ;* about 200, or one-tenth of the population, died. "Sickman's Lane " marked the most fatal spot.
'51	*Paris.* A contagious epidemy.
'51	*Italy.* Quinsey, with oral ulcerations, was very fatal to children.— SHORT.

Plagues and Pestilences affecting the Human Race—Contd.

A.D.

1652 ...... *Copenhagen.* Malignant fever after an unusually dry and hot summer.—BARTHOLINE.

'52 ...... *Saxony.* An idiopathic miliary fever, subsequently known as the "Picardy sweat," appeared as an epidemic.—HECKER.

'52 ...... *Leipsic.* Prevalent and fatal scarlatina.—(CHRIST. JOAN. LANGIUS, *Prax. Med.*, part 2, cap. 14, § 9.) This outbreak often mistaken for the first appearance of miliaria in Europe.—DE HAEN, *de Divis. Feb.* § 4.

'53 ...... *Ireland.* Plague in Galway.—*Life of Bishop Kirwan.*

'54 ...... *England.* Pestilence severe in *Chester* in April.

'54 ...... *Europe.* Severe visitation of plague. It raged in *Denmark, Turkey, Russia, Presburg* (?), *Hungary, Italy, Egypt, Malta,* and *Sardinia.*

'54 ...... The mortality in four cities is given :—

Moscow	200,000	Amsterdam	13,200
Riga	9,000	Leyden	13,000

'55 ...... *England.* Plague in *Colchester* carried off 4,731 persons; also at *Sunderland.**

'55 ...... *Europe.* Various parts of the continent affected.

'56 ...... *Italy.* Pestilence carried off in *Naples* 240,000 persons ; *Benevento,* 9,000 ; *Genoa,* 10,000 ; *Rome,* about 10,000 ; and in the *Neapolitan* territories generally, about 400,000. Cardinal Gastaldi affirms that this was the most horrible pestilence ever experienced in Rome.— *Univ. Hist.,* xviii, 318.

'58 ...... *England.* Prevalent influenza.—WILLIS's *Pract. Phys.*

'58 ...... *Spain.* Severe visitation in *Gerona.*

'58 ...... *Europe.* Epidemic catarrh prevailed in the spring, and in the autumn malignant fever followed. It raged with great severity in *England,* being as destructive as the plague. The seasons were very intemperate. On the day of Oliver Cromwell's death (3rd September), "there arose a dreadful storm in England, which was felt all over Europe, and from its severity seemed to threaten all nature." Cromwell it is said died of this fever.

'58 ...... *North America.* Epidemic disease prevailed.

'60 ...... *England.* Plague prevailed at various places. At *Woodbridge* (Suffolk), 300 inhabitants carried off by the plague.—DUGDALE'S *England,* vol. I., p. 1562.

'61 ...... *England.* An epidemic constitution commenced in England in this year, and lasted until the end of 1664, characterised by continued and intermittent fevers.—SYDENHAM : *Works (Latham Edit.).*

'62 ...... *Northern Europe.* In the cities of *Leipzig* and *Copenhagen* plague prevailed.

'62 ...... *Venice.* Lost 60,000 inhabitants by pestilence.

'63 ...... *Southern Europe.* "The whole *Venetian* territories were seized this year with a malignant epidemic, which infected 60,000 people. They began with horror and a fever ; some died quickly, the rest recovered. It proceeded from monstrous and incredible numbers of small worms."—See SHORT, p. 338.

'64 ...... *England.* Great plague visitation at *Yarmouth,* 2,500 died.

'64 ...... *London.* A malignant epidemy, which subsequently developed into the great plague.

'65 ...... *London.* On 26th April the plague broke out.—(BOYLE, i, 652.) In July the king and court removed to Salisbury. The plague carried off 68,596 souls in London.—(*Ibid.*) In September fires were kindled

---

* The following entry occurs in the parish register of Bishopwearmouth :— "Jeremy Reed, Billingham, in Kent, bringer of the plague, of which died about thirty persons out of Sunderland in three months. Sepult. July 5th, 1665." *Vide* FORDYCE's *Durham,* 1857, vol. ii, p. 402.

Plagues and Pestilences affecting the Human Race—Contd.

A.D.	

~ 1665	*London—Contd.*
	to purify the air, which had continued remarkably calm during the plague.
	The following account of the circumstances attending this last plague visitation in London is compiled from various authorities—chiefly BASCOME and SHORT :—
	    In 1663 a "severe pestilence" prevailed. In May, 1664, it became a malignant fever; in June it assumed an aggravated form; and on the 2nd of November the true plague broke out. The antecedent events were the appearance of a *comet ;* multitudes of flies ; swarms of *ants,* which could be taken from the highways in handfuls ; numberless frogs and insects, which filled the ditches ; eccentric behaviour of animals, which forsook their accustomed haunts ; unusual absence of swallows ; and a *drought* of seven months' duration in the spring. Morton says that for several years before this outbreak of the plague, fevers were prevalent. They were checked somewhat by the cold weather, but always appeared again in other forms. The way in which the plague commenced is described by Mr. Boghurst, a medical practitioner, who resided in the metropolis during the whole period of its prevalence. "The disease spread not altogether by contagion at first, nor began only at one place, and spread farther and farther as an eating' and spreading sore doth all over the body, but fell upon several places of the city and suburbs like rain even at the first, as St. Giles's, St. Martin's, Chancery Lane, Southwark, Hounditch, and some places within the city, as at Proctors' Houses." He says in another place, "This year, 1665, in which the plague hath raged so much, no alteration nor change appeared in any element, vegetable, or animal, besides the body of man, except only the season of the year and the winds ; the spring being continually dry for six or seven months together, there being no rain at all, but a sprinkling shower or two about the latter end of April, which caused a pitiful crop of hay in the spring ; in the autumn there was a pretty good crop, but all other things were healthy and sound, and all sorts of fruits, such as apples, pears, cherries, plums, grapes, melons, cabbages, &c.; all roots, as parsnips, carrots, turnips; all flowers and medicinal simples were as plentiful, large, fair, and wholesome, and all grain as plentiful and as good as ever." In 1666 the disease was extirpated by the great fire. For two years after fatal dysentery was very prevalent.
	    I now resume the detailed narrative.

'65	*London.* The plague broke out about the beginning of May. In the first week there were 9 deaths from it ; the week after, 3 ; and in the next, 14. In June the number increased to 470 a-week, and in July to 2,010 a-week. The first week in September the burials numbered 6,988 ; the second week, 6,544 ; and the third, 7,165. After that the mortality gradually decreased.—(CRUTWELL's *Gazeteer*). In all, 100,000 persons are said to have died in the course of the year (LYTTLETON's *Hist. of England,* vol. ii, p. 592). According to another account (HOWE's *Epidemic Diseases,* p. 110), the victims numbered 68,596. In Pepys's *Diary* (3 Sept. edit. Colborn, 1848, iii, 79) mention is made of the "child of a citizen in Gracious St., a saddler," who was saved by being given by its parents into the arms of a friend, who carried it to Greenwich, they having lost all their other children by the plague, and being in despair of escaping it themselves. There was a picture of this incident in an exhibition of the Royal Academy.
'65	*Derby.* Very severe visitation of plague. No supplies brought into the market, but expedients for the exchange of commodities against each other, or for coin, were devised.

Plagues and Pestilences affecting the Human Race—Contd.

A.D.	
1665	*Derby—Contd.* It was said to have been observed on this occasion that the houses of tobacconists, tanners, and shoemakers were exempted from plague visitation.—GLOVEE.
'65	*Ireland.* The great plague which devastated London at this time, reached Kilkenny, and possibly other parts of Ireland. In April, 1668, the Bishop of Ossory made a grant to one of the inhabitants of Kilkenny of a "messuage or mansion house, uninhabited and ruinous, by reason that the same was converted in the *late* visitation of the city of Kilkenny into a pest house."—(BUTLER'S *Notes* to CLYN's *Annals.*) Petty (then Surveyor-General) says, in the *Political Anatomy*, that there were in Ireland before the great plague, above a million of people, and, alluding to the great mortality of London in 1665, adds: "Wherefore, if the plague was no better in Ireland than in England, there must have died in Ireland 275,000. But 1,300 dying a week in Dublin, the plague of London was but two-thirds as hot, wherefore there died in Ireland 450,000." Again, writing of the same plague, in his *Verbum Sapienti*, he thus calculates the actual pecuniary loss which a State suffers by the diminution of its population: If each head in England be worth 69*l.*, it "follows that 100,000 persons dying of the plague above the ordinary number, is near 7,000,000*l.* (sterling) loss to the kingdom; and, consequently, how well might 70,000*l.* have been bestowed in preventing this centuple loss? and, therefore," he adds: "the late mortality by the pest is a great loss to the kingdom, and estimating the value of the Irish people destroyed between 1641 and 1652 as slaves, and as negroes are usually rated, viz., at about 15*l.*, one with another," he calculates the loss to this part of the kingdom at 10,355,000*l.* The burials in Dublin, as given by Petty, in his *Observations on the Dublin Bills of Mortality*, in the year following (1666) were 1,480. This is the first recorded account of the number of Irish burials, and probably the first Dublin bill of mortality, although Grant alludes to one in 1662. See *Irish Census*, 1851 (part 5, v. i, p. 111), and *Assurance Magazine*, April, 1853.
'66	*England.* There was a plague outbreak at *Cambridge;* Sir Isaac Newton fled before it. It was very severe at South Maperton (Dorset); also at Eyam (Derbyshire). In connection with this outbreak there is the following remarkable circumstance:—The linen of the plague patients was buried without being first disinfected. In 1757 it was disinterred, and the plague revived.—CORBY and EVANS'S *Hist. of Bristol*, ii, 248.
'66	*Europe.* In *Holland* and *Prussia* plague prevailed. "Miliary Pestilence" in *Bavaria.*
'66	*Malta* visited with plague.
'66	*Spain.* Epidemic pestilence in all the provinces. Salamanca and Lisbon are specially mentioned. The symptoms were those of quinsy.
'66	*West Indies.* Yellow fever in St. Domingo and other islands.
'67	*England* (Nottingham). Much greater ravages in higher than lower part of town; attributed to the protective influence of the effluvia from tanyards in the lower part, where there were then forty-seven of them. *Vide* THOROTON's *Nottinghamshire*, edit. 1797, vol. ii, p. 60.
'67–69....	*England.* "Regular small pox."—SYDENHAM.
'68	,, Plague in *Winchester.*—DUGDALE.
'68	*America.* Yellow fever prevalent. Especially destructive in the cities of New York and Philadelphia.
'69	*England.* Measles and small pox rife.
'69	*Norway* visited by malignant measles.
'70	*France.* "Gangrenous ergotism broke out in Aquitaine, in Sologne, and in the Galinois district; it continued until 1674, by which time it had extended to Montargio and the neighbourhood."—BASCOME, p. 111.

Plagues and Pestilences affecting the Human Race—Contd.

A.D.	
1672	*Hungary.* Miliary pestilence prevalent.
'72	*Spain.* Sterility of the land and epidemic disease prevailed. In May the Council of One Hundred were informed that pestilence had broken out on the French frontiers. In May and June of the following year (1673) a mild form of the epidemy (described by Valcarcel as of a tertiary type) appeared in Spain. It increased in malignancy during August, September, and October. Nearly half the inhabitants of Barcelona were destroyed by it.—BASCOME, 111.
'75	*England.* Influenza followed warm autumn.—SYDENHAM.
'75	There was published *England's Passing-Bell; or a Poem written soon after the year of the Plague, the Fire of London, and the Dutch War.* By Wm. Gilbert, Noncomformist Divine. 8vo.
'75	*Hamburgh* suffered from a miliary pestilence.
'75	*Spain.* Epidemic tertian fevers prevailed in *Carthagena.*
'75	*Malta* lost 11,300 of its inhabitants by plague.
'75-76....	*England.* Virulent small pox and measles again prevalent.
'77	*Europe.* Various parts suffered with plague.
'77	*Spain.* Pestilence broke out in Murcia and Carthagena, and prevailed throughout the country till 1679. The capitals of Granada, Cordova, and Seville suffered severely.
'77	*America.* Great mortality from small pox in Charlestown, near Boston, Mass.
'78	*Algeria* and *Morocco* ravaged by plague.
'79	*England.* Cholera first appeared in England.—(BASCOME.) This statement, originally advanced by Sydenham, is refuted by the learned Dr. Wells, who places the epidemic of this year under the head of dysentery, due entirely to local influences.
'79	*Europe.* Pestilence and famine rife in Germany. Pestilence at Vienna and Plague at Dresden. Continued from June to December, 1680.
'79	*Spain.* Great epidemy in Andalusia.
'81	*England.* Bronchial disease prevailed.
'81	*Ireland.* Petechial fever in Dublin and other places.
'81	*Europe.* A mortal angina, which caused death in twenty-four hours, raged in *Italy, Poland, Switzerland,* and *Germany.*
'81	*Sardinia* suffered from disease.
'81	*Spain.* Pestilence first appeared in different parts of *Castile.* It then broke out in the city of *Esmirna,* extended to *Carthagena, Murcia* and *Oran;* from thence spread to *Malaga, Antequera, Granada, Moron, Ronda, Lucena, Andujar,* and other districts, and finally reached *Xeres, Santa Maria,* and *Cadiz.*
'82	*Dublin.* Petechial fever.
'83	*Europe.* The *Hungry Fever* raged, especially in *Germany.* This sickness "began with a coldness," and an intolerable hunger followed. "Most, if not all, that satisfied their hunger died."— (SHORT.) Malignant fevers and epidemic diseases prevailed throughout the continent. The winters were very severe, and the other seasons inclement.
'83	*America.* Fevers and epidemic diseases.
'84	*Greece.* The Venetian army, soon after the siege of Santa Maria, suffered greatly from disease.—FINLAY'S *Hist. of Greece,* p. 211.
'85-6	*India.* War and drought in the Dakhin, followed by pestilence.
'86	*Greece.* The Venetian army, which was encamped in low ground between Tyrinthus and Nauplia, suffered from an autumnal fever, which continued to make destructive ravages after 29th August.— FINLAY'S *Hist. of Greece,* p. 218.
'86	*West Indies.* Yellow fever caused great mortality, especially in the island of Martinique. It was called the "Maladie de Siam," from the supposition that it had been imported from that country. See *Despatches,* quoted by COPLAND, *Dict. Pract. Med.*

Plagues and Pestilences affecting the Human Race – Contd.

A.D.

1688 .... *Great Britain.* Epidemic catarrh. About the middle of May began a fever in London, and all over England, which reached and spread all over Ireland in July. The symptoms were the same in all. It was called the "hot catarrh," and began and ended its course in seven weeks. Though not one of fifteen escaped it, yet not one of a thousand that had it died.

'88 .... *Europe.* "The fever spread all over Europe from east to west."— SHORT, i, 455. See also Dr. Thompson's *Annals of Influenza*, Sydenham Society, 1852; and Forster's *Atmos. Origin of Epid. Disorders*, p. 162.

'88 .... *America.* Pestilence prevailed with great severity in America; it was preceded by hot and moist weather.—BASCOME, p. 113.

'89 .... *England.* Spotted fever, small pox, and other diseases prevalent.

'89 .... *India.* The plague and pestilence which for several years had extended through the Dakhin as far as Surat, broke out violently at Béjápúr, and in the royal camp. Its virulence was such that those attacked gave up hope. The visible symptoms were swellings "as big as a grape or banana, under the arms, behind the ears, and in the groin, and a redness was perceptible around the pupils of the eyes." Thousands lacked burial. This pestilence lasted for seven or eight years.

'90 .... *Europe.* Disease both in the vegetable and animal kingdoms. Miliary or sweating pestilence committed great ravages in Stuttgart, Dusseldorf, Erfurt, and Jena. Epidemic diseases also prevailed in various parts of Spain, especially at Perpignan and Bellagardi. Italy suffered at the same time.

'90 .... *America.* Bilious remittent or yellow fever prevalent. It raged with great violence in Charleston, South Carolina.

'91 .... *York.* In August great mortality occurred in the city, 11,000 persons dying from the contagion.—BOYLE, i, 701.

'91 .... *Europe.* Small pox prevalent. "Not only were young people attacked, but even the aged, and especially those who were pregnant."—(RAMAZZINI, *Const. Epid. Op.*, edit. Geneva, pp. 157—86.) Fever and influenza, travelling westward and reaching *London* and *Dublin.*—RUTTY, *Weather and Seasons.*

'91 .... *South America.* In the town of *Ibarra*, a putrid fever raged, ascribed to the decomposition of fish ejected from the volcano of *Imbaburu.*—HUMBOLDT, *Cosmos* (Bohn), i, 231.

'92 .... *Leicestershire.* There was an outbreak of the plague at Rothwell, which gave rise to the publication of several pamphlets of a controversial nature. (See *Literature.*)

'92 .... *West Indies.* An earthquake in Jamaica destroyed 2,000 citizens of Port Royal; mosquitos and flies appeared in swarms, and yellow fever carried off 3,000 more of the citizens. Yellow fever was also very fatal in the Barbados for several years at this time. It was called "the new distemper, or Kendall's fever."

'93 .... *Europe.* Epidemic catarrh and "a general cough and cold." "It spent its fury in five weeks. It was three weeks sooner in England than in Ireland. It not only affected these, but the whole of the continent, though not all at the same time."—(SHORT, i, 395; WEBSTER, i, 335; FORSTER, *Atmos. Origin of Epid. Disorders; Phil. Trans.*) "The same disease (influenza) appeared in *London* and *Oxford*, and also passed through *France, Holland*, and *Flanders.*" —(MOLYNEUX.) A mildew—"ros valde corrosivus"—is mentioned by HOFFMANN as infecting vegetables this year, whence the cattle died in multitudes.—*Temp. Ann. Insalub.*

'93 .... *Hesse* (Germany). "At the end of July and the beginning of August, besides dysentery and malignant fevers, a certain intermittent fever, like tertian fever, attacked man."—VALENTINI, *Const. Epid. Hassiaca. Ephem. Nat. Curios. Syd. Op.*, edit. Geneva, i 276.

Plagues and Pestilences affecting the Human Race—Contd.

A.D.	
1694	*Scotland.* A plague in the south. It found its way to the parishes of Kirkmichael and Killicudden, in Ross and Cromarty, where it raged with unrelenting fury, whole villages being depopulated by it.—*Stat. Account of Scot.*, xiv, 44.
'94	*Europe.* Epidemic catarrh raged among men and horses in various parts of the Continent. Miliary fever broke out in Berlin, and continued for some time, but was not very fatal.
'94	*The Navy.* The seamen and troops of Sir Francis Wheeler's expedition to the island of Martinique suffered dreadfully from yellow fever.
'94	*North America.* The same disease raged, carrying off the inhabitants of *Boston, New York,* and *Philadelphia* in great numbers. In the following years it was especially fatal in Connecticut and New Hampshire.
'94	*West Indies.* Yellow fever in *Barbadoes* and elsewhere, called *Kendal's Fever.*—BASCOME, pp. 114 and 115.
'95	*Italy.* Apoplexy epidemic through the excessive heat. *Hesse.* Apathæ.
'95	*West Indies.* Yellow fever in Bermuda.
'95	*America.* Pestilence among the American Indians.
'97	*Wales.* "Epidemic of dysentery, which, for more than three years, ravaged the sea coasts of many parts of South Wales, raged so fatally, and caused so much mortality, that in some families scarcely one survived to bury the dead."—JONES's *Diseases of Ireland.*
'97	*Germany.* Epidemic small pox at Augsburg, Stuttgart, Bâle, &c. It continued during the year following.
'98	*France.* Epidemic catarrh.
'98	*England.* Fatal catarrh prevailed. " A severe and awful catarrh." (See FORSTER, *Atmos. Origin of Epid. Disorders,* p. 163.) A fatal spotted fever.—SHORT.
'99	*Spain* suffered again from epidemic disease. It was very fatal in Cerdena. Don Manuel de Alsivia wrote a work describing the malady.
'99	*Europe.* Plague in various places in the *Levant. France* also suffered from pestilential catarrh, and an epizoötic among the cattle, especially among the horses. Capmany describes the disease as being a bilious plague, which at this time prevailed in Liorna, Geneva, Cerdena, Narbonne, and Nismes.—BASCOME, p. 115.
'99	*South America.* The disease was supposed to have been taken out to *South America.* Various parts of the coast having suffered severely from this pestilence, Buenos Ayres especially, it spread to a considerable distance, and Lima was nearly depopulated by it, for it nearly devastated the country, sparing neither Spaniard, white, creole, mustee, mulatto, nor negro.
'99	*North America.* At this period a dreadful disease affected the Anglo-Americans. The inhabitants of Charleston and Philadelphia suffered....." The disease which affected the Anglo-Americans was considered to be similar to, and as severe as, the epidemic which had devastated the Barbadoes a few years previously."—BASCOME, p. 115.
'99	*India. Tatta* (Scinde). A plague carried off 80,000 of the people.
1700	*British Isles.* The barking mania epidemic. Its last appearance here. See WILLIS and CALMIEL.
1700	*Spain.* The civil wars about this time were succeeded by a malignant exanthematous fever, which produced great mortality. It was attributed to the corrupt and irregular habits of the soldiery, the men being of different nationalities. Escobar speaks of the disease as being contagious. "Pestilential angina," says Bruno Fernandes, "was so fatal to children, that at the commencement of this century but few escaped

Plagues and Pestilences affecting the Human Race—Contd.

A.D.	
	Spain—Contd.
1700	its ravages, and the disease was in every way the most fatal that had been experienced for a long time : it was called miliary or sweating sickness at Breslau, and was very destructive to the inhabitants of the island of Milo, in the Levant. In the north of Europe it was followed by small pox. During the subsequent seven years of this century epidemic pestilence prevailed in various parts of the world —England, Scotland, Friesland, the United States, &c."—BASCOME, p. 116.
'01	*Germany.* " The summer induced great relaxation of the bowels. Infants were first attacked in the month of June, more in the month of July, in which month a kind of griping diarrhœa affected adults, and at last *cholera* appeared, with vomiting and cramps in the legs."—CAMERARIUS, *Ephem. Nat. Cur.*, pp. 66 and 67.
'02	*North of Europe.* Plague.—(*Univ. Hist.*, vol. xxxv.) Gottwald traced the origin of the *Dantzic* plague to *Pinozow*, soon after the battle of the Swedes and Saxons in this year.—INGRAM, *Hist. Plagues*, p. 86.
'03	*England.* A very mortal summer.—SHORT.
'03	*Switzerland.* Ergotism prevailed through the cantons, especially at Friburg.
'03	*America.* Small pox and scarlatina raged at *Boston*, and in other parts bilious plague broke out in *New York*, and was very fatal, being termed " the great sickness." Extreme drought prevailed about this period.
'05	*Ceuta* (Africa). An epidemic fever caused great mortality. The appearances on dissection were described by Don Antonio de la Locha, *Protomedicus*, as follows : " The blood was observed to be coagulated in the ventricles of the heart, especially in that of the right side, and also in the vena cava (in the immediate neighbourhood of the heart) ; the pulmonary artery was similarly engorged. In the aorta the blood was also very thick, but in moderate quantity ; the pulmonary veins were nearly empty. These phenomena were not observed in all cases, since in the majority the blood was only thickened and not coagulated ; and the cause of this difference was according to the greater or less degree of power of the malignant ferment." Pestilence broke out at *Tunis* in April, at *Malaga* in May, and in the island of *Cerdena* in August.
'07	*England.* Epidemic influenza.
'07	*Germany.* Malignant catarrh.
'08	*Ireland.* Sir Thomas Molyneux gives an account in his *Memoirs*, of an influenza, and Dr. Rogers, in *Epidemic Diseases*, records epidemic small pox and dysentery, as prevalent this year.
'08-9	*England.* Puerperal fever in *Yorkshire*.—HEY.
'08	*Europe* suffered first from universal catarrh, and then from pestilential fevers. " Lanciscus relates that a similar epidemic appeared and raged with much severity in Italy, principally at *Rome :* he describes the malady as beginning with a running at the nose, or coryza, attended with pains in the limbs, extending over the whole body, but felt more especially in the chest. In the spring, peripneumonia prevailed ; chills and flushes suddenly seized persons, and were accompanied by severe cough, spitting of blood, and turbid, scanty urine ; the respiration was laborious, and a general yellowness of the body was observed."—BASCOME, p. 119.
'08	*America* suffered from the like pestilence.
'08	In *Silesia* and *Poland.* A phthous fever in spring and summer.
'08	In *Dantzic* and in *Seville.* Plague.
'08	*India.* When Bahádur Sháh arrived at Burhánpúr (on his march against Khan Bakhsh), a severe pestilence broke out among the royal troops. Those attacked suffered from such unnatural heat that they generally died within a week, but those who survived the first

Plagues and Pestilences affecting the Human Race– Contd.

A.D.	*India—Contd.*
1708	week recovered. The mortality while the army continued its march was such that pioneers were sent ahead to dig graves ; and when the army halted to camp, "tents were filled on one side and graves on the other."
'09	*Ireland.* Influenza in Dublin.
'09	*France.* In *Sologne* gangrenous ergotism, a fourth part of the rye crop having been infected with the ergot or spur. This disease also appeared in the cantons of *Lucerne, Zurich,* and *Berne.* It prevailed there again in the years 1715 and 1716 ; and epidemically four or five times in ten years at *Orleans.*—BASCOME, p. 119.
'09-11....	*South America.* Various places on the coast suffered from yellow fever. In the Brazilian territory vast numbers of all complexions were carried off.
'10	*North of Europe.* Copenhagen and many parts of *Sweden* suffered from sweating sickness. Stockholm lost 30,000, and Copenhagen 25,000 people between 10th August, 1710, and February, 1711. —(LAUTZLAER, *Mem. du Royaume de Suède,* t. i, 29.) 13,000 perished in *Carlskrona* —(BROBERG.) Pestilence raged in *Lithuania* (Russia).
'10	*Spain.* Dire pestilence. A prodigious number of insects appeared at *Seville* about this time. Disease prevailed among the cattle. ·
'10	*Canada.* An epidemy carried off great numbers of General Nicholson's troops (employed in the reduction of Canada), which were encamped at a place called Wood Creek, N.Y. No cause for the outbreak is assigned.
'11	*England.* Small pox epidemic. There was published—*Discourse occasioned by the Small Pox and Plague now raging, the substance of Two Sermons in Bristol, by* Strickland Gough, minister there. 8vo.
'11	*Northern Europe.* Plague.—*Univ. Hist.,* vol. xxxv.
'12	*France.* At *Mümpelgart,* epidemic, miliary, or sweating pestilence. Catarrhal fever or influenza in various places.
'13	*England. Stirling* "almost laid waste" by an epidemic dysentery, which was "caused by the inhabitants using water wherein flax was laid to steep."—SHORT.
'13	*Ireland.* The Dunkirk Fever, so called by reason of its importation thence by the troops.—RUTTY, *Weather and Seasons.*
'13	*Austria.* The plague.
'13	*Constantinople.* Small pox. INOCULATION was practised at this time.
'14	*Vienna.* Plague.—NICHOLSON's *Brit. Encyc.,* vol. iv, art. Leibnitz.
'15	*Europe.* Small pox and measles epidemic in many parts. Miliary fever at *Breslau* and *Turin.*
'15	*America.* Yellow pestilence prevalent, causing mortality, it is said, equal to the plague in London in 1665.
'16	*Spain.* At *Aquilar des Campos* epidemic variola, consequent upon cold and damp weather, broke out in March, and proved the prelude to a pestilential sore throat, or quinsy, which lasted until December, 1719.
'17	*Scotland.* Fever and confluent small pox.
'17	*Ireland.* Fever and small pox.
'17	*Europe. Germany* suffered from a fatal small pox. Likewise *Ferrara.*—SHORT.
'17	*France.* Jaundice became epidemic at Marseilles, also ergotism.
'17	*Spain.* In the autumn, after extreme changes of weather, jaundice became so general that nearly a tenth part of the population of *Asturias* (Spain) suffered from it.
'17	*Aleppo* (Syria). Plague, 60,000 victims.
'18	*Wismar* (Mecklenburg-Schwerin). An epidemic fever (enteritic) broke out.

Plagues and Pestilences affecting the Human Race—Contd.

A.D.

1718 .... *Switzerland.* Hot weather induced "a variety of rheumatic fevers and pleurisies, as well as diarrhœas and dysenteries," in October and November.

'18 .... *Europe.* An epidemic miliary fever in France and neighbouring countries, particularly *Piedmont*, while England remained almost entirely free from it. It first appeared in Picardy this year, and then became known as the *Picardy Sweat*, being thought analogous to the English sweating sickness.—HECKER.

'19 .... *England.* "One of the hottest summers remembered; putrid, continual, remittent, and intermittent fevers." An epidemic of white hives.—SHORT.

'19 .... *Provence.* Early in the year "all kinds of fevers, small pox eruptions, dysentery, rebellious coughs, and diseases of a gouty character. . . . In March, affections of the lungs; in April, fevers and small pox; in May, tertiary fevers; in August, eruptive fevers on the skin, as if one had used cupping glasses; and dysentery."—SCHEUCHZER, *Beschreibung der Provencalishen von Astruc.* Zurich, 1721.

'19 .... *Peru.* An epidemy commenced at Buenos Ayres, and spread to Central Peru. The disease only lasted a month. It was called by some a "malignant catarrh," but seems to have been a deadly form of typhus.—*Trans. Epidemiological Society*, vol. ii.

'20 .... *Marseilles.* Plague, 60,000 victims, of which 18,000 persons carried off in the month of September. The disease said to have been introduced by a ship from Sidon, which arrived 1st August. "In order to mitigate the disease, the king's ministers commissioned Don Josef Fornós, a native of Hostal-Rich, to proceed to the university of Montpelier, in order to consult with the physicians of that university as to the best means of prevention and cure. All social affection became extinct, the consequences being as dreadful as those of the disease itself. Husbands and wives, parents and children, and the dearest friends and connections, hastened to escape from each other, and an exclusive selfishness took possession of every heart. The symptoms of this terrible scourge were variable: shiverings were often followed by a quick pulse, which soon gave way under pressure. The warmth of the skin was generally natural, whilst a burning heat was felt within, and an almost inextinguishable thirst. The tongue became white, the speech faltering, eyes glaring, face red or congested, and sometimes livid; pains at the heart were frequent; nausea and bilious vomitings, with looseness of the bowels and hemorrhage, were always fatal symptoms. The most characteristic sign of the malady was buboes in the groin or arm-pit, but these were not always attendant, especially when the disease proved rapidly fatal, as was the case in many instances. *Toulon, Aix,* and *Arles* also suffered greatly from this pestilence; the deaths were estimated at one-third of the whole population! In a district of *Provence*, where the population amounted to 247,899 persons, 87,659 perished. Miliary fever was exceedingly prevalent and fatal in the canton de Bray, in Lower Seine."—BASCOME, pp. 121 and 122. See also TULLEY's *Plagues of the Mediterranean;* CHICOYNEDU, *Traité de la Peste;* BERTRAND, *Relation Historique de la Peste de Marseilles.*

Plague caused by filth about galleys and slaves.—(SIR RICHARD BLACKMORE, *Treatise on the Plague.*) Out of 230 galley slaves employed on burials, 220 perished.—(CHICOYNEAU, *Relat. Hist.*) Immorality consequent upon this plague very great.—BERTRAND, *Hist. Rel.*

'20 .... *Provence.* "In January, lung diseases, fluxes, and affections of the limbs; in February, dangerous small pox among children; in March, violent fevers, and inflammation of the throat; in April,

Plagues and Pestilences affecting the Human Race—Contd.

A.D.	
	Provence—Contd.
1720	agues, ophthalmia, and spasmodic diseases. In May and June, when the epidemy in Marseilles broke out, tertiary duplices reigned; in September, all along the Rhine there were extraordinary, and, in some cases, very bad, fevers."—SCHEUCHZER, *Beschreibung der Provencalischen von Astruc*, Zurich, 1721.
'21	*Northern Europe.* In *Silesia* epidemic ergotism during this and the following year. Scarlatina at *St. Petersburg, Courland,* and *Lithuania.*
'22	*London.* A malady, of which the chief symptoms were a sore throat, dizziness, and pain in the limbs, proved fatal to numbers.
'22	*Europe.* Plague caused much mortality at *Vienna,* in *Hungary, Moscow,* and in the *East.* Dysentery raged in *Upper Saxony;* ergotism in *Silesia.*
'22	*Spain.* An epidemic pestilence, accompanied with exanthematous eruptions, broke out in *Granada.* Pestilence fever also appeared in the city of *Placentia.* Dr. Morena found the best remedies to be stimulants, such as wine.
'22	*America.* An epidemic of measles prevailed.
'23	*Spain.* Yellow pestilence prevalent, especially in the cities on the coast. At Lisbon a disease prevailed, the predominant symptom of which was black vomit. Don Vincente Boibid, a celebrated physician of Madrid, attributed these distempers to the use of fruit and snow water. Miliary fever at *Frankfort-on-Maine.*
'23	*Lisbon.* Plague.—COPLAND's *Dict. of Med.,* iii, 156.
'23	*Port Royal* (Jamaica). Deadly yellow pestilence succeeded an inundation in the previous year.
'24	*England.* The Devonshire Colic epidemic and fatal.—HUXHAM.
'24	*Spain* and at *Lisbon.* Yellow fever, attributed to the use of fruit and snow water.
'24	*Frankfort-on-Maine.* Miliary fever.
'24	*Asturias* (Principality). Epidemic catarrh amongst children.
'25	*Europe* and *America.* Malignant fevers.
'26	*England.* A general small pox; a calm, hot, and dry May, which caused remitting and intermitting fevers : then a confluent small pox, from August to June following.—SHORT.
'26	*Granada* suffered from "a series of anomalous diseases," which caused great mortality.
'27	*England.* A fatal and malignant epidemy prevailed in *North Lancashire ;* also during part of the following year. At *Plymouth,* coughs, with great defluxions and swellings of the glands.—SHORT.
'27	*Spain.* Epidemic mania. Dr. Casal mentions the death of many members of the council of Pilona from it.
'27	*Carthage* visited by a pestilence similar to that of 1637.
'28	*England.* Chincough very prevalent. Fevers, quotidians, tertians, quartans, remittents, putrid, and spotted.—SHORT.
'28	*Scotland.* Scarlet fever raged in Edinburgh.
'28	*Ireland.* Chincough and sore throat epidemic in Dublin. Dysentery.
'28	*Europe.* About this period, miliary fever, or sweating pestilence, prevailed with great mortality at *Chambery, Annecy, St. Jean de Maurienne* (Savoy), at *Carmagnola, Vercelli, Ivrea,* and *Biella.* Epidemic pestilence was rife in Poland, Austria, and Siberia. The island of Bourbon, as described by Don Udloa, was afflicted with plague.
'28	*Spain.* Influenza was epidemic. It was called by Pedro de Rotundis, "un catarro sufacativo."
'28	*America.* " Yellow fever was very fatal to the inhabitants of Charleston, United States ; it was termed 'a bilious plague,' from its severity. A similar disease carried off great numbers of the population of Carthagena and Portobello, in South America ; the most fatal symptom was black vomit. This disease made great havoc

Plagues and Pestilences affecting the Human Race—Contd.

A.D.	*America—Contd.*
1728	among the crews of the vessels under Don Domingo Justiniani, and of the galleons under Lopez Pintado."—BASCOME, p. 123.
'28	*Asia.* Plague prevailed in *Tropoli, Damascus,* and *Aleppo.*
'29	*London.* In the month of November people were seized with colds, and afterwards fevers, which carried them off in a few days; 1,000 a week died in London.
'29	*Ireland.* Influenza.
'29	*Europe.* An epidemic catarrhal fever travelled from east to west. It seems to have been the "influenza" of our own day. RUTTY says that the epidemy was in Britain in December, 1728.—(GLUGE, *Influenza,* p. 73.) Intermittent fevers.—RUTTY.
'29-35....	*Europe.* During these seven years pestilence raged in *Vienna, Pignerol, Fossano, Nizza, Rivoli, Asti, Larti, Acqui, Basle, Silesia, Thrasburg (Lower Rhine), Prino, Frésneuse (Lower Seine), Vimeux (Seine et Oïse), Orleans (Loiret), Meaux, Villeneuve, St. George (Seine et Maine),* and in *Bohemia, Denmark, Sweden,* and *Russia.*—BASCOME, p. 124.
'30	*South America.* Yellow fever at Carthagena and Portobello.
'30	*England.* Jail fever first recorded as appearing at Blandford Forum.
'30	*Dorset.* "Sir Thomas Pengelly, Lord Chief Baron of the Exchequer, died here, on his return from the Western Circuit, of the gaol distemper, brought from Ilchester to Taunton by the prisoners. Sir James Shepperd, knight, member for Honiton ; Thomas Morley, Esq., Serjeant-at-Law ; John Pigot, Esq., sheriff of Somersetshire, &c., died of the same distemper a few days before."—HUTCHIN's *Dorset,* i, 79.
'30	*Spain.* A formidable epidemic disease commenced at Cadiz, named the black vomit ("el vomito negro"); it was supposed to have been brought thence from South America, and, extending over the continent, continued its ravages until 1738. It was probably this pestilence which, during the seven years 1729-35, "raged in Vienna, Pignerol, Fossano, Nizza, Rivoli, Asti, Larti, Acqui, Basle, Silesia, Thrasburg (Lower Rhine), Trino, Frésneuse (Lower Seine), Vimeux (Seine et Oïse), Orleans (Loiret), Plouviers (Loiret), Meaux, Villeneuve, St. George (Seine et Maine), Bohemia, Denmark, Sweden, and Russia."—*Vide* BASCOME, pp. 123 and 124. Also, probably about the same date:—
'31	*England.* Small pox epidemic at *Plymouth.* Miliary fevers epidemic, and chincough among children ; in September *cholera morbus* which lasted till October, when the colic prevailed ; also an epidemic fever, with swelling of the neck, among children, in some parts of England.—(SHORT.) At *Blandford Forum* (Dorset), a severe small pox epidemic was raging, when, on 4th June, the greater part of the town was destroyed by fire. The sick patients were removed to the fields, and afterwards placed in tents. None of them died ; but many speedily recovered. This gave rise to the treatment of the disease in sheds and tents.
32	*Foggia* (Naples). Many persons perished from vapours escaping from rents in the ground caused by an earthquake.
'32	*London.* Pestilential fever destroyed 1,500 persons in one week in April. Towards the end of the year an epidemy of influenza affected nearly the *whole world,* travelling from east to west.—(GLUGE, *Influenza,* p. 81.) "It invaded Saxony and the neighbouring countries in Germany about the 15th of November, and lasted in its vigour till the 29th of the same month. It was earlier in Holland than in England, earlier in Edinburgh than in London. It was in New England before it attacked Britain ; in London before it reached some other places westward, as Oxford, Bath, &c. ;

Plagues and Pestilences affecting the Human Race—Contd.

A.D.	*London—Contd.*
1732	and, as far as I can collect from accounts, it invaded the northerly parts of Europe before the southerly. It lasted in its vigour in London from about the middle of January, 1732-33, for about three weeks. The bill of mortality from Tuesday the 23rd to Tuesday the 30th of January, contained in all 1,588, being higher than any time since the plague. It began in Paris about the middle of their February, or the 21st of our January, and lasted till the beginning of their April, or the 21st of our March ; and I think its duration was longest in the southerly countries. It raged in Naples and in the southern parts of Italy in our March. The disease, in travelling from place to place, did not observe the direction, but went often contrary to the course of the winds."—JOHN ARBUTHNOT, M.D., *An Essay concerning the Effects of Air on Human Bodies.* London, 1751, p. 193.

"This epidemic distemper [influenza] spread itself all over Europe, and also infected the inhabitants of America ; so that it was, perhaps, the most universal disease upon record. The first accounts we have of anything like it this last year in Europe was in the middle of November, from Saxony, Hanover, and other neighbouring countries in Germany. It raged at the same time in Edinburgh, and Basil, in Switzerland. It appeared in London and in Flanders after the first week in January, towards the middle of which it reached Paris, and about the end of the month Ireland began to suffer. In the middle of February Leghorn was attacked, and near the end of it the people of Naples and Madrid were seized with it. In America it began in New England about the middle of October, and travelled southward to Barbados, Jamaica, Peru, and Mexico, much at the same rate as it did in Europe."—*Medical Essays and Observations*, published by a Society in Edinburgh. 3rd edit., vol. ii.

This epidemic was made the subject of several other learned treatises.

'32	*Scotland.* Edinburgh was attacked.—*Medical Essays.*
'32	*America.* Epidemic yellow fever.
'33	*Ireland.* Fever, dysentery, and small pox.—PUE. Agues and anginas, followed by sporadic petechial fevers.—RUTTY.
'33	*France.* The Picardy sweat was epidemic at *Abbeville.*—HECKER.
'34	*Great Britain.* Epidemic fever (scarlatina ?). Anginas throughout England.—(SHORT.) Chincough began in *England*, and was epidemic throughout Europe. Scarlatina appeared at *Edinburgh.* Canine madness prevailed.—WEBSTER.
'34	*Egypt.* Plague destroyed many thousands.
'34	*North America.* "An epidemy affecting the throat and respiratory organs nearly exterminated all young children."—(FLEMING'S *An. Pl.*, i, 258 and 259.) Yellow pestilence or fever ravaged America, especially the cities of New York, Boston, Charleston, Philadelphia, and Albany ; it extended also to the tribe of the Mohigan Indians, and was rife in the West Indies. In Barbadoes it caused great mortality. During the winter in North America, which was cold and wet, a distemper affecting the throat and respiratory organs nearly exterminated the young children. — BASCOME, p. 125.
'35	*England.* January was characterised by a continued north wind ; a colic, with severe rheumatic pains, and sometimes a palsy of the arms and hands ; cough, ophthalmia, and erysipelatous fever ; in February a spotted fever, which raged until May ; the summer unpropitious ; fruits did not ripen ; many singing birds died ; very little honey ; the leaves fell in August ; small pox, scab, measles, cholera, diarrhœa, and hydrophobia prevailed.—SHORT.
'35	*Scotland.* Epidemic measles and fever.—WEBSTER.

Plagues and Pestilences affecting the Human Race—Contd.

A.D.

1735 ...... *America.* Epidemic fever, with ulceration of the mouth and fauces.   .

'35 ...... *Europe* and *Asia.* Plague destroyed thousands in Egypt. Various pestilential epidemics raged for more than ten years, afflicting France, England, Scotland, Ireland, Holland, Calabria, Switzerland, New Spain, Aleppo, Tangiers, and Smyrna.

'36 ...... *England.* Influenza. Severe outbreak of small pox at *Nottingham.* The burials of the year exceeded the baptisms by 380. Malignant fever in *Cornwall.*

'36 ...... *Europe.* At *Seville* the lower orders suffered much from disease, especially in the suburban districts. Ergotism broke out in *Silesia* and *Suborth*, and at *Wealtenburgh,* in Bohemia. "Dr. Saine describes the disease as beginning with a disagreeable titillation of the feet, as if ants were creeping on them (formication), which was soon succeeded by a violent cardialgia, or pain in the stomach ; the hands were next affected, then the head ; many cried out that their hands and feet were on fire ; epilepsy was one of the concomitants of the disease."—BASCOME, p. 125.

'36 ...... *Grand Cairo* suffered from a violent pestilence from the 1st of February to the 12th of March. 7,000 were buried daily for some days. The victims altogether numbered 100,000.

'37 ...... *England.* Influenza in the spring. In November *Plymouth* and its vicinity invaded by a disorder which spared no constitution or age. —(HUXHAM.) *Yorkshire* severely attacked.—RUTTY.

'37 ...... *Ireland.* Dysentery prevalent. Chincough and catarrhal fever.

'38 ...... *Spain.* Drought, followed by famine and pestilence. A murderous dysentery spread over all the sea-board of Andalusia. It affected animals first, especially those that were domesticated. Poultry, pigeons, and birds which fed on grain suffered greatly. It was remarked that numbers of the insects called by the Spaniards "largostus" appeared before the outbreak of the disease.

'38 ...... *Tobolsk* (Siberia). An epidemy of pestilential carbuncles, so contagious that the healthy were attacked upon merely approaching the sick.—*Flora Siberic.,* vol. ii, p. 89, Fab , 41.

'39 ...... *London.* A disease known to the Italians and the Spaniards under the name of *Garrotilla pestilentiorum, Angina maligna,* or *Morbus strangulatorius,* appeared in London, and was described by Dr. Fothergill under the title of "the sore throat attended with ulcers."

'39 ...... *Ireland.* Fever and dysentery.

'39 ...... *America.* Epidemic measles.—WEBSTER.

'39 ...... A plague having destroyed the Emperor of Austria's (?) army, peace was concluded with the Turks.—BOYLE, ii, 89.

'40 ...... *England.* Petechial fever and malignant sore throat. Itch prevalent. —HUXHAM.

'40 ...... *Ireland.* A total failure of the potato crop was followed by famine and disease. Very fatal in *Dublin.* Dysentery.

'40 ...... *Europe.* Fevers, attended with convulsions. Epidemic in *Germany.* The "vomito negro" prevalent in *Spain.*

'40 ...... *Asia.* Pestilential carbuncle broke out at *Tobolsk* (Siberia), first attacking horned cattle and horses, and afterwards human beings.

'41 ...... *England.* Catarrhs and anginas. Small pox at *Cirencester* and elsewhere. White hives were very common. This is one of the first notices of infantile *Pemphigus* in England.

'41 ...... *Ireland.* February. Fluxes and fevers, from want of proper food. —FAULKNER'S *Dublin Journal.*

'41 ...... *West Indies.* Yellow fever.—COPLAND.

'42 ...... *England.* Epidemic influenza.

'42 ...... *Scotland.* Religious mania, with convulsions, epidemic.

'42 ...... *Ireland.* "Colds and chincoughs, and the measles."—RUTTY.

Plagues and Pestilences affecting the Human Race—Contd.

A.D.

1742 .... | Spain. "In the archives of the Franciscan Convent of San Diego de Carthagena it is recorded that pestilence prevailed amongst the members, nearly all of whom suffered severely; three only escaping."—BASCOME, p. 125.

'43 .... | England. Scarlatina.

'43 .... | Ireland. Influenza; pemphigus; epidemic angina maligna.

'43 .... | Europe. Epidemic influenza. Plague at Moscow.

'43 .... | Messina (Sicily). Plague ravaged the city. "The dead bodies lay in the streets mangled by the dogs, for want of persons to bury them, as the galley slaves who had been set at liberty for that purpose sickened and died; neither were there any servants, surgeons, or chaplains left in the hospitals to attend the sick." It broke out in Calabria, and threatened the adjacent provinces.— BOYLE, ii, pp. 110 and 111.

'43 .... | Asia. Plague in Aleppo.

'44 .... | Europe. Severe catarrh throughout Europe.—(WEBSTER.) Very fatal in London.—SHORT.

'45 .... | Great Britain. Scarlatina.—SHORT.

'45 .... | Ireland suffered from fever and small pox.

'45 .... | Messina. Suffered severely by pestilence.

'45 .... | Turkey. A murrain amongst the cattle, succeeded by a dire plague. It raged with especial violence in Constantinople. Vide DR. MUR- DOCK MACKENZIE, Phil. Trans., 1764.

'46 .... | Ireland. "In May several inflammations and abscesses in ears occurred, and chincoughs were very epidemic among children."— RUTTY.

'47 .... | England. Putrid fever raged in July.—SHORT.

'47 .... | Spain. In the spring, epidemic catarrh broke out in the territory of Huesca of Aragon; petechial fever succeeded. In the Asturias, an epidemic icterus, or jaundice, attended with malignant fever, caused great mortality between the months of March and May. The weather in March had been very variable.

'47 .... | Constantinople lost 200,000 of its inhabitants by pestilence about this time.

'47 .... | America (North). Dysentery prevailed in various parts, especially at Hartford and New Haven. Yellow fever followed, and continued until the year 1755.

'48 .... | England. An epidemical malignant fever; very fatal in Dorsetshire. Cornwall severely visited by the morbus strangulatorius.

'50 .... | London. The lord mayor, one alderman, two judges, the greater part of the jury, and a number of spectators, caught the jail dis- temper in the month of May at the Old Bailey.

'50 .... | France. Puerperal fever epidemic.—CHURCHILL.

'50 .... | Constantinople. Plague; 70,000 died.—BOYLE, ii, 165. WEBSTER says 200,000.
         Note.—In September, 1751, "an Order in Council was issued, that all ships coming from the Levant into any port of his majesty's dominions were to perform quarantine for forty days."

'50 .... | Fez (Africa). Above 30,000 persons carried off by the plague. 3,000 perished at Tangiers, including the alcaide and British consul. Of 130 Jewish families, only 15 Jews remained alive.—BOYLE, ii, 165.

'51 .... | Plymouth. Malignant sore throat, continuing during the two ensuing years.—HUXHAM.

'51 .... | In 1751 famine and pestilence were rife in the kingdoms of Isen and Cordova. The outbreak was attributed to the arrival of mendi- cants at the port of Malaga. From this period until 1760 epidemic pestilence prevailed in various parts of the globe: dysentery of a malignant type in the Northern States of America, malignant fever in Normandy, gangrenous sore throat in Ireland and France, and a petechial fever in Constantinople, which destroyed 150,000 persons.

Plagues and Pestilences affecting the Human Race—Contd.

A.D.	
1751	Famine and plague carried off great numbers in *Syria, Smyrna,* and *Cyprus.* In the latter place disease destroyed 30,000 victims. *Aleppo, Jerusalem,* and *Damascus* also suffered from epidemic pestilence." 60,000 deaths occurred at Aleppo. "Yellow fever of extreme malignity swept the West Indian Islands and the coast of Africa, as recorded by Lind, who describes the mortality to have been produced by a pestilential vapour which arose in the south-east of the *Guinea* coast, and traversed immense swamps. In several towns among the negro population the mortality was so great that there were not sufficient left to bury the dead, and the gates at Cape Coast Castle were shut for the want of sentinels to guard them, the whites suffering equally with the blacks from the fatal scourge. Yellow fever was also rife in America, especially in *New York* and *Philadelphia.* An atrabilious fever raged at *Senegal.*"—BASCOME, pp. 128 and 129.
'52	*Ireland. Angina maligna.* — (WEBSTER.) Great havoc among children.—RUTTY.
'52	*Switzerland.* Gangrenous sore throat and malignant postula prevalent. Small pox, scarlatina, anginas, and other epidemic diseases common in the human species.—HECKER.
'53	*Dublin.* Raucedo and mumps were epidemic.
'54	*England.* Gangrenous sore throat epidemic.—WEBSTER.
'54	*Ireland.* Petechial fever, and a very mortal epidemy of gangrenous sore throat. Scarlatina.
'54	*France.* Ergotism began at Cologne, and spread through the Llandes, Flanders, and Artois. The epidemy was almost as severe as those of the middle ages.—VERHEYEN, *Dict. de Med., &c., Vet.*
'54	*America.* Gangrenous sore throat.
'55	*England.* Catarrhs and malignant sore throat were prevalent.—WEBSTER.
'55	*Algiers.* The plague raged so dreadfully that the European consuls and merchants shut themselves up in their houses.—BOYLE's *Chron.,* ii, 211.
'56–7	*Ireland.* Agues, influenza, fever, dysentery, small pox, scurvy, and diseases of the eye, followed famine.
'56	*Constantinople.* July. Plague raged violently.—BOYLE's *Chron.,*ii, 214.
'57	*Europe.* Dysentery and putrid fevers prevalent in many countries.
'57	*Constantinople.* February. The plague broke out again and carried off great numbers. Prince Mahomet, the heir to the Ottoman throne, died of it.—BOYLE, ii, 218.
'58	*Ireland.* Gangrenous sore throat.
'58	*Scotland.* Influenza in the north during September and October.—(WHYTT, *Medical Obs. and Inquiries,* vol. ii, p. 192.) Prevailed at *Edinburgh* to an unparalleled extent.—*Memoirs, Med. Phil. Soc.*
'58	*Smyrna.* September. Plague.—BOYLE, ii, 230.
'59	*England.* Violent and fatal epidemy of contagious scarlatina.—SHORT.
'59	*Ireland.* Dysentery.—RUTTER.
'59	*Copenhagen* devastated by small pox.
'59	*Peru.* An epidemy commenced in the same way and at the same place as that of 1720.—UNANUAE, *Sobre el Clima de Lima, Trans. Epid. Soc.,* vol. ii.
'60	*England.* In *Cleveland* (Yorkshire). Scarlatina, sometimes complicated with malignant sore throat.
'60	*Scotland.* Puerperal fever was epidemic in *Aberdeen* this year and the following.—GORDON, *Puerp. Fever.*
'60	*Ireland.* Ophthalmia.
'60	*Spain* (Carthagena) suffered from a tertian fever, which became very virulent during the dog days, causing great mortality in the city and adjoining provinces. The epidemic lasted until 1763.

Plagues and Pestilences affecting the Human Race—Contd.

A.D.

1760 .... *Cyprus.* Plague. "Many places were left so destitute of inhabitants as not to have enough left to gather the fruits of the earth." The plague ceased in July.

'60 .... *Ottoman Empire.* Plague prevailed at Constantinople, Aleppo, Smyrna, Salonica, Broussa, Aden, Antioch, Antab, Killis Ourfah, Diarbekr, Mensel, Jerusalem, Damascus, and many other large towns and villages in the *Ottoman Empire.* The Frank settlements on the sea coast of Syria were exempt, with the exception of Tripoli and Scanderoon. At the latter place the plague appeared for the first time in the century.
     This plague " was one of the most malignant and fatal that Syria ever experienced, for it scarcely made its appearance in any part of the body when it carried off the patient."—ABBE MARITI, *Travels through Syria, Cyprus, and Palestine,* vol. i, pp. 278—96.

'61 .... *England.* Unusual seasons. Influenza appeared, and "sometimes proved periodical and of the tertian type." "It nowhere observed any fixed law, but pursued its uncertain course in a desultory manner; yet infecting cities and large towns earlier than the surrounding villages."—BAKER, *Treatise on Epid. Catarrhs and Dys.*

'61 .... *Scotland.* Influenza of the same type as in *England.*

'61 .... *Ireland.* Cholera morbus, inflammation of the bowels, and bilious purgings, were very frequent. Petechial fever epidemic among the soldiers, but favourable.—SIMS, *Observations on Epid. Disord.*

'61 .... *Toulon* (France). The epidemic distemper, which lasted two months, carried off one-third of the inhabitants.

'61 .... *Venice.* Virulent influenza.

'61 .... *America.* In the north severe catarrh prevailed in the spring; yellow fever ensued in the summer and autumn.

'61 .... *West Indies.* Yellow fever prevalent.

'62 .... *Europe.* An epidemy of catarrhal fever or influenza. Pestilence in France.

'62 .... *England.* In the *Phil. Trans.* for this year a case of ergotism which occurred in Suffolk is described by Dr. Charlton Wollaston, F.R.S. It was confined to one family, and seemed to have arisen from bread made of spoiled wheat. "Many people have been lately afflicted by colds, which attacked them with violent pains in the stomach, head and bones. It is the opinion of the faculty that it is in the air, the distemper being so common."—(*Annual Register.*) Seldom fatal.—(RUTTY.) This was known as the " wormy year." —THOMPSON, *Annals of Influenza.*

'62 .... *Edinburgh.* Influenza.—WEBSTER.

'62 .... *Ireland.* Scarlatina was common in the beginning of May. The weather was very wet. In *Dublin,* about the middle of May, began the catarrhal fever or feverish cold, scarce sparing a family, or any age, sex, or condition, except that it rather spared children.

'62 .... *Copenhagen.* Influenza.—RUTTY.

'62 .... *North America.* Great heat and drought prevailed. Bilious remittent fever raged in the following autumn, especially at *Philadelphia.* A similar epidemic caused great mortality at *Havannah.*

'62 .... *The East.* Pestilence was prevalent in Siam, Bengal, Syria, and various parts of Egypt.

'63 .... *Europe.* Epizoötic diseases in France, Spain, Italy, Denmark, and Sweden, followed by pestilence. Malignant fever, after a famine, destroyed it is said 20,000 of the inhabitants of Naples.

'63 .... *North American Indians.* Several epidemics. The Nantucket Indians were attacked by a bilious fever, which was very fatal. It broke out in the autumn. White people were not affected.— WEBSTER, i, 412.

'64 .... *Scotland.* Much disease.

Plagues and Pestilences affecting the Human Race—Contd.

A.D.

1764 .... *Ireland.* A disease characterised by all the symptoms of yellow fever.

'64 .... *Austria.* Lethal epidemic disease.

'64 .... *Copenhagen.* Plague.

'64 .... *Holstein.* Plague.

'64 .... *Spain.* A miliary fever, attributed to the distress arising from the Portuguese war, broke out in the principality of Estremadura and extended to various other parts of the country, proving especially fatal at Cadiz. Carthagena suffered from tertian fevers consequent upon heavy rains during the months of April and May. 2,000 deaths occurred in the city in those two months. Pestilence was prevalent about this time in *Swabia.*

'64 .... *Italy.* Famine and plague.

'64 .... *Naples.* Plague.—COPLAND's *Dict. of Med.,* i, 777.

'64 .... *America.* Yellow fever distemper.

'65 .... *Scotland.* Dysentery prevalent.—WEBSTER.

'65 .... *India.* Much sickness prevalent.—ANNESLEY, *Diseases of India.*

'66 .... *Ireland.* A vesicatory fever.—(MCBRIDE's *Practice of Physic.*) Seemingly *Pemphigus gangrænosus.*

'66 .... *Europe.* Malignant catarrh. In the preceding winter the temperature fell to − 20°

'67 .... *Ireland.* Influenza and puerperal fever.—MCBRIDE and CLARKE.

'67 .... *Europe.* Catarrhal fever (influenza) spread from Madrid over the greater part of Europe. It was not remarkably fatal.

'67 .... *France.* Scarlatina prevalent.

'67 .... *Normandy.* Puerperal fever.

'67 .... *China.* Small pox destroyed 100,000, principally young children; chiefly in *Pekin.*

'68 .... *Ireland.* Influenza severe.—O'BRIEN.

'69 .... *Leyden.* Malignant fever.—SILVIUS DE LA BOE.

'68 .... *Carthagena* again visited by violent pestilence.

'68 .... *America.* Hydrophobia very frequent.

'69 .... *England.* There was published—*The City Remembrancer of the Great Plague,* 1665, &c.

'69 .... *Egypt.* "Those diseases which in mankind could be attributed to the use of unwholesome bread, were frequent."—FLEMING's *An. Pl.,* i, 429.

'69 .... *America.* "Vast numbers of caterpillars infested Northampton and Massachusetts, and destroyed all traces of verdure. The summer following was hot and rainy. Small pox, dysentery, and hydrophobia prevailed in Boston" and elsewhere; anginas were also rife. Yellow pestilence raged in the island of *Jamaica.*—BASCOME, p. 133.

'69 .... *India.* Famine and pestilence carried off this year upwards of 3,000,000 of the inhabitants of *Bengal.* Want of rain caused the failure of the grain crops, and famine ensued.

'70 ...... *England.* Ulcerous sore throat epidemic at *Manchester.*

'70 .... *Europe.* In *Poland* and *Russia* 20,000 persons died of famine and pestilence. In *Bohemia* 168,000 persons succumbed to disease. For some weeks tertian fever broke out at *Carthagena;* pestilence again appeared in the convent of St. Diego; and puerperal fever became fatally epidemic at *Vienna.*

'70 .... *India.* Cholera was endemic among the natives in the Amboo Valley, in Arcot, and throughout the Travancore country.—CURTIS.

'70 .... *Turkey.* Pestilence afflicted the frontiers and the adjoining provinces of Podolia, Volhynia, and the Ukraine. It is said to have swept off 250,000 of the inhabitants.

'70 .... *Constantinople.* Plague. More than 1,000 deaths per day.—BOYLE, ii, 258.

I

Plagues and Pestilences affecting the Human Race—Contd.

A.D.

1770 .... *Siberia* (?). A disease producing boils and ulcers, called by the people *Moravia Vasva* or plague. It was only a gangrenous esquinancy. See PALLAS's *Voyages dans Plusieurs Provinces de l'Empire de Russie*, vols. iii and iv.

'70 .... *West Indies. St. Domingo.* The cod fishery failing, the Spanish colonists were compelled to salt or smoke the flesh of their cattle, which were dead or dying of anthrax, said to have been caused by mephitic vapours from an earthquake. A carbuncular epidemy resulted, and carried off more than 15,000 black and white people in six weeks.—LYELL PLACIDE JUSTIN, *Hist. d'Hayti*, p. 120.

'70 .... *America.* Anginas and catarrhs.

'71 .... *Ireland.* An epidemic nervous fever, "entirely different from any of those formerly mentioned, and claiming the prerogative of the plague," almost all other disorders vanishing before it.—SIMS's *Observations.*

'71 .... *Wallachia.* Plague.

'71 .... *Germany.* An epidemy of ergotism.

'71 .... *Moscow.* Plague; treated in SAMOILOWITZ *Sur la Peste.* Reinfection frequent.—MERTEUS, *Obs. Med.*, p. 123.

'72 .... *Scotland.* Small pox.

'72 .... *Spain.* Pestilence.

'72 .... *Moscow.* The plague, it is said, carried off 133,299 persons within eighteen months.

'72 .... *Persia.* At *Bussora* and *Bagdad* 80,000 fell victims to plague, and in the whole peninsula of the Ganges, famine and disease destroyed vast numbers of lives.

'73 .... *Edinburgh.* Severe epidemy of puerperal fever.—YOUNG, *Med. Comm.*

'72 .... *America.* Epidemic catarrh and measles.

'73 .... *Mexico.* 30,000 persons carried off by the plague in May.—BOYLE, ii, 264.

'74 .... *England.* Epidemic catarrh.

'74 .... *France* was afflicted with epidemic convulsions, "sur un epue d'epilepsie qui reconnoit pour cause le virus exanthematique malaire."—BARAILLON.

'74 .... *Vienna.* Puerperal fever.

'74 .... *America.* A similar malady to that in *France* this year.

'75 .... *Europe.* Epidemic influenza from March until January, 1776.

'75 .... *Aix.* Small pox very prevalent.

'75 .... *Finland.* Anthrax extended from animals to mankind.

'76 .... *Dublin.* A malignant fever, supposed to have originated in the gaol, caused great mortality.—BOYLE, ii, 271.

'76 .... *Lower Austria* and *Wilna* (Poland). Anthrax frequently communicated from animals to mankind.

'77 .... *England, France.* Scarlet fever, complicated with malignant sore-throat or diphtheria.

'78 .... *England.* Epidemic angina at *Manchester* and elsewhere.

'78 .... *Holland.* Scarlet fever.

'78 .... *Carthagena* (Spain). Plague.

'78 .... *Constantinople.* Plague.

'78 .... *North America* (now *United States*). After the vacation of *Philadelphia* by the British army there was great mortality by yellow fever.

'80 .... *Spain.* Epidemic pestilence appeared in various parts of the peninsula. It first broke out in May in a village of Passages, and was supposed to have arisen from intramural burial, the stench from the over-crowded graveyards being intolerable.

'80 .... *North America.* Yellow fever continued to rage at Philadelphia and in other places. A fever called "break-bone fever" was also prevalent, but did not prove fatal.

Plagues and Pestilences affecting the Human Race—Contd.

A.D.

1780 .... *South America.* The "Andalusian fever" broke out among the Spanish colonists at Rio Janeiro and other Brazilian settlements.

'81 .... *Europe.* The crews of the channel fleet suffered greatly from epidemic disease. 11,732 sick were sent to Haslar Hospital. 1,457 had scurvy, 240 dysentery, and 5,539 severe fever. "This may be taken as a specimen of the health of the British navy down to the close of the eighteenth century."—BASCOME, p. 138.

'81 .... *India.* Cholera was prevalent in Ganjam. 1,143 men of the Bengal troops were attacked.

'81 .... *America.* Epidemic puerperal fever. Measles prevailed at *New York, Philadelphia,* and elsewhere. Numerous cases of hydrophobia occurred further south. The summer was excessively hot.

'81-82.... *Universal.* An epidemy of influenza overspread *the World.* It commenced in China in September, travelled through Asia, and reached Moscow in December. In February (1882) it had reached Revel and Eastern Prussia, and by August and September it was in Spain and Italy. It broke out in America in the spring.—(GLUGE, *Influenza.*) According to Forster (*Atmos. Origin, &c.,* p. 171) the disease appeared in America in the spring of 1781, not occurring in Europe until a year later. In Utrecht 3,000 persons were ill at one time.

'82 .... *France.* Two provinces are mentioned (Languedoc and Rousillon) as having been visited by a "terrific epidemic," which caused great mortality. Epidemic distemper at *Brest.* The *Picardy Sweat* carried off 3,000·persons in a few months in *Languedoc,* according to HECKER.

'82 .... *Spain.* An epidemic broke out at Lerida, and ran through Tarragona, Manresa, Llasanes, Solsona, Iqualada, and Villafranca del Panades. Variola appeared in Tortosa, and soon overspread the kingdom of Aragon.

'82 .... *Constantinople.* Famine and pestilence prevailed. A fire had destroyed 7,000 houses, and the remaining dwellings were consequently overcrowded.

'82 .... *India.* Cholera, incorrectly called spasms by Dr. Girdlestone, appeared among the troops at Madras. Within a month upwards of a thousand men had been attacked. It appeared also on the Coromandel coast.—FRA P. DE S. BARTHOLOMEW, *Viaggio alle Indie Orientali.*
In May, cholera was raging at Trincomalee, and the fleet at anchor there was severely affected.

'82 .... *Chili* (South America). The country desolated by an epidemic distemper.—BOURGOING'S *Modern Spain,* vol. i, p. 256.

'83 .... *Europe.* The plague in various places, as *Greece,* the *Crimea,* and *Constantinople.*

'83 .... *India.* Cholera carried off 20,000 persons at *Hurdwar* during an annual festival there, and assailed a division of the Bengal troops stationed at Garigani.

'83 .... *Asia.* The plague in *Smyrna,* and in *Egypt* and *Dalmatia.*

'83 .... *America.* Epidemic scarlatina and measles.

'83 .... *Iceland.* Famine and pestilence. Eruption of Mount Hecla.

'84 .... *Spain.* The summer was hot, and a great scarcity of water was experienced. In November, epidemic tertian fever prevailed in the province of Alcarria. Small pox appeared, first in a mild form, but afterwards malignant. The following spring being rainy and damp, exanthematous fevers, rheumatisms, and intermittent quotidians broke out all over the country. The diseases of this period are described in works by Dr. Don Felix Ibañez, and Dr. Don Juan Manuel Alvarez.

'84 .... *Smyrna.* Plague. 20,000 deaths.

'84 .... *Tunis.* 32,000 deaths from plague.—BOYLE, ii, 287.

Plagues and Pestilences affecting the Human Race—Contd.

A.D.	
1785	*Spain.* Epidemic tertian fever prevailed throughout Andalusia, especially at Carthagena, where the disease raged with unprecedented severity ; 2,500 deaths. Levida suffered from variola.
'85	*Northern States of America.* Measles.—COUBANT, 1st August, 1785 ; WEBSTER, i, 455.
'86	*Spain.* Carthagena lost 1,300 more from pestilence. The city of *Viso* had a great mortality.
'86	*Levant.* 800,000 persons perished by a plague.—BOYLE, ii, 291.
'86	*West Indies.* At Havannah the "vomito negro" prevailed ; believed to have been produced from putrid hides.
'87	*India.* Cholera committed terrible ravages in October in the provinces of Arcot and Vellore.
'88	*India.* Arcot (Madras). Pestilential *cholera* very destructive.
'88	*England.* Influenza prevalent.
'89	*The Levant.* The plague raged dreadfully this year.—BOYLE, ii, 295.
'90	*North America.* "The most severe pestilences on record occurred all over the United States, in the form of anginas, croup, ulcerated sore throat, putrid bilious fevers, &c. Dr. Manson describes one of the epidemics thus : ' Slight influenza, stinging pain in the jaws and limbs, soreness of the muscles of the neck, attended with severe fever.' The measles, which occurred the year previously, appear to have been the prelude to a series of epidemics which raged for thirty years. Influenza was very severe in the cities of New York and Philadelphia, and rapidly affected the other parts of the States wherever the same conditions of weather and atmosphere prevailed. This disease also traversed the barren wilderness, seizing on the Indian population, attacked seamen at sea, and raged with great mortality through the western hemisphere from the 15° to 45° of northern latitude. Scarlet fever was also prevalent at Philadelphia, and carried off great numbers of the young. These epidemics generally exhibited as the predominant feature the superabundance of biliary secretions which were vomited."—BASCOME, pp. 140 and 141.
'91	*England.* Typhus fever.
'91	*Egypt.* Plague. *Smyrna*, plague.
'91	*Africa.* Bilious remittent fever in towns on northern coast.
'91	*North America.* The winter was early and severe ; the spring dry and cold. Catarrh again prevailed. Yellow fever broke out in *New York*, and carried off numbers. Scarlatina and hooping cough were also prevalent. The bilious plague raged at *Philadelphia*.
'91	*West Indies.* In the island of *Grenada* bilious plague. Yellow fever was fatal at *Havannah*.
'92	*Egypt.* 800,000 souls swept off by a plague.—BOYLE, ii, 314.
'92	*United States.* In July yellow fever raged, causing great mortality in the city of *Charleston*. In the following month scarlet fever carried off great numbers in *New York*, *Philadelphia*, and *Bethlehem*.
'93	*Europe.* Dysentery very prevalent.
'93	*United States.* "The spring was dry, the summer intensely hot and showery, with hail, and the autumn dry and cold. A fatal dysentery swept off vast numbers in Georgetown, Coventry ; a nervous fever was prevalent at a place called Fairfield ; yellow fever raged to an alarming extent at *Philadelphia*, carrying off in the course of four or five months upwards of 4,000 persons ; it was also fatal in *Boston*. In the following year it prevailed at *Baltimore* and at *Norfolk* in Virginia.
'93	*East Indies.* "About this period a similar epidemic caused great destruction in the island of Dominica and other of the West Indian Islands. In Dominica it continued for three years, until 1796."—BASCOME, pp. 142 and 143.

Plagues and Pestilences affecting the Human Race—Contd.

A.D.

1794 .... *France.* The horses and mules of the French army being affected with "mange," the disease was transmitted to and propagated among the soldiers.

'94 .... *United States.* Yellow fever raged with great violence in Philadelphia, New York, Charleston, and other cities, continuing until 1800. "In the whole course of my life," says Professor Kemp, writing to Dr. Baily on yellow fever, "I never experienced a state of air so distressingly debilitating and unfriendly to my spirits." The atmosphere was warm and humid.

'94 .... *India.* During October, cholera very prevalent in Arcot and Vellore.

'96-97 .... *United States.* Yellow fever prevalent at New York, Charleston, Boston, Newburyport, Philadelphia, and in other States. The year following, 1797, it caused great mortality in Norfolk, Providence, Portland, and Savannah, extending from thence to New Orleans, where it commenced with the symptoms of common remittent fever.

In Trinity Church, Salford (by Manchester), is a monument with inscription to memory of Major Thos. Drinkwater, who perished at sea on his return from West Indies, 1797 :—

"Thrice had his foot Domingo's island prest,
'Midst horrid wars, and fierce barbarian wiles ;
Thrice had his blood repell'd the yellow pest
That stalks, gigantic, through the Western Isles ! "
&c., &c., &c.   —*Manchester Historical Recorder.*

'97 .... *England.* In spring, catarrh prevalent.

'98 .... *Wurtemberg.* Anthrax severe, sometimes affecting the people.

'98 .... *Europe.* "Catarrhs, anginas, and pleurisy were frequent in mankind."—FLEMING'S *An. Pl.,* i, 546.

'98 .... *United States.* "The preceding winter was severe and long. The summer this year was remarkably dry and sultry ; the rivers afterwards inundated the adjoining country, heavy rains falling at the same time. Catarrhs, pleurisies, and sore throats prevailed, with bilious fevers. In the autumn, grasshoppers infested the country round about Pennsylvania and New England, and a pestilential yellow fever commenced and spread dismay among the inhabitants ; many were carried off by it. The citizens of New York, Philadelphia, Wilmington, Newport, Albany, Boston, Portsmouth, and New London suffered greatly from this disease, which exhibited both bubo and carbuncle, with many other symptoms of the true plague. A peculiar fog or vapour was observed in New York during the most fatal period of this pestilence, especially in the month of September. Lake and marsh fevers prevailed also about this period in the low and swampy districts, such as Milford, &c. This yellow pestilence was less generally characterised by inflammatory action, and venesection was attended with less salutary effects than on former occasions."—BASCOME, p. 145.

'99 .... *Egypt.* Plague in the French army.—See *Memoires de la Peste observée en Egypte pendant le séjour de l'armée de l'Orient dans cette Contrée ;* Baron Larrey's *Description d'Egypte.*

'99 .... *North Africa.* In Barbary 3,000 deaths occurred daily. Fez alone lost 247,000 citizens. At Mogador the pestilence broke out in the form of virulent small pox in April, degenerated into plague in July, and ceased in October. In Morocco it was preceded by famine. For details, see BASCOME, p. 145.

'99 .... *Jaffa* was taken by the French army. The sacking continued for two days, and immediately afterwards the plague appeared among the troops.—BOYLE, ii, 351.

'99 .... *India.* In *Bombay* 3,000 deaths daily.

Plagues and Pestilences affecting the Human Race—Contd.

A.D.	
1799–1800	*Europe.* In November (1799) influenza broke out in *Russia;* in January it reached *Prussia,* and soon after it became epidemic throughout the continent.
1800	*Morocco.* Glandular or bubonic plague devastated the empire.— COPLAND.
1800	The *British fleet,* with 18,000 troops on board, was visited off *Cadiz* by an epidemic disease.—BOYLE, ii, 361.
1800	*Spain.* In the autumn the same disease appeared at Cadiz, the deaths from it in the middle of September numbering 200 daily. It spread to Xeres, Malaga, and other parts of the country, persisting until 1804.
1800	*United States.* Malignant yellow fever broke out at Baltimore, and raged at Boston and other places in the States.
1800–01....	*Spain.* Yellow fever broke out at Cadiz, and attacked nearly all the inhabitants. "It was observed that most of those who were born in the West India islands, or in Spanish America, escaped its influence ; that it was not quite so dangerous to the old inhabitants as to those who had recently settled at Cadiz; and that the majority of foreigners fell victims to its fury." It was also remarked that it raged with much greater violence among men than among women. "This difference was likewise observed in 1804: it was asserted to have been in the proportion of 48 to 1, and the extreme inequality of the two sexes which was perceived in the churches, in the public walks and assemblies, seemed to confirm the accuracy of this calculation. It was on the 12th of August and the 31st of October that the contagion committed greatest ravages at Cadiz. During this interval it attacked 47,350 persons, and carried off 7,195 of that number, exclusive of the troops who had recently arrived for the defence of the coast, and who alone lost 3,000 men. Winter seemed not to check the calamity, as had been hoped. Cadiz and the other cities of Andalusia were not free from it till the end of April, 1801. Every measure tending to prevent the spreading of the contagion was resorted to. Every apartment, and every place to which it had penetrated, was whitewashed and fumigated. Care was taken to burn the clothes and goods of the infected, and to inter the dead at a considerable distance from the city, and in graves of a sufficient depth. When the contagion was at its height, in September and October, 1800, from 140 to 170 persons died every day at *Cadiz.* The infection was at the same time making terrible ravages in the adjacent places, at *Port St. Mary,* the *Isle de Leon,* and *Rotas.* The gates of Cadiz were kept closely shut. The contagion extended to *Chicklana, Puerto Real,* and *St. Lucar.* It even spread to *Xeres, Seville,* and by degrees over the whole province of Andalusia. A cordon was placed at the foot of the Sierra Morena, and was not withdrawn till the spring of 1801, after it had been ascertained that every part of the country was free from infection. About the end of 1801 a new alarm was excited. At *Medina-Sidonia,* and in its neighbourhood, several putrid fevers appeared, but it was discovered that they were not of an epidemical nature."—BOURGOING'S *Modern Spain,* vol. iii, p. 189.

The population of Seville in 1800 was about 800,000 ; of these 76,488 were attacked by the contagion, which carried off 14,685 persons between the 28th of August and the 30th of September. [FULLARTON says that nearly half of these were *gitanos,* or gypsies, in the suburb of Triana.] This scourge renewed its ravages in the beginning of the autumn of 1801, and spread over all Andalusia, but at Seville it proved much less destructive than in the preceding year.—BOURGOING'S *Modern Spain,* vol. iii, p. 130.

Plagues and Pestilences affecting the Human Race— Contd.

A.D.	
1801	*England* and *Ireland.* Typhus fever prevailed. Dr. William Heberden, the younger, M.D., F.R.S., published—*Observations on the Increase and Decrease of Different Diseases, and particularly the Plague.*
'01	*Europe.* Egyptian ophthalmia broke out.
'01	*Paris.* "An infectious fever rages at present so violently at Paris that it has caused a void in almost every society in that city."— FAULKNER : *Journal.*
'01	*Germany* and *Röttingen.* An epidemy appeared which HECKER thought bore a close resemblance to the English sweating sickness. See 1802.
'01	*United States.* Anginas, pleurisies, and yellow pestilence prevalent.
'02	*Central Germany.* "A very hot and dry summer was succeeded in November by incessant heavy rain; thick fogs spread over the country, and enveloped such places as were inaccessible to ventilation; amongst others the small Franconian town of *Röttingen,* situated on the River Tauber, and surrounded by mountains. Towards the end of the month an extremely fatal disease broke out, which was without example in the memory of its oldest inhabitants, it being totally unknown to them previously. The young and strong were suddenly seized with pain and anguish at the heart, with violent palpitations and lacerating pains in the nape of the neck; profuse, sour, ill-smelling perspiration broke out over the entire body, and a suffering, as though a violent rheumatic fever had seized on the tendinous expansions, accompanied this terrible malady. In the worst cases a spasmodic trembling ensued, the patient fainted, the limbs became rigid, and death closed the scene, frequently within twenty-four hours from the commencement of the attack."—(BASCOME, p. 147.) HECKER, to the same effect, adds that it was called the sweating sickness.
'02	*Atlantic Emigrant Ships.* A dreadful mortality occurred in the ships with Irish emigrants on board, bound for America, half the number dying in many of the vessels.— BOYLE, ii, 371.
'02	*Philadelphia.* Yellow fever raged with much violence.—BOYLE, ii, 374.
'03	*Great Britain.* Influenza prevailed in the spring, causing great mortality.
'03	*France.* Influenza.
'03	*Spain.* September. Yellow fever.—(BOYLE, ii, 378.) Appeared at *Malaga.*—AREGRILA, on *Epid. Fev. Malaga.*
'03	*West Indies.* The army of General Rochambeau was ravaged by the fever in St. Domingo.
'04	*Andalusia.* Towards the end of the summer, the yellow fever, called the *vomito negro,* broke out at Malaga with terrible severity. "It extended its ravages along the coast of the Mediterranean to Carthagena, Alicante, and even to the vicinity of Barcelona. It proved particularly fatal at Gibraltar, where, in the month of October, 120 persons daily died." Cadiz did not entirely escape, but the mortality there was comparatively insignificant.—BOURGOING'S *Modern Spain,* vol. iii, p. 189.
'04	*Leghorn* and *Lucca.* Yellow pestilence.
'04	*West Indies.* Yellow fever, especially in the Islands of Martinique and Grenada.
'05	*Gibraltar.* The plague raged.—BOYLE ii, 389.
'05	*United States.* Spotted typhus, or petechial pestilence, caused great mortality. Malignant yellow fever in *New York.*
'06–07....	*Ceylon.* A fatal epidemy, probably of an anthracoid nature.
'07	*Europe.* Anthracoid diseases exceedingly prevalent.
'08	*Ireland.* Cholera.—TUOMY, *Diseases of Dublin.*

Plagues and Pestilences affecting the Human Race—Contd.

A.D.	
1809	*Walcheren Expedition* (to an island at the mouth of the Scheldt). "About the 20th August the soldiers fell ill, staggered, dropped in the ranks, seized by dreadful fevers, and with such rapidity did the malady extend, that in fourteen days 12,086 soldiers were in hospital, on board ship, or sent to England." The natives, it was found, were ill every autumn, one-third of them generally being confined to bed until the frost set in. In the preceding autumn, of 200 French quartered in the village, 160 took fever, and 70 of them died.—*Naval and Military Gazette*, 1829.
'09	*British Army in Portugal.* Epidemic pestilence broke out amongst the British troops occupying Portugal.
'09-10....	*India.* A severe epidemy at Coimbatore and other places.—See AINSLIE'S *Report of the Epidemic Fever of Coimbatore, Madura, &c.*
'10	*Ireland.* Typhoid. Puerperal fever epidemic.
'10	*Gibraltar.* Population of 14,000 reduced to 28, by yellow fever. Of the 28 who escaped 12 had had the disease before.
'11	*England.* Puerperal fever prevalent in Somersetshire.
'11	*Quarantine.* The port of *Balaclava* was prohibited on the ground that the plague originated in the culpable negligence of the inhabitants, in not clearing away the weeds that accumulate at the top of the harbour.
'12	*England.* A severe frost was followed by influenza and a malignant fever.
'12	*Southern France.* Intermittent fever followed extensive inundations. Dry gangrene was very severe among the British troops at *Ciudad Rodrigo*.
'12	*Constantinople.* Plague carried off 160,000 persons.
'13	*London.* "During the months of October and November typhus fever became more frequent than it had been for several years previously; it prevailed mostly in the filthy courts of Saffron Hill, near Hatton Garden, which are almost exclusively inhabited by the lowest kind of Irish labourers. Scarlatina was also rife, but was not very fatal. These diseases were not, however, confined to the places where they first appeared: they soon showed themselves in the crowded districts in the eastern and north-eastern parts of the town, and in the borough, and were greatly prevalent in the alleys about Essex Street, in Whitechapel, near Golden Lane, Old Street, and in many filthy courts about Cow Cross and Chick Lane, in the vicinity of Smithfield; they were also rife in the districts near Kent Street, in the parishes of St. George and St. Saviour, in Southwark, in the courts running into Shoe Lane, Clare Market, the Strand, at Somers Town, and, singular to say, they broke out last of all in St. Giles's, the district proverbially the receptacle of beggary and vice."—BASCOME, p. 149.
'13	*French Army.* On the French frontiers an epidemic broke out in Napoleon's army, which carried off 60,000 men in six weeks.—BOYLE, ii, 453.
'13	*Gibraltar.* During this year the yellow pestilence again broke out here, raging from October to December, and destroying many soldiers and civilians.
'13	*Malta.* Plague made its appearance in this island, where it had not been known since 1675. Here a few Greeks and some French and Italian prisoners of war were induced, by the offer of rewards and liberty, to wait on the sick, bury the dead, whitewash the infected houses, burn the furniture, &c., as nobody on the island would undertake the task. Comparatively few of these "children of despair" fell victims to the disease. Between April and November 4,483 persons were carried off by it. See 1820.
'13	There was published—*History of the Plague in the Islands of the Mediterranean, as it lately appeared.* By J. D. Tully. See 1837.

Plagues and Pestilences affecting the Human Race—Contd.

A.D.	
1813	*Gozza, Corfu,* and other places were affected with pestilence.
'13	*Bucharest.* Plague.—TULLY's *Plagues of the Mediterranean.*
'14	*Italy.* At Noya an epidemic resembling the plague broke out. It also appeared at Cagliari.
'14	*Gibraltar.* Yellow fever broke out in August, and disappeared about the end of October. It was not again heard of on the Rock for fourteen years.
'14	*Altona.* Unparalleled pestilence.—STENHEIM, *Uber den Typhüs.*
'14	*Siberia.* A deadly epidemy caused considerable mortality.— WRANGELL, *Le Nord de la Siberia,* vol. i, p. 265.
'14	*Dantzic.* During the investment an epidemic carried off 20,000 men.—BOYLE, ii, 457.
'14	*India.* Cholera appeared in an epidemic form among the recruits at Fort William and also at Jaulna.
'14	*Smyrna.* Plague carried off 35,000 persons.
'15	*France.* Dysentery at Ivanbege.
'15	*Italy.* A hot nervous fever, with gangrenous boils and carbuncles, broke out at Noya on 27th December, and raged for six months, affecting all except old persons. Women were the first and most frequent victims. It spread to *Cagliari,* and was very fatal there. The outbreak was preceded by a famine. A south wind which prevailed seemed to aggravate its violence.
'15	*Corfu* lost more than a fourth part of its population in a few days by a destructive pestilence which broke out at a small village called Marathea, in the district of Lefchimo. The village was situated near stagnant pools and marshes, which were first swelled by unusual rains and then evaporated by unusual heat and a constant sirocco or south-east wind. Of 700 persons attacked in this little place only 78 recovered.
'15	*Mauritius.* A disorder similar to the yellow fever caused great mortality.—BOYLE, ii, 477.
'16	*Dublin.* Severe fever outbreak.
'16	*Naples, Venice.* Plague.
'16	*Antigua.* Yellow fever broke out.—BOYLE, ii, 486.
'16	*Constantinople.* Plague.
'16	*Guadaloupe.* Pestilence.
'16	*India.* Anomalous weather induced low fevers of a typhoid character, accompanied by malignant sore throat—a disease previously unknown in Bengal.
'17	*Dublin.* Contagious fever appeared in Dublin, and made alarming progress. The number of beds provided for the reception of patients in hospitals, and the buildings connected with the House of Industry amounted to 1,000, which were always occupied.
'17	*Ireland.* Contagious fever prevalent.—BOYLE, ii, 494.
'17	*North America.* Yellow fever produced great mortality at Savannah, New Orleans, Mobile, Natchez, Havannah, Baltimore, Charleston, and in various parts of the States.
'17	*Europe. Poland,* and *Italy* suffered a contagious fever resembling typhus.—SAUNDERS' *News Letter.*
'17-24....	*India, China,* and the *Eastern Nations.*—Pestilential **CHOLERA** broke out in the month of August at Jessore, a populous town in the centre of the delta of the Ganges, crowded and filthy, and surrounded by marshy jungles. 10,000 of the inhabitants died in the course of a few weeks. In September it broke out in Calcutta, and spread thence along the banks of the Ganges in a north-westerly direction, not extending farther east than Muzufferpore. The English army assembled at Bundelcund, on the banks of the Sinde, lost 9,000 men by the disease. The roads were covered with the dying and the dead. In 1818, the epidemic extended to Jaulnah, on the Madras side of the peninsula. In March, 10,000 perished from it at Banda, and a

Plagues and Pestilences affecting the Human Race—Contd.

A.D.	*India, China*, and the *Eastern Nations—Contd.*
1817-24....	similar proportion at Hutta, Saugur, Ougein, and Kotah. Allahabad lost an equal number in the same month. In April and May, Cawnpore, Meerhut, Agra, Delhi, Lucknow, and Fyzabad were attacked, 30,000 succumbing at Gorukpore alone. In August it reached *Bombay*; October, *Madras*; and in December, *Ceylon*. It was also raging by this time in the Mauritius, the Burmese Empire, the kingdom of Aracan, and the peninsula of Molucca. The following year (1819) Penang, Sumatra, Singapore, the kingdom of Siam, and the isles of France and Bourbon were infected. At Bankok, the capital of Siam, 40,000 persons perished. During 1820 the disease spread to Tonquin, Cambogia, Cochin-China, Southern China, Canton, the Philippines, &c. In 1821 Java, Bantam, Mendura, Borneo, and various other parts of the Indian Archipelago. In Java it is reported that 102,000 persons were carried off by it, 17,000 of whom belonged to Batavia, one of the most unhealthy towns in the East. "This same year this dreadful pestilence, in the month of July, reached Muscat, in Arabia, in its western course, where 10,000 persons lost their lives, and during the remainder of the year committed great ravages in various places in the Persian Gulf. In the following month (August) it appeared in Persia, and raged ·with violence at Bassora and at Bagdad. .In Bassora 18,000 lives, being one-third of the population, were sacrificed in eleven days, and a similarly fearful destruction befell Bagdad. In Bushire, where it broke out in July, 1821, its ravages were most fearful. The bazaars were closed, the houses abandoned, the unburied dead lay in heaps in the streets, and the surviving population sought safety in flight. In Shiraz one-eighth of the population perished. In the years 1822-24 it revisited Tonquin and also Pekin, Central and Northern China, the Moluccas or Spice Islands, Amboyna, Macassar, Assam, and most of the other eastern countries. In Ispahan the epidemic did not inflict much damage, but at Erzeroom it attacked the army of the victorious Abbas Mirza, and swept his ranks from front to rear, the terror stricken soldiery throwing away their arms and flying from before the invisible destroyer. During these years, 1822-24, extending to 1827-30, this pestilence prevailed in many of the principal cities of Persia, and also in Chinese Tartary; it ravaged most of the populous cities of Mesopotamia, Syria, and Judæa, and reached within 150 miles of the Georgian frontiers of Russia; it was also rife at Orenburg and Astrachan, beyond which it seems not to have extended until the years 1828-29, when it appeared at Orenburg, the capital of the province of that name, situated on the Tartar frontier, 400 miles north of the Caspian Sea. During this period disease was rife in various other parts of the world."—BASCOME, pp. 151—55.
'18	*Ireland.* Great mortality occasioned by typhus fever. Reports from the south of Ireland in September described the epidemic fever as affecting one-fifth of the population.—BOYLE, ii, 502.
'18	*India, Ceylon,* and the *Mauritius.* Asiatic cholera. It reached Bombay in August.
'18	*United States, South America, West Indies.* Yellow fever.
'18-20....	*America, &c., &c.* Yellow pestilence rife in the United States, West Indian Islands, Bermuda, British Guiana, and various parts of the South American Continent.

About 1819 there was prepared for the Indian Government:—

(1) *Report on the Epidemic Cholera Morbus in the Presidency of Bengal in the Years* 1817-19. By James Jameson, Esq.

In Bombay : (2) *Reports on the Epidemic Cholera of Hindostan and the Peninsula of India, since* 1817.

(3) *Report on the Epidemic Cholera as it appeared in the Presidency of Fort St. George.* Drawn up by William Scot. (See 1824.)

Plagues and Pestilences affecting the Human Race—Contd.

A.D.

1819 .... | *Europe.* Epidemic diseases in many countries :— Russia, Poland, Prussia, &c., scurvy. *Bavaria.* Malignant fever.—HENKE, *Zeitschr. für de Staatsarz-neik,* vol. x, p. 18.

'19 .... | *Africa.* The plague raged with great violence on the coast, especially throughout the empire of Morocco. *Tunis,* it was estimated, lost half of its population.—BOYLE, ii, 507.

'19 .... | *Mauritius.* Cholera was brought to the island by H.M.S. "Topaze" from Trincomalee.

'20 .... | *Eastern Asia.* Indian cholera.

'21 .... | *France.* In *Paris* a violent epidemic disorder broke out in the Royal Military School of St. Cyr.—BOYLE ii, 528.

'21 .... | *Barcelona.* Yellow fever caused from 200 to 300 deaths per day.—BOYLE ii, 527.

'21 .... | *Xeres* visited by yellow pestilence. The British troops suffered severely, but the civilians in greater proportion.

'21 .... | *Cadiz.* Yellow fever.

'21 .... | *America.* There was a protracted drought, which withered vegetation and dried up the springs. Fevers and dysenteries prevailed ; then yellow fever broke out at New York, and soon extended to Boston, Philadelphia, Baltimore, Charleston, New Orleans, Natchez, Mobile, Alabama, Havannah, and along the low banks of the Mississippi river.

'21 .... | *China.* Cholera, formerly unknown in this country, "first appeared on the shores of the Yellow Sea, as a mist which gradually rose from the water, winding its course along the hills and valleys ; and wherever it passed men found themselves suddenly attacked with a frightful disease, which was incontestably the cholera. It ravaged first the province of Chamtung. then turned northward to Pekin, striking on its march the most populous towns ; it then crossed the Great Wall. It is probable that it followed the route of the caravans as far as the Russian station of Khiaktha, and afterwards passing through Siberia, invaded Russia."—HUC, *Travels in Tartary.* China, vol. ii.

'21 .... | *Arabia.* A considerable body of European and native troops were sent to the assistance of the Imann from Bombay. Cholera followed in their track and committed terrible ravages. The Arabian historian, SALIL-IBN-RAZIK, says : "This year a plague broke out in Oman, and proved fatal to a great many. Some who are seized die at once ; others after two or three days ; and only a few survive. God preserve us from so dire a disease ! Great numbers in Oman fell victims to it ; it prevailed also in India, in Sind, and Mekrain."

'21 .... | *Siam.* Cholera morbus carried off 40,000 persons.—BOYLE ii, 526.

'21-22.... | *Persia.* Cholera appeared at Bassora with extraordinary violence. From 15,000 to 18,000 persons died from it in eighteen days. From this city the disease was carried by boats and caravans up the Tigris to Bagdad. A war had broken out at this time between Persia and Turkey, and Mahomed Aly Mirja led his army in person against Bagdad ; but just as he was on the point of possessing himself of the city, he was carried off by cholera, and his army suffered frightfully from the disease.—MACNAMARA.

'22 .... | *Syria.* Cholera came by way of the Persian caravans, and reached Aleppo in November. M. de Lesseps, the French Consul at this town, took refuge with some two hundred friends in his country house, and planted themselves in a regular state of siege during the period cholera lasted in the place. This party escaped the disease, as did also M. Guys and his friends under similar circumstances at Lattaquia.—MACNAMARA.

'22 .... | *Ireland.* Typhus fever in Queen's County, and in County Kilkenny.

Plagues and Pestilences affecting the Human Race—Contd.

A.D.	
1822	*Paris.* Typhus and spasmodic yellow fever.
'22	*New Orleans.* Epidemic yellow fever in September and October.
'22	*Chili.* An upheaval of the sea-bed on the coast exposed oysters, mussels, and other shell-fish to the sun. They rapidly putrified, causing a most offensive effluvia to pervade the air. Disease followed.
'23	*Alexandretta.* Cholera appeared here and in the neighbourhood of Laodicea and Antioch, whence it spread along the shores of the Mediterranean. It disappeared at the end of the year, nor did it reappear either in Persia or Turkey during the next five years.
'23	*Ireland.* Small pox. "The malignity of the epidemic constitution of the air was very remarkable at this time ; it interfered with the recovery of patients after surgical operations. Slight punctures, received while dissecting, were often succeeded by suddenly fatal attacks of typhus disease."—STOKES, *Sketch of Epidemic Fever.*
'23	*Lisbon.* Yellow fever, and at the *Island of Ascension.*
'23	*Africa.* Yellow fever in various settlements, especially at *Sierra Leone.*
'24	*England.* The arrival (in March) of quantities of grain from places infected with the plague caused great alarm. *Quarantine* was strictly enforced.
'24	*Rome.* Colds, apoplexy, and diseases of the chest were alarmingly prevalent. The theatre Argentina was closed for lack of singers.—BOYLE, ii, 570.
'24	*Calcutta.* Typhoid and exanthematous fever. Malignant cholera also broke out near the city. In 1824 there was published at Madras—*Report on the Epidemic Cholera as it appeared in the Presidency of Fort St. George.* Drawn up by William Scot. This contains an appendix of sick returns and meteorological tables. (See 1818-20 (3).)
'25	*Hamburg.* Great mortality from small pox.
'25	*Paris.* Small pox made dreadful ravages in November. The *Journal de Paris* asserted that the disease was not small pox, but a malady imported from Asia.—BOYLE ii, 672.
'25	*Grand Cairo.* Pestilence killed 30,000.
'25	*South America.* Yellow fever epidemic. Very deadly at Rio de Janeiro. In the settlement of Aracaty, the deaths in a short time were estimated at 30,000. Great numbers died when endeavouring to reach the coast for water.
'26	*Ireland.* Epidemic typhus very fatal. Dr. Graves mentions several cases "which, in their symptoms and morbid anatomy, agree essentially with yellow fever."
'26	*Europe* (North Western). Epidemic influenza. In *Holland* nearly the entire population was affected.
'27	*England.* Severe remittent fever.
'27	*Europe* (North Western). The summer of 1826 having been moist and rainy, in the early part of this year influenza became epidemic at Groningen, in Friesland, North Holland, Belgium, and Lower Germany. The mortality was so serious that the Dutch Government "found it necessary to adopt strong measures to relieve the sickness which affected nearly the whole population."
'27	*West Indies.* A sort of rheumatic fever broke out in *St. Thomas,* and affected every one of the population, amounting to 12,000 persons. It was exceedingly painful, but seldom fatal. It spread over the other islands.
'27	*United States.* Yellow fever prevalent.
'28	*Paris.* A rheumatic ailment, similar to the above, appeared in the city. A writer thus describes the malady :—"It was generally unaccompanied with any great degree of fever, but affected the whole nervous system in a most peculiar manner ; especially by a most painful sense of formication in the hands and feet, as well as

Plagues and Pestilences affecting the Human Race—Contd.

A.D.	*Paris—Contd.*
1828	a degree of numbness which seized first upon the members, and thence extended over the whole body. The formication and painful numbness of the extremities were so characteristic of the complaint, that at Paris and elsewhere in France it was known by the name of ' mal des pieds et des mains.' " Unlike its West Indian predecessor, this disease proved fatal in many cases. Its course was sometimes completed in a few weeks, sometimes not for several months.
'28	*Italy.* The *French army*, encamped before the city of *Naples*, lost great numbers by pestilence.
'28	*Gibraltar.* Yellow pestilence broke out in September in the filthiest and most crowded parts on the Rock, and soon attacked all classes of the military and civilians. " It was observed to prevail to a greater extent and more severely in some situations than in others, particularly along the line of wall facing the sea—few of the soldiers stationed there escaping an attack, so that it was soon found necessary to withdraw the sentries stationed in the neighbourhood." —BASCOME, pp. 157 and 158.
'29	*Orenburg* (Russia). In August, epidemic pestilence broke out, having been preceded by the appearance of dense swarms of small green flies, which in Asia are called plague flies.
'30	*Europe* and *Asia.* GREAT **CHOLERA** EPIDEMIC. About this period cholera " showed itself on the borders of the Black Sea, penetrating thence into the centre of European Russia, where it continued throughout the winter. Towards the beginning of autumn it commenced with great violence in the Georgian frontier of Persia, having appeared in June, 1830, in the Persian province of Ghilan, on the Caspian shore ; from the southern parts of which it extended northward, along the west Caspian shore, until it reached Baku, Tiflis, Astrachan, and numerous other places, in its progress into the very heart of the Russian empire. At Astrachan, from July to the end of August, 4,000 died in the city, and 21,270 in the entire province. 2,367 persons died of it in Saratov ; and shortly afterwards, of 1,792 Don Cossacks attacked, 1,334 perished. At Penza, situate about 140 miles north of Saratov, 1,200 of the population were seized in the course of a fortnight, and 800 sunk under it. At Nijni Novgorod, where the epidemic soon afterwards broke out, 1,863 persons were taken ill, of whom nearly 1,000 died. The mortality in Bessarabia and Moldavia was appalling. Jassi, the capital of Moldavia, was almost depopulated. This insatiable malady continued to spread, carrying death in its course, westward and northward, through Russia, Poland, Moldavia, the Duchy of Posen, Silesia, and Austria, visiting Warsaw, with other towns in Poland, and extending, May, 1831, to Riga and Dantzic ; and in June and July to St. Petersburg and Constradt ; it reached Berlin on the last day of August, Vienna in September, and Hamburg on the 7th of October."—(BASCOME, p. 159.) " Malignant cholera showed itself on the frontiers of Europe, towards the borders of the Black Sea, and spreading, passed into the centre of European Russia ; while from the Georgian frontier of Persia it extended into the very middle of the Russian empire, and travelling westward, swept away hundreds of thousands of people in its course."—(FLEMING, *An. Pl.*, ii, 150.) At *Moscow*, the atmosphere was suddenly filled with dense masses of small green flies (which are in Asia thought forerunners of pestilence, and called plague flies) before the outbreak. See *Englishman's Magazine*, No. 2. Dr. Reimona, of St. Petersburg, in a letter to Dr. Marc, communicated to the Academy of Medicine at Paris, says :—" That the cholera was brought to Astracan by ships, and spread itself over Russia by the emigration of the inhabitants, principally those of the lower orders. This is the sole cause of its propagation into Russia. It has never shown itself in

Plagues and Pestilences affecting the Human Race—Contd.

A.D.	*Europe* and *Asia—Contd.*
1830	any place, except where it has been brought by travellers who came from infected places."—A. NEALE, *Researches, Animate Contagions* (London, 1831), p. 198. CHOLERA MORTALITY. The mortality caused by cholera during the pestilential period 1817-30, has been thus stated :—At *Erivan* and *Tauris* one-fourth of the population were destroyed. In *Syria* its ravages were extremely varied : in some localities one-half of the populace were carried off ; whilst in others, as in *Tripoli,* only one in about 200 died. At *Tiflis* three-fourths of those seized perished ; at *Astrachan* two-thirds were carried off. Out of 16,000 attacked. in the province of Caucasus, 10,000 fell victims; at *Moscow* one-half and at *Orenburg* only one-fifth of the inhabitants perished. Out of 54,000 and upwards attacked in the Russian provinces more than 31,000 died. In *Hungary* 400,000 were said to have been seized, and more than half were destroyed. In this country (*England*) and in *Wales,* according to the tables furnished by Dr. Merriman from the reports sent in by the Privy Council, out of 62,000 attacked, 20,578 died. In *Ireland,* out of 54,552 who were taken ill, 21,171 fell victims. In the countries of *Asia* not subject to European dominion, the data respecting the ravages of this disease were extremely vague and scanty, although there is reason to believe that in some of them they were more extensive than in India. Throughout the Indian peninsula 1,800,000 persons are said to have fallen victims, out of a population of somewhat over 4 millions.
'31	*Great Britain.* On 26th October **CHOLERA** appeared at Sunderland. A month later it broke out at Newcastle-on-Tyne, and subsequently at Houghton-le-Spring, North Shields, Tynemouth, South Shields, Gateshead, and other places. In *Scotland,* at Haddington, 28th December of the same year ; and in *Ireland,* at Belfast, 14th March, 1832.
'31	*Europe.* Epidemic of ergotism in many northern countries.
'31	*Paris.* In May, an epidemic called " la grippe " made its appearance. The disease generally lasted for eight or ten days, and was not very fatal.
'31	*Russia. Mandrosos* was afflicted with an extraordinary epidemic—gangrene of the spleen. The disease is fully described by Dr. BASCOME (*Hist. Epid. Pest.,* p. 162). " *Cholera* followed the Russian army employed in the subjugation of Poland ; it also proved very destructive in Warsaw, and in many other places during the months of April and May. In June it prevailed in Cracow and other adjoining places, extending in its course to Gallicia, Hungary, Smyrna, and Constantinople ; it raged with such intensity at Cairo, that 10,400 Mahomedans, besides Jews and Christians, were carried off. During this year, whilst cholera was progressing over the continent of Europe, it appeared at Mecca, where it proved very destructive to the ' Hadji,' or pilgrims. In August it broke out at Alexandria, and nearly at the same time, all the towns in the delta of the Nile suffered from its violence."—BASCOME, p. 159.
'31	*Bagdad.* " In March the plague was officially declared to be in the city. 7,000 perished in the first fortnight of the awful visitation, the population being probably 75,000. 150 persons often died in a day. The malady whetted its edge, and widened its circle of operation, so that in April some days witnessed from 1,000 to 1,500 deaths. In two months 50,000 are supposed to have been cut down."—EADIE'S *Life of Dr. Kitto,* p. 194.
'32	CHOLERA continued to spread. Its first appearance in London was reported in February, in the immediate vicinity of the shipping ; but isolated cases had been met with in the previous December. Edinburgh and Leith suffered greatly in January. France and

Plagues and Pestilences affecting the Human Race—Contd.

A.D.	
1833	Holland were also affected. In the summer the epidemic prevailed throughout England, Scotland, Ireland, Wales, and in the Channel Islands. First case in Manchester, 17th May. Its effect on the mortality of Glasgow is shown in the *Insurance Cyclopædia*, art. Glasgow, subheading Mortality.
'32	*Paris.* 18,654 deaths were reported to have occurred between March and October.
'32	*Canada* and *United States.* Some emigrants carried cholera to Quebec, whence it extended to Montreal—where, out of a population of 30,000, nearly 3,000 fell victims—to Kingston (Lake Ontario), New York, Newcastle, on the Delaware river, New Orleans, and Havannah.
'32	*Ceylon.* Spasmodic cholera. — See PRIDHAM'S *Ceylon and its Dependencies*, vol. ii, p. 693 ; FORBES'S *Eleven Years in Ceylon*, vol. i, p. 397 ; ii, p. 43.
'33	*Great Britain* and *Ireland.* Influenza very prevalent in the spring. "The disease was ushered into London during the prevalence of a bleak wind and a cold vernal atmosphere, succeeding to a long, warm, moist winter."—*Lond. Med. Gazette*, vol. xii.
'33	*Europe.* Epidemic influenza passed over the continent from east to west. In *Dalmatia* the influenza assumed a rheumatic and catarrhal character.
	The disease appeared in *Bohemia* in March, and in *Saxony* in April.
'33	CHOLERA.—There was a general fast in England on 31st March. " On the 26th of March, Paris was again invaded by it, and the inhabitants of *Calais* also suffered greatly ; in *Paris*, at least 20,000 persons had fallen victims to this scourge by the end of September. During this year and the following it raged throughout *Spain*, and was especially destructive in Madrid. Numerous places on the borders of the Mediterranean were visited by this pestilence, and it reappeared in London and in other places in this country, as well as in North America."—BASCOME, p. 163.
'34	*Constantinople, Cairo, Alexandria,* and *Smyrna.* Plague.
'34	*Gibraltar.* Cholera attacked nearly every one on the Rock.
'34	*Sweden* reached by the cholera.—LLOYD, *Scandinavian Adventures*, vol. i, p. 432.
'34	*Vienna.* Puerperal fever very fatal.—BARTSCH.
'34	*Egypt.* In the beginning of the year plague broke out at Alexandria, where it was said to have been introduced from Malta. It next appeared at Grand Cairo, and thereafter extended up the banks of the Nile. The town of Fua lost 1,800 out of a population of 2,500. The distemper subsided as the year advanced ; but its ravages, together with the long-continued military exertions of the Pasha, left Egypt almost depopulated.
'34-39....	*United States.* Yellow fever prevalent in various parts, especially at Charleston, which was crowded by strangers employed in rebuilding the city after its destruction by fire. The outbreak was attributed to the extreme heat of the summer.
'35	*Leghorn.* Cholera carried off 60 or 70 persons daily.
'36	" In Europe, America (North and South), and in the greater part of the West Indian Islands, an apoplectic, pernicious fever, as it was termed, was prevalent in the northern hemisphere."—BASCOME, p. 167.
'37	*Europe.* Influenza broke out in London in the first week of January, and lasted for six or seven weeks. It prevailed generally (?) in *England* by the middle of February. *Scotland, France, Spain, Denmark, Sweden,* and *Russia* also suffered great mortality from it. About the end of the previous year a sort of influenza was rife at *Sydney* and the Cape of *Good Hope.* All over the eastern hemisphere the weather was cold and tempestuous.

Plagues and Pestilences affecting the Human Race—Contd.

A.D.	
1837	*Roumelia.* Epidemic plague broke out in July, and was general by the month of September.
'37	*Rome.* Epidemic cholera. 200 or 300 deaths daily. In the four months July, August, September, October, no less than 5,419 deaths occurred in the imperial city, out of a population not exceeding 156,000.
'37	*Berlin.* Asiatic cholera.
'37	*India.* The plague at *Marvar.*

In 1837 or 1838 Captain A. M. Tulloch and Mr. Henry Marshall, Deputy Inspector of Hospitals, prepared for the Secretary-at-War a *Report on the Sickness and Mortality among the Troops in the West Indies :*—

" The negro race suffer to a much greater extent than white troops by epidemic cholera. When this disease made its appearance at the Bahamas, though none of the white troops died from it, there were 20 of the black troops cut off out of 62 attacked, and it ran very rapidly to a fatal termination. *The same has been observed wherever the native troops in the East Indies have been attacked by this disease.*"

'38 .... *England.* The deaths registered from cholera were 331, against no less than 2,482 from diarrhœa. Dr. Boehm, of Berlin, published an able work on the cholera, which attracted much attention in Europe.

About this date Major Tulloch prepared a *Statistical Report on the Sickness and Mortality among the Troops in the United Kingdom,* from which we draw the following :—

Epidemic Cholera.—During the three years that this disease prevailed, about 2·8 per 1,000 of the strength were annually cut off by it. This epidemic appears to have exerted its fatal influence in all localities with undeviating regularity ; for we have here instances of different bodies of troops quartered in various situations throughout the kingdom, and yet the proportion of deaths is within a fraction the same in all ; but it did not prove equally fatal to all classes, the mortality having increased progressively with the advance of age, as is shown by the following table :—

Ages.	Aggregate Strength of Cavalry and Household Troops during the Three Years which Cholera Prevailed.	Deaths by Cholera in that Force during the Three Years.	Annual Rate of Mortality by Cholera at each Age.
Under 18	548	—	—
18 to 25.................	14,103	32	2·3
25 „ 33.................	13,336	33	2·5
33 „ 40.................	7,223	29	4·0
40 „ 50 and upwds.	2,229	11	4·9
Total	37,439	105	2·8

Of 171 treated for this disease among the Dragoon Guards and Dragoons, 54 died, or about one-third of the whole number attacked. Among the other troops the proportion was much the same.

'38 .... *Ascension* (Island). Yellow fever broke out in the garrison, and committed great ravages. The epidemic extended to the crews of several ships of war which touched at that island, and many of the seamen and officers perished. The disease was attributed to the effluvia rising from stagnant pools.

Plagues and Pestilences affecting the Human Race—Contd.

A.D.	
1839	*South America.* Pestilence. " This frightful epidemic, which the Llaneros have appropriately styled *peste*, or plague, is supposed to have originated in the great primeval forest of San Camilo, at the head waters of the Apura, from the decomposition of the vegetable detritus accumulated there during centuries. From thence, travelling eastward along the course of the river, the epidemic continued its ravages among the inhabitants of the towns and villages situated on the right bank, attacking first one place and then another, until the whole province scarcely escaped depopulation. Even when the mortality abated, the country, which until then had possessed a most healthful climate, never recovered its former salubrity."—RAMON PAEZ, *Wild Scenes in South America.* London, 1863.
'39	*Russia.* Petechial fever and measles prevailed at St. Petersburg.
'39	*France.* A disease, called " sudor miliaris," in the district of Coulommiers.
'39	*The Alps.* In the month of February an epidemic broke out at *Mount St. Bernard*, and " proceeded with the rapidity of lightning." It was characterised by typhoid symptoms.
'39	*Algiers.* Epidemic erysipelas raged here.
'39	*Texas.* Yellow fever at *Galveston.*
'41	*Sweden.* " During this period, extending to the year following, 1842, an epidemic religious ecstacy, as it was called, prevailed in Sweden. This singular epidemic malady was distinguished by two prominent and remarkable symptoms—one physical, consisting of spasm, or involuntary contractions or contortions, &c. ; the other mental, being an ecstasy, more or less involuntary, during which the patients fancied themselves divinely inspired, and felt impelled to speak of supernatural things which they fancied they saw ; they were occasionally moved to preach. It was the female portion of the community that suffered most. Anything offensive to the mind reacted convulsively on the body, causing a sort of chorea, which it was attempted to distinguish or divide into two distinct forms of the disease, called mental and physical chorea. Several thousand persons were attacked by the disease ; it was rarely fatal. Persons who had been affected, when convalescing, felt languid and debilitated, both in body and mind."—BASCOME, p. 172.
'41	*Asia.* Plague at Syria and at Erzeroum.
'41	*The African Fleet.* Remittent fever very fatal amongst the crews of the ships employed in suppressing the African slave trade.
'41	*New Granada.* Small pox very fatal.
'41	*United States.* Yellow fever at Key West, eastern Florida.
'42	*England.* There was enacted the 2 William IV, cap. 10, *An Act for the Prevention, as far as may be possible, of the Disease called the Cholera, or Spasmodic or Indian Cholera, in England.* The mode of its operation was by the framing of laws and regulations regarding infected districts.
'42–43...	*Persia.* Cholera in a sporadic form prevailed in many parts of the country.
'43	*United States.* Epidemic erysipelas, popularly called " the black tongue," broke out in Ripley county (Indiana ?), and soon extended to other parts. *Boston* was visited in the autumn by an epidemic fever. A like malady prevailed at a little place called *Erie* (N.Y.), where it was attributed by some to the poisoning of the wells. Yellow fever appeared at a little inland settlement in Wilkinson county (Mississippi) under somewhat peculiar circumstances. The disease could not have been imported, for it was not prevalent at New Orleans, nor at any place along the river (Mississippi) at the time. The town itself occupied a healthy position, being situated on high and well-drained ground.
'44	*Goree* (Senegal). Yellow pestilential fever.

Plagues and Pestilences affecting the Human Race—Contd.

A.D.	
1844	*African Fleet.* Remittent fever broke out on board the "Eclair" while on the coast of Africa. 74 lives were lost.
'45	*India.* In the early part of the year cholera prevailed with great violence along the banks of the *Indus.* At Kurrachee, near the mouth of the river, there were 8,000 victims in a few days. About the same period it proved very destructive in *Affghanistan.*
'45	*Persia.* Cholera extended into this country from east to west, " spread northwards into *Tartary,* and southwards into *Kurdistan,* and also into the pashalic of *Bagdad.* In September it prevailed at Herat and Samarcand, and in the November following at Bokhara."—(BASCOME, p. 177.) See 1846-47.
'46	*Spain.* In *Galicia* fearful mortality from famine and epidemic pestilence.
'46	*Canada.* The weather was distressingly hot, and numbers were carried off by fever.
'46	*On the Plains* (United States). The Mormons, during their march from Nauvoo to Utah, suffered greatly from remittent and yellow fevers, and a scorbutic disease which they called the "black canker." Their track across the desert was marked by the graves of those who perished.
'46-47....	*Scotland.* Epidemic remittent fever prevalent. In Glasgow about 15,000 persons perished.
'46-47 ...	*Asia, Europe.* CHOLERA. " Epidemic cholera, after raging with very great violence for two years in *Persia,* towards the end of the summer of 1846, broke out at *Tauris* and *Teheran,* and during the autumn advanced to places nearer the *Russian* frontiers. On the 16th of November, 1846, cases occurred at the village of Ialiany, and also in the same month at Leukoran; and it is worthy of remark that these were the places first attacked in 1830. The disease also appeared at Bakrou, and advanced in December to Schehêmakha and Derbent, and in the month of February, 1847, to the town of Konba. Its appearance at Ialiany and in the district of Talyseh was marked with that malignity which for the most part characterises the commencement of cholera. We observe at Ialiany a remarkable instance of the influence of the trade and locality tending to foster it. Selecting for its victims those who had but recently recovered from the fever of the country, the cholera almost invariably carried off every one attacked, nine-tenths falling victims to the disease. In the localities where the trans-Caucasian provinces the attacks became less violent, and without the towns the disease no longer presented a malignant type. Towards the end of February it was supposed that the disease had ceased ; but in the following month, March, it recommenced with redoubled violence, and in April spread destruction with fearful rapidity. Traversing the shores of the Caspian Sea, it reached Tiflis in May. It also appeared in this month on the other side of the Caucasus, at Kizliar, whence, reascending the Terek, it penetrated to Mozdok ; at the end of June to Piatigorsk and to Georgierk, and entered Staowpol in the first week in July. From October, 1846, to June, 1847, there occurred in the Caucasus and trans-Caucasian provinces no less than 17,055 cases of cholera, of which 6,318 died. Astrachan suffered greatly from cholera, great numbers of the inhabitants having been carried off, as was also the case in Moscow. From official accounts received from St. Petersburg, it appeared the inhabitants of the western town Alexandrof were attacked with cholera, and also the district of Olgapol, in Podolia. The latter is about thirty miles distant from the Austrian frontiers."—BASCOME, pp. 178—80. The registrar-general in his report on the public health for the third quarter of 1847 said :—

Plagues and Pestilences affecting the Human Race—Contd.

A.D.	*Asia* and *Europe—Contd.*
1846–47....	"The great historical epidemics have diminished in intensity; and there appears to be no reason why they should not be ulti- mately suppressed with the advance of the population amongst which they take their rise. Their origin is obscure, but influenza appears generally to have become first epidemic in Russia, cholera in India. *It is in India that the source of the latter disease must be attacked.* If the health of India become sound, Europe might be safe, and hear no more of the epidemic which is now traversing Russia. The attention of the Indian authorities has been for some time directed to the subject . . . . *Asiatic cholera has taught us that the lives of thousands in England may depend on the condi- tion of the pariahs of Jessore.*"
'47	*England.* Throughout the year influenza raged all over England. At *Liverpool,* 103,000 Irish paupers having accumulated there, virulent typhus broke out, and caused great mortality. Lord Brougham presented to parliament a petition thereupon in May. In six weeks, at the end of the year, 11,339 deaths occurred from it.
'47	*Scotland.* "During the last fortnight of November an epidemic of rather a remarkable character broke out, and prevailed in the north of Scotland, commencing in *Dundee,* travelling over the entire coast as far as Kinnaird's Head, and extending westerly, involving Huntly, Keith, Elgin, and Inverness. It first affected the system by pain in the throat, followed by headache, sickness at stomach, and expectoration of a dark, bilious-looking substance. To such an extent did this malady prevail [in *Aberdeen*] that the University and King's College, then in session, were closed; half the students at Marischal College and the University were laid up; those at the grammar schools were afflicted in the same proportion. At *Edin- burgh* and *Montrose* the malady prevailed to an alarming extent, the schools generally having been visited; 810 scholars belonging to the schools in the latter place suffered at one time. The weather, which had been damp and rainy, was considered to be the principal cause."—BASCOME, p. 181.
'47	*Ireland.* Virulent small pox followed by typhus caused great mor- tality.
'47	*Europe* and *Asia.* INFLUENZA afflicted various parts of Europe, notably *Copenhagen* and *Marseilles.* It was of a mild character however. At *Prague* typhus prevailed from 16th December, 1847, with some severity. CHOLERA was rife during 1847 at *Moscow, Stockholm, St. Petersburgh,* and *Cronstadt.* Famine and pestilence were experienced in *Silesia.* CHOLERA raged at *Trebizond,* and a fatal pestilence at *Constantinople.* Asiatic cholera killed more than 30,000 of the *Damascene* pilgrims.
'47	*United States.* Yellow fever was prevalent at *New Orleans* from 5th July to 22nd October, 1827, carrying off 2,544 victims.
'47	*Java* suffered from epidemic diseases about this time.
'47	INFLUENZA. In the month of January (1847) influenza pre- vailed on the coast of Portugal, in the south-east of Spain, in Newfoundland, and New Zealand; in March, at Valparaiso; in April, on the coast of Syria; in July, August, and September, on the west coast of Africa, south of the equator; in August, in Hong Kong, and in December, at Paris and Madrid. Half the population of Paris was attacked by the disease. In June, 1848, cholera prevailed in St. Petersburg and Berlin; by September it had reached Hamburg; in October it was at Edin- burgh. It is thus seen to have followed much the same course as in 1830-31. The Board of Health showed this clearly by the fol- lowing simple diagram :—

K 2

Plagues and Pestilences affecting the Human Race—Contd.

A.D.	*Asia* and *Europe—Contd.*				
1847	Astrakan	July 20, 1830	....	June,	1847
	Moscow	Sept.,	'30	.... Sept. 18,	'47
	Petersburg	June 26,	'31	.... June,	'48
	Berlin	Aug. 31,	'31	.... ,,	'48
	Hamburg	Oct.,	'31	.... Sept.,	'48
	Sunderland............	,, 24,	'31	.... Oct. 4,	'48
	Edinburgh	Jan. 22,	'32	.... ,, 1,	'48

'47 .... | *The East.* More than 30,000 of the pilgrims bound to *Damascus* perished from Asiatic cholera. See *Gazette Medicale*, 1847.

'48-49.... | *England.* Cholera. It reappeared in Sunderland on 12th August, 1849, and committed considerable ravages for several weeks. The total deaths in England and Wales were returned by the registrar-general as 53,293. From diarrhœa, in addition, 18,887. This may be said to be the first time that really authentic details were available.

'49 .... | *England.* The cholera outbreak continued.

'49 .... | *Europe.* Cholera prevailed in many parts of the Continent.

'49 .... | *Hull* (Yorkshire). Cholera; deaths at the rate of 241 to each 10,000 of population, which was the highest rate experienced by any town in the kingdom. Total deaths, 1860, viz., males 885, females 975, being at the rate of .1 in 43 for both sexes. Dr. Henry Cooper, M.D., read a report before the British Association *On the Cholera Mortality of Hull during the Epidemic of* 1849.

In 1849 Dr. John Snow, M.D., published a work *On the Mode of Communication of Cholera,* which attracted a good deal of attention, and passed through several editions. He therein enunciated the theory that *Cholera becomes epidemic through the medium of our water supply.* Dr. Farr said :—" Dr. Snow's theory turned the current in the direction of water, and tended to divert attention from the atmospheric doctrine, which in London had received little encouragement from experience."

It was in this year also that Dr. Budd, of Bristol, announced that he had discovered microscopic fungi in the water used for drinking when cholera prevailed. About the same period Dr. Brittan and Dr. Swayne also published an account of certain " annular bodies," or " cholera cells." Professor Mitchell, of Philadelphia, announced a similar theory. These discoveries are believed to have been all independently made ; and they demonstrate the large amount of scientific investigation which was being bestowed upon the subject.

'50 .... | *West Indies.* Cholera in *Jamaica* for the first time. It occurred in the autumn of the year, and it was estimated that 50,000 persons died from it. This led to the publication (in 1853) of *Report on the Cholera in Jamaica, and the Sanitary Condition and Wants of that Island.*

'52 .... | *England.* Scarlatina and diarrhœa were unusually prevalent. The deaths from the former were 18,887, and from the latter 17,617.

'52 .... | *Croydon* (Surrey). Great outbreak of epidemic fever.

There was issued from the office of the registrar-general (from the pen of Dr. W. Farr), *Report on the Mortality of Cholera in England,* 1848-49—a most exhaustive volume, from which many of the preceding details are drawn.

In 1852 also, Dr. W. Farr read before the Statistical Society a paper on the *Influence of Elevation on the Fatality of Cholera.* The paper is printed in the *Journal* of the Society [vol. xv, p. 155].

'53 .... | *England.* The report of the registrar-general for this year contained the following :—" The outbreaks of cholera in Russia demand the attention of the people of England, and should accelerate all the arrangements for the supply of pure water, the drainage of towns, and the removal of nuisances."

Plagues and Pestilences affecting the Human Race—Contd.

A.D.	*England—Contd.*
1853	In August the cholera broke out in *Newcastle-upon-Tyne;* and Dr. Farr declared that " the evils at which the above warning was directed were found extraordinarily rife " there. The total deaths from cholera in England were 4,419, of which 1,927 occurred in Newcastle and Gateshead.
'53	*Europe.* Cholera prevailed in Russia, in Sweden, Norway, and Denmark. About 15,000 persons died in the three last named countries.
'53	*Western Arabia.* Plague.
'54	*Great Britain.* The *third cholera epidemic.* It was not nearly so severe as that of 1849. The mortality from cholera and diarrhœa in 1848-49 was at the rate of 41 in 10,000 ; while the mortality in 1854 was at the rate of 22 in 10,000 of the population, or but a little more than half. The rate of mortality by diarrhœa in the two epidemics were equal, viz., 11 in 10,000 of the population. Thus in 1854 the mortality from cholera and diarrhœa were equal ; while in 1849 the mortality from cholera had been 30 in 10,000, or nearly three times its force in 1854.

The following is a table of the districts and towns which suffered most severely from the cholera epidemic of 1854, arranged in the order of the rates of mortality experienced :—

Districts, &c.	Deaths Registered.	Deaths to 10,000 Populatn	Districts, &c.	Deaths Registered.	Deaths to 10,000 Populatn.
Milton	116	91	Cardiff	225	42
Towcester	86	67	Richmond	69	41
Thanet	206	65	Stockton and Hart-⎫	239	39
Merthyr Tydfil	455	59	lepool................⎭		
Wisbech...........	176	49	Auckland	114	32
Gravesend	84	49	West Ham	124	31
Maldon	102	46	Liverpool and West⎫	1,290	30
Brentford	196	45	Derby ....⎭		
Romford	113	45	Brecknock..............	54	30
London	10,738	43	Norwich	193	28

	The total deaths in *England* from cholera were 20,097 ; from diarrhœa 20,052.
'54	*Europe.* Cholera raged in *Italy* and *Sicily;* above 10,000 are said to have died in *Naples.* It was also very fatal to the allied troops at Varna in the autumn of this year.
'58	*Tripoli.* Plague.
'59	*England.* Great outbreak of *Diphtheria.* The deaths from it in the previous year had been heavy (6,606), but they now rose to 10,184, of which 5,300, or more than one-half, were of children under 5 years. The greater portion of the remainder were of those varying in age from 5 to 15. In 1860 the deaths receded to 5,212, which was still above the average.
'59	*Scotland.* Diphtheria caused 415 deaths.
'59	*Northern Africa.* Plague.
'62	*China.* CHOLERA in Pekin. It first appeared in the village of Taku, where many of the Chinese died, and some of the European soldiers in the garrison. It also visited various towns on the river. In Pekin people were seen dead in the streets. They had been seized and were unable to reach home. The Chinese quarter of the city was very filthy, and great numbers died there. It next visited the Tartar portion of the city, passing through it from south to north. In the hospital nearly all the attendants suffered,

Plagues and Pestilences affecting the Human Race—Contd.

A.D.	*China—Contd.*
1867	some severely, but none died. Almost every day persons were seen in the dry bed of the canal or in the streets who had lain down and died in the night. These were removed by the police. The recorded deaths were 15,000, out of a population of 1,500,000, being 1 per cent. The mode of enumeration was by counting the coffins taken out of the city gates. As many as 20 coffins were seen on one road out of the city ; and frequently 8 to 10 were to be seen. This was in July and August. The Tartar portion of the city was very unhealthy, from the fact of all the offal and filth being thrown into the river, the stench from which during the summer was fearful, and cholera remained here much longer than in other parts of the city. Cholera is said to visit the city every year.—*Chinese and Japanese Repository,* i, pp. 476 and 477.
'63	*England.* Measles, which for the preceding five years had shown some considerable increase, now further augmented the deaths, of which 11,349 were attributed to it in the returns of the registrar-general.
'63	*Persian Kurdistan.* Plague.
'63-64....	*Arabia.* After an absence of twenty-eight years, the plague showed itself again.
'66	*England.* The deaths from cholera were 14,378 ; from diarrhœa 17,170. Deaths from measles showed a considerable increase.

Regarding the days of the week most fatal to cholera, during the epidemic of 1866, the fewest deaths occurred on Saturday ; the next fewer on Sunday. The greatest number occurred on Wednesday, and the next greater on Tuesday. In 1849 the deaths on Tuesday and Saturday stood highest ; on Thursday and Friday lowest. The popular belief as to unlucky Friday did not apply, as Dr. Farr has already pointed out, to either of these epidemics. He adds, with great sagacity, " If the temperate or intemperate habits of any of the working classes of London had any effect on this series of facts, they therefore raised the deaths on Monday, lowered them on Friday." |
| '66 .... | *Dublin.* There appeared in March this year a form of pestilence locally termed " Black Death," from the purple blotches which appeared on the skin, and were supposed to resemble the symptoms of the Black Death of the fourteenth century. Many persons of all ranks died within a few hours after seizure.

An international conference was held at Constantinople for the purpose of considering epidemic cholera in its various aspects. |
| '66 .... | *United States.* Some of the principal cities in the States suffered from a severe visitation of Asiatic cholera. In St. Louis, on the Mississippi, which sustains some deaths by cholera almost every summer, the deaths in that year are said to have reached 200 per day in a population diminished by flight to 180,000. |
| '67 .... | *Europe.* Cholera prevailed in *Rome, Naples,* and *Sicily* in August and September, and in some parts of *Switzerland* in October.

In 1867 a " cholera conference " was held at Weimar, and there were present many of the leading epidemiologists and mycologists, including some from England. An opportunity was afforded for "the interchange of ideas," as the diplomatists say, on this and other important theories, such as the local relations of cholera to soil as regards its geological character and its conditions of moisture, and the alleged efficacy of disinfection, the communicability of cholera, the meteorological aspect of the case, and the like. Whether cholera is a fermentation of infinite microscopic self-multiplying organisms in the bowels, drawing the serum from the blood with excruciating spasms, leaving the clot to coagulate throughout the body as in a bruised surface, and thus producing the blue and livid colour which marks the fatal stage of this terrible |

Plagues and Pestilences affecting the Human Race—Contd.

A.D.	
	Europe—Contd.
1867	malady, or whether any other theory be preferred, the practical effects as regards the human subject and the practical means of prevention are in the present state of our knowledge the same. Be the cause of cholera what it may, excremental pollution of air and water will develop it anywhere and everywhere, and the abolition of these will remove it.—*Vide* Dr. SIMON's *Report to the Privy Council*, 1867.
'67	*India.* Cholera outbreak at the first Hindu fair at Hurdwar.—See text, "Plague Spots."
'67	*Persia.* Plague at Bagdad and in Euphrates valley, also in *Mesopotamia.*
'68	*England.* The mortality from measles large. 11,630 deaths.

There was published, by way of supplement to the twenty-ninth report of the registrar-general, but in a separate volume—*Report on the Cholera Epidemic of* 1866 *in England.* This report was prepared by Dr. Farr under direction of the registrar-general, and is a most exhaustive and valuable work.

In December, 1868, the "Scientific Review" contained the following :—

" *Cholera Fungus.*—After a series of ·long botanical researches, Professor Ernest Hallier, of the University of Jena, has convinced himself of the presence in the excreta of cholera patients of a microscopic fungus which exists in them in considerable quantities. On submitting this minute plant to a careful microscopical examination, the distinguished botanist found that it has all the characters of *Urocistus oryzæ*, which in India is found sometimes in the rice plantations. Professor Hallier then manured some rice plants with the excreta in question, and finds that they perish rapidly. A whole plantation may be thus destroyed by the *Urocistus* in a very short space of time."

| '68 .... | *India.* During the religious fair held at *Kamsat* (in *Maldah* district, Bengal) cholera broke out severely, and was thence widely disseminated through the district by the 8,000 or 10,000 Hindus who had come to bathe in the Ganges.—*Hunter's Imperial Gazeteer of India.* |

Dr. Guy, in his valuable work, " Public Health," published 1870, has pointed out that *between the epidemics of cholera and plague there is an unmistakable resemblance*. They are, he says, evidently diseases of the same class. The figures on the death registers rise to an unwonted height in certain years only. They harmonise with the theory of an imported disease. But there is this difference : the cholera of 1854 attained its maximum in eight weeks, and subsided in thirteen ; while the plague (of 1665) took twenty-two weeks and seventeen weeks to accomplish the same feats. The figures for the cholera are suggestive of a disease carried chiefly in currents of air ; those for the plague of one spreading more slowly by direct contact, and exposure of the healthy to the sick. He adds :—

" This disease too, like others of its class, is most fatal when it first breaks out, least fatal when it is passing away. How it selects its victims we do not know, and cannot expect to learn. Some whom it kills quickly seem in the rudest health, others who are longer dying are obviously less vigorous. Whether a man is to succumb or recover probably depends in part on the strength of the dose, but in part upon his having or not having some unsound organ which will not bear the congestion of the cold, or the quickened circulation of the hot stage. The intemperate man is taken always at a disadvantage, and the chances of escape lessen with age. Another fact must be specially noted, as common to all epidemics—the poison, when it does not kill by sudden shock, remains for a variable

Plagues and Pestilences affecting the Human Race—Contd.

A.D.	India—Contd.
1868	period, in some shorter, in others longer, inert. The seed is sown, but takes time to germinate. The interval of real or apparent inaction is known as the period of *incubation*. It is not easy to fix the limits in these maladies. In cholera it is thought to extend from three days to a week; in typhus fever from a few minutes or hours to a few weeks or months. The fact that there is this period of inaction, or incubation, helps to explain some apparent anomalies. The cholera, considered as a type of the class to which it belongs, has one or two other characters worth noting. It has been more than once preceded by the milder epidemic influenza; it has given something of its own character to other diseases prevailing before, during, and after its own visitations; it has seemed to require time to develop itself in the several places which it attacks, for several weeks will sometimes elapse before the weekly deaths exceed one or two; and it is certainly, as a general rule, fostered and promoted by overcrowding and uncleanliness." Vol. ii was published in 1882.
'71–72....	*England.* There was a very serious outbreak of *small pox.* The deaths increased from 2,620 in 1870 to 23,126 in 1871, and were 19,094 in 1872. In 1873 they had subsided to 2,364, being about the annual average. The causes of this outbreak are considered in the current reports of the registrar-general; but much special and valuable information will be found in a paper by Dr. Guy, read before the Statistical Society, viz., *Two Hundred and Fifty Years of Small Pox in London,* vol. xlv of the *Journal of the Statistical Society,* p. 399. I take one passage from it only :—" There is nothing in the numerical surroundings of the great epidemic of the year 1871 (less severe, be it understood, than the epidemics of the past centuries) which ought to shake our confidence in the preventive efficacy of *vaccination;* for the years which preceded, and still more those which followed it, show by the smallness of the figures to what a low degree of mortality some cause or causes could reduce this formidable malady small pox" (p. 426).
'71	*Persia, Kurdistan.* Outbreak of plague. In the autumn of 1871 medical commissioners were sent both by the Persian and by the Ottoman Government into Kurdistan, to ascertain the nature of the disease reported to be the plague. The members of these commissions satisfied themselves upon two important points—first, that the disease was true plague; and next, that the outbreak had probably begun late in the autumn or early in the winter of 1870, before the commencement of the famine. The commissioners were unable to ascertain the extent to which the disease had prevailed and was then prevailing; for when they attempted to carry out their investigations in the remoter villages of the infected district, the inhabitants (fearing doubtless that the commissioners carried the poison of the plague with them) took to their arms, and the commissioners had to save themselves by flight.
'71–73....	*China.* Plague very prevalent in district of Yunnan.
'72	*India.* At the great fair held at *Karagola* (Purniah district, Bengal), epidemics frequently break out, and since 1871 cholera has spread over the district from Kárágolá, with fatal results.—HUNTER'S *India.*
'72	*The East.* Plague in *Mesopotamia, Western Arabia,* and the district of *Bengazi.*
'74	*England.* The deaths from measles were again large, being 12,255.
'74	*Tunis.* Plague. Dr. Laval, a famous French physician, lost his life in attempting to give aid.
	From 1865 to the year just ended [1874], Asiatic cholera has been uninterruptedly present in Europe. Twice within that period

Plagues and Pestilences affecting the Human Race—Contd.

A.D.	*Tunis—Contd.*
1874	the disease was generally diffused over the continent. This long continued prevalence of the malady would appear to be now coming to an end; if indeed it be not already ended : for several months have passed without news as to the presence of cholera in any continental State. Before, however, there is distinct assurance of the epidemic having ceased, another extension of the disease from the East is threatened. Cholera is reported to be seriously prevalent in the Dutch Malaysian possessions. From these possessions every year a large number of Mahomedan pilgrims visit Mecca. It is commonly believed that the starting point of the great westward extension of cholera, which is only now dying, or has but lately died, out in Europe, was the introduction of the disease into Mecca by pilgrims from the Straits Settlements in 1865, at the time of the pilgrimage of that year. There is reason to doubt that belief : but the Ottoman Government, probably entertaining it, regards the danger to which Mecca—and through Mecca, Egypt and the whole Turkish empire—will be exposed from the introduction of cholera by pilgrims from the Dutch Malaysian possessions in the approaching pilgrimage of 1875 as a very real one. It has accordingly commissioned the vice-president of the general board of health of the Empire, Dr. Arif Bey, to proceed to Mecca and take precautionary measures.*—*Times,* 1st January, 1875.
'75	*Persia.* Plague. Also in Mesopotamia, &c.
	The scene of the present diffusion of plague in Mesopotamia was on the lower Euphrates, south of Musseyib. The disease first showed itself at the close of February or the beginning of March last among the Aflij Arabs, who occupy the northern portion of the great marshes on the east bank of the river. The infection quickly spread to the neighbouring tribes, and, attacking both banks of the river, it extended along the stream from Devanieh upwards to Hillah. On the west bank of the stream the infection spread also to Nedjef (Meshed Ali) and Kerbella (Meshed Hussein)—to the edge of the desert, in fact, traversing the district which was the scene of the outbreak of 1867.—*Times,* 17th August.
	During this year the plague prevailed at *Bagdad,* and the Privy Council of Great Britain consulted its medical officers on the expediency of prohibiting the exportation of wool from Mesopotamia into this country ; but were advised that there was really no danger of infection from this cause. See 1879.

* It was reported that at the International Sanitary Convention held in Vienna, 1874, it was resolved that a commission should be appointed to inquire into the causes of plagues and pestilence : the commission to hold its sittings in Vienna, and it was understood that it would occupy itself chiefly with an investigation of cholera and its causes. It was to be composed of physicians and members appointed by foreign governments. Its office to be permanently established at Vienna. The governments were expected to defray the expenses. The first measures intended were to establish stations at different points in Asia and Africa. At these stations meteorological observations in general were to be made, but their principal office was to make observations in regard to certain designated atmospheric changes which affect the origin and propagation of the cholera. The commission would serve as a centre for the collection and distribution of materials for scientific purposes Suitable governmental sanction having been first obtained, it would despatch physicians into such countries as had no regular sanitary organisation of their own. The particular lines of investigation to be followed would be carefully marked out in advance. It would be the duty of these agents to report promptly the breaking out of epidemics whenever they occurred. Hopes were entertained that much good would be accomplished by the commission.

Plagues and Pestilences affecting the Human Race—Contd.

A.D.	
1876	*Turkish Arabia.* Euphrates valley, &c. Upwards of 20,000 died of plague.
'76	*Persian Kurdistan.* " Black plague."—At the instance of the highest medical authorities, the chancellor of the German Empire created a commission to investigate the nature of this disease, the causes to which its owed its origin, and the best means to prevent its development and propagation. Professors Pettenkofer and Hirsch were appointed upon it, and conducted their researches with a thoroughness and ability worthy of their great reputation. The result of their inquiries are of great value. The considerations presented in their report deserve serious attention, not only with reference to the regulation of the ordinary habits of life, but also and *especially, on account of their bearing upon life insurance.* Cholera was not the only subject upon which their inquiries threw light. They related to all similar pestilences and diseases. Among these latter were reckoned the so-called chlorine, diarrhœa and dysentery. The recommendations were sanitary measures and personal cleanliness.—*Vide Deutsche Versicherungs Zeitung.*
'77	*Astrakhan.* Plague pestilence prevailing.
'77	*China.* A species of plague, very fatal.
'78	*London.* Diphtheria prevailed extensively in the northern and north-western portions of London, on high ground.
	There was published—*Diphtheria : its Nature and Treatment, Varieties and Local Expressions.* By Morell Mackenzie, M.D., London. He says the disease is the same as the *Cynanche trachealis* described by Dr. Cullen (Edinburgh) in 1802; and by M. Breton-neau in 1826.
'78	*Asia* and *Europe.* Diphtheria prevailed largely (as indeed it had done during the two previous years) in *Hungary.* In one town, out of a population of 20,000, no less than 2,135 persons were attacked, of whom 927 died. In *Germany* it was also epidemic. Amongst its victims were the Princess Alice (Duchess of Hesse) and one of her children.
	Battle Fields. The insurance companies appealed to the Austrian Government to obtain a satisfactory " disinfection " of the fields of the late battles in Bulgaria and Roumelia. A number of dead bodies were unburied in Turkey, and an epidemic was dreaded in Vienna, which might seriously affect the calculations in the actuaries' tables. Apprehension is certainly not unreasonable ; the frightful form of typhus which is now raging in south-eastern Europe and in Armenia may well make the directors of insurance offices uneasy, to say nothing of the insurers themselves, who have probably hitherto given little thought to the matter........It is a mis-fortune that epidemics will not avoid the prudent man and fasten only upon the reckless. The only thing to be done is to neutralise this malign influence at its root. But the interference might be beneficially carried further. In the ordinary business of insurance why should not a man's drains be examined as well as his chest ? The interest of insurance offices in sanitary improvement has not yet been fully apprehended. With their powerful organisations and command of capital, the offices might do much to lengthen the lives of their insurers, and thus secure that " mutual " profit which is the reason of their being.—*Pall Mall Gazette.*
'78	*Russia.* Typhus prevailed very severely in many places.
'78	*Siberia.* Plague carried off large numbers.
'78	*Arabia.* Cholera reported from Jeddah and Mecca. The *Lancet* hereon said :—" Since 1875 epidemiologists in this country have had an uneasy feeling that we were about to witness another diffusion of the malady beyond the boundaries of India. This feeling seemed to receive confirmation from the ascertained spread

Plagues and Pestilences affecting the Human Race—Contd.

A.D.	*Arabia—Contd.*
1878	of the disease eastwards into the districts of China, and probably also into parts of the Eastern Archipelago, and northwards into Beloochistan and Afghanistan to the frontier of Persia. Although no facts were known of extension to the countries westwards, yet it was to be inferred that what had been observed to the north and east of India might also be taking place at the west, and the recent carriage of the disease by a French transport from Saigon into the Red Sea gave some countenance to this view. This happened when the tide of the Mecca pilgrimage flowing from India and the Eastern Archipelago was in full flow."
'78	*Salonica* (Turkey). Severe typhoid fever outbreak; deaths 30 to 50 per day.
'79	*Astrachan.* Plague assuming serious proportions early in January in consequence of thaw.
'79	*Russia.* In February, plague reported to prevail here; Europe in great alarm. Germany appointed a medical commission to proceed to Moscow and report. The clothing of the travellers coming from Russia into Germany was ordered to be disinfected with sulphur. In Austria and Hungary steps were taken. The English College of Physicians called a meeting to consider what steps should be taken. A special meeting of the Epidemiological Society was held, and the following papers read:—(1). *On the Characteristics of Plague in Mesopotamia in* 1876 *and* 1877. By Dr. E. D. Dickson, Physician to the British Embassy in Constantinople. (2). *Observations on the Reappearance of Plague in Europe.* By Mr. J. Netten Radcliffe. A British medical commission was sent out to investigate. Finally it was announced that "the Russian Government has taken determined steps to isolate the province of Astrachan, and a cordon of 18,000 troops has been posted around that province so as to prevent all egress until after the purification. Villages were burnt to the ground, the inhabitants being lodged in tents and compensated for their loss."* Soon after which it was reported that the disease had disappeared.
'79	*England.* The Privy Council again [see 1875] consulted its medical advisers on the question of the fear of contagion from imported commodities. On this occasion attention was mainly turned to imported rags—not wool. Dr. Simon had (in 1875 or earlier) expressed an opinion that there was reason to suppose that disease gives a long-lasting infectiveness to absorbent articles which have been in use by the sick; but he did not feel himself entitled to say that under no circumstances could danger in that respect arise through the commercial relations of Europe with the East. It was therefore resolved to call the attention of Russia and the Eastern Governments to the question—a case in the Tyne seeming to indicate infection from a cargo of rags. On the other hand, after inquiry some time since at eighty-six paper mills visited by a government

---

* The recent epidemic in Astrachan has cost Russia the sum of 80,000*l.* This reckoning includes the expenses from January, 1879, when General Loris Melikoff was appointed Governor-General of the governments of Astrachan, Saratof, and Samara, up to the month of April, when all danger had disappeared. The budget of the plague presents some features of interest; the sanitary cordons and quarantine arrangements cost 40,000*l.*; the surveillance of the Volga, in suspected situations, and the measures necessary to isolate them, cost 2,400*l.*; the medical staff, and salaries of the employés amounted to 10,000*l.*; drugs, &c., to 3,600*l.*; assistance and indemnities to the inhabitants of the villages, &c., destroyed as a precautionary measure, and the transport of troops, have naturally absorbed the major portion of the sums of money appropriated to arresting the invasion of the scourge.—*Sanitary Record*, February, 1880.

Plagues and Pestilences affecting the Human Race—Contd.

A.·D	*England—Contd.*
1879	inspector, no case of infection was heard of. See *Sanitary Record*, x, p. 228.
'79	*Zurich* (Switzerland). Pulmonary typhus; believed to have been imported by animals and birds purchased for a menagerie.
'79	*India.* Cholera amongst the pilgrims returning from *Hurdwar* fair; between 20,000 and 30,000 hillmen, from the Himalayan districts near Nynee Tal died on their homeward journey. Railway carriages had been used by infected pilgrims. The government forbade the holding of *Chiragan* fair. See text, "Plague Spots of the World."
'79	*United States.* Yellow fever at Memphis, on the Mississippi.
'80	The Statistical Society of London put forward as the subject of competition for the "Howard Medal," with 20*l.* added, awarded by it, the following subject:—"The Oriental Plague in its Social, Economical, Political, and International Relations; special reference being made to the labours of Howard on the subject." The successful competitor was Mr. Henry Percy Potter, F.R.C.S. The essay is published in the *Journal* of the Society, vol. xliii, p. 605.
'81	*Mecca.* Cholera broke out amongst the pilgrims. Out of 3,500 detained at Etwedj to perform quarantine, only 27 died. "Constantinople, 27th September. In consequence of the receipt of a despatch from Jeddah reporting the outbreak of cholera at Mecca, the Sanitary Board have resolved to enforce ten days' quarantine against vessels from the Red Sea. Ships from Egyptian ports will be visited by medical inspectors, and such as have passed through the Suez Canal after undergoing quarantine in Egyptian ports will be subjected to forty-eight hours' observation."—*Times.*
'81	*Aden.* Cholera. A letter in the *Times*, under date 30th August, said :—"There is a disease here which is causing considerable alarm—it is entirely confined to Mussulmans—which the doctors pronounce to be sporadic cholera, being sometimes fatal in two hours. I do not believe it is anything of the kind, but is, I think, entirely due to Ramadan—the Mahomedan month of fasting, now just over. The deaths have been very large ; the symptoms being griping pains and vomiting. The last returns show a sudden decrease of mortality. It is only reasonable to suppose that men who work all day without food and eat a heavy meal at night, and keep that on for a month, would suffer very seriously, especially in this climate."
'81	*India.* A severe FEVER EPIDEMIC in Umritsur; 200 to 300 deaths occurred daily. In eleven days there were 2,265 deaths, of which 1,138 were children. The Punjaub Government made every endeavour to stop the pestilence. which, it is thought, was caused by the late heavy rainfall.—*National Reformer.* "A standing medical board has been constituted at Bombay to report weekly on the amount of cholera in the city. This step has been taken with the view of attempting to procure the removal of the very harassing and vexatious quarantine restrictions now imposed in Egypt on arrivals from Western India."—*Times.* HUNTER, in his "Imperial Gazetteer of India," published this year, says :—"Cholera is the principal epidemic with which Balnsor District (in Orissa) is afflicted, and this disease is doubtless often induced by the stream of pilgrims which annually flows along the trunk road." Very severe outbreaks in **1853** and **1866** (i, 331).
'82	*England.* Enteric fever of a virulent type broke out amongst the workmen in the Severn tunnel, two of whom died.
'82	*England* (N.W.). Serious attack of typhoid fever, preceded by diphtheria.

Plagues and Pestilences affecting the Human Race—Contd.

A.D.	
1882	*Persia.* Plague at Saoutch-Boulak in the Kurdish mountains. This was the fourth time of its appearance in this district during the last twenty years. In 1863 it decimated the Djetalis in the district of Makrion, and in 1872 it made its appearance among the Mekris of Saoutch-Boulak, and thence spread to Bana, while in 1878 it was very violent in the district where it is now reported to be raging. These precedents show that there is a predisposition to its breaking out in the Kurdish mountains to the north-west of Persia, just as there is in the north-east of the Khorassan and in Mesopotamia itself. But while in Mesopotamia the plague increases as the weather gets hot, and disappears when the cold sets in, it invariably makes its appearance in the Persian districts during the winter, when the tribes are huddled together in wretched huts and underground caverns to take refuge from the snow. The Kurds themselves so well understand the importance of isolation in the case of any outbreak that each village is jealously guarded in the time of the epidemic, and Dr. Thalozan, a French physician to the Shah, who accompanied him during his last tour in Europe, attributes the comparative rapidity with which each epidemic has been got under to this fact alone.—*Daily News,* 2nd May, 1882.
'82	*Alaska.* Pestilence caused great mortality in July.

HARRISON AND SONS, PRINTERS IN ORDINARY TO HER MAJESTY, ST. MARTIN'S LANE